THE LOVE FIXERS

UNLUCKY IN LOVE

ANGELA CASELLA

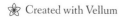

ALSO BY ANGELA CASELLA

Unlucky in Love

The Love Fixers

The Love Bandits (July)

The Love Losers (October)

Finding You

You're so Extra

You're so Bad

You're so Basic

You're so Vain

Fairy Godmother Agency

A Borrowed Boyfriend

A Stolen Suit

A Brooding Bodyguard

A Reluctant Roommate

Bringing Down the House (Nicole and Damien's story)

Highland Hills

(co-written with Denise Grover Swank)

Matchmaking a Billionaire

Matchmaking a Single Dad

Matchmaking a Grump

We all want a badass book boyfriend, and here you go, you're welcome. But why should the hero be the only one who gets to be a badass?

CHAPTER ONE

CLAIRE

"It's not a big deal, right?" I ask Lainey. We're sitting on my green velvet, curb-find couch with a couple of sweating beers. It's barely three o'clock on a Thursday, but I've decided it's happy hour in my apartment. "People get fired all the time. I mean, it wasn't even a good job."

"No," she agrees, "it was a terrible job. That woman abused you." She waves around my one-bedroom apartment, which looks particularly sad in the bright July light flooding through the cracked single-pane windows of the sagging Brooklyn brownstone. It's as if every speck of dust has been magnified, every brown cardboard box made to look larger. "But this palace of yours isn't going to pay for itself."

The woman has a point.

"I'm not one to talk, though," she adds morosely, tugging on her short black hair. "I'm hardly contributing."

Lainey's allowed to be down in the dumps. Her very rich, big-dicked fiancé left her a month ago, and she got the boot from his penthouse apartment in the Upper East Side. I told her to come sleep on my couch, which was a great idea in theory—best friends since childhood and college roommates, together again—and I'm glad she's here. Truly glad. Especially because she's going through something, and I want to be her scaffolding. But I didn't account for all the crap that has flooded my tiny living room. There are so many boxes that I feel like I'm making my way through a maze every time I try to go to the kitchen or bathroom, and I nearly injured myself last night in the dark. I need to have a calm, reasonable discussion with her, but every time I try, I chicken out. Because I know it has to feel like a pretty bad comedown, going from that to this. She has a job at a fashion boutique, but she's making less than I was at my job for Agnes Lewis.

I heave a sigh, thinking of all the pointless hours I spent in a dark, miserable cubicle, trying to satisfy someone who took pleasure in being chronically disappointed. "It wasn't even my fault," I mutter. "It only said it was alcoholic in the fine print, and you know what Agnes said about my reading glasses."

"She was right," Lainey replies. "They *do* make you look like a bug. But a cute bug, like your dad's nickname for you."

"Thanks." I give her shoulder a shove, and she gives me the sad smile of someone else who feels like they're on the gallows, waiting for their turn. Sighing again, I add, "She actually forbid me to wear them at the office. So I didn't."

"She basically did it to herself."

I smile at the encouragement. "You know, if it had been a normal day, it would have been okay. She would have slept it off in her office. Maybe she would have even been nice to everyone for a change."

"It's okay, Claire. Everyone will forget what happened before too long. You know how it goes, another day, another crisis."

But she's wrong. It's not every day a world-famous lifestyle guru —the woman known as the next Martha Stewart—stumbles onto a morning show drunk at nine a.m. because her assistant mistakenly gave her an alcoholic fizzy juice drink someone had sent over as a sample. A drink she'd enjoyed so much, she'd downed three cans before lurching onto set, calling the host a mealy-mouthed fuck-tart on camera, and then vomiting on her own shoes.

"Doug convinced her I did it on purpose," I add spitefully, wanting to grind him into the ground with one of Lainey's high heels.

"Of course he did," she says with a groan. "Doug is a spiteful prick."

He's my ex...situationship. When you work twelve to fifteen hour days, you don't have time to mess around with anyone who doesn't work with you. Or at least in the same part of the city as you. Which is my only explanation for why I started sleeping with the head of PR, a man who's fifteen years older than me and, yes, named Doug.

At first it was fun in a forbidden, will-they-or-won't-they way, but it didn't take very long for me to realize I really shouldn't have.

He wasn't very good in bed—or in supply closets—and he always talked down to me, like I was a little girl, even though I'm twenty-eight, thank you very much.

He didn't take it well when I told him I was ready to call it quits. He started closing elevator doors on me and going out of his way to make me look stupid in meetings. Honestly, I wouldn't be surprised if *he* sent those juice drinks, knowing it was exactly the sort of thing Agnes would suck down.

Lainey rubs my back. "We both have bad taste in men. Go us. Hey, why don't we consult the Tarot about what you should do next?"

I try to hold back another groan. A client of the boutique gave the cards to her a few days ago, and she acted like she'd been gifted a winning lottery ticket. She's been trying to figure out a business idea that'll make us bank, but can't seem to narrow in on one plan. Last week, after scrubbing Todd off her social media, she speculated that "love erasing"—getting rid of all evidence, online and in real life, of a lying, cheating snake—should be a service someone offers, and maybe we should be the ones who offer it. But I pointed out it wouldn't be very healthy for her psyche right now. Then she moved on to the idea of becoming "really good" with the tarot cards, even though I haven't seen her practice once since she brought them home.

I have zero interest in a reading, but right now nothing's going to make me happy, so she might as well enjoy herself. I take another swig of my beer and nod. "Go for it."

She gives a squeal and reaches into one of the fifty boxes stacked up around the living room. Really, something's got to give.

She gets the cards out and starts shuffling them as if we're about to play Go Fish.

"Do you know what you're doing?" I ask with some interest.

"No," she says with a snort, "but I Googled it, and I've heard you can do a reading with just one card." Shoving a spread toward me, she adds, "Pick one with intention."

I suck in a breath and slowly let it out. When I got a job working for *the* Agnes Lewis, I felt invincible. The other students in my graduating class from NYU were jealous or impressed. I figured I'd pay my dues, and then she'd help me launch my own business, same as she'd done for past assistants. My dream was to open a bakery and create confections special enough to make busy New Yorkers pause and lose themselves in wonder, and I was certain the bakery would be mine if I just held out for long enough. Years passed, promises were made, but it never happened. I just kept paying my dues as one year went by, two, three, seven. Now, here I am at almost thirty, unemployed, broke, single, and living in a maze of boxes.

I want something exciting to happen, I think as I pull the card.

I turn it over on the palette-wood coffee table, which presides over two short boxes. The card has a drawing of a skeleton riding a horse, and the word DEATH is emblazoned beneath it.

"Yeah, I really wish I hadn't done that," I say, but Lainey scrunches her mouth to the side and picks up her phone. A second later, she lifts a finger. "This says the Death card is usually about big changes, not death per se."

"That's super helpful." My phone buzzes in my pocket. I tug it out and frown at the UNKNOWN NUMBER readout on the screen. "Another phishing call. Great."

"Why don't you answer and tell the person off? I did that after Todd broke up with me. It made me feel fantastic for at least three minutes." She tucks her own phone away and gives me a long look. "You're too much of a people pleaser, Claire. It would be good for you."

I hesitate for a long moment. The person on the other end of that call is probably a peon with a terrible boss, same as I had. Why ruin their day? On the other hand, maybe they find it entertaining when people flip the script. Lainey's still looking at me, her expression suggesting she doesn't think I'm going to do it, so I shrug and answer the call.

"Is this Claire Rainey?" asks the woman on the other end. Her voice is confident and throaty.

"Yes, who's this?" I say, lifting my eyebrows at Lainey, who mimes for me to put the phone on speaker.

I do, smiling at her.

"Nicole," says the woman.

"And what are you trying to sell me today, Nicole?" I ask, my tone haughty, the way Agnes talks to everyone. Lainey stifles a laugh and gulps her beer. "Because I can assure you I'm not interested in buying tinctures or Tupperware, and I don't have a car, so I'm pretty damn sure the extended warranty hasn't expired for the five hundredth time."

The woman on the other line laughs, which I hadn't expected.

"Good, you have a sense of humor, that'll make this much easier. But I'm not calling to sell you something. I'm calling to give you something."

"Jesus?" I ask, raising my eyebrows at Lainey. "Because I think he'd object to cold calls on principle."

My friend snorts and then flinches and covers her face, as if she can stuff the sound back in.

"No, but it's cute that you enjoy guessing games. I'm actually calling about your inheritance."

I nearly drop the phone but manage to keep hold of it, trying to swallow the feeling of unease creeping up my throat. "What are you talking about?"

"Your inheritance." There's a pause, then she says, "I'm bad at sharing shitty news in a soft way, so I'm just going to level with you. Your father died."

Now, I *do* drop the phone, my fingers turning slack in an instant. My whole body revolts against the notion, my stomach sinking, my limbs trembling, everything within me hot and cold and shocked as if I were zapped and frozen in the same instant. My dad can't be dead. He called me this morning to commiserate about my job loss and then gave me a five-minute lecture about eating bran. He's the only person who cares enough about me to give me stupid lectures. No, he *can't* be dead.

My whole body trembling, I glance at Lainey—or at least I try to. That damn DEATH card is still lying out on the coffee table, making me shake harder.

"What happened?" I say, my voice quavering, hot emotion pressing into me. *No, no, no, this isn't happening. This can't be happening.* "I talked to him just this morning. I—"

"Oh, sorry. Not that guy," says the woman on the phone, her voice muffled slightly by the rug. "Yeah, he's fine. I mean, probably. I'm talking about Richard Ricci. *He's* definitely not okay. He died about a week ago."

I pick up the phone, confused, panicky, and on edge. Relieved, too, but I have a strong urge to call my dad and hear his voice, the same way I did as a kid, after waking up from a nightmare about him dying. "I don't know any Richard Ricci. You must have the wrong number."

"I don't," Nicole says, sounding not the slightest bit fazed. "You're Claire Rainey. Five foot seven, blond with hazel eyes. Your mother is Lana Williams. You have an overly enthusiastic Instagram account, and you used to be the personal assistant to that orange woman who was on TV yesterday morning." Her laughter is like nails raking across my skin. "But something tells me you're not anymore. Seems to me you're pretty lucky I'm calling, actually."

"Who *are* you?" I ask in shock.

Lainey is practically thrumming with energy next to me, pointing at the tarot card as if a piece of cardboard could have brought on whatever this is.

"I'm the executor of Richard's will," the woman continues, "and he left you his house and a little chunk of change. You'll have to come to Marshall, North Carolina to check it out. There are some interesting terms that we can discuss when you get here."

"But *why?*"

"Weren't you listening?" she asks. "Dick was your father. I'm guessing your mother had a little fun on the side. It happens. From what I can tell, *he* had a lot of fun with a lot of people."

"This is some kind of scam," I snap, pissed and confused. I answered this call so I could feel like I had control over something, but I've completely lost control over *everything*. "You want to lure me to this Marshall place so you can kidnap me or put a gun to my head and make me enter all of my passwords."

"Do you have any money for me to steal?" Nicole asks, her tone derisive.

No.

"I'm not going to tell you that."

She sighs. "Talk to your adopt-i-dad. The closest city's Asheville. If you need help buying a plane ticket there, it can be covered by the inheritance." She snorts. "What am I talking about? Of course you need the money."

I have about five hundred questions for her, maybe a thousand. Especially about this man she claims was my father, which obviously must be impossible. I have a father. A father I adore. But I'm so baffled by her that I find myself asking again, "Who *are* you?"

She said she's the executor of this Richard's estate, but she's obviously no lawyer. Or at least I'm pretty sure a lawyer wouldn't talk like this.

"You'll find out soon enough," she says. Dead air hangs over the line for a moment before she adds, "I look forward to meeting you, Claire. I'll be in touch."

"But wait—"

When I look down, I see only my phone's wallpaper. She hung up.

"What the fuck?" I ask no one in particular. "She never even gave me her number."

"Look the guy up," Lainey says, her eyes wide. "Now."

So, I type his name into a search with shaking fingers, adding Marshall to the end. An obituary pops up from *The News Record.*

It says Richard Ricci died in an accident at age sixty-one, but it's not the article that commands my attention—it's the man's photo.

Despite both of us being blond, my dad and I have never looked alike. My mom used to joke about that when I was little, particularly because she and I didn't look much alike either. But the joke isn't funny anymore, because this guy, this guy who's already gone, *does* look like me. Our eyes are the exact same color, our brow lines are the same, and—

"Holy shit," Lainey says, giving me an appraising look. "*Holy shit*. He looks just like you did when you used the 'guy' filter on Instagram."

She's right.

"What just happened?" I ask, my voice shaking as much as my fingers still are.

Lainey takes my hands and squeezes, staring into my eyes. "This, my friend, is what they call a game changer."

CHAPTER TWO

CLAIRE

"Bran muffin?" my father asks, giving me a brave smile. He doesn't know why I'm at his apartment for breakfast, other than that I no longer have a job that requires me to show up at 7 a.m. every morning. For me, it was inevitable that I'd come here. Whenever anything big happens in my life, my father is the person I go to. Always. I don't see why that should be different now, when the something big has to do with my parentage.

Even if my mother were in New York City and available, I never would have gone to her for the truth. Truth for her was always a fluid thing, something that could be influenced by her feelings or mood.

"Yes," I say. The last thing I want to do right now is eat, let alone eat something that tastes like sawdust, but Lainey's right—I can't seem to say no to anyone, even when I'd really like to. That's why it took me six months to break things off with Doug.

Maybe it's my father's fault, because he's a people pleaser like me. Or maybe this Richard Ricci was a people pleaser, too, and I got the disease from him. An unpleasant shiver goes down my spine, because I'm having trouble wrapping my head around the possibility that this man I never knew, and never will know, provided half my genetic material.

I take a deep breath and slowly let it out as I lower into a chair at my dad's round, lemon yellow kitchen table, and watch him serve us muffins that smell like mulch.

My dad had a reality check at his last physical, and his baking has taken a turn for the healthy. I want him around forever, so I'm glad he's taking his doctor's warnings seriously. Still, it's been a hard adjustment. Butter and sugar are the love language of my soul, one *he* taught me. In fact, I stayed up until four in the morning making Bronuts last night like some kind of manic house elf. Bronuts, a cross between brownies and donuts, are my signature bake. They're essentially fried brownies, crispy on the outside and gooey and chocolatey and soul-affirming on the inside.

Lainey decided on the name, which will absolutely be changed in the unlikely event that I ever get to open my dream bakery. She got the idea when we were drunk, because of the infamy of the cronut, the croissant-donut smashup creation that made Dominique Ansel's bakery a famous New York institution, with a line out the door every morning.

The baking might have relaxed me more if I'd been alone, but Lainey stayed up with me, Googling Marshall—small town in the Blue Ridge Mountains, nineteen miles from Asheville, population of 792—and my maybe-father. I think she meant for it to be comforting, but each thing she said made my nerves prickle more.

"The obituary doesn't say what he used to do for work. It's actually weirdly vague, don't you think?"

"It doesn't say anything about who he left behind, either. Don't they usually say stuff like that?"

When I got up this morning after a few hours of sleep, I checked my emails and found a message from Nicole that lacked any kind of greeting or signoff—

I booked you a flight on Sunday from JFK. The info's below. I figured that would be enough time for you to get over your existential crisis. They say to arrive an hour early, but that's mostly bullshit. Bring a big bag.

My mouth fell open at the audacity. I was tempted to send a scathing reply—who was she to order me around and buy a ticket without even consulting me about my schedule? Admittedly, I had no schedule and nowhere to be, but somehow that only made it worse. I even pulled up a message box, but I kept looking at the blinking cursor and not writing. It took me a minute to realize why...

I knew I was going to get on that flight, and I didn't want to find myself face-to-face with this intimidating woman after telling her off online. Because even if I had no personal connection to Richard Ricci, I wanted to know more about him.

Frankly, I also couldn't afford to cover the ticket myself—another reason why I couldn't chew her out for buying it without consulting me. But maybe, just maybe, my money troubles were over. If I'd inherited this guy's house, I could sell it. It might not give me enough startup funds to open my bakery, but at least I could afford to live in my shitty apartment for a while without worrying about where I'd get the rent.

I wanted to show Lainey the message this morning and ask her what to do—there's nothing like passing the buck when you're emotionally drained—but she was still asleep after our all-night-baking-and-worrying session. So instead I'd texted my dad and asked him if I could come over to talk.

And here I am now, struggling to think of what to say, or how to say it.

Dad sits down across from me and pats his belly, glancing at the framed photo of my mother on the wall, the same way he does about five hundred times a day.

Mom left a couple of years ago to visit an ashram in California. She was supposed to come back in six weeks, but six weeks turned to six months, and then two years. The last time we heard from her was at Christmas about seven months ago, when she called to tell us the guru had ordered everyone to give up their phones. She'd miss talking to us, but we were on different paths anyway. She was one of the chosen, and since we'd neglected to give up all of our worldly possessions and join the ashram, we were celestially fucked.

Dad had tried to get her to come home. He'd contacted the cops, who'd told him they could do nothing, and a private investigator, who'd joined the ashram undercover and then chose to stay. So, ultimately, Dad had needed to accept she wasn't coming back this time.

This wasn't the first time my mom had left home to find herself. There'd been yoga retreats, girls' weekends that had extended into girls' months, and a couple of years before she left for the cult, an affair with her "twin flame"—a fast food "chef," her word, who was only two years older than me, white, and had cornrows. Given what I'd learned yesterday afternoon, I was guessing she'd tried to find herself in North Carolina twenty-nine years ago.

"Your mom's like a cat," my dad had told me when I was a kid and she'd missed some major life event. *"She loves us, but she doesn't love the same way we do."*

Because, it went without saying, both of us are dogs.

It hurt—watching her hurt him, feeling her push me aside like I was an overly demanding pet—but it didn't hurt as much as it might have, because I had him.

My dad was the one who took care of me. Mom brought me to the occasional yoga or art class, but she wasn't reliable. Dad was the one who'd bought me my first box of tampons, hugged me while I cried about stupid boys being stupid, taught me how to bake, and wrote my resume before I sent it to Agnes Lewis, adding ten bullet points about all of the supposed marketing work I'd done for his event planning business.

My father was everything to me, and he'd never really been mine.

Or at least that's how it felt right now, with the injustice of the whole thing pounding through my veins. My mother had let him raise me even though she knew I wasn't his kid.

"You sounded upset on the phone, bug," Dad says, his brow furrowing. "I'm sorry about your job, but maybe it was for the best. Agnes was always so demanding. I didn't want to say so while you were working for her, but she might not be a very nice sort of person."

I almost laugh. For my dad, this is the same as saying she's a secret devil worshipper who spends her night dancing nude around a bonfire. Instead, I sigh and say, "Yeah, you might be right about that."

"She sure didn't seem inclined to help you out. Maybe you could work with me for a little while, honey. I can always use help at—"

"Dad, I'm not here because of Agnes," I blurt, because I can't let him offer to help me, again, without saying what I came here to say. I suck in a breath and hold it, worry pounding through me. Will he still think of me as his daughter if he didn't know about Richard Ricci?

I'm hoping he did, that my mother was honest with him in this, at least, but that would also mean he's been lying to me for my whole life. It would mean it's *true*.

I take a quick bite of the muffin, buying myself half a second, because suddenly I'm *terrified*. I regret the bite, but I chew and swallow it, sucking in more air.

Not enough.

Suddenly, I feel like I'm choking. I let out the breath and suck in more air, but it doesn't feel enough. It feels like an anvil is sitting on my chest, and I can't breathe. I can't function. I can't—

I've had panic attacks at work, so I recognize what's happening and lean forward, putting my head between my legs and trying to slow my breathing.

"Bug," my dad says in alarm. "Is it the bran? I knew I put in too much. They were dry, weren't they?"

He pushes a glass of water toward me so aggressively it falls off the lip of the table and nearly hits my head, dousing my feet instead—and as soon as I catch my breath again, I find myself laughing. Laughing in the hysterical way people do when they're in serious trouble.

"Claire, what's going on?" Dad asks, standing in front of me.

That won't do. The laughter dries up, and I get up to grab some paper towels and mop up the mess. "Dad, take a seat," I tell him as he hovers. "We need to have a serious talk."

"You're making me nervous," he says, but he does as I ask.

I sit down too, and force myself to just come out and say it. "Dad, someone got in touch with me about a guy named Richard Ricci. Do you who know who that is?"

The look of horror on his face tells me he does, and also makes me worry about his heart health. Can any amount of bran counter the effect of something like this?

"He got in touch with you?" he says, looking down and pushing his muffin around like it might magically become edible.

"No...he's dead."

He looks up, eyes wide. "Really?"

"I saw his obituary. Dad...you obviously know who this guy is. Did Mom tell you..." My voice starts quavering, but I force myself to continue. "Is he my father?"

"*I'm* your father," he says firmly, his brown eyes holding mine. And even though I'm upset and on edge and really screwed up, I feel my eyes heat.

"Of course you are. But he's my, he's... The other half of my DNA comes from him, doesn't it?"

His jaw tightens, and he gives a slight nod. "Your mother told me as soon as she found out she was pregnant."

So at least she's only a partial piece of shit.

"But Dad." I don't realize I'm crying until I feel the tears coursing down my cheeks. "Why didn't you tell me? Why did you pick up so much slack for her when you knew I wasn't even—"

He grabs my hand and holds it tightly. "Didn't you hear me, bug? I wanted to be a dad, *your* dad, and I am. I was there from the moment you were born, and I haven't missed a minute. *I'm not going to miss a minute.* That's what being a parent is."

"But Dad..." I'm full-on crying now, and he sighs and gets up, surprising me when he comes back with two snifter glasses with an inch and a half of bourbon each.

"It's eight thirty," I say through my tears.

"So long as neither of us go on a morning talk show, I think we'll be just fine."

I laugh as he hands me the bourbon and then a napkin for my waterworks, pausing to squeeze my shoulder. Comfort courses through me, because *thank God.* I didn't think he was going to throw me out on the street and cross my photo out of all of his albums, but it would have been painful if he'd looked at me, for even half a second, as if I were a stranger.

He sits across from me and lifts his glass, and I hoist mine up to clink it against his.

It only occurs to me after we drink that he may be toasting Richard Ricci's death. I'm guessing he wasn't on friendly terms with the man who cuckolded him.

"Dad," I say haltingly. "Did you ever meet him?"

"No," he says, his tone is about as salty as it gets. "I didn't have that pleasure. But your mother told me he didn't want to be a father, honey. I'm sorry if that's hard to hear."

It wasn't. When I thought of Richard Ricci, I felt nothing but the confusion attached to his existence, and maybe regret that I'd never get to ask him any questions, especially since my mom was almost equally out of reach.

"Not really," I say. "I have you." I clear my throat, then tell him about the strange communications I've received from Nicole.

By the time I finish, we've both downed our bourbon, and I feel a bit tipsy, because the only other thing in my stomach is a bite of bran.

"What do I do, Dad?" I ask.

He smiles at me. "You go. Can Lainey go with you?"

For some reason I hadn't even thought of this possibility, but now it seems obvious.

"Shit, I don't know." I lift my hand to my mouth. "Sorry. I blame the bourbon."

"You're twenty-eight," he says with a soft smile. "You can swear around me."

"She probably wouldn't be able to come right away," I say, considering, "but maybe she could borrow her parents' car." Why they have one is anyone's guess—my father doesn't. It's cheaper to pay for deliveries and taxis than to keep a car in the city, and juggling city parking is an exercise in insanity. But Lainey's parents aren't the kind of people who'd let that stop them from having a luxury they can't really afford. "I'll check out what's going on, meet with the executor, and if I have to stay for more than a few days, I'll ask her to join me."

"I think you should." He pauses, studying me. "Unless you'd like me to come?"

I consider, then shake my head slowly. "No, Dad. I don't think that would be right. I don't want you to have to go through this guy's things or whatever."

I mean, for all I knew, he'd kept photo albums or videos of all of his conquests. While I'm not exactly excited by the prospect of finding a stash of nudes of my mother, it would be worse if my dad found them.

"I respect that," he says. "But I'm here if you need me."

He obviously means it, and again, I let myself soak in his goodness. My life might be pretty messed up right now, but at least I have a dad who'd do literally anything for me. That's a pretty good thing to have going for you as a person, and I'm determined never to take him for granted.

He hugs me for a solid minute, and then I go home and pack. And drink some more bourbon.

Lainey sleeps like the dead, so I don't worry much about waking her, and by the time she finally stirs, I'm on my third drink of the day. It's ten o'clock.

"Did I sleep until evening?" she asks, rubbing her eyes and yawning as she glances at my tumbler glass.

"No, I get drunk during the day now. It's a thing."

Understanding dawns in her eyes. "You talked to your dad."

I nod slowly. "Yes."

"And Dick's your bio dad."

"Unfortunately, yes. I have something to show you." It takes me a few seconds to pull up the email on my phone, but then I shove it toward her face. "That Nicole woman got me a plane ticket for Sunday."

Lainey studies the screen, then scrolls down, her brow furrowing. Her gaze darts up to meet mine. "Claire, this is for *today*. For twelve o'clock."

"Twelve p.m.?" I ask stupidly.

"Yes."

I heave a breath of relief. "Okay. I wasn't banking on a middle of the night flight, but at least I have time."

She shoves my arm. "Twelve p.m. is in two hours, you day drunk."

Well, shit.

CHAPTER THREE

DECLAN

Here's a life motto that makes sense: if you're going to do something stupid, make sure you get something out of it. This trip was one of the stupidest things I've ever done, and I feel worse than I did when I left home. So there's that. All I want to do is pick up my dog, go home, and get drunk on the porch while I watch the sun go down. I want it bad enough that I feel it pounding through me—*dog, home, drunk*—while I wait in a torture-chamber plane seat at a gate at JFK airport. Doesn't help that the weather took a turn, and it's almost as black as night out even though it's midday in July. Rain is pelting the winds and windows, and the anxiety I was already feeling is pulsing outward, infecting all of me. At least no one's sitting next to me.

The old woman next to the aisle took one look at my face and resorted to reading the in-flight magazine so she didn't have to take another. Her stark white hair, curled under around her chin, and sharp-eyed expression look vaguely familiar, but not in a way that sets off any alarm bells.

"You've got skills, Dec," I can hear my brother Seamus saying with a snort. *"All you need to do is look at someone to make them want to turn around and leave."* And he's just the kind of jackass

who'd take one look at me and dramatically creep out of the room after saying it to make everyone laugh. Truthfully, though, we'd both know he kind of means it. My brother's the comedian, the joker, the one with charisma—and he'll never quite forgive me for not being like him. Or for making decisions he wouldn't have made.

I went to see Seamus and our sister, Rosie, because something fucked up happened, again, and I was hurting. I felt a bone-deep need for them—the way a wounded dog finds its way home—but I knew I couldn't stay. We're safer if we stay apart in exile. Rosie keeps trying to change my mind about that, but she's right when she calls me a mule. I can be guided, but when I set my heels in, neither hell nor heaven can sway me.

Truth is, it hurt to see them more than it helped. There are so many memories attached to my brother and sister, and the good ones are harder to carry than the bad. Because our parents are gone, and the life we had is gone too. Forever. Part of me is grateful for that, because the life we'd had was built on a foundation of quicksand, and each year, I felt myself sinking in deeper, becoming someone I didn't want to be. But the way it all fell apart left a mark on my soul, or tore it up completely.

Yes, the trip was a mistake—no two ways about that. They're better off without me, and safer if I stay away.

I'm thinking about lifting the armrest between me and the empty seat beside me so I'll feel less like I'm being squeezed to death when a blonde woman comes stumbling down the aisle toward me. Her hair, loose around her shoulders, is a bright, sunny blonde, and for a second my eyes are glued to it.

"Please take your seat," the flight attendant calls to her, as if it weren't perfectly obvious that's what she's trying to do.

My luck's the kind that guarantees her seat is the one between me and the lady who's currently reading about the snack preferences of some smiley fuck in a flight suit.

"I'm so sorry," the blonde woman says as she reaches my companion.

The woman gives a theatrical sigh, as if she were really enjoying the space-filler article, and heaves herself up and into the aisle. Blondie squeezes in and sits next to me, bringing a whiff of bourbon with her, chased by a botanical scent of rosemary and apples.

I give her a second look, surprised. She doesn't seem like the kind of woman who'd be a few drinks in at noon. She may look a bit frazzled, but she's what Seamus would call the wholesome type. Blonde and pretty, dressed in the sort of neutral clothes a person wears because they don't want to be noticed. Beige shorts. A plain red T-shirt. Maybe it seems odd that I'd pick up on a thing like that, but if you want to avoid getting noticed, you get to learn what clothes will help you do the job. Especially if you're a six-foot-tall bearded man who can accidentally scare people into reading in-flight magazines.

The blonde woman sighs as she buckles her belt, then murmurs something under her breath.

"What?" In-Flight Magazine Lady says. "You're going to have to speak up. I'm partially deaf in one ear."

"Oh," Blondie says, turning toward her. "I wasn't... I was just saying, 'You made it.' You know...to myself."

"Yes," the older woman says slowly. "We all made it, most of us well before you did. Would you like a pat on the back?"

I hold back a laugh. Laughter's an invitation, and the last thing I want is to be drawn into conversation with either of them. You start talking to someone on a plane, they might keep you talking right up until you land, and I don't have two hours of conversation in me right now.

I learned that with my neighbor. I laughed at one of his jokes, and I couldn't quit him after that. He was always inviting himself over for a beer, telling stories with no beginning or end or perceivable point. I started expecting it, wanting it. Now that he's gone, and

I've got myself a new neighbor, I'm more cautious. No point in getting attached. Especially when the whole point of my self-imposed exile is to be alone.

"No," Blondie says. "I was talking to myself. I didn't invite anyone else to join the conversation."

This time a half laugh does escape me, and the older lady at the aisle isn't as humorless as she seems, because I catch her lips twitching.

Blondie glances at me. Her eyes widen, and I'm tempted to ask if she's also going to develop a sudden interest in the in-flight magazine that's going around these parts.

The flight attendant leads us through a presentation everyone ignores, and finally it's time for this tin can to become airborne.

I hold my jaw tight and grip the armrest as the plane taxies and then lifts into the air. I don't like giving up control, never have. It requires the kind of trust a man would be stupid to give—especially to a pilot he's never seen, who could very well have been doing shots at the bar with Blondie.

"Here," Blondie says, surprising me by thrusting a pack of gum at my chest. "It helps if you have something to do with your mouth." Her eyes widen, and then she shakes her head. "Wow, Claire, really?"

"You talking to yourself again?" I ask, drawn in despite myself.

"It's a bad habit." She reclaims the pack before I can take a piece, which is just as well. It's some fruit flavor, not mint, and chewing it would have made me feel worse than the little spastic bumps wracking the plane every twenty seconds or so, as if it's caught the hiccups.

"Would you like to know what I think a bad habit is?" asks the older woman who's the hubcap on our little group. Somehow, without wanting to be drawn into conversation, I'm being engaged by both of them. It's like being suckered into one of those group chats without being able to pull the plug.

Without waiting for either of us to respond, the older lady sniffs and says, "Alcoholism."

Claire blushes and gives me a sidelong glance.

"What? I'm not an alcoholic," I say for some damn reason.

"Neither am I," she hurries to say. "I just...I got some upsetting news, and I didn't realize I'd be getting on a plane this afternoon. It all happened so quickly. It's not like I usually drink before noon, honest to God."

Whatever she's saying has all the marks of a long, complicated story. I can't afford to be interested in it. Long, complicated stories lead to long, complicated conversations, and I want to put this trip behind me and pretend it never happened.

I want to go back to feeling numb, or putting up a good front of it.

"You didn't realize you were going to be on a plane?" the older lady asks scornfully. She's apparently all about long, complicated conversations.

"Well, the woman who bought me the ticket told me the flight was for Sunday," she says.

The older lady's scowl deepens. "There's your problem. You let someone else do for you what you should have either done yourself or directly overseen. You young people are always letting others do your dirty work, and then you're surprised when it doesn't turn out the way you wanted. Why, in my—"

The plane gives a dramatic shake that sends a jolt of fear through me. I grip both armrests and feel a crack beneath my palm.

Claire gasps. "You broke that."

But I don't respond. I *can't*. The plane's still shaking as if it's a toy being manhandled by a giant-ass toddler.

I can feel her watching me, and I hook onto her gaze, needing to latch onto something other than the feeling of being shaken around by someone so much bigger. My first conscious thought other than *—the gig is up* and *fuck, fuck, fuck*—is that her eyes are beautiful.

Golden, with little flecks of brown and green. The play of colors is almost hypnotizing. I'd much rather keep staring at them than think about dying next to her, both of us hooked into these cheap plastic chairs, positioned too closely together to be comfortable for anyone but a child.

She says something else, and it takes a moment for the words to register through the buzzing in my ears.

"Do you want me to get you a drink?"

A drink. *Yes.* I can't have more than one, because I'll need to drive home in a couple of hours, but I'm not going to make it through this flight without something to settle my nerves.

I swallow. I nod. The older lady sighs.

"Not alcoholics, huh? Why, in my day—"

"It's still your day, isn't it?" Claire asks pointedly. "Would you like a drink too? My treat."

There's static over the loudspeakers, then a voice announces. "Folks, this is your captain speaking." He chuckles; I'd want to punch him in the face if I didn't need him to fly the plane. "You may have noticed a few little bumps, huh? It's not pretty out there today. There's no need for concern, but I'm sorry to report that we're going to experience turbulence all the way to Charlotte airport today. So stay in your seats if you can, and keep those seatbelts fastened. Have a pleasant flight!"

I grit my teeth. Flying is hard for me most of the time, but right now, with all my nerves raw and scraped, it's worse.

The older lady is still scowling at Claire, but then the plane gives another jolt that has my hand hugging the cracked plastic, and she gives a self-righteous nod. "You know, under the circumstances, I suppose I wouldn't mind having a Pimm's Cup."

Claire looks at her in disbelief. I'd smile if the plane didn't give another jolt.

"Ma'am, I don't think they'd even have that in business class.

My guess is that you're stuck with bad red wine or bad white wine. Maybe a Budweiser."

"They might be willing to mix your bad white wine with sprite," I suggest, momentarily forgetting my vow of silence. The look on the woman's face is nearly worth it.

"My word. You're a heathen, aren't you?" Again, though, there's a glimmer of humor in the way she says it.

"What's your name?" Claire asks her.

"Mrs. Rosings," she says primly, then cuts off Claire before she can speak, "and we all know *you're* Claire."

Both she and Claire turn toward me, their expressions expectant, and my gaze shoots to the aisle. A flight attendant is approaching us with her cart, just a few people in front of us, which is good, because the plane gives another jolt that has me digging my hand into the fractured plastic of my armrest.

"Well, young man?" Mrs. Rosings says.

"Name's Declan." It feels like I should offer up something else —*good to meet you*, or something along those lines, but it's not really true. There are few places I wouldn't rather be. Still, I like Claire, and I don't mind Mrs. Rosings.

The plane's man-handled by the air again, and I must have flinched, because Claire surprises me by placing her hand on my arm. Maybe it's my fear of dying here, in this metal tube, but the sensation feels amplified—as if every point of contact has been tattooed into my skin. I glance at her in surprise, my gaze again finding those nearly golden eyes. They beat into me, steadying me. "You don't need to be scared."

"I'm not scared," I say gruffly, the response so immediate it's an obvious tell, the kind that could get a guy in trouble or lose him a lot of money.

Soft, that's what my uncle used to call me when he felt like taunting me. Then again, next to him, steel was soft. He'd prided himself on that.

Other people had called me soft too, though, enough times that it had burrowed under my skin. When I was a kid, a few guys had dared to say it to my face after finding out that I kept a greenhouse with my mother, and they'd learned the hard way that a guy can love growing flowers with his mother and still know how to throw a punch.

Claire shrugs uncaringly. "Call it what you will. You know, my dad always tells me turbulence is just like driving over a bumpy road. They're just, like, air bumps."

"My husband died in a plane crash," Mrs. Rosings comments with a sigh.

Jesus Christ. "Really?" I ask, arcing my neck toward her so quickly I hear it crack.

"Is that the kind of thing someone would joke about, young man?"

No, probably not. But it doesn't make me feel better about our chances. I read once the odds of dying in a plane crash are one in a million, whereas the odds of dying in a car crash, like my parents did, are one in five thousand. But here's the thing about odds: someone's at the bad end of them. Those are real people who died, and here's the proof.

"Oh, thank goodness, the drinks cart is almost here," I hear Claire murmur. Her hand is still pressed against my arm, her fingers long and delicate but firm. Maybe she's forgotten it's there, or maybe she realizes it's my lifeline right now. Because it is: the soft press of her fingers and thumb is the only thing helping me push back the panic as the plane bucks.

There's a static crackle, then the captain's voice graces us again: "Sorry folks, we're going to have to suspend the beverage service. That turbulence is going to get worse, and we don't want anyone getting hurt."

My eyes probably look wild as they track the retreat of the drinks cart.

Claire swears under her breath, and Mrs. Rosings gives her a stern look. "I heard that, young woman."

But the words have barely passed her lips before the plane lists to the side and then shakes so hard the drinks cart goes flying down the aisle and collides with the back wall with a bang so loud it seems to shake the plane a second time.

A couple of swears and exclamations of surprise fill the air, and it is not at all comforting when I note that one of them came from the flight attendant who lost her cart. She races forward to reclaim it, her face pale and drawn. Also not good. Flight attendants are on multiple planes everyday—if she's nervous, there's a reason for *me* to be nervous.

My heart is pounding wildly in my chest now, and without thinking about it, or knowing why, I find myself looking into Claire's eyes again.

"It's going to be okay," she says calmly, almost like she means it. I'd believe her if not for her fearful expression. She has eyes that tell a person how she's feeling, and today hasn't been a banner day for her.

"You don't really believe that," I say flatly. "You're just saying that to make me feel better." It blows my mind that she'd bother— that she'd pause in the middle of a crisis to worry about what other people might be feeling—and it makes me feel strangely protective of her.

"I *do* believe it," she insists. "It's like my dad told me. They're bumps in a road." Her lips lift slightly in the corners, and I register that they're *very nice* lips. Rosy and soft, with a pinprick mole at one corner. "Focus on me," she says, and I decide I'm going to do exactly that. If I'm going to die, I might as well do it looking in the face of a beautiful woman.

Mrs. Rosings chuckles and pulls something out of her purse. I don't glance at her, and neither does Claire, because we're still locked onto each other. The plane shakes again, and Mrs. Rosings thrusts whatever she has toward me, reaching across Claire to do it.

I finally break the stare, feeling a strange heat pulsing in my temples, and look down at what Mrs. Rosings has clutched in her hand as I reflexively take it.

I frown at her. "It looks like a bracelet." An ugly bracelet, I think but don't add. It's chunky and metallic and large and heavy for no perceivable reason.

"Open it," she says with a nod toward the bling on one side.

"I've seen these before! *You* have a flask, Mrs. Rosings?" Claire announces. "I guess I should be pissed at you for being a hypocrite, but that's honestly too delightful."

"Shhhh," the woman says fiercely, glancing down the aisle as if the flight attendant, or anyone else, might currently give a fuck about whether she snuck alcohol onto the flight. The other customers are murmuring to each other or themselves, and a woman a few rows up is weeping. *Weeping.* Fuck.

Claire's hand flexes on my arm. "Open it," she says.

My gaze shifts to Mrs. Rosings. "What's in it? Pimm's Cup?"

"Gin."

Not my favorite, but yes, I am at a *drinking gin from an old lady's bracelet* level of desperation. The last thing I want to do is have a panic attack. I take a pull of the gin, then another, before handing the flask off to Claire. She takes it with the hand that's been pressed to me, and my skin feels cold from the lack of her.

When she wraps her mouth around the opening, I feel a pulse of awareness of those pink lips wrapping around the place where mine just pressed. I shake it off as she holds the flask out to Mrs. Rosings, who primly recaps it and returns it to her bag.

"I don't know what kinds of germs you have," she says. "My cousin Jennifer caught herpes from sharing a drink with a stranger."

"I'm pretty sure that's not the only thing Jennifer shared with the stranger," Claire says, laughing—and then laughs harder when

Mrs. Rosings only watches her with a flat expression. "Oh, come on, Mrs. Rosings. I can tell you have a sense of humor. You can't hide it from me."

This time a small smile breaks through on the woman's face. Claire has a way with people and probably doesn't even realize it. She's got the gift of the gab, like my brother, something that bypassed me, and an understanding of the ocean of things left unsaid beneath each thing that's shared. But the plane seems to take offense, because it gives a bigger dip, then feels like it's free-falling. Screams rip through the air, and I feel my heart trying to pound its way out of my chest. I feel the same way I do every time I hear the kind of bad news there's no backing away from—*they're dead, dead, dead*—except this time, I'm the one who's about to be shoved into the unknown. This is it. This is it. This is—

A warm hand presses to my chest, against my racing heart, searing my skin through the thin fabric. It slides upward, cupping around my jaw and turning my face. It's her. It's Claire. And now her golden, color-flecked eyes beating into mine. The smile on her face doesn't meet them, which tells me that even though she's seeking to comfort me, she knows we're in trouble too. Regret tugs at me, because she'll be gone too, and the world needs more bright things, not fewer.

She says my name, and I don't really think, I just do what feels natural, what it feels like I need more than breathing, because the plane is bouncing again, and it's going to fall, and this is going to be it, and I lean in toward her—

She meets me halfway, and I reach behind her to wrap a hand in her sunshine hair, which is the source of the apples and rosemary smell. I kiss her. It's not a gentle kiss, it's an *I'm about to die, so fuck it* kiss. I suck in her lips, her smell, her taste of gin and bourbon and something sweet, and I try to make sure this last moment is as good as any moment can be. It would be better if Mrs. Rosings weren't muttering something beside us, but I guess we don't get to choose how we go out, at least not in detail. And kissing this woman whose last name I don't know seems like a pretty good deal to me.

Her hair is soft and silky against my hand, and she makes a sweet little moan in my mouth, and for half a second I don't even care that I'm going to die, and all of this sorry shit I've gone through will have been for nothing, because this feels so good. Better than it should, probably because it's the last time I'm going to feel *anything*. My whole body is waking up, as if it's been asleep for months, years, but it wants to be awake for this—the big finale.

Then a pair of hands slaps in front of our faces, and I pull away, stunned as I hear Mrs. Rosings say, "Quit your fornicating, kids."

It takes me a second to realize the plane's evened out—and everyone within view of us is staring.

CHAPTER FOUR

CLAIRE

How awkward is it to spend the rest of a two-hour flight sandwiched between a disapproving older woman with surprisingly fine taste in gin and a *very attractive* stranger who just kissed you like you were a winning lottery ticket?

I'm about to find out.

When Mrs. Rosings clapped her hand in front of us like we were a couple of dogs going at it through a chain-link fence, Declan jolted away from me as if he'd been informed that I was the source of Jennifer's herpes.

I look up, dazed, and am surprised to see we haven't died—or if we did, hell truly is other people. Because everyone within a five-seat radius is staring at us, and one woman is covering her son's eyes, as if he hasn't seen worse in G-rated movies.

"Uh, sorry," I say, because it seems like something needs to be said. But it doesn't take long for the other passengers to lose interest in us and return to doing whatever it is they were doing before it started to seem like we were all going down.

There's a crackle of static, and then the pilot comes over the loudspeaker again. "Well, folks, that was a doozy!" He laughs, joined by no one. "But we've circled around the weather system, and the rest of our trip should only have a few little bumps. We've added an hour to our flight time."

Which means I'm going to miss my connecting flight to Asheville, probably, but I can barely register that right now.

I glance at Declan—at that big, strong man who is clearly terrified of flying, and remember what his racing heart felt like beneath my hand, his lips pressed to mine, consuming me. Is he as affected by what happened as I am? Because one touch was enough to make me want many, *many* more—unlike Doug of the unsatisfying supply cabinet gropings. But when I look at him, he has the in-flight magazine spread open across his lap—the in-flight magazine! It looks like it has some sticky red substance on it from a child's lollipop, but apparently even that is preferable to looking at me.

Holy Jekyll and Hyde!

The change is enough to give a girl whiplash, never mind the turbulence, and I can't help but feel disappointed. Like I'm an in-flight convenience that has been used and discarded.

To be fair, he'd clearly wanted nothing to do with me or Mrs. Rosings until it seemed like we'd be spending our last minutes on earth together. Now that he's been granted a reprieve, he probably figures he'd rather be done with us.

Or maybe he has a girlfriend, a voice whispers in my head.

Shit, does he have a girlfriend?

I wouldn't be surprised if he did—hell, he probably has five of them. He's got this tall, muscular, brooding thing going on, with black hair that's the perfect length for a woman to wrap her hands in, and a short, trimmed beard that's so completely perfect it probably makes pubescent boys jealous. And don't even get me started on his eyes—a deep, warm brown fringed with lashes that would make a baby deer jealous. He's in work pants and a white T-shirt that hugs his muscular arms and shows an outline of a black tattoo on his chest. The second I saw him, I checked my ticket number, because when I fly, I'm usually seated next to people who smell like cheese or small children who pepper me with questions and kick my feet. But, no, some greater power sat me next to this fine specimen. It no longer seems like such a gift, though.

Crap. What if he has a girlfriend waiting to pick him up at Charlotte, and she takes one look at him and knows his tongue was in my mouth?

I could be the Richard Ricci in this scenario, a thought that is frankly unbearable.

"Do you have a girlfriend?" I hiss at him.

His eyebrows wing up, and he nearly fumbles the in-flight magazine onto the floor. It's open to a spread about socks. I can hear Mrs. Rosings laughing softly to herself beside me.

"I'm not really looking for a relationship," Declan says after an uncomfortable moment. "I'm sorry for..." He gestures toward my mouth, and I feel an unfair tingle in my lips. "But...yeah, I figured we were done for, and it seemed like a good idea at the time."

"Excuse you," I say, feeling the sting of his words. "What makes you think *I'm* interested in *you*?"

He glances from me to Mrs. Rosings next me, as if I've asked a trick question and she's his help hotline. "You just asked if I have a girlfriend."

"Because she wants to know how much of a scoundrel you are, boy," Mrs. Rosings says helpfully. "Not every woman who gives out cups of sugar wants to bake cookies."

I've never heard that one before, but it sounds accurate enough, so I nod. "What she said."

He rubs the back of his neck, wincing as the plane gives a little bump, this one as gentle as a baby's burp compared to earlier. "No, no girlfriend." His brow furrows, and he tilts his head slightly, studying me with a bottomless gaze. A woman could get lost in it if she weren't careful. Since it's starting to look like I'm going to survive this trip, I think it's time for me to start being careful.

"What about you?" he asks. "Is some guy in a suit going to track me down?"

I snort. "Why do you assume he'd been in a suit?"

"Wouldn't he?"

I suppose he's right. Most of my exes *have* been guys in suits, but that's purely situational. I worked in a high rise office building, around the clock, so guys in suits or khakis and button-up shirts were the people I met.

"No, no guy, in a suit or not. But I don't like being put in boxes."

"Feels like we're all in one now," Declan says with a sigh. "I shouldn't have kissed you, though. Whether there's a suited guy or not. I'm sorry."

I'm not. Maybe I should be, but getting kissed by a hot stranger has been the highlight of my shitty week. I don't like what this says about me, but it might have been the highlight of my year.

"Thanks, I guess," I say, trying not to sound sullen.

He gives me a small nod, then reaches into the backpack under the seat in front of him and pulls out a pair of earbuds and puts them in. Duly noted, conversation over. He doesn't even pull out a device to play music on, so presumably he's just using them for sound cancelling.

As messages go, this one is loud and clear.

I lean back and look away from him.

But I only get about halfway through a good and pouty sigh before Mrs. Rosings touches my arm. "He's *embarrassed*," she says conspiratorially. "My son is the same way. Doesn't like anyone to know he's afraid of anything. But we saw past the veil, didn't we? He's having a hard time forgetting that."

It's an interesting perspective, and I turn to get a better look at her. She's wearing one of those kaftans rich people favor—the kind that look like they cost maybe twenty bucks from Walmart but were probably handwoven from silkworm threads. Agnes has a hundred of them. "I guess we did."

She smiles at Declan's figure to my left, and I can *feel* him. His skin was hot and hard beneath his shirt, nothing like Doug from PR, who took off his shirt with great fanfare, only to reveal a pasty chest that hadn't seen the light of day since the last fiscal crisis and had as much definition as a popover that had failed to rise. That quick touch was enough to give a woman *an imagination*.

"Who are you, Mrs. Rosings?" I ask, because I don't want to think about Declan.

"Are you inviting yourself to my Christian name?" Mrs. Rosings asks as if she hadn't just pulled out a bracelet flask she'd snuck past security.

"No, I want to know who you are. I'm asking...you know...what your deal is."

"You're drunk," she says flatly.

I almost say *I wish* but settle for, "Only mildly tipsy. It'll pass soon."

Her lips twitch, fighting a smile, and she says, "I was a Mary Kay saleswoman for thirty years. Now is that the truth or a lie?"

I study her face, taking in the slight twitch of her nose as she watches me and the fine wrinkles around her shrewd blue eyes.

"Lie."

She nods as if we've settled something and says, "Well, at least you have more sense than I thought you did when you sat down stinking of a bar."

"We're back to this, are we?" I ask. "I thought we'd trauma-bonded."

She makes an aggrieved sound, then settles back in her seat and picks up the in-flight magazine. Is that thing made of crack? Are there golden tickets in it that will take me somewhere better than here?

The last thing she says to me before settling in for what's bound to be a perfectly boring read is, "That wasn't trauma, girl. It's like you said—just a couple of bumps in the road."

WHEN THE DIVERTED plane finally lands, I shoot up out of my seat the instant the captain cleared us to take off our seatbelts. My enthusiasm earns a comment from Mrs. Rosings, who tells me I didn't have any God-given sense if I don't realize we aren't getting off the plane for *at least* another five minutes, and there's no cause for me to loom over her like a bird of prey...

Then the line moves along and she walks off without a backward glance at Declan and me, which makes me feel a twinge of regret even though she made it clear she doesn't consider us friends.

Lainey says I want everyone to like me, and that's my fatal flaw.

She says her fatal flaw is to make hasty judgments and then cling to them until their final, dying breath—like how she decided Todd was going to be her endgame even though she kept finding out distressing new things about him. Like the fact that he'd had a secret text chain going with his childhood girlfriend for four months, and had been secretly meeting up with her for the last two.

I reach for my bag in the overhead compartment, but Declan gets to it first, pulling it down as easily as if it were full of feathers. He pauses, then his lips quirk into a small smile, and he nods at me and says, "Thanks for the sugar, Claire. I won't forget you."

Then he turns and leaves, and even though I'm eager as hell to get off the plane, it takes me a solid ten seconds—full of plenty of grumbling from the people behind me, to follow him. By the time I get off, he's gone, nothing but a whisper against my skin, where his short beard had rubbed against it.

Ten minutes later I'm standing in front of the help desk at the airport, where I've been informed that my connected flight is already halfway to Asheville, and the next five flights from this airport to that one have been cancelled. I won't be able fly to Asheville until tomorrow afternoon, earliest.

"But we're only, like, two or so hours from Marshall, right?" I ask the woman behind the counter, who has frizzy hair and a nametag so bedazzled with gem stickers I can't tell what her actual name is. "Two hours driving?"

"I don't know what Marshall is," she says, patting a bunch of brochures so they'll align more perfectly. It has the added bonus of allowing her to avoid my desperate gaze. I'll bet those brochures have gotten a lot of pats today.

"It's this little town right next to Asheville."

"Asheville is about two hours away by car, yes."

"So I can rent a car?"

"If you don't mind driving in the rain. Follow the signs to the rental counter."

It's not a helpful response, but my dad's always said you get more flies with honey. Admittedly, I have no idea why anyone would want flies, but the precept stands.

"Thank you, ma'am. But what about my luggage?"

"That's not a problem at all," she insists with a knowing nod. "They'll bring it directly to your location."

She has a tone that doesn't brook questions, but I *need* that bag. "Are you sure? Is there someone I should call?"

"You can call the airline help number," she says unhelpfully, "but they'll tell you just what I did. As long as you put your information on the tag, they'll bring it to you."

She sounds pretty sure of herself, so I don't question her again. I'm about to ask something else, when she shifts her gaze to the next person in line. "Ma'am?"

I turn from the counter, take a couple of steps away to lean against a pillar, and pull out my phone to send an email to the executor woman, telling her she made "a little mistake" with the plane ticket, explaining my current situation, and asking whether I need to book a hotel room. I hope to God she'll say no, or offer to pay for it. It's the only reason I keep the FU so implicit, although Lainey would probably tell me that I'm just rationalizing my inability to be assertive.

Sighing, I tuck away my phone and do my best to follow the signs, although it turns out the ticket attendant had a lot of unwarranted confidence in the airport's signage. It takes me about half an hour to find the car rental counter.

Once there, I'm pleasantly surprised that I only have to wait in line for about five minutes—and unpleasantly surprised when I get to the front of the line, because it turns out they've nearly been cleaned out of vehicles, and the only one-way rental they have left is a single enormous van.

I grew up in New York, so it's only thanks to Lainey's parents' ill-advised Dodge Dart that I know how to drive at all. A van would really be pushing it.

Only...if I don't rent it, I'll be stuck at the airport for twenty-four hours, and I've already established that there's nothing to do other than sit around in a rocking chair and eat a giant pretzel. Don't get me wrong, I'd enjoy the hell out of that for fifteen minutes, but twenty-four hours? Not with the way adrenaline is dumping into me, insisting I *do* something.

"And you're sure this is the only one available?" I ask the attendant. "No little compact cars hidden behind it?"

He laughs, even though I'm definitely not joking, and picks his nose. "Nope. She's a girthy thing, huh? Even bigger in person than in the pictures. Not used to driving big cars?"

"No," I admit.

"Nothing to worry about," he says, flicking whatever he found in his nose onto the carpeted floor with confidence. "You'll be queen of the road. No one would dare hit you if you're out in one of our Deluxe Plus models."

"It's not myself I'm worried about," I say, checking out the photo of the vehicle, which reminds me of one of those perspective pictures that shows a dinosaur next to a six-foot-tall man. "How busy is the road to Asheville?"

He laughs again. "Starts as a six-lane highway."

I think of the last time I drove Lainey's car, and how it took me seven minutes, sweating, to parallel park in a space so large I should have been able to just pull in. If I take this van, I could accidentally mow people down. I could be the inspiration for one of those *Based on a true story* Lifetime movies.

A throat is cleared behind me. I glance over my shoulder and shock pulses through me, settling not unpleasantly between my legs, because it's *Declan*.

I'd figured I'd never see him again. My gaze darts to his mouth, which is more generous than most men's.

He sticks his hands into the pockets of his work pants and rocks on his feet, nodding to me. "I could drive."

"It's a one-way rental to Asheville," I say. "You're going there too?"

His answer is a nod, his gaze on me, and a hot shiver works through me. It hits me that I've only heard him say maybe twenty words. Would it be foolish to get into a van with a stranger?

"You're asking me to put my life in your hands?" I ask.

His lips lift into a reluctant smile. "Or to let me rent the van and go by myself. I need to get home and pick up my dog."

Not exactly the most flattering invitation, but I decide to focus on the positive aspect...

"You have a dog? What kind of dog?"

"A quiet one."

The guy behind the counter grunts. "Do you want the van or not?

Declan raises his eyebrows, leaving the choice to me: stay here and eat delicious pretzels until they stop being delicious, or drive to Asheville with a hot guy who could win a kissing competition.

Turning back to the man behind the counter, I say, "We'll take it."

CHAPTER FIVE

DECLAN

Kissing Claire was another stupid act, but I figured I was owed one final mistake before dying. Not everyone gets that chance.

I don't have a good excuse for why I invited her to drive to Asheville with me. Sure, there was only one van left at that particular car rental place, but there were a few other car rental places to the left of the one she'd found. I could have told her so, she could have gone off and rented her compact clown car, and that would have been that. But I *wanted* her to come with me. I could still feel her lips against mine and the silky slide of her hair against my hand. I could hear the little noise of surprised approval she'd made in her throat—as if I'd swallowed it, and my chest had become an echo chamber.

Rosie would have a romantic view of that, no doubt. She has notions about shit like that. Maybe it's from the books she reads, half of them with a waxy-chested guy on the cover. My brother, who's always seeing a different woman, would say it's proof of nothing except that I need to get laid, and I'm more inclined to take that view of things. I have a few...friends in Asheville, women whom I see with no strings attached on either side, but it's been several weeks since I bothered calling any of them.

Maybe I'm fooling myself, but I'd much rather believe that's the issue than that I want to be around this woman because I'm curious about her. Because I like her.

Either way, here I am, sitting next to Claire again, only this time in a big, dark-blue van with a console between us, the rain beating against the windshield.

"So, was the in-flight magazine really that interesting?" Claire asks as I turn onto the highway toward Asheville. "Both you and Mrs. Rosings seemed *really* into it, so I figure the quality must have gone up. You know, my friend Beth used to sell articles to the in-flight magazine for American Airlines. Isn't that funny? You don't think about people actually writing those things. They'll probably give her job to A.I. soon, and no one would notice except for you and Mrs. Rosings."

"I wasn't reading it," I admit, partly to stop the stream of words coming from her, so fast I can barely keep up between the rain beating on the windshield, the traffic, and the bewilderment of being here, with her. "No one reads it. They could probably type the same word forty times, and no one would notice."

In my peripheral vision, I can see her eyes widen—and I imagine the golden sparkle of them. "I didn't think you'd admit to that." A pause lingers between us, surprisingly heavy, then she says, "Were you really that desperate not to talk to me?"

She seems a little upset about it, and for some reason I don't want to upset her. It's either that or my cock, wanting to test the waters, that has me saying, "I'm going to level with you. I was hard. I didn't want anyone to notice. That lady with the kid looked about ready to call the air marshal on us."

"Ooooh," she says, her voice a little breathy in a way that sends a pulse of pure need through me. Yes, it's definitely been too fucking long. Although I can't deny that this isn't aimless lust. It's lust that's firmly anchored to the woman beside me. "Well, I guess that explains why you didn't turn any of the pages."

"You sure paid attention to what me and the old broad were up to," I say, amused. The plane ride was a blur for me after kissing Claire. I'd stayed trapped in my mind, hostage to shitty thoughts, even though I could feel her there, at the edge of my awareness. The sun, burning me and inviting me out to soak it in.

"Something tells me she wouldn't appreciate being called that."

"I'm guessing you're right about that."

She looks out the side window. "It's kind of strange, thinking we'll never see her again. I was sort of fond of her and her gin bracelet." Her gaze darts back to me. "I didn't think I'd ever see *you* again either."

"And yet, here we are. Maybe you'll get lucky and run into Mrs. Rosings at the liquor store in Asheville."

I meant it as a joke, but she straightens in her seat as if I'd pinched her. "I'm really not the kind of person who drinks during the day. This was an isolated incident. And I—"

I lift a hand from the wheel. "Hey, no judgment from me."

She turns fully toward me, and awareness of her blasts through me—her scent, her warmth, *her*. I don't know why I figured it would be a good idea to bring a woman who got me hard from one kiss into this van—inches away but untouchable—but I don't feel any regret. I'm glad she's here. I'd figured I wouldn't see her again either—a thought that had filled me with a strange melancholy. Then again, my mood has been all over the place lately.

"I got fired on Thursday, and then I found out my father isn't my biological father, and my biological father is dead. I figured I was owed a couple of day drinks." She says this with a warm, self-righteous fury that makes me feel a thrum of sympathy and, for some godforsaken reason, also turns me on.

I feel an itch to look at her, and I scratch it, giving her a sidelong glance that takes in more of her—her sunshine hair, the golden glow of her eyes, the curve of her cheekbone. "Why'd you get fired, Claire?"

"You're not going to ask why my dad's not my dad?"

"I'm guessing it's because your mother fucked someone else, if you'll forgive my language."

Laughter bursts from her, and it's impossible not to smile. "You don't talk a lot, but when you do, you sure have a way of choosing your words... Yeah, that's exactly what she did." She pauses, watching the rain patter against the windshield. "I got fired for getting my boss drunk."

"I'm sensing a pattern," I tease.

She reaches out as if to shove my arm, remembers I'm driving on a busy highway being beaten by rain, and holds back. "It was a mistake. She's this lifestyle guru so people send her product samples all the time, and I gave her this canned drink that turned out to be alcoholic. She drank, like, three of them before we realized the problem—and then she went on a morning talk show."

I laugh lightly. "I actually know who you're talking about. My sister watches that show."

I mentally kick myself, then mentally pummel myself, because goddamn—a few minutes with her, and I've already revealed more than I should have. At least I didn't use Rosie's name.

"You have a sister?" she asks, leaning toward me.

"Sure, and she saw the show," I say, trying to deflect. "Said she's never laughed so hard in her life."

"Thanks," she says, her mouth puckering. "I'm glad it amused somebody. So what do you do for work?"

"Landscaping. Need a job? I could use someone to help me haul manure."

"Very funny. No, I need to deal with a personal crisis before I even think about getting another job."

Something about the way she says it suggests she wants me to ask questions. I'm surprised by how much I'd like to. But if I ask her questions, she'll feel obliged to ask me questions, and I won't be able to answer them with complete honesty. So I settle for saying, "So you're not here to enjoy our beautiful summer weather?"

I can sense her smiling as she looks out the windshield at the aggressively grey day, as if the clouds decided they'd like to swallow western North Carolina whole.

"No, but it *is* beautiful here," she says, her tone almost wistful. "I don't get out of the city often."

I almost laugh, because we're barely out of Charlotte, the highway congested with cars, smog all around us. It's not beautiful yet—but it'll get beautiful, and I'm glad I'll be the one to see her face when the mountain views start to assert themselves. I can almost see it now, her pretty pink lips parted, her eyes fixed on the far-off vistas.

I felt that way when I first saw it too. Like I was still lost, but I'd found something worth keeping.

"Just wait," I say, giving her another sidelong look.

She gazes back at me for a long moment before speaking, maybe even a minute or two. Then she surprises me by saying, "Did you really get hard from kissing me?"

A groan escapes me, because her words shoot straight to my cock. It takes a second for me to land on an answer that's not a request to pull over so we can make use of this excessively large vehicle. It would be so easy to touch her. To reach out and put a hand on her bare thigh, beneath the bottom hem of her shorts. To inch it upward and...

I cough. "Yes, but it's nothing you have to worry about. I'm perfectly capable of controlling myself. It's just been a while."

"Like a few months?"

"A few weeks, maybe."

She laughs, her eyes dancing with it. "And that's what you'd call a while?"

"Yeah."

"So, did you have a girlfriend three weeks ago?"

"No," I admit. "I had a few no-strings friends in Asheville."

She shakes her head, her mouth in a mirthful line. "Why am I not surprised?"

"I don't know," I say, stealing a glance at her. "Why aren't you?"

"You look like a player." She waves a hand at my body. "From my experience, men who spend a lot of time at the gym are always players. My friend actually wrote an article about that...you know, the same one who writes for the in-flight magazine. Do you take selfies in your bathroom mirror?"

There's a teasing lilt to her voice. Although what she said was obviously not meant as a compliment, I like that she's been noticing me.

"I've never taken a selfie," I say, "whether in the bathroom mirror or not. And I'm not a player. I'm just not looking for a girl-friend. The women I see aren't looking for relationships either."

"So they're players too," she says. "You're all players."

"Who's putting people into boxes now?" I ask, sneaking another look at her. "Anyway, I disagree. Saying someone's a player implies there's a game. There's no game. No disappointments. Just needs."

Fuck, I shouldn't have said that. Because that word seems to spark something inside of her. She leans toward me slightly, her eyes alight. My awareness of her in my peripheral vision becomes almost painful, and I shift in my seat, wishing I'd brought the damn in-flight magazine.

"So you have a lot of needs?"

"I do," I agree, barely aware of what I'm saying. My throat thick, I add, "Do you?"

"Depends on whether I have someone around who's any good at fulfilling them."

Fuck me.

She licks her lips, and I'm about two seconds away from pulling over to the side of the road and—

"Why are you so afraid of flying?" she asks, her about-face

shocking me. It's like she threw a bucket of ice water on my dick, so that's good, at least.

Loss of control.

I can see my uncle in my head, grinning at me. There'd always been something menacing about his grin, even when he was trying to charm people, like he was a wolf constantly busting the seams of his sheep suit. My mother hadn't liked him much, so I'd barely seen him when I was a kid. A few holidays, maybe. And gossip, whispered when Seamus, Rosie, and I were out of sight. *Organized crime. Drugs. Bad news.* It wasn't until my parents died that he became a central figure in my life—the one pulling the strings. Making me think I could still tug on them when I needed to.

"I don't know," I hedge. "It's an irrational fear." I shrug. "Or maybe not so irrational. You heard Mrs. Rosings. Bad shit might not happen frequently, but it does happen."

"I know, right?" Her eyes widen. "I couldn't believe it when she said that. I had questions for her—"

"I believe that."

I see the hint of a smile on her face. "But she opened her in-flight magazine too, so I didn't get to ask."

"You must just have that effect on people."

"Very funny...but why didn't you just drive if you're afraid of flying? It's far, but it's not, like, in California."

"I'm not going to let something like that hold me back," I say. "I figure I'll get over it eventually."

The expression on her face makes it clear she doesn't believe me. "What?" I ask defensively. "That's how people get over shit like that. My uncle always told me to feel the fear and do it anyway." I feel a tightness in my throat, the same way I get whenever I talk about someone who's gone for good. I'm glad he's gone, mostly, but there are dozens of other emotions wrapped around that one. "He was wrong about a lot of things—most things—but he was right about that."

"Sure," she says, making it obvious she doesn't buy it. "It just reminds me of how I told Lainey's parents I was afraid of roller coasters when I was a little kid, and they took us to this amusement park with a seriously terrifying ride, with tons of upside-down turns. Her dad spent twenty minutes hyping it up, and I got into line with them. But at the last minute I wanted to leave. I was in tears. But he told me that if I found the gumption to go on that roller coaster, I'd never be afraid to go another. I could do anything."

"And what happened?" I asked, drawn in.

"I went on it." She pauses, reflective, then finishes, "Lainey and I clung to each other the entire time, screaming, although she was screaming for a different reason. I never wanted to go on another roller coaster again."

I'm surprised into laughter for a second, and then my mood sobers. "I wasn't upset I missed my connecting flight. I'm not looking forward to getting on another plane ever again. I thought we were done for. You?"

"Only for a few seconds. But I never think something terrible is going to happen until it already has. It's the optimist in me."

I smile at her, because I can't *not* smile at her. I'd like to know more about her situation. About the father who's not her father and the job that's no longer her job, but it still doesn't seem right to ask for personal information when I can't really reciprocate. So I settle for turning on the radio.

She smirks at me. "Is this like the in-flight magazine of the car?"

"Maybe," I acknowledge. "But I don't have a hard-on this time." *Yet.* "I think I just need a minute to absorb everything. The whole near-death experience."

She nods and then surprises me by touching my arm—a quick touch, but she might as well have sparklers for fingers, because I feel it up and down my body.

"Trust me, I get it," she says. "It's been one hell of a day."

Silence falls between us. But a little while later, when the road changes and the rolling blue mountains become visible in the distance—soft and lovely and layered instead of jagged and snow-topped, like the behemoths out west—I let myself look at her again and soak in the quiet wonder on her face.

It's beautiful, to have a face like that—one that registers everything and leaves nothing to the imagination. It's also dangerous.

She catches me looking and turns to smile at me. "So this is what you told me to wait for, huh?"

"Yeah," I say. "And it only gets better. The view from my back deck is so good, my neighbor used to sneak his dates back there and pretend it was his place."

She snorts. "Sounds like *he's* a player."

"He was, actually, but...he's dead," I say before I can stop myself. It's the thought that's been trailing me all week—the grief that brought me to New York City to see my brother and sister, even though I'd intended never to visit them. People in hiding are supposed to hide, not gather together and throw parties. True, they're hiding together, and I'm on my own, but that's because I'm the reason for it. It's the penance I've been paying. But when you've only made one real friend in two years, and you find his broken body, you seek out familiar things. I still see him like that whenever I close my eyes, and it's bringing back other memories, buried ones. It's enough to drive a man mad.

Claire's giving me a horrified look, like I might have killed him myself, when I feel the back tire of the van pop. Her eyes widen, and she reaches out to grab my bicep, her hand wrapping around it like it's a handlebar. "What happened? Did someone hit us?"

"One of the tires popped," I say, pulling to the side of the highway.

Claire's eyes widen as a couple of cars whizz past us on the narrow road, and she releases my arm. The wipers on the windshield are fighting a losing battle with the downpour pinging off the van in all directions; the sound making it almost impossible to hear her as she asks, "What are we going to do?"

She sounds so helpless over a popped tire that I have to laugh. "You've never been in a car with a busted tire before?"

She's already shaking her head. "We didn't have a car growing up. Lainey's parents have one, but it's this teeny-tiny old thing and they hardly ever use it. Should I call Triple A? Or maybe the highway patrol?"

Without thinking, I reach forward and tuck some of her sunshine hair behind her ear, finding it as silky as I remember it. "It's okay, Claire. I can change the tire. I'm happy to. Makes me feel good that I can be the one who takes care of you this time."

"I didn't mind helping you," she says, looking a little startled. "I had panic attacks at the office sometimes. I know what it feels like, so when I saw you..." She swallows, and maybe she's thinking of that kiss too—of the electric pull that made me forget I was on a plane, or that planes existed, because she trails off. Then she swallows again and says, "Are you really going out in this?"

She gestures to the rain beating down on the windshield. It's still falling hard, like it's taken offense to the day and wants to wash it away.

"Sure. Wouldn't be the first time. I've camped in worse."

Sometimes I pack a bag and take to the mountains.

Sometimes, when I'm out there, I wonder if I'll bother coming back.

Her eyes gleaming with purpose, she reaches into her tote bag, the only luggage she has until her bag comes in, and removes a small pink plastic umbrella.

"No way," I say, laughing.

"You'd rather get wet than stand under a pink umbrella?" She sounds borderline offended that I don't want to balance her tiny umbrella against my shoulder while I work on the van.

"It's not the color I object to. It's just too small, and I'd have no way of holding it."

"I'll hold it over both of us."

A smile works over my face, because she said it with such determination, but if she tried, we'd both be soaked, no two ways about it —and she'd be even harder to resist if her T-shirt was wet and plastered to her chest.

"Let's put that in our back pocket, okay?"

"Is that your way of saying no?"

"My dad's. But it works well enough." I reach out and touch her hand, just above where it's hooked around the umbrella. "Thank you for the offer all the same. You're going to feel the car lift up, by the way."

I'm thanking her for the offer of the umbrella, but it's not just that. She made me feel better on the plane, even before the kiss. She's a person who cares about other people when she has no cause to. There aren't a lot of people like that in my life, at least not anymore, and I have enough sense to value those people when I come across them—even if our acquaintance is only going to be the length of this car ride.

Truth is, I'm not all that upset the tire popped, because it means I get to keep her for a few minutes longer.

CHAPTER SIX

CLAIRE

Another car whizzes by, making me flinch. I don't like the thought of Declan out there in the rain, alone, so I pull out my phone as a distraction. I haven't texted my dad and Lainey yet, and they're probably worried.

Sure enough, half a dozen notifications are waiting for me. The first, a response from the estate's executor—

Nope, didn't get the tickets wrong. It was a little test. You passed, BOOM. Come straight to the cabin. We have business to discuss. Plan on staying here. The only hotel in town smells like feet, and I have it on good authority that the carpet only gets cleaned once a year. You're welcome.

There's no greeting, no signoff.

Anger and confusion churn in my gut. Is this woman a psychopath?

Why else would someone blow hundreds of dollars on a last-minute plane ticket as a test ninety percent of people would probably fail? In fact, why go to the trouble of testing a perfect stranger in the first place? Could it be part of some weird codicil in my birth father's will?

I guess I'm a popped tire and an Uber away from finding out, although I'm suddenly wary of showing up at the house by myself and being alone with this woman. Maybe Declan—

Don't start asking him for more favors, Claire. He doesn't owe you anything.

Sighing, I text my dad and then Lainey, letting them know there was some trouble with the connecting flight, but I'm making the rest of the trip by car.

Lainey texts back immediately:

> Oh no, you're a terrible driver. Are you sure you're okay?

> Don't text me back if you're currently driving. I'd feel immense guilt if you died because you were answering me.

I glance out the window, see nothing but rain, and text back:

> I have a story for you...I can't tell you now, but it involves the hot guy who's driving this van.

My phone instantly rings. Sighing again, I decline the call and text her instead.

> Lainey, what if he'd been right next to me?

> Why isn't he?

> He's fixing the flat tire. That's part of the story.

> Goddamn, you really DO have a story.

> The only thing that happened to me today is that a woman shoplifted from the boutique. She stuffed a shirt into her bra and then bought a cheap bracelet. It was incredibly obvious, but I didn't know what to say, and she looked like she could murder me without breaking a sweat. So I rung her up for the bracelet and didn't say anything.
>
> On a related note, I might get fired. It was an expensive shirt.

Crap. We'll need the money from Richard's estate even more than I thought. While my dad offered some financial support after I called him crying on Wednesday afternoon, I'm less inclined to take it now that I know the truth. He's already done so much for me, *given* so much, and...

He assured me that I'm as much his daughter as ever, but I feel beholden to him in a way I can never repay. Because without him, I would have nothing. I'd be as good as an orphan, since my mother seems to be in no hurry to come back from the ashram, now called the Tribe of Light.

I send off a final text to Lainey—

> stay strong, I'll call later

Then I peer out the window again, craning my neck to try and get a look at Declan in the rain. The flat tire is on the side facing away from the highway, at least, so there's minimal chance he'll get hit by a car. I heard him retrieve the spare and whatever doo-dads are needed for tire changing, so presumably Operation-Change-a-Tire is moving forward, but nothing has happened since. No movement of the van, no sound except the rain and an occasional car.

Another minute ticks by, the pounding against the windshield escalating. Intrusive thoughts worm into my brain. What if Declan

left, or someone took him? What if he's being attacked by a mountain animal right outside of view? It feels wrong to continued sitting
in here, bored, while he's out there getting attacked by a cougar or a
black bear or whatever.

I also don't like being left in here with my worry, wrapping
around me like rubber bands being squeezed tighter and tighter. So
after a few more minutes tick past, I pull the pink umbrella out and
get out of the car. Within seconds, I realize why Declan was so
dismissive of the umbrella. The rain is falling at an angle that makes
protection impossible. Everything is soaked, the ground a thick
sludge of gravel. I move around the side of the vehicle, breathing
hard, worried I'll find him in some kind of distress. But when I make
it to the back tire, he's sitting on his haunches beside it, examining
the spare with a scowl.

He glances up at me, his hair soaked, his shirt glued to his chest
in a way that outlines every ridge of muscle and the swirl of ink on
his chest. Is this what happens when people in books are always
talking about forgetting to take a breath? I thought it was B.S., but
now I'm not so sure. Because I'm speechless. All I can do is look
at him.

"You came out here to save me?" he asks with a slight upturning
of his lips, then shakes his head. "The spare's no good. Changing it
won't get us to Asheville. We'd be better off with the flat."

"Time for highway patrol?" I ask as the rain showers me with
hot spray.

He smiles at me, his hair dripping into his eyes. Drops of water
cling to his long eyelashes and beard and drip down his neck. My
mind tries to track all of them. "I know a guy. I already texted him.
We're less than an hour away."

I step forward with the umbrella, intending to cover us both, but
I slip on a muddy patch of gravel and go down like a stack of bricks,
falling right onto Declan. Although he'd be more than capable of

catching me, he wasn't prepared, so he goes down too. Suddenly we're both splayed out on the gravel and mud and falling rain by the side of the highway, the insufficient umbrella on top of us. I'm on top of *him*—well, his back anyway—but he rolls to face me, his arms going up around me, holding me as if there's a chance he can retroactively save me from going down. My hands grip his biceps as if they've just been waiting for the excuse my clumsiness has provided.

The umbrella tumbles a few feet away, getting stuck in one of the trees next to us. But my focus is on Declan. His nose has a slight bump on the bridge.

"Are you okay?" he asks hoarsely.

I'm better than okay. My body is stretched out on top of him, and he is hard and hot. I'm so close to his face that I see the surprise fade from his eyes, overtaken by something else.

I remember him talking about his needs, his voice husky and deep, and then his hand is moving over my back in a caress that makes me want to arch into him like a cat. My breasts are pressed to his hard chest, and my nipples suddenly feel hard and achy. The rain's still coming down hard, soaking us more. The warm water is actually cool against my overheated skin, but the goosebumps washing across my skin have nothing to do with it. Neither of us attempt to get up. His arms are still around my back, pressing me closer.

"You should have let me come out with the umbrella sooner," I say, my voice strange and breathy to my ears. "You're all...wet."

He reaches up and captures a lock of my hair in his hand, tracing his fingers over it. "But you're wet too. Your hair is dripping with it." A jolt of pure lust zips through me and settles down low.

"So maybe the umbrella sucks," I admit.

He laughs, and I laugh with him, and it's absurd—being out here and covered in dirt and rain, with this man whose existence I wasn't aware of this morning. It's a pure moment. A *good* moment, and I want to clutch onto it even harder because I have no idea what's going to come after it. All I know is that it won't feel as good as this does.

I push myself up, palms against his hard chest, thighs on either side of him, straddling him basically. I'm ready to push to my feet when I feel something that makes me pause. Liquid heat courses through me, and it has nothing to do with the rain. I look at Declan, and find his eyes on me, his fixed focus sending more heat through me. "I don't think the magazine would have covered it," I say, my voice coming out ragged.

He curses through his teeth but doesn't try to push me off.

"You told me it's been a while since you've...fulfilled your needs."

A sound of disbelief escapes him. I'm not sure he's even aware of it, but his hand is moving up and down my back, the slight pressure pushing me closer to where I'm desperate to be. "*Claire.* We should get up and wait in the back of the car. We can change into dry clothes."

"No one's kissed me like you did...not for a long time." Maybe ever, I think but don't say. Doug kissed like a fish gasping for air. There were other men, of course, but none of them were anything special. None of them made me feel special either.

His gaze sharpens on me. The water patters on my back, but it feels good, like I'm running out into a rainstorm and dancing. "Why not?"

"No one's wanted to, I guess."

"That's not true," he says, his eyes beating into me, his hand moving in that same rhythm down my back, his hard cock captured between us. There's so little space separating us—we're even closer than on the plane, his face inches from mine, his mouth in a near smile, beads of rain caught in his beard.

"You were the last person I wanted to kiss before I died," he murmurs, his head so close to mine that I can feel the words *and* hear them, "and I'd only known you for half an hour. There must be plenty of people who want to kiss you."

"Not like *that*," I say.

"Then they're stupid," he insists firmly. "There's no curing stupid."

I lower my head slightly, my lips only a whisper above his mouth. Everything inside of me is focused on him, on now.

"Are you inviting me to kiss you again, Claire?"

"Yes," I say, feeling fire in my cheeks because I don't think I've ever had to say it before. To ask for it. And also because his voice is husky and deep and *dirty*. "I think I need you to."

And the hand he still has on my back lifts up and spears into my wet hair, pulling me to him as he lifts up to meet me—and this time I'm positive. No other man has ever kissed me like this before—like I'm a delicacy, but he's too starving to savor me the way he'd like to. My whole body aches and pulses, and I feel alive in a way I can't remember *ever* feeling.

All those years of pushing paper, staring at a computer screen, listening to Agnes drone on...how much living did I miss? I could have been doing this—taking planes to mystery places, making out with a sexy landscaper in the rain on a road in the mountains.

Declan sucks on my bottom lip and guides me up to sitting with his hand, my legs weaving around his waist so his hard cock is captured between us, the rain bucketing down on our heads—and I start rocking against him before I even realize I'm doing it, my hands buried in the wet hair at the nape of his neck. It feels natural, it feels *good,* and from the breathy swear he utters in between hard, desperate kisses and the way the hand that isn't speared into my hair settles on my hip, guiding my movements with slick confidence, he thinks so too.

Then someone beeps a car horn three times, and horror washes over me.

What's the matter with me? We may be mostly hidden by the huge cargo vehicle, but we'd be visible to anyone driving this way. It probably looks like I'm...

I jolt off of Declan's lap, and his eyes follow me, heavy-lidded in a way that has me thinking about his *needs*. Normally, the knowledge that he's a player, the kind of guy who has a list of women, would put me off. But right now...

My head's still spinning from the last couple of days, and it feels like it'll never stop. No, this isn't going to lead anywhere, but what does it matter? Does *anything* matter?

There are no guarantees. I put in all those years with Agnes because I thought they were leading somewhere, and the only thing I got was a box full of personal items before I was escorted out the door. Only three or four personal items, since last fall she decided it looked gauche for each of us to have different and unmatching tchotchkes out on our desks, so everyone had to color coordinate and run our final choices by her.

But Declan's still staring at me, the rain dripping off the ends of his messy black hair. His shirt is completely plastered to his chest now, and I can make out more of the tattoo on his pec—a bird of some kind. *A bird of prey*, my mind supplies, even though it doesn't really look like that. His cock is a hard, delicious outline in his pants, and he's so appealing it's physically painful to look at him without jumping right back onto his lap.

"I've never..." I start, then trail off.

"I know...it's... Maybe it's the near-death experience," he says, his voice gruff. Almost embarrassed again, reminding me of what Mrs. Rosings said on the plane. He reaches for my hand as if to take it, then lets his hand drop. I'm too startled to tell whether or not I'm disappointed. "Let's get inside the back of the van so we can change."

"I don't have anything to wear," I admit as we get up—neither of us in a particular hurry since we're both soaked through and couldn't get any wetter. I *definitely* couldn't get any wetter. "All of my clothes are in my checked bag."

Everything's in there, a fact I'm trying not to freak out about.

"I have something for you," he says, opening the back of the cargo van. I climb in, my whole body prickling with awareness, because he's going to follow me in.

Because he's going to change in here, too.

My breath sounds obscenely loud, even more so than the water pinging off the metal body of the beast we're in, as I sit on the floor of the van and watch him climb in behind me and close the cargo door. His duffel bag from the plane is already back here, and I watch as he opens it, riveted, as if it might contain evidence about who this man is. Because I don't know a whole lot other than that he's a landscaper who has a dog, a sister he doesn't talk about, and a fear of flying.

Except that's not entirely true. I know that he's funny and an observer—the kind of person who watches others and picks up on things most people wouldn't notice. I know that he has secrets he doesn't want to disclose to anyone. That he's vulnerable with me, and he's not used to it. I also know that he has a big dick and is a good kisser and...

I swallow as I catch the T-shirt he just tossed me. It's bright green, but I couldn't care less about what it looks like, to be honest, because he just peeled off his shirt, letting the soaked fabric slap onto the floor. He's hard and tan and built, with a sprinkling of dark chest hair. I was right about the tattoo. It's of a crow with a sprig of something clutched in its claw.

When he glances over at me—probably sensing me staring at him like an obsessed fan—he swears again. "Don't look at me like that, Claire."

"Why not?"

He pulls on a dry white T-shirt, robbing me of my view. This is a disappointing development, because I'd hoped we'd be keeping our clothes off for longer. "I don't have great control over myself right now."

"Does that mean you're going to turn around while I change my shirt?" I ask, grabbing the hem of my sodden shirt. It's mid-summer and warm despite the rain, but it's still not pleasant to sit around in wet clothes.

"No," he says, his jaw working. "Not unless you want me to."

"I don't," I say, because I'd honestly like him to look. I feel like a different person right now—freer, wilder, more *alive*.

I pull the shirt off, feeling his gaze beating into me. But I don't put the green shirt on. Not yet. Partly because I have a gorgeous black lace bra on, purchased after I finally worked up the nerve to break up with Doug, and this is the first chance I've had to show it to anyone. Excitement zips through me, and even though I should be more cautious—even though Declan's a near-stranger, and I shouldn't be flashing him in the back of a van by the side of the road —I feel completely safe.

"Why are you so worried about self-control?" I ask. "You told me you have half a dozen women at your beck and call, so you obviously don't care about controlling yourself most of the time. Why does it matter with me?"

He gives his head a little shake, his mouth lifting into a half smile. "I said I had a few friends with benefits. That doesn't mean they're at my beck and call."

"If you're okay with sleeping with them, why not me? From the way you're acting, I'd assume you weren't attracted to me if you didn't keep..." I wave my hand in the direction of his dick, which is still a very pronounced bulge in his wet pants.

Will he be taking those off too?

I steel myself and then say something completely unlike me.

"We'll probably never see each other again after today. I think we should have some fun."

He edges closer on his knees, everything in me tracking his progress as he slides across the metal floor of the van. He's so close, I can hear his breathing—deep and measured, like he's having a hard time maintaining control. I can see his pupils expanding as he watches me, taking me in. I'm expecting him to touch me—my whole skin is prickling in the anticipation of it —but instead he picks up the shirt. He looks like he's about to dress me as if I'm some kind of baby doll, not an adult woman perfectly capable of putting on a shirt, when he pauses and eyes my bra.

"It's soaking wet," I confirm. "It'll make the shirt wet."

"So you're not going to wear a bra?" He swallows.

"I don't want to ruin your shirt."

"From what you've said, there's a very low chance I'll be getting it back."

"Why are you holding back with me?" I press, because every-thing in me wants him, even if it's insane. This isn't normally the way I behave around men, but Declan makes me feel almost wild with abandon. And I can tell he's attracted to me—it's all over him, from his eyes to what's between his legs. The problem solver in me needs to understand why he's holding back.

He wraps his hand around the side of my bare abdomen, a choked sound escaping him. "I like you."

I give myself a second to be pleased by this, even though it's lukewarm praise at best. "So?"

He sighs, his hand rubbing up and down my side, sending waves of sensation through me. "I can't let myself get attached to anyone."

"You don't like the women you're sleeping with?" I ask, incredulous.

"Slept with. I didn't dislike them," he says, his mouth in a firm line, "but there was no temptation for more. On either side."

Maybe I should be worried about why he'd be that desperate to push people away. For all I know, he could be a murderer, a bank robber, a villain. But I'm caught up on his certainty that his "friends" aren't interested in more. I frankly don't think that's possible. Maybe he's not tempted, but they'd have to be. Their ovaries wouldn't allow them any peace until they locked it down.

"How do you know?"

A smile plays at his lips. "Not a lot of women want to date someone who shovels dirt and shit all day, but sex is different."

"You can't cure stupid," I say.

His head arcs down, a single drop of water falling from his dark hair, and he kisses my neck, his lips hot and soft, while his hand reaches around to unclasp my bra.He has the kind of skills that come with experience, another red flag, and a second later, my wet bra is on the floor of the van next to our soaked shirts.

A pleased sigh escapes me, and I weave my hand into the back of his wet hair, pulling him closer as his mouth blazes a path down my neck to my breasts. He kisses between them, his hair brushing against my chest—wet and hot and *oh my*.

"Declan," I say, my whole body liquid with need in a way it's never been before, not in my entire life. He may not want to veer out of control, but suddenly I do. It feels too good for me to care about anything else right now. Right now, right here in this old van, on the side of a highway, I feel like a goddess. "*Declan.*"

I want to climb into his lap again. I want to climb him like a tree.

He gazes up at me, his head still bowed over my breasts, like they're his life's work. Then he takes my nipple in his mouth and sucks, and I honestly I have no control left. I fumble down, reaching for the button of his work pants, and he doesn't try to stop me, thankfully. Seconds later, I have them unzipped, and I'm reaching down to wrap my hand around him through his underwear. He groans as he shifts to the other nipple, his wet hair brushing against my chest and sending another wave of sensation blazing through me.

Then my gaze catches on the green shirt, which landed face-up on the floor.

Keep Marshall, NC Green

"Oh," I say, my hand flexing around him. "You know Marshall? That's where I'm going. I just inherited a house there."

He pulls away from me so quickly, I'll probably get whiplash.

CHAPTER SEVEN

DECLAN

Fuck. *Fuck.*

I swallow, trying to reclaim some of my body's blood flow from my dick. But it's hard as hell with Claire's chest on display, her nipples glistening from my mouth and her wet hair plastered against her shoulders like liquid gold.

Taking a deep breath, I zip up my pants, my dick protesting the uncomfortable trap. Then I reach for the green shirt on the floorboards and gently tug it over her wet hair. She puts her arms through the sleeves, because I've given her little choice.

"What the hell just happened?" she asks, staring at me in disbelief. She's owed her disbelief. I've been an asshole, an idiot, and here's my punishment—a throbbing dick, and a beautiful woman who wants to do something about it but has just been rendered untouchable.

"Claire, we can't. I'm…" I swallow. "Where's the house?"

She gives me an incredulous look. "Why does it matter?"

"Where's the house?"

"1465 Sheriff Lane."

I run my hands through my wet hair, swearing under my breath, because what are the fucking odds?

It's that bad luck that likes to dog me around, saying you thought *that* was bad? Well, here's something worse.

"What's going on?" she asks, touching my arm. Even that slight contact's enough to make my dick pissed off at the rest of me. Maybe it was our experience on the plane that did it, but I want this woman in a way I don't fully understand. And now...

I make myself meet her eyes. "Richard Ricci...he was the biological father you were talking about?"

Her eyes widen with surprise. "How'd you know that?"

"I'm..." I swallow. "I was his next door neighbor." *His friend...* sort of. I hadn't meant to be his friend, but he hadn't left me much of a choice. He was the kind of person who made decisions about that kind of thing and then refused to take no for an answer.

The first time he snuck onto my deck, he'd done it alone—probably testing the waters. I'd threatened him, and he'd held out a second can of beer from the grocery bag at his feet. *"Yes, we both know you could beat the shit out of me, but why bother? Wouldn't it be more fun to have a drink with an old timer and watch the sun set?"*

He was right—it was.

His death last weekend, so sudden, so fucking senseless, had made a mark on me, when I'd thought I was past the point of being surprised or saddened by anything. When I'd thought I was mostly dead inside. It was thanks to Dick that I'd started living my life again, such as it is, instead of just existing. And now he's gone.

Claire gives my arm a gentle shove, her eyes wide. "Get out. Richard Ricci was seriously the pervert who used to sneak women onto your deck?"

Surprised laughter escapes me. "I didn't say he was a pervert. Just that he enjoyed the view...and some female company."

"Oh my God," she says, shaking her head, her hand lingering on my arm for a beat before she drops it. "You're seriously my next-door neighbor?"

I can't help but smile at the situation we're in, even though my dick is far from happy that Claire is now completely off limits. Liking her was dangerous enough, liking her and fucking her, and then having her move in next door is unacceptable. Besides, there's every chance Dick Ricci would haunt me if I were to start something I can't finish with his daughter. Even if he never told me he had a daughter. So my dick will just have to accept its strangulation. And I'll just have to suffer through the next several days knowing this woman I like, this woman who drives me past the point of control without even trying, is living, eating, and sleeping next door to me. "Guess so."

I think of the couple who've been staying next door, off and on. Nicole and Damien. The woman, who has pink hair and an attitude problem, is the executor of Dick's estate, although I don't know why he picked her. Before last week, I'd never seen her before in my life. We've only had one real interaction—she walked over Dick's dog, now mine, and said he'd been willed to me. I took him, then asked if there'd be a ceremony or celebration of life for Dick. According to her, he'd specified that he didn't want one, which I'd found hard to believe. He'd lived for celebrations—for drinking, especially, a problem that everyone thinks did him in, since he fell down a flight of stairs.

Pain tugs at my chest, with the fortunate side effect that it finally deflates my hard-on.

"What was he like?" Claire asks softly, tugging me out of my head. I feel guilty for a moment. I've been moping around because of what happened Dick, but he was just my interfering neighbor. He was more to her, and she'll never know him.

"You really just found out about him?" I ask, remembering what she said earlier.

"Yesterday," she confirms.

"I would have been day drunk too," I say. And even though I

know I shouldn't, I let myself tuck some of her wet hair behind her ear. "I'd offer you a pair of shorts, but they wouldn't fit."

"No, probably not." She swallows, her neck bobbing slightly, making me remember the way it felt against my lips, her skin soft and fragrant. My dick gives a half-hearted twitch. "Do you want to change your pants?"

Yes. They're soaked and uncomfortable as hell, but I can't take my pants off around her. Not now. Because if she so much as glanced at my dick, I'd blow off my own convictions as easily as if they were dandelion seeds. And if she looked at it and licked her lips, God forbid, I'd throw off every scruple I've ever had.

"Your pants," she says again, as if there's any chance in hell I didn't hear her the first time.

"I'm okay." I pause, then add, "Your dad...your bio-dad, I mean...he was a complicated guy, but I liked him. I'm going to miss him a lot."

Saying it, *thinking it*, puts that choked up feeling back in my chest. It's like I'm sitting on the plane again, feeling it shake.

She nods and then looks away, but not before I see the tears welling in her eyes. "Sorry," she says. "Wow, I can't believe I'm crying. I didn't even know he existed until yesterday afternoon, and it's not like I've never had a father. I have *the best* father. It's just weird to talk to someone who actually knew him. It makes it more real. This is all so..."

"Fucked up?" I offer. I move so my back's against the partition separating us from the front of the vehicle, the rain still pattering on the roof as if it's not aware of all the things that have changed over the last ten minutes. Maybe it's another piece of stupidity, but when she sits next to me, her back inches from mine, I take her hand and squeeze it. "It *is* fucked up. Now, before you ask, he didn't tell me about you, but it was like that with us. He knew I had my secrets, and he kept his close too. We didn't test each other's boundaries. That's why we got along."

That's was true in the beginning, but it didn't stay true. Still, it's all she needs to know.

"Oh," she says, staring at the closed cargo doors. "Honestly, I'm surprised he wrote me into his will at all."

"I'm not. He cared about people in his way. I'm guessing he checked up on you more than you think. Maybe he knew you had a good dad, a dad who could give you what he couldn't, and that's why he stayed away. You know...he gave me something too."

"What?" she asks, turning toward me.

"His dog, Rocket. My dog, I guess." I pause, feeling a pulse of guilt. It's not my fault, that I knew Dick and she didn't. But for a second, I feel like I'm the one who took something away from her. "But if you want the dog, you can take him." My heart beats an unnatural rhythm. If she says she wants Rocket, I'll let her have him, but it'll feel like another loss—something else stripped away from me. I'd never thought about getting a dog or even a cat. If you'd asked, I would have said I didn't want one, didn't need anything else to take care of, but something inside of me eased when Nicole brought him over on his leash and he licked my hand for the first time.

Rocket hadn't shown any particular affection for me before Dick passed on, but I guess he sees me as the only thing he has left, same as he is for me. I don't want to lose him.

"No, of course not," Claire says, squeezing my hand. It feels so good I instantly release it. Liking a stranger I was never going to see again was pretty low stakes. Liking *her* is impossible—or at least acting on it is.

She gives me a sidelong look, her soft breath warming my face. "So I take it we're done having fun?"

"Yeah," I say, regret heavy in the word. "It's like I told you...I can't get close to anyone."

"You don't have any friends?" she asks incredulously.

"A couple, I guess. But they don't live next door."

"My father did."

"Another reason why I can't spend time with you. Dick wouldn't have liked it."

"I thought he was your friend?"

"He was, and I'm guessing there's a reason he didn't tell me about you."

She huffs. "He never saw fit to say anything to me while he was alive, so I don't see why his opinion should matter now that he's gone."

"I'm sorry for that," I say, giving her a sidelong look. Letting myself soak in the sight of her in my T-shirt. I like it more than I should. I like *her* more than I should. Clearing my throat, I say, "But you said you're close to your dad. That's good. A person should have at least one parent who's not a piece of shit. I was lucky enough to have two."

Even if I didn't get to keep them for as long as I would have liked, and my father had secret debts that bit me in the ass long after he died. But I don't tell her any of that, because the more I say, the harder it'll be to stop talking. So much of it has built up inside of me, waiting for a release, pushing, always pushing.

"They're gone, aren't they?" she asks, then grimaces. "Sorry, I guess that's one of those things you'd rather keep to yourself. But I could tell from the look on your face."

I nod once before falling into silence, my mind a mess, because it feels like I've lost the ability to zip myself up. Or I've lost it around her, anyway, which gives me more motivation to keep my distance.

Then there's a loud engine sound from outside, audible even over the rain, and I open the back of the cargo van to see the resident Marshall auto-repairman and handyman, Rex Carlson, getting out of his tow truck.

He glances into the back of the van, his eyes alight with humor as he takes in the discarded shirts and Claire's sexy-ass bra on the floor. Damn it. He clearly thinks we fucked in the back of the cargo van. Even though it could have gone down like that, it didn't, and I feel strangely protective of her. I don't want him thinking about her like that. He's a nice guy, but I'd prefer it if he never thought of her at all, truthfully—a stupid thought that I bury down deep.

"Got caught in the rain, but I had some dry stuff in my carry-on," I say with a grunt as Claire scoots out behind me.

"Sure," he says easily, as if he couldn't give a shit one way or another, and I guess he probably doesn't. "Who's ready to go to Asheville?"

I glance at Claire, taking in the words on her T-shirt and the message they convey—she's going to be living next door to me, *next fucking door*, and say, "If you can drop me and the van off at the airport, I'd appreciate it. Could you also give Claire a ride up to Dick Ricci's old place so she doesn't have to wait for me to pick up my car? She'll be staying there for a while."

From the look on his face, he thinks the situation is weird. I've given him a few reasons for that. The biggest, I'm guessing, is that I'm not going to bring her myself. Not just because of whatever happened in the back of the van but because Dick's cabin is literally next door to mine.

I can't bring myself to look at Claire and find out whether she's more pissed or upset. Pissed, I can handle. A lot of women have been pissed at me, because even friends with benefits occasionally make demands. The thing is, when I say I can't get close to anyone, I mean it.

More lives than mine might depend on it.

CHAPTER EIGHT

CLAIRE

Conversation with Lainey

> This is the weirdest day of my life, but I can't talk yet. I'll tell you everything tonight.

Now you're just being a tease.

> Did you get fired?

Undecided. Prospects are murky.

> Have you moved on from the Tarot to Magic 8 Balls?

"Soooo," Rex says as I pocket my phone. I hold back a sigh. He's a nice enough guy who looks to be my age, late twenties or early thirties, with hair that exists somewhere between red and brown, a handsome face, and a slight twang to his words. But I don't have much bandwidth left for a new person right now.

Declan barely said two words to me the whole way from the van to the airport. When we left him off, he saluted us and that was that. I would have felt bad about leaving him to deal with the rental agency alone if he hadn't been such a dick. It's hard not to feel a little resentful that he just passed the buck and made me someone else's problem, as if it was no big deal and we hadn't spent all day together.

Still, if he thinks his bad behavior is going to make me less curious about him, he doesn't understand much about women, especially women who have just developed a taste for trouble. I want to know what his deal is, and what happened to him that sent him running, because something obviously did.

At least it stopped raining. The sun came out about twenty minutes ago, right about when we left Declan off—as if he took his storm with him—and there are two rainbows arcing off in the distance. Two rainbows are supposed to mean good luck, right?

Rex gives me a sidelong look. "You knew Dick?"

"I will never not find it weird that there are men in this world who've asked people to call them Dick," I comment.

"Oh," he says with a laugh, as if caught off guard. "He didn't ask anyone to call him that, as such. He was kind of a dick, so people thought it was funny. It stuck. Same way the guy who owns the gas station goes by Billiard, because he's as bald as one. So, how'd you know Dick?"

"He was my father," I say.

The *oh shit* look on his face is so classic, I almost laugh.

"I'm so sorry," he gushes. "I say what I'm thinking most of the time, and at least half the time it's a mistake. You know, he might've been a dick, but there were plenty of people who liked him." He points one of his fingers back toward the airport, keeping his hands on the wheel. "Declan there was one of them." His face creases into a frown. "But maybe you didn't get the best impression of Dec."

I laugh, thinking of our wet clothes in the back of the van. I had to strain the water out of my bra and shirt before I put them in my carry-on bag with the shitty umbrella, which I saved from the trees that had claimed it. "He's nice enough," I say. "But he's too closed-off. I'm more of an open book."

There, that's true, although it's a pretty small thing to say—my feelings are more confusing. Declan claimed he didn't have any friends who asked questions, but this Rex doesn't strike me as Mr. Reserved, and he very willingly called him to come save the day. So what was his deal with me?

Rex nods. "Can't say that's not so. But he's a good guy, mostly. I'm sorry for what I said about your father. We were all really sorry to hear the news."

"You don't have to worry about saying bad things about *Dick*," I say, glancing at him. "I didn't know him personally. I didn't even know he existed until yesterday." It's only after I say the words that I realize I should probably be a little less of an open book. I'm used to living in a city that's so big you can break up with someone and never have the misfortune of seeing them again—but that's obviously not the case in Marshall.

"Ohhh," he says, "I see." From the way he says it, he doesn't, not totally, but the basics have fallen into place. There are probably a hundred words for what I am, but the one that comes to mind first is baseborn, probably because I've been reading a lot of romantasy for an escape from the tense atmosphere at Agnes Lewis's offices.

"Do you know how he died?" I ask. "All I know is that it was an accident."

He casts a quick glance at me, as if trying to judge whether I'm the squeamish type. I try to look like I'm not, but I'm guessing he can see right through me. People usually do. "It was," he says. "Fell down the stairs. The coroner figured it happened instantly. No suffering. One of those freak accidents that happen in the home."

I nod, but it makes me uneasy, partly because I'm going to be staying in that home, and partly because that kind of accident could happen to anyone, any time. Get distracted at the wrong second, and it could be your last.

"I'm guessing you've talked to Nicole?" Rex says her name warily, as if he's talking about some wild beast escaped from the zoo.

"What's she like?" I ask, because this man's the talker Declan's not, and if I can get him going, he might forget to stop.

"Well...she's an interesting woman. I met her a couple of times at the bluegrass bar."

"Is she..." I can't think of a polite way to ask him whether she's a psychopath, so I clear my throat to buy time. "Is she...easygoing?"

He laughs. "I wouldn't say so, no. But she *is* interesting. I can't say more. Don't know her well enough to consider myself a judge."

Damn it. He may be a talker, but he's obviously feeling overly cautious after he accidentally told me that my bio-dad's a dick.

For the rest of the ride, I ask Rex questions about Marshall. He answers me readily enough and then pulls off the highway. A few minutes later, he gestures out the windshield. We're moving slowly down a stretch of street lined with colorful buildings, most of them businesses with signs—I see a bookstore, a record shop, a flower shop, and a couple of bars and restaurants.

"Here it is," he says with a grin. "Downtown Marshall."

"Wow, this is so cute," I say, smiling out the window. It feels like a town hand-plucked from a holiday Christmas movie where the high-strung blonde lawyer learns what's really important in life—finding a man who's willing to wear a Christmas sweater.

A little voice in my head whispers that it might be easier to open a bakery in a place like this than it would be in New York, where food service businesses come and go so quickly, you can miss them if you walk a different direction from the subway station for two weeks. It's a ridiculous voice, of course, because I'm not staying. I can't. This place isn't home, and it never will be.

There's only three or four blocks worth of "stuff" before the buildings become nondescript and grey, no more storefronts. "Oh, that's it?" I blurt before I can think better of it.

I'd known Marshall was small, but you'd have to run around it five times to get a mile.

"It's not New York City," Rex says with a knowing grin, "but it does us just fine. And Asheville's only twenty minutes away."

"Sorry," I say, and this time I know I'm the one who put my foot in it. This is his home, and I just insulted it, however unintentionally.

"You're good," he says. "We're used to people from New York around here. It feels like Asheville is fifty percent people from New York these days."

"And the other?"

"California or Florida," he says with a snort. "There's only a handful of people who are actually from these parts anymore."

"It's like that in New York too," I say. "Only I *am* from there. Born and raised."

"Well, if you're Dick's kid, you're from here, too. Honorary. He may not have always lived here, but he was one of us." He taps the steering wheel again as he directs the truck up an ascending road. It's as if he's sending up a wish or adding to the mass of thoughts and prayers that must be gathered somewhere in the ether, like hopeful pink clouds.

We're leaving the little downtown area behind, the scenery around us becoming rural more quickly than I'd anticipated.

Shit. Will there be internet at the house? I'd assumed so, since Nicole emailed me, but I can already tell it's a mistake to make any kind of assumptions with that woman. Besides, pretty much everyone has data on their phones.

"Will there be internet at the house?" I ask, my voice coming out strangled.

My new friend Rex laughs. I'm relieved for thirty seconds—*of course there's internet, Claire, how could there not be internet?*—before he says, "No, ma'am. Your daddy was only the sociable type when he wanted to be, and he was a cheapskate, too. Proud of it.

The one thing he wasted money on, besides gambling, was his long-shelf-life food. Always said he was planning to survive the apocalypse."

"He was some kind of prepper?" I ask, fascinated. Maybe a little a horrified too, because I already have one parent who's in a cult. Is this genetic? Will I wake up one day and start thinking some stranger on the internet is the reincarnation of God?

"Nah, not really. He never did set up a bunker. Said it would be too much work. Same reason he never accepted an invitation to go deer hunting with me."

I make a face that he hopefully doesn't see. What can I say? I watched *Bambi* when I was five, and it made an impression.

He gives me a sidelong look, probably misinterpreting my expression. "He was a fun guy, but he didn't have much up and at 'em energy. Still, I bet you'll find some interesting stuff up there."

That sounds about right—one parent a cultist and the other too lazy to bother being much of anything. But I don't have time to over-think the genetic lottery and how it's probably shafted me, because he takes a turn and starts edging up a rolling peak. My breath gusts out because it's so beautiful. The mountains are a rolling blue expanse in either direction, and there are conifers and maples and poplars everywhere. I can't remember when I last saw so many trees —*wild* trees that weren't planted by city planners. Trees that don't give a damn about which way they go or about things like up and down, because some of these trees are growing partially sideways.

"I know, right?" Rex says with a grin. "They picked a good spot."

"Dick Ricci's house is up here?" I ask. I can't decide whether that's a good thing—it's beautiful, but there's no internet, and it's a bit secluded. How hard will it be to sell this place? Will I have to spend a few weeks here?

He turns a corner, and two cabins come into view on the right side of the road, built side by side on the edge of a large hill. They're both wood, and they look like the search results you'd get if you had access to the internet and Googled log cabin. I've never spent the night somewhere so rustic, and my heart beats faster in my chest. This is...well, it's exciting.

Rex slows the car, and even before he puts on his blinker, I can tell the cabin on the right is Declan's. For one thing, it's much nicer, and for another it has an expansive back deck, visible from the road, that looks out over the mountains. The other has a view partially blocked by trees. It also looks like it's seen better years, or even decades, although it has more rustic charm than its partner. There are a couple of Adirondack chairs arranged on the front porch of Dick's place, plus a huge plate glass window that looks out on the road. When Rex pulls into the driveway, smiling broadly, I flinch—because there's a woman standing directly behind the window, watching us. She has short, neon-pink hair and is dressed all in black—like she dressed for a stealth mission but forgot to cover her hair.

Rex must catch my flinch, because he smiles at me again. He won't be winning any poker games, particularly not if he's playing against Declan, because it's a *worried* smile. "That's Nicole."

"Hey, will my cell phone work up here?" I ask, chewing on my lip. If you're going to be holed up in a house with a psychopath, it seems like the responsible thing to do to ensure you at least have a working phone.

"Should do, although you might need to find a few sweet spots in the house." He grabs a receipt and pen from the well beneath the dash and writes down a number. Handing it to me, he says, "Call or text if they give you any trouble. Or even if you just need someone to talk to."

"They?"

"She's up here with her husband, Damien. Nice guy." He glances at the car in the drive. "Don't see their vehicle, though, so he must be out doing something. The Jeep was Dick's."

It's an old red, rust-bucket Jeep—more tank than car.

I'm tempted to ask him to drive me back to Marshall, or maybe even Asheville, but I'm more curious than I am nervous. This whole situation is so far out of my comfort zone, it's in a different solar system, one that seems to be revolving around this house, or maybe the intimidating woman who's standing in that window. I could retreat. It's what I've done most of my life—stepping away from arguments, placating people, *waiting*. But the afternoon I spent with Declan made me realize how damn tired I am of nothing happening.

So I say goodbye to Rex, get out of the car, grab my carry-on, and head to the front door.

I'm suddenly deeply self-conscious of not having a bra on—as if a bra might protect me from Nicole—but it's better not to be wearing one than to have two boob-sized wet spots on my shirt.

The door opens before I knock, and the woman with bright pink hair stands in front of me. There's something familiar about her eyes, although I couldn't say what. I *know* I've never seen her before. She's not a person who'd be easily forgotten.

"Well, well, look what the cat dragged in," she says with a sharp grin. "Welcome home, sis."

CHAPTER NINE

CLAIRE

"Sis?" I repeat, gawking at her. Because it hits me like a piece of fallen scaffolding that *this* is why she looked familiar—her eyes and mouth...they're similar to what I see in the mirror each morning. "You're his daughter, too? Why didn't you say anything?"

She reaches for my carry-on bag, and I let her take it, because I'm numb. Too much has happened, one revelation snowballing with another, forming a snowmageddon that's avalanched my brain. It's impossible to form a logical thought beyond the press of—*I have a sister, now?*—but there's room enough for illogical ones. I figured she took the bag as a friendly gesture, the way someone will offer a chair to a person they've just slapped with big news, but she tosses it carelessly into the interior of the cabin, which looks like wood on top of wood.

"Hey," I say, flinching, a protest making it through my sloppy brain. "My laptop's in that."

She ignores the comment and pulls me into the house, and even though I'm more intrigued than ever—could she really be my sister? —I feel like a fly being tugged into a spider's den.

"Come on," she says. "I've got some bourbon in the kitchen with your name on it."

What is it with people feeding me alcohol today?

I'm not about to complain, though. If ever there's a day for drinking it's today, even more so now than at eight this morning. So I follow her down a wood-lined hallway to a cozy kitchen, the walls half wood and half a chalky, grey color that probably used to be white. The stove's small but no more so than the one in my apartment in Brooklyn, and the thought of baking in here is pleasant.

Nicole waves me toward a round table with four chairs pushed up to it—each of them different, as if scavenged from freebies left out on people's stoops—and I sit on one that's painted blue. Sure enough, there's a bottle of bourbon sitting out with two juice glasses.

It's almost impossible to wrap my head around what's happening. Just this morning, I was sitting with my father in his kitchen. Now I'm in a kitchen that belonged to my other father—a man I'll never know—about to have a drink with a half-sister who may be crazy.

"Well, shit," Nicole says, filling up both glasses to the brim. "It's good to finally meet you. Damien—that's my husband—told me not to do the thing with the plane ticket. He said you might not make it on the flight and it would be a waste of money, but I knew you'd pull through. You couldn't help it. You've got those Ricci hustler genes." She puts out her fist, presumably for a bump, and for some godforsaken reason, I give it to her.

You just can't say no, I hear Lainey telling me. *It's pathological.*

So I put on a stern face. "I almost missed it. Do you know how long it takes to get to JFK Airport from my apartment?"

"No, not really," she says as if she couldn't care less. "I'll bet it was kind of fun, though, huh?"

"No," I object, although she's not entirely wrong. It gave me an adrenaline rush, making the mad dash and getting there in time, and it was definitely a thrill to board the plane at the last minute and find myself next to *him*. "How do you know you're my sister?"

"The will was the first I'd heard of you," she says with a sigh.

"My husband and I are private investigators, so you can imagine how embarrassing that was for me. If you're wondering how we can know for certain that you're really a Ricci—Dick said in his will that there was a DNA test when you were little."

"Oh," I comment, the word falling out of my mouth. Because part of me had hoped this was all some strange mistake, despite my resemblance to him, to her. Despite what my father had told me. "You're really a private investigator?"

I'd never met one before in real life. It had always struck me as the kind of job people have in TV and in books, not real life.

"But I didn't go looking for Dick after he left," she continues, ignoring the question, which is probably just as well, "because I didn't want to find him. I would have wanted to find *you*. He may be dead, but I'm pissed at him for keeping you secret."

For half a second, I'm thrilled by this—by the fact that I have a sister, and she wanted to find me. Lainey's like a sister, but I'd always wondered what it would be like to have a sibling with the same parents. Someone I could bitch to about the Tribe of Light or Dad's relentless positivity. Of course, the only thing I can bitch to Nicole about is being abandoned, which doesn't sound like much fun at all. Then I absorb the rest of what she said.

"You knew Dick?"

She nods and takes a swig of the bourbon, giving a sigh of enjoyment as she sets the glass down. "You know, I used to think drinking shit bourbon was a mark of character, but when Damien's right, he's right. The good stuff just hits different. Don't tell him I said so, though. I don't want him to get a big head. His anniversary present to me was much better than mine to him, and we both know it."

"You knew Dick?" I ask again, getting annoyed. She's no more straightforward than Declan, but at least he had the good grace to seem to feel bad about it.

"Yeah," she said. "I had that misfortune. I'm sorry to report that his name was accurate."

"So I've heard," I mutter.

"He cheated on my mother constantly—with your mom, too, it turns out." She lifts her glass, and I find myself mechanically lifting my drink to clink it with hers.

There you go again, says Lainey in my head.

Nicole shrugs. "I'm a few years older than you. He left when I was seven, sent divorce papers, and never came back. Like I said, my mom and I didn't bother to look for him."

"He raised you?"

She laughs as if this is the funniest thing she's heard all month, or maybe in her whole life. "Now, let's not get to free-wheeling with words, Claire Rainey. That man didn't raise shit. But he *did* leave us this crappy house, so I suppose he wasn't totally useless."

"Us?" I repeat, feeling sweat bead on my temples. "So it's not mine?"

"It's *ours*." She grins at me. "We got it halfsies, just like sisters should. And there's an insurance payout, too. With a caveat…"

"A caveat?"

She sighs. "You keep repeating everything I'm saying. Did you hit your head? Or maybe you just inherited Dick's brain along with his sense of style."

I glance down at Declan's shirt, my soaked shorts, and ruined shoes. I'm guessing she didn't mean it as a compliment to me or our bio dad. "I didn't know either of you existed yesterday morning," I say as soon as I'm confident I can say them in an even tone. "I'm just trying to keep up."

She snorts. "Anyway, back to the caveat. Yeah, the insurance company thinks he committed suicide."

"Did he?" I ask, feeling a squeezing sensation in my chest. Honestly, if this day keeps going on the way it has, I'm going to have a heart attack at twenty-eight.

"Oh, I think not. You know how it is." She waves her hand in a gesture that's supposed to convey something, although I have no idea what. "They don't like to pay up. They'll think of any excuse not to. He fell down the stairs—accident, right?—but he had a ton of alcohol in his system, plus some pills, so they think he did it on purpose. You know, drugged himself up and then took a fall so he could make it look like an accident. Fucked up, no?"

"Why would he do something like that?"

"To get his beloved daughters a payout, of course," she says with a sarcastic smile.

I pause, trying to think of a tactful way to ask what I need to ask. But she's not tactful, so maybe I don't need to be either. "How much money are we talking?"

"Not too much," she says, and my spirits fall. "Something like two-hundred-and-fifty grand each."

My mouth drops open. "Not too much?"

I'm used to living on a personal assistant salary in New York City. Sure, it wouldn't be enough for me to open my bakery without any external backers, not in New York City, but if I did it somewhere else...

I could finally do something with my life instead of daydreaming about it. I could stop waiting—watching sand fall to the bottom of the hourglass.

Then I remember the rest of what she said. "But they're not going to give it to us..."

"Unless we can prove it was an accident or someone offed him."

My eyebrows rise. "Didn't the police do some kind of investigation?"

A pfft of air escapes her. "They're incompetent as hell, but they didn't find his death suspicious."

I sigh, my dreams of the bakery floating away. "I suppose that's that. I guess we can still sell the house. That'll be worth something."

Her expression hardens. "I don't give up so easily, and starting now, neither do *you*. Maybe it was an accident." She shrugged her shoulders. "Damien's looking into that angle. He's meeting with a structural engineer who took a look at the stairs, and we already have our lawyer working on the insurance company, but there is a chance someone did this to him, Claire, and you and I will be working on that. Because if anyone had a right to kill that salty bastard, it was you and me. I didn't do it, and I know for a fact that *you* didn't do it, so it's only right if we're the ones who look into it."

"You really think someone murdered him?" I ask in awe. The rest of the message penetrates a beat later. "And you want me to look into it? You're the P.I. I'm just—"

"Oh, I know all about your sad little job," she says dismissively, lighting a flame of anger in my gut. Because who the fuck is this woman, anyway? But years of Agnes have dampened my spirit of resistance, and I don't step in to tell her off. "This is your chance to prove you're worth more than that."

"To whom?" I find myself sputtering. "To *you*? Why do you think I care about proving anything to you?"

"Good," she says with a grin. "Your spirit isn't entirely broken yet. I'd prefer to be the person to do that. We can rebuild from there."

"You're crazy," I say before I can think better of it.

"A lot of people think so, sure," she says with a sly grin. "But no one would ever call me a pushover. Can the same be said of you?"

I don't say anything, because I can't. I *am* a pushover, and we both know it. Maybe I've always been that way, or maybe seven years of Agnes Lewis did it to me. Either way, there's no denying the truth—a truth that's even now seeping into my bones and making me feel weak. *Small.* I don't like her for that. I don't like her for taking my world and shaking it like it's a snow globe she might choose to throw in the trash.

"No, I didn't think so," she says. "Drink your bourbon."

My hand lifts the glass of its own accord, and for a second, I think I'm going to sip it—that I'll do what she told me to, for no other reason than that she told me, but then she says. "What'd you think of your companions on the plane?" Her gaze lowers to my shirt, and a lazy grin crosses her face. "I see you met Declan."

I don't plan it, I just throw the contents of the glass onto her face.

I flinch after I do it, my hand clutching against the empty tumbler as if I can retroactively take it back, because I've never done anything like that before. Ever. My dad always taught me to avoid conflict at school. Two kids in his middle school wailed on each other, and one of them ended up hitting the other in the head with a rock and giving him a concussion so bad he missed two months of school.

It's not worth the risk, he'd say. *It's always better to walk away with your body and dignity intact.*

But Nicole doesn't hit me in retaliation. She doesn't even yell or jump to her feet. Instead her smile stretches wider—it's genuine and terrifying, and I feel like I made a big mistake by coming here. A bigger one by throwing that drink on her.

"Good," she says, grabbing a dish towel that's sitting on the middle of the table and sopping up most of the liquid. "I wish you'd wasted a shittier bourbon, but I'm glad to see you're not all rose petals and butterflies on the inside. I'd hoped for more."

"You don't get to control my life," I say, rising to my feet. "How'd you know my seat would be next to Declan's?"

"You should be thanking me," she says, smirking now. Her shirt has to be as soaked as mine was earlier, but she doesn't seem uncomfortable in her skin. I'll bet this woman is never uncomfortable in her skin. "He's a sexy beast, and it's obvious you noticed." She waggles her eyebrows up and down. "The second I saw him, I knew I couldn't let him go to waste."

"We were both stranded, and we got caught in the rain. So he gave me a shirt to change into. Big whoop," I say. "I can see you're very concerned with how I got here from the Charlotte airport, and why I arrived in a tow truck."

She waves a hand in unconcern. "What matters is that you're here. Besides, I've met that guy. Roy is a harmless non-entity. The perfect person to drive you around."

"His name is Rex."

"I don't care." Her gaze narrows on me, calculating. "What happened with Declan? Why wasn't he the one who dropped you off? Did you piss him off? Because that wouldn't be good for our plans. I was banking on you charming him with your blonde hair and Pollyanna personality."

"What plans?" I ask through my teeth.

She sighs, and rocks back in her chair, balancing it on its back legs. I hope it falls. "I put you between him and Mrs. Rosings for a reason, Claire. Declan's the one who found our father's body, and our dad was screwing Mrs. Rosings. If someone offed him, it was probably one of them. And you're going to help me find out which."

CHAPTER TEN

Declan, a murderer?

I think back to the look on his face when he told me he'd liked my dicky dad. That he was going to miss him a lot.

There'd been genuine grief in his eyes. But had he been grief-stricken because he'd lost a friend or because he'd murdered one? He certainly has secrets—a whole bucketload of them. Maybe two. But I can't believe it. Frankly, I don't want to.

And the thought of Mrs. Rosings killing anyone is laughable... until I consider the way she had that flask hidden away in her bag but kept getting on my case about the bourbon I'd drunk before coming to the airport. She's capable of deceit.

I run my hands through my hair—still wet—and lower back into the chair. Nicole's still tipped back in hers, looking utterly unconcerned by what she just told me, even though she's blown my world apart, again, for what is probably the third time in twenty-four hours.

"Wait," I say, putting two and two together and finally getting four again. "We're not going to even get into how you did it...but you seated me next to two people you think could be killers?"

She barks a laugh. "Oh, come off it. If they did it, they're not the kind of killers who'd randomly off people for the fun of it. If they did it, it was personal. Trust me, Dick was a guy who had an uncanny ability to piss people off."

"Runs in the family, huh?"

Her eyebrows rise. "You're part of that family."

My mind works away at what she's told me, and I find myself thinking of something she said earlier. Dick might not have been my father in any sense but DNA donorship, but he was hers in every sense. For a while, at least. He probably wasn't the best father, judging by the fact that he left her and never bothered introducing himself to me, but he did mean something to her. It makes me feel bad for her for half a second, before I remember that she's been pulling my strings.

"It's fucked up that you did that," I say. "Really fucked up."

"I know," she says, rocking. "So was it worth it? Did you buddy up to them, or are you one of those people who zips up in planes?"

"You know, it was a pretty rough flight. We thought we were going to crash."

The look on her face tells me I'm not going to get any sympathy or remorse from her. "Oh good," she says. "People say all kinds of shit when they think they're on death's doorstep."

"Thanks for your concern," I say tightly. "But yes, I talked to both of them. Does this mean Mrs. Rosings lives in Marshall too?"

"Just outside, but yeah. She's got herself a big old mansion."

Troubled, I tap the edge of the table. "But Declan didn't seem to recognize her."

She snorts as she lowers her chair to four legs. "Why would he? He's a hot piece, and I'm guessing it's never occurred to him that women over forty exist."

Her take on him doesn't resonate, but I'm guessing she knows a lot less than she thinks she does—while also knowing more than I'm comfortable with.

"Dick was shallow too," she says. "No way he was tapping that for any reason but the money in her bank account. I figure maybe he ripped her off, and she got salty about it. Poison is a woman's weapon, and—"

"Do you know this from experience?" I ask, glancing at the empty glass in front of me.

"No," she says, laughing. "But if there was poison in it, it would be all over my shirt. You don't have anything to worry about."

"I can't stay in this house with you."

She presses a hand to her chest in mock disbelief. "Are you scared of me, Claire?"

Yes. Any sane person would be.

"No, of course not. But you're..."

"Crazy, we covered this. But it's a deceptively large house, and you won't be here alone with me. My husband Damien is staying here too, and most people like him. Besides, your bedroom door locks, and I have it on good authority that you couldn't even afford a room at the motel with the feet smell."

"This is exactly what I'm talking about," I say, waving a hand at her. "You've been looking up my private, personal information."

She lifts her eyebrows, staring into my eyes with her hazel ones, so uncannily like my own. "Wouldn't you have done the same if you found out you had a sister, and you had the power to learn about her?"

"Maybe," I admit, "but that doesn't make me any more comfortable with you messing around with my private life."

"Speaking of private life," she says pointedly, checking out my T-shirt. "Did you bang our father's weed dealer and steal his shirt?"

"Excuse you," I say, crossing my arms over my chest, feeling the lack of a bra. "I already told you what happened." For a second, I can see Declan in my head—his hair soaked from the rain, his eyes latched onto me like I was someone he wanted to keep looking at for a long while. I can feel the brush of his beard against my face. It's only then, with Declan in my head, that I register her accusation. "Weed dealer?"

She shrugs carelessly. "Grower, dealer. Who knows what they're calling it these days. It's barely even scandalous anymore now that it's practically legal."

"I thought he was a landscaper," I say faintly, my voice coming out weak, because that was one of the only things I thought I knew about him for sure, and it's probably not even true. I don't mind that he grows weed, really, but it speaks of a kind of moral ambiguity. There's a difference between smoking it and growing it, right?

"He is," Nicole says, "and he happens to be very skillful at growing things."

"How do you know all of this?" I ask, frustrated.

"That's my job," she says, tapping her temple with two fingers. "Knowing things and using that knowledge to benefit myself."

"So you think Declan killed our bio-dad over...weed? That's a stretch. You're right, it's practically legal now. In New York, it *is* legal."

"Not here, yet. But yeah. I wouldn't think that was why. That guy's got secrets, though, and Dick liked to use information as currency, same as me. He might have been trying to bribe him."

She's right about the secrets, but from what I could tell, Dick was maybe the only person Declan had felt comfortable sharing his secrets with. In so much as he's comfortable sharing them with anyone. But I doubt she'd take my word for it.

Still, I feel compelled to say, "I don't think it was him, or Mrs. Rosings."

She lifts her eyebrows and angled her head. "No one suspects women, but she could have pushed some pills down him, then given him a shovey-shove. Should be easy enough to prove or disprove, especially now that you're best buddies with her."

"I wouldn't say we're best buddies," I mutter. Although, truthfully, I would have been happy to see her again if not for the murder accusation. "But she's..."

I was about to call her nice, but that's not strictly true. *Interesting* is a better term for her, which is the same word Rex used for Nicole.

"Regardless, you're our in. We'll go see her tomorrow."

I swallow, trying to appear unaffected, like I couldn't care either way, and say, "What about Declan?"

"Oh, you'll be seeing him," she says. "You'll be seeing a lot of him."

That sounds a bit ominous, and suddenly I really do need a drink.

"Do you have any sealed bottles?" I ask.

She gives a slight nod as if in approval. "You want a beer?"

Not really, but I nod. She gets up and grabs me a can from the fridge, hands it over and takes a seat again.

"Buchanan Brewery," I comment. "I've never heard of that before."

"I'm starting to think there's a lot you haven't heard about, sweet summer child. But don't you worry, I'm going to show you the way."

I'll bet that's what they told my mother before she transferred her bank account to the Tribe of Light.

"What happens if I don't want to stay here?" I say, even though I know she's right—I can't afford a hotel. Not without taking the money from my dad.

"Well, I wasn't shitting you about Dick's will. It *is* interesting. Our inheritance is contingent on both of us staying in this house for a month. If you leave, this heap of shit is all mine. The insurance money too, presuming we're even able to get it."

"A month," I ask, my mouth gaping open. I'd figured I might need to stick around for a week or two to get the house ready for market. But a month, with *her*? I've been here for less than an hour and I already feel like a chess piece being glided around on a board.

Still, the news isn't totally terrible. Declan's next door, and if I'm here for that long, maybe I'll have time to figure out what his deal is. And yet... "*Why?*"

She shrugs, her mouth pursing to one side. "It's like I told you, our father was kind of a dick. Maybe he wanted to inconvenience us one last time."

"I don't know if I can stay here for a month..." Unless... "You have your husband here. Could my friend Lainey come stay with us?"

She shrugs again. "As long as she doesn't hit on Damien. If she does, I'll have to kill her. Same goes for you."

"I'm going to take that as a yes."

"Half of the house is yours. Have an orgy if you want."

"No thanks." I sigh and take a sip of the beer. "You know, speaking of orgies, Declan said Dick used to sneak women into his back yard because he had the better mountain view."

She gives a muffled laugh. "Yeah, he really couldn't keep his dick in his pants. We probably have half a dozen other siblings, and we're the only two he knew about."

I give her a half smile. She's probably nuts, this whole situation is definitely nuts, but I feel surprisingly *energized* given all the excitement and lack of sleep. I take a moment to consider why and decide that part of it is because I don't know what's going to happen five minutes from now, let alone in five days. It's surprisingly nice to feel unmoored when I'm used to my days and weeks and months and years following a similar and frankly uninspiring pattern. Sometimes you don't know you're stuck in a rut until someone blows up the rut, and you with it.

I look around the kitchen, taking in a few surprising touches—a framed photo of a scrappy looking mutt and a dried flower arrangement. The man who's taken shape in my head—a lazy wannabe prepper with twenty girlfriends and who-knows-how-many illegitimate kids—wouldn't hang either of those things up.

But here's the evidence that Richard Ricci, or someone close to him, did.

It's strange and arresting to think that the man who was living here a week ago—my father—is dead. He'll never walk through this kitchen again, or sneak into Declan's backyard. He'll never be anything more than a photograph to me. *An idea.* Stories told by other people. Stranger yet: these things he left behind outlived him. Hell, the burned food stuck to his stovetop outlived him. It's the kind of thought that shakes a person and makes them want to clear their browser history.

"I guess I missed his funeral," I say softly.

She snorts. "There wasn't one. We're supposed to throw a party for him at the end of the month."

I nod. "I can help with that. My father's an event planner."

"I know. Chuck Rainey. He has a four-point-eight average on Yelp."

I roll my eyes, preparing to get up, then pause and look at her. "Are you sure he didn't kill himself, Nicole? This...it seems like he had it all worked out, what he wanted to happen after he went."

"I'm sure," she says, staring me down even though she's shorter, sitting or standing. It's a kind of super power I'll never possess.

"He was your father. You wouldn't want to think—"

"Look," she says firmly. "I'm very well aware of who and what he was. He didn't do it. He was paranoid. The lawyer's office told me he kept changing the will, adding codicils and what have you."

I'm tempted to point out that there's a reason cops don't work on cases for blood relatives or close friends, but I doubt she'd take it well.

"Okay," I agree. "What did he do for a living anyway? I don't know anything about him."

Or you.

"He was a contractor," she says. "He worked on houses and shit, but he was really bad at it."

Of course he was.

"Can you show me where I'm staying?"

She grabs her glass of bourbon, her shirt still wet and reeking of a bar, and I feel a stab of contrition. "I'm sorry about the dr—"

A finger is waved in my face. "Never apologize after taking a stand. Never. It undermines the whole gesture."

"Ohhh-kay."

"I'll take you on a tour of our shit heap."

I keep the beer and reclaim my bag, and Nicole leads me on a tour of the downstairs part of the house, which lasts all of five minutes. There's the kitchen; the living room we passed to get to the kitchen, with the large plate glass window; plus a dining room with a large table that looks like it was used as a work table rather than for eating. There's also a bathroom and a small sitting room lined with books. The sight of the armchair in that room, a faded blanket layered over it, makes my eyes feel hot. Because I can tell it was a favorite chair—one he enjoyed sitting in—and he's gone, but it's not.

I was expecting photos, maybe even a photo of my mom, or a baby picture of me she might have sent him, but there aren't any. Not a single one. The only other things on the walls are a framed cross-stitch of an eagle and a line drawing of a marijuana leaf.

"Let's move this party upstairs," Nicole says jovially. So we do. Each step is attended by a healthy creak, and I can't help but think about Dick Ricci and his last trip down them. The thought gives me a whole body shiver.

She said Declan found him. It must have been awful, beyond awful. It's no wonder he's feeling the weight of it. I'd like to ask him about it, but a person shouldn't go around poking at other people's trauma. So I pat the thoughts down and tell them I'll attend to them later. After I've seen the house.

There are three bedrooms. One of them—the one Nicole and Damien have claimed—has a bathroom attached, and there's also a small bathroom in the hall, between the two others. I'm satisfied that the house is plenty large enough for Lainey and maybe a quarter of her boxes, if she chooses to come.

"Is that all you brought?" Nicole asks, eyeing my small carry-on as I bring it into one of the two open rooms. It's wood paneled, and there's a queen-sized bed with a comforter that looks like it came from a discount bin somewhere. The only other furniture is a dresser I have nothing to fill and a desk with a chair.

"No, I brought a suitcase, but the plane I took to Charlotte got re-routed, and it came in too late for me to make the connecting flight to Asheville. They said they'd deliver it to me when it comes in."

She laughs, holding the wall to brace herself. "Yeah, you're definitely never getting that back."

"They seemed pretty confident about it," I say, mostly because I want to disagree with her.

"I give it a ten percent chance of happening. Maybe seven. I'll bring you some clothes." Her gaze lingers on the green Marshall shirt. "Unless you want to keep wearing your sex shirt as a token."

"It's not—" I cut myself off, because there's obviously no point in continuing to protest. But I feel very justified in glowering at her. "I don't know why you want me to have sex with Declan if you think he's a murderer."

"There's a reason Mata Hari was a successful spy," she says with a wink. "I'll leave you to unpack your five things."

She's back a few minutes later with an all-black outfit that'll make us too matchy-matchy for my taste, not to mention she's several inches shorter than me and one pant size smaller. I'm in no position to protest, and I don't have a car that I can use to get something else. There's the Jeep, which probably has keys somewhere, but it's almost as intimidating as the van was earlier.

I had the presence of mind to bring some of my toiletries in my carry-on, at least, but I'll need to buy some basics I can use before my bag shows up.

If my bag shows up.

My bag needs to show up.

Of course, I'll have to borrow or rent a car to get anything from town, which would be much easier if I didn't have to do it on my phone, with its tiny font.

My reading glasses were in my suitcase, too.

"Can we get the internet installed?"

She winks. "Already on my bucket list, sis. Although maybe it'll do you good to stay off Instagram for a few days. Normal people only like looking at so many photos of cake."

With that, she's gone.

I lock the door, then change into the damp bra and Nicole's clothes and sit on the bed and drink my beer with my back to the wall, suddenly too tired to call the airline or Lainey or my dad or do any of the things I need to do to be a responsible adult.

When I finish the beer, I lie down and stare at the watermarks on the ceiling, thinking about Nicole, the father I didn't know and the mother I knew less than I thought. I'm tempted to poke around in the house—to learn more about him that way—but I don't have the physical or metaphysical energy to try. I also think about Declan.

Is he back home?

Is he thinking about me?

Is he jerking off to what happened earlier?

Is it totally screwed up that I'm still into him?

He's very good-looking—*painfully* good-looking—but if it were just a matter of hotness, it would be easier to let it go. No, it's something else that has me on the hook...maybe it's the near death experience we shared or the fact that he knew my bio-dad.

Or maybe there's a part of me that's sick of being agreeable and *good*, and I want to grab one of Declan's shovels and dig up all of his dirt until he's laid bare to me.

CHAPTER ELEVEN

CLAIRE

I must have fallen asleep, because the next thing I'm aware of is a soft knock on the door. It takes me a moment to orient myself—the room is completely dark and musty and decidedly not mine.

"Come in," I call out, cringing at the hoarse sound of my voice. I have a dehydration headache, and my whole body feels like it's been through a washing machine.

"Door's locked," says a deep male voice I don't recognize.

"Who are you?" I ask, mentally reviewing the supplies I have in my carry-on for whether or not any can be used as weapons.

My mind catches up with the situation a second later. I remember that Nicole has a husband I haven't met yet—and also that a murderer probably wouldn't knock.

"Damien," the visitor responds helpfully, confirming his identity. "I've got some food for you."

Earlier, I didn't want to eat anything unpackaged in case these people prove to be murderous in addition to crazy, but I'm so ravenous at this point I'd eat anything—even something that's been sitting in Dick's fridge for over a week.

I pad over to the door and turn on the light switch next to it, blinking from the sudden assault. Then I open it, revealing a tall, broad man with light brown skin, black hair, and blue-grey eyes. He's very attractive but much more refined than Nicole—he's like the William Henry knife to her shiv.

"*You're* Nicole's husband?" I ask in surprise.

"You were expecting someone white?" My mouth gapes open, but he laughs. "Sorry, I had to. It's been a long week. Can I come in for a minute?"

I glance at the door, remembering how Nicole said she'd kill anyone who hit on Damien. It was probably a joke, but why take chances on a probably?

"Let's keep the door open," I say.

He nods and hands me a brown paper bag that smells promisingly of tomato sauce and cheese. "Neither of us would hurt you," he promises.

"It's not you I'm worried about," I tell him.

His chuckle is probably not as reassuring as he thinks it is. He waves to the old desk. "Go ahead and eat. Don't stand on ceremony for me. I just ran into Rex, and he said you and Declan got caught out in the rain with a flat tire. Sounds like it's been a long day."

"Does everyone know everything about everyone around here?"

"They try," he says, watching as I lower into the chair and take out the sandwich and soda. It's eggplant parmesan, my favorite. I glance at it in wonderment, then suspicion, my gaze shifting to him.

"You posted about it on social media," he says with a shrug. "I'd argue it's not an example of her overreach."

"Did Nicole send you to talk to me as a kind of good cop-bad cop thing?"

"Nah," he says, leaning against the wall just inside of the door. "My wife's fast asleep." From the way he says it, it's a reminder. His way of saying, *she may be a little crazy, but I love her*.

He cocks his head, watching me. "She barely slept at all after she learned about you, you know. It's been days. Nicole might come off as someone who couldn't care less, but when it comes to the people in her life she couldn't care more."

This gives me pause for a second, then I think about the way she Machiavelli-ed the whole plane ticket situation. "Maybe I want her to care less if caring more means stalking me and putting my life in danger."

He lifts his eyebrows. "You want to know the truth? I think what happened to Dick was an accident, and this is Nicole's way of trying to make sense of it. If it weren't for you, I would wish he'd gone right on hiding. Not much of a man, to leave his kids and then expect them to set everything aside and come running as soon as he makes the shitty decision that finally kills him."

"Whoa," I say, setting down the sandwich. I hadn't expected him to be so honest with me, either about Dick or the situation with Nicole. It's refreshing, yet I can't shake the feeling that I'm *still* being manipulated. "Tell me how you really feel."

One side of his mouth lifts in a smirk that's truly devastating, even though I don't feel any kind of pull toward him—thank God, because my half-sister is a terrifying woman.

"You're family," he says. "I don't see any reason to B.S. you."

"If you're so sure he wasn't murdered, then it seems like a pretty thankless task for me to run around town with Nicole and ask people questions."

He lifts his eyebrows. "If I were you, I wouldn't just throw out her hunch and trust mine. I'm right plenty of times, and I don't let her forget it, but she's right more often than I am."

I take a bite of the sandwich to avoid responding, but the truth is, I don't have a ton of choices here. If I want any of the money, I'm stuck in this house for a month. I *need* the money. I need to regroup and figure out what happens next, because what's been happening wasn't working out.

He taps the wall. "The sheets on the bed are clean, and I wasn't sure if you had a toothbrush and toothpaste, so I put a set in the hall bathroom for you." He lifts his hands, grinning. "Sealed."

"Thanks," I say, feeling a blush try to exert itself. "I appreciate the sandwich and the toothbrush. Even if it's your way of telling me I already smell like garlic."

"Oh—" he snaps his fingers, "—I almost forgot, but the Jeep out there is yours. Nicole and I have our own car here, and another at home, so we don't need it." He pulls a key fob from his pocket and sets it on the desk next to my food.

Relief washes through me, chased by fear, because the Jeep really is a beast, big enough that I could mow over a squirrel without hearing the thump.

"Sleep well," Damien says with a nod. "We're glad you're here, Claire."

"You too." It's a rote response, delivered without thought, and after he leaves the room, shutting the door behind him, I have plenty of time to be embarrassed by it.

You too? You too, what?

But I dial the airline's hotline as I finish my sandwich, then spend the next twenty minutes on hold while I explore the bedroom. Which isn't as interesting as it sounds. There's not much to explore beyond the dresser—empty—and the desk, which has a single drawer. I'm excited about the drawer for a second because it's jammed, but when I finally wiggle it open, the only thing I find inside is a crumpled napkin which looks soiled in a way that I'll only dare to touch it if I find rubber gloves.

Finally, the call connects. I'm assured that my bag will indeed be brought to me...once they find it.

"It's very important," I say for the third or fourth time.

"It always is, sweetheart," says the man on the other line with a beleaguered sigh. "It always is."

After we hang up, I call my dad and tell him a very sanitized version of the story—turning Declan into a helpful stranger, Nicole into someone who's definitely not a psychopath, and Dick's maybe-murder into a total accident, although I do tell him Nicole and I are related.

Once we get off the phone, I get ready for bed and slip under the sheets before calling Lainey, whom I give a completely unedited account.

"It's the DEATH card," she says, sounding thrilled by my misfortune.

"You genuinely believe all of this happened because I pulled a card out of a stack?"

"No, dummy," she says, "I think the Tarot really works. I'm going to watch some online tutorials tonight."

"You really think you're getting fired, don't you?" I ask, reading between the lines. Lainey's work schemes come in hot and hard when something big happens in her life.

Her sigh gusts over the phone. "Probably. The sweater that woman stole was made of cashmere from some grass-fed goat."

"Don't all goats eat grass?"

"I'm guessing it was organic grass, watered by tears. The owners are really pissed off. It had mother-of-pearl buttons. It was hideous but very expensive."

This time I'm the one who's excited by her misfortune. "You should come stay with me, Lainey. It would be so much better if you were here too. We could have fun. The mountains are gorgeous, and you've always talked about taking up hiking."

I must be truly desperate, because I've never had any desire to hike.

"I might like hiking more on a theoretical level," she says. "What about the boxes? And the apartment?"

I hold back a groan, because it's hard as hell to find a new apartment in New York, but I'm going to have to let the place go. Given my current financial situation, I can't cover a month's rent if I'm not actually living there. Still, I can't kick Lainey out. I offer to help her cover the next month's rent but admit that I'm going to have to let the unit go after that.

She sighs. "I figured as much. I'm going to have to figure out what to do with all my shit."

"Why don't you ask your parents if they can take some of it, and you can bring the rest over here in their car?"

"Let's see if I get fired over the grass-fed yarn first." She pauses. "Do you have a photo of Declan?"

"Wouldn't it have been weird if I'd asked to snap his picture?"

"Look one up," she says. "If he's a landscaper, he probably has some kind of website."

My heart starts thumping as I turn the phone on speaker and draw up the search window. But I only have one bar of service in this room—two, if I stand on the bed and lean toward the window, and after I enter in "Declan, landscaping, Marshall," it takes the phone forty seconds or so to think about it before spitting up results. I get a couple of hits—none of them him. I don't know his last name or any other thing about him, besides Nicole's pot accusation.

"No photos," I report to Lainey, trying not to sound disappointed.

"That's okay," she says carelessly. "It's not like he's far. I'm sure you can get one later."

My pulse jumps again at the thought of seeing him. Of walking out the door and bumping into him.

"That would be creepy," I tell her, my throat dry.

"You're wearing his T-shirt right now, aren't you?" she asks pointedly.

Yes. I told myself it was because I didn't want to wear the clothes Nicole had lent me to bed if I also have to wear them in the morning, but that wasn't the only reason. I like the T-shirt—the way it smells, the soft fabric, and the thought that it was stretched around his hard, broad chest at some point.

Am I hoping he'll look in through the window before I change and see me in it?

The thought had occurred to me.

"I'm in trouble on so many levels," I say with a groan.

"Remember the Death card," she says again. "OK, I'm going to go watch those tutorials. I'll give you an update in the morning." She's silent for a second, then she says, "Honestly, maybe I'll quit if they don't fire me. What you've got going on sounds way more interesting than what's happening here, and I wouldn't mind putting a few states between Todd and me. He...he put up some Instagram posts."

"That fucker," I say, mostly to make her laugh.

She laughs. "They're not about *her*. Actually, it's sort of worse. They're about letting go of the things that were holding you back so you can self-actualize. I'm guessing I'm *what was holding him back.*"

"Sounds like he should join the Tribe of Light with my mother," I say with a laugh. "Yes, come here. *Please God* come here. And we'll figure all of this out. Maybe we can finally do something meaningful with our lives if we get that insurance payout."

My mind starts spinning, forming a future made of spun sugar—delicate and breakable but so beautiful it takes my breath away. My bakery, with a red-and-white-striped awning like in a movie and a line out the door, the smell of chocolate and vanilla scenting the air. Lainey, with me. The two of us, doing it together.

"We?" Lainey interrupts. "As far as I know, Richard Ricci wasn't my father too."

"This might be my chance to start a bakery, and I refuse to start a small business without you." I don't want to oversell it, because the spun sugar in my brain is so fragile that even a hairline fracture can send it all crashing down, so I add, "I've heard there's a high rate of failure, and whenever possible, I'd prefer to share my failures."

"You're too good to me."

"Impossible."

We hang up, and I plug in my phone, grateful I'd stuffed the charger in my carry-on, and snuggle into the covers. I figured it would take me a long time to get to sleep—from the plane to Declan to finding out Nicole is my sister, it's been the craziest, fullest day I can remember. So I'm not surprised when my thoughts keep pinging around inside of my skull like sugar-high toddlers.

I do what I always do when I can't relax—I head down to the kitchen and bake. It's not my kitchen, and it's poorly stocked, but there are enough ingredients for cinnamon muffins. By the time I'm finished, it's past midnight, and I'm not really hungry, but I pack the food away and head back upstairs. I still can't sleep...

My mind keeps summoning up random, unrelaxing thoughts—*a man died in this house, did I remember to book Agnes's chemical peel? I hope I didn't, and she shows up anyway*—until my mind turns to Declan. Declan, kissing me like he'd die if he stopped. My lips remember what it felt like and want more of it. It's dizzying to think he's right next door, lying in his bed.

Does he sleep naked?

My mind is full of images of Declan in some implausible California king bed with black silk sheets, when I finally ease into sleep.

When I wake up, it's bright outside, light streaming in through the cheap blinds, and I have an even worse dehydration headache. It feels like a dog is barking *inside of* my head.

Groaning, I get up and slide on my shorts from yesterday, dry by now, and more me than the outfit Nicole lent me.

There's another shrill bark, and it hits me that the sound isn't only inside of my head—it's from a real dog, and moreover, the dog must be in this house. Do Nicole and Damien have a dog? I wouldn't put it past them to have kept something like that from me, but *why*?

I open the door, and a little mutt comes flying at me. Dogs aren't on the long list of things I'm afraid of, but it lunges at me like a little missile made of teeth and flesh, and I'm not ashamed to admit I scream. When the missile reaches me, though, the dog is transformed into a little tornado of affection, licking and sniffing me as his tail wags.

I crouch down to pet him, and it strikes me that he has a remarkable resemblance to the framed art in the kitchen. He also seems to take interest in the bottom hem of my T-shirt.

Could this be Dick's old dog? Maybe the little guy got confused and wandered into the wrong house?

I didn't notice a doggie door, but then again, I was probably in shock during my tour of the house.

"Nicole?" I call out tentatively.

There's no answer, so I pad down the hall and then down the stairs, taking them cautiously. There's a tell-tale creak in the middle, and I have to wonder...was that the last sound Dick heard before the end? The thought makes me shiver and glance down at my innocent, sweet little friend, who might have borne witness to the whole thing.

If only he could tell us if there'd been anyone else here to see it too...

I shake off the dark feelings, and when I get to the bottom of the steps, make my way to the kitchen, where a note is skewered to the kitchen table with a pocket knife.

So my sister has a flair for melodrama. After our talk yesterday, I'm not surprised.

Sighing, I free the note.

Sleeping beauty,
Damien tells me that he gave you the keys to the Jeep,
so you've got wheels. Hope you know how to drive stick shift,
sweet cheeks; neither of us do. When you wake up, head to
Main Street. It's small enough that you shouldn't have any

trouble finding us. Be there no later than noon, we have work to do today.
    Your sister

My first thought is *Am I really related to this unholy terror?* My second is that I definitely don't know how to drive stick shift, which means the key Damien gave me is essentially worthless.

There's no phone number, so I guess I'm supposed to use my detecting skills to find a couple of private investigators, who make it their business to be shady. There's no mention of the little dog or what I'm supposed to do about him.

A quick glance at the clock over the stove tells me I have a couple of hours to figure out a way to Main Street. Does anyone work for Uber here? God knows if the app will even work. I tried to pull up Wordle, and I gave up on the day's puzzle quicker than I usually do, because it took twenty seconds to chew over each of my wrong guesses.

I glance out the side window of the kitchen and flinch. Declan's walking around outside, his expression brooding. He's even more appealing out here, in his element—a strapping, handsome mountain man wandering around outside of a wooden cabin. I should probably be pissed at him—I *am* sort of pissed—but it's at least novel to be rejected by a man because he likes me too much. In my long, checkered dating history, no one's thrown that one at me before. If it's an untruth, it's at least a flattering one. He turns toward the patch of trees behind our houses, his gaze panning to either side, and that's when it hits me…

Oh, crap. He's looking for his dog. *This* dog. If I don't catch him now, he could spend hours on a worthless search of the woods.

I entertain the shallow thought that I just rolled out of bed without putting on makeup, brushing my teeth, or combing my hair, then sigh and head for the kitchen door, the dog trailing me like I'm made of bacon. It's as I reach it that I realize this door no more has a doggie door built into it than the front.

Nicole did this.

She kidnapped Declan's dog so I'd be forced to talk to him—and just like yesterday, I'm falling right into her plan.

CHAPTER TWELVE

DECLAN

I call out Rocket's name again, feeling a familiar tightness in my chest. Dammit. I've been home less than twenty-four hours, and I've already lost him. Maybe I'm still not cut out for pet ownership. Could be I'm not cut out for much of anything anymore.

I don't like the way I left Claire yesterday. My mother always told me that even though women can take care of themselves, men should still be gentlemen. It wasn't a very gentlemanly thing to do, sucking her tits and then handing her off to Rex to bring her home, especially after she got me through the flight from hell. Thinking about my screwup kept me up half the night, and the other half was spent dreaming about her soft skin and sunshine hair, kissing that little mole next to her mouth and sucking on her hard pink nipples while she made little sounds of pleasure she didn't even seem aware of...

I'd wanted more.

I'd abandoned control entirely when we were out on the side of the road, and so had she, rocking against me. And sure, I'd been with women—a lot of women, if I'm being honest—but I'd never felt so lost to it. The only explanation that made sense was that our experience on the plane had created a bond, and the desire to fuck like two people who'd been given a temporary reprieve from death.

But the loss of control had made me uncomfortable, and then more uncomfortable after I found out she's my next door neighbor. So I'd forced some distance—space in which I could breathe and remember why I'd come here to hide. It wasn't so I could make friends or find a girlfriend, and it could be argued that I didn't deserve those things. Didn't deserve the dog, either, or the peace I get from growing things. From sitting out on the deck with a beer, the mountains spread out before me.

Maybe the things I deserved would come for me, the same way they'd come for Dick.

By the time I'd left them at Asheville Airport, my head felt like it had been stuffed with barbed wire and cotton fluff. The kid at the desk at the car rental agency looked about ready to shit his pants when I complained about the flat and the irresponsible and unforgivable lack of a spare. They'd issued a refund, not that I gave a shit, and then I'd driven back to Marshall, my mind full of Claire. What were she and Rex talking about? Was she asking him about me?

That was another thing about Claire. She was too curious. Leave her alone with anyone in town for half an hour, especially Rex, and she'd probably know more local gossip than I did. It was dangerous to get to know someone else like that.

I knew I should just let it be, but as soon as I got done picking Rocket up from the dog sitter, I'd called Rex to make sure she'd gotten home okay.

"Yeah," he said, "I'm just pulling back into the auto shop right now. Thanks for the introduction, man. We're going out to dinner tomorrow night."

"No, you're not," I'd all but growled while Rocket pawed my shoulder in the seat next to mine.

"Is there any reason I shouldn't?" he asked pointedly—and it hit me like a brick to the gut that I'd let Rex become a friend too. A friend who knew me well enough to call me out on being full of shit. Then again, he knew Claire and I had stripped down together in the back of that van. Maybe it was only logical to assume that a man who'd seen her half naked would be feral for her.

"She's only in town for a little while," I told him, my voice choked.

"Doesn't matter to me, friend. We'll have some fun while she's here."

"You're fucking with me," I said flatly.

"Sure," he admitted. "But the real question is why you got me to drop her off at her house—*next door to yours*—if you're into her. I don't think Dick would mind, if that's your holdup."

I had a feeling he was wrong about that, but I didn't say so. Dick was gone, and what he would and wouldn't have minded can only be guessed. Besides, it wasn't really Dick I was worried about. My brother and sister have made new lives for themselves, and I'm not going to fuck with that by making stupid decisions. Because if I let myself get attached to Claire, I'll let things slip without meaning to—and it'll keep happening until she knows everything.

She's a good person. A *law-abiding* person. If she finds out what we ran from, she might feel inclined to do something about it. She'd certainly have opinions.

Or judgements, a thought that puts a knot in my throat.

I can't take that risk.

My sister found a job at a bakery, and Seamus works for a mechanic. It's honest work—the kinds of jobs where you do your thing, you get paid, and then you get the fuck out. Safe.

Sure, Shay doesn't much like that he works for a body shop instead of running one, and Rosie doesn't exactly seem happy, but *they're fine.* No one's going to come for them, and they're not in a position where they're likely to piss off anyone with the power to do something about it.

I'm the one who's not okay, but the struggle should fall heaviest on me.

When I let Rocket out to take a piss this morning, it took me half an hour to realize he hadn't scratched on the door to come in yet.

I'm supposed to bring a bed of plants to a shop downtown, but I can't leave my dog out here, wandering around in the heat. Totally alone, because Damien and Nicole's car is gone. He could get nabbed by a hawk, hit by a car. Hit with heatstroke.

"Rocket?" I call, feeling the worry pounding a steady beat inside of me, the sensation as familiar as my own heartbeat.

But the only thing I hear is a rustling sound behind me that prickles the hairs on the back of my neck. Most of my jumpiness faded a few weeks after I got here. In the beginning, every cricket chirp, every broken twig was someone who'd come for me. But no one did come, and eventually that particular worry faded into the background, but right now, my skin feels oversensitized, my brain strangled and wrong. My vigilance, higher than normal. It's probably just a squirrel. Or maybe even Rocket, but it could be someone else. Someone who's bided their time.

I don't have a weapon, other than my fists, and if it's someone who came here with a vendetta, they didn't show up for a fistfight.

I turn around quickly, because if this is the end, I'd rather see it coming.

But it's not a big sweaty guy behind me. It's Claire, holding Rocket to her chest, a T-shirt plastered around her. *My* T-shirt. For a split second, my mind goes to a strange place, because it hits me that this is the way she'd look on a Sunday morning if she stayed over, rumpled and sweet, having just risen from my bed. But the thought leaves me shaken, because no one's *ever* stayed over at my house.

"I have your dog." She holds him out, and relief radiates through me, because he's unharmed.

I take Rocket from her, and he licks my face, his tail wagging so hard he nearly falls on his ass. "You scared the shit out of me, buddy," I tell him, then look up at Claire. Her hair is loose around her shoulders, spilling around her face, and her eyes are the same magnet they were yesterday, daring me to look. Commanding me to at the same time.

She lifts a hand to her hair. "I must look terrible. I literally just rolled out of bed."

I should tell her the truth—she looks like the first ray of daylight sneaking around the curtains in the morning and smells like apples and rosemary. I should thank her. I should apologize for ducking out on her yesterday. But I hear myself saying, "You're wearing my shirt."

She plucks at it. "Yeah, I still don't have my suitcase, and it was comfortable to sleep in."

"It's yours," I say, immediately feeling like an idiot. I'm not granting her anything of worth—it's a freebie T-shirt I got for plucking weeds at town hall.

"Thanks," she replies.

For a second, I think that's going to be it—this awkward run-in will end, and I'll have to watch the woman I spent all night thinking about walk away, but she blurts, "I didn't kidnap your dog."

I nearly drop him. "The possibility hadn't occurred to me."

She bites her bottom lip, then says, "But I think my sister did."

"Your sister?" I ask in disbelief. "Are you talking about Nicole?" My mind trips over that unexpected detail before faceplanting over the accusation. Why the hell would Nicole kidnap Rocket after giving me Rocket?

Claire glances back at Dick's cabin, then says in an undertone, "Yeah, I guess Dick was her father, and he left her and her mom when she was seven. She's my half-sister. I didn't know any of this until last night." She tucks a few strands of hair behind her ear. "Look, I know you want to keep your distance. You've made that perfectly clear, but

I need help getting down to Main Street to meet Nicole, and I'd *really* like to talk things over with someone who's familiar with this situation and isn't crazy. I feel like my whole life is spiraling out of control."

"How do you know I'm not crazy?" I ask, my blood pumping faster, because I want to give myself this. I want to talk to her. To sit with her. To soak her in. To feel something good and normal. Rocket bats a paw against my beard to reclaim my attention, and I scratch his ears.

"I don't, I guess," she says. "But you're definitely less crazy than my sister. She sets a low bar. I mean...I really think she kidnapped your dog so I'd be forced to talk to you."

"Why would she give a shit if we talk?"

She rubs a hand over her mouth, drawing my gaze back to her lips. I'm remembering what they feel like against mine, fucking bliss, when she says, "I get the feeling she just does things to see what happens next. Like rolling the dice. Do you really grow weed?"

I feel like I did that time I went ice-fishing with my dad and got a dunk in the frozen lake. How does she know? Did Dick leave something lying around the house? A smoking blunt instead of a smoking gun? I looked around before the cops showed up, but I didn't find anything damning.

My brows lift. "I don't think I should answer that."

"I know all about evasions and passive aggression," she says with a sigh, "and I have to say that sounds an awful lot like a yes."

I catch the look of disappointment on her face, and fuck, if she thinks growing a few weed plants in my greenhouse is bad, she'll really take issue with what I used to do for my uncle. Even though I should *want* her to think the worst of me, I find myself saying, "It's not like I hide behind trees on school grounds to sell it to kids. I did it as a favor for Dick. I've got a green thumb. I've always been able to grow anything."

Her lips part in a look of surprise. "But why risk it? Nicole says it's still illegal here."

More so than in Pennsylvania, but it was illegal to grow there, too. *Definitely* illegal to grow in large quantities.

I shift on my feet, still holding Rocket. I make a split-second decision. Staying away from Claire was the right call—she and her sister know too much about me—but now I have to convince her not to tell anyone else about the weed. I also have to find out what else this crazy sister knows.

"You said you need someone to bring you to Main Street. I'll do it. I have to head there anyway to make a drop-off."

"Of weed?" she asks, her eyes wide.

"Plant starters."

"Oh," she says, blushing.

I swallow, trying not to notice the way her chest flushes too, and say, "But you should change out of the shirt. If you wear it downtown, people will notice. They'll talk."

"And you don't want me to mess with your rep as a player?" she asks pointedly.

"I don't want them talking about me at all if I can help it. I like to keep to myself." In all honesty, I don't like the thought of them talking about her either, and they will. The thought makes me bristle. But I'm not going to be the one to tell her she's too much of an open book, too trusting. She's beautiful the way she is—and I'll be damned if I'm going to be the one to change that.

"Good luck," she mutters. "I've been here for less than a day, and I can already tell the people here gossip about everything."

She's right about that. But there's an art to avoiding gossip—to fitting into the mold the town's made for you. *Shut-in. Loner.* Something tells me that Claire and her sister are going to mess with the status quo around here.

And that means this life I've carved out for myself might be over just after it finally got started again. The thought makes my chest burn.

"Be out front in ten minutes," I say, my voice coming out gruff. This situation isn't her fault, but she's still part of it.

"We need to work on your people skills."

"No thanks. You get people skills, suddenly people want to talk to you."

"God forbid," she says, but the corners of her mouth are twitching with laughter—and I find my own mouth wanting to smile back.

"I'll see you in ten minutes." I head back to the house, Rocket licking my ear, since I've still got him up over my shoulder, and I don't let myself glance back at her. I stick to the self-imposed rule all the way to the back door, when I feel an itching between my shoulder blades that has me turning around. It's not her watching, though. Not anyone watching. It's just her presence, behind me, that commands me to get a final glance of her in the green shirt—engulfed in something that's mine. I watch as she makes her way inside the house, then I step through my own back door and lower Rocket to the ground.

He wags his tail tentatively.

"Well, buddy," I tell him. "I'm fucked."

He barks once in agreement.

———

TEN MINUTES LATER, my truck is parked in front of Dick's house, and Claire emerges in a black shirt and black pants with a tote bag over her shoulder.

"You sure you want to wear that?" I ask as she gets in. "It's a high of eighty-five today."

"You really take an interest in what I'm wearing, don't you?"

"Sorry," I mutter, my gaze roaming out the window and landing on Dick's Jeep. "You don't have the keys to the Jeep?"

She secures her belt, her mouth scrunching to the side. "I do, actually, but I don't know how to drive stick shift. Honestly, it's a miracle that I know how to drive anything considering how I learned."

"In your friend's parents' little car," I comment.

"You remember that?" she asks in surprise.

"Nothing wrong with my memory." I don't know what possesses me—insanity, must be—but I find myself offering, "I can teach you if you like. It'd be easy to learn out here. Not many cars coming by."

"Thank you," she says, clearly surprised, and why shouldn't she be? I keep saying we can't spend time together, and here I am, offering to spend hours in a car with her. *Idiot.* But I don't like the thought of her being stuck at the house, and I like it even less to think of her taking that tank out without being able to maneuver it, so I don't try to take the words back. If she accepts, I'll find a way to fulfill my end of the bargain.

She pulls a wrapped baked good out of the tote bag and hands it to me.

"Do I look like I can't feed myself?" I ask with a half-smile.

Her gaze travels to my arms. "You must manage somehow. But I figured I'd share. There's no way I'm going to eat twelve muffins before they go stale. Since you live next door, I might as well warn you—I like to bake way more than I can eat, and you're probably going to get plenty of leftovers."

"I'll have to try the muffin before I agree to that," I tease, although I don't doubt it tastes better than anything I'd put together.

I steer the car out onto the road, then unwrap the muffin with one hand and take a bite.

Fuck, it's good. So good, I probably shouldn't be trying to steer a car while trying to eat it, because it's the kind of food that makes you think about what you're eating instead of just shoveling calories into your mouth.

"This is the best muffin I've ever had," I say, glancing at her as I balance the rest of the pastry in my lap. She's watching me, eyes sparkling, and I know I've pleased her.

"You've got something there," she says, pointing to the little pinprick mole at the corner of her mouth. I lift one hand from the wheel and try to wipe my mouth, but I must do a half-assed job of it, because her hand reaches out and swipes away the crumb, her touch brushing millimeters from my lips. For a second, my control slips. For a second, all I can think about is yesterday afternoon—Claire in the rain, Claire rocking against me, Claire with her chest bared to me. *Claire.*

I hear a creaking sound from the wheel and abruptly loosen my grip, which I'd unintentionally tightened.

Claire's looking at me, her eyes dilated, but she clears her throat and says, "What's your frame of reference?"

"My sister likes to bake," I say. "Don't tell her I said yours are better."

She smiles wider, and I feel a puncture wound in my chest, because she's never going to meet Rosie. Of course she won't. The surprising thing is that I actually want her to.

"Thanks," I say between bites, because I can't stop eating the damn thing. "I'll accept your reject baked goods anytime."

"Glad to hear it."

We sit there in silence for a second as I finish the muffin and maneuver down the road. Then I ask, "So, are you going to turn me in?"

"For what?" she asks, giving me a sharp look.

"Growing. You strike me as a rule follower."

Her expression turns contemptuous. "I know you don't mean that as a compliment. No one ever means that as a compliment. Even people who want you to follow the rules."

"There's nothing wrong with following the rules when they make sense."

She makes an amused sound. "And who gets to decide if they do? You?"

I give her a sidelong glance, taking in the curve of her cheek, her soft golden hair. "Sure. I guess we each have to make that call on our own and hope we're not caught by someone who disagrees with us and has the power to do something about it."

She's watching me again, and her gaze sends a hot shiver through me. I shouldn't be enjoying this—shouldn't be doing it—but at least this time I'm only breaking my own rule, I guess.

"You know, I think you're the kind of guy my dad used to warn me about. Tattoos. Drugs. Your own set of rules."

This gets a laugh from me. "I wish I could tell you he'd be wrong."

"Why'd you grow weed for Dick?"

I pause for a second, thinking of giving her a non-answer, but he was her biological father. She deserves to know something about him, and maybe it would help her to know that life hadn't treated him easily. "Dick had bad dreams and chronic pain, and CBD wasn't strong enough to help."

"You sure he didn't just con you into doing something illegal for him?" she asks, watching me again. "If he and Nicole were anything alike, I wouldn't put it past him."

"No way of knowing. But I get what it's like to carry around hard memories. I felt for him. So he got me the seeds, and I grew it for him. He couldn't keep a succulent alive."

"Do you honestly expect me to believe you don't sell to anyone else?" she asks hotly. "I'm guessing you could make more with the homegrown stuff than you could landscaping."

I don't blame her for thinking so. It's what I would assume if I were in her shoes. But it still burns, and I find myself saying, "I've never sold the stuff I grow here to anyone, him either. I wouldn't."

It's true, although not for the reasons she's probably thinking. She's full-on staring at me while I drive, and I hurry to say, "I didn't do it to be a nice guy, Claire. He was doing favors for me too."

"Like what?" she asks, much too interested. This was a mistake. I should have let her believe what she wanted to about the weed. I couldn't have left her stranded at the house, obviously, but I could have ordered her an Uber.

Except Rex is the only Uber driver in town, and even though he admitted he was joking about asking her out to dinner, I still feel a little...territorial. I don't want him driving her around, doing her favors. I'd rather be the one to do that.

She's still looking at me, still waiting for an answer, so I say, "Doesn't matter anymore. Is Nicole really your sister?"

"I guess," she says with a sigh. "She told me it was in the will. Dick got a DNA test and everything."

"Did you see the will?" I ask. Because that's not the kind of shit you take for granted. I don't want this sister taking advantage of her. Claire's the kind of woman who believes what people tell her. There's something beautiful about that—something pure—but it's the kind of beautiful that can bite you in the ass.

"No," she says. "Shit. I should have asked. But how do I know she didn't mess with it?"

"Find out which attorney he filed with. There are only a few of them in town, unless he went somewhere in Asheville. If you find his lawyer, you can ask to see a copy of it since you're named in the will. At least I think that's how it works."

I'd been the executor of my parents' will, so I'd been the first to find out how deep of a grave my father had dug himself before my parents' car accident. He'd probably told himself there would be time to adjust course—he'd always believed he could turn things around in his favor. My parents' favorite story, repeated so many times we all knew it by heart, was about how their first date had been a total disaster. Dad had spilled an entire beer on Mom, but somehow he'd convinced her to go out on a second date. If he could achieve that, then what was recouping thousands or even hundreds of thousands of dollars in debts?

But we all run out of time eventually.

"Thanks," she says. "I'll do that." Giving me a sidelong look, her lips tipped up slightly, she adds, "You know I never thought I'd be taking legal advice from someone who grows pot."

"Here's the rest of my legal knowledge. I'm only someone who *allegedly* grows pot. Speaking of allegations, do you really think your sister kidnapped Rocket? She seemed happy enough to hand him over the other day."

Her mouth forms an apologetic line. "Maybe kidnapped was a strong word, but she definitely put him in our house and shut the door. She guessed something happened between us because of the —" She plucks at the shirt she's wearing, my head following the movement, and I need to force myself to look away. "You know, the shirt."

I swear under my breath. "So you think she's trying to play matchmaker or something?"

"Maybe? I told her I wasn't interested, but clearly that didn't stop her."

Well, shit. That shouldn't sting, but it burns like whiskey on a bullet wound. Then again, I don't know why Claire *would* be interested in me for any reason other than what usually draws women in. The only solid things she knows about me are that I'm afraid of flying—*soft*, I hear my uncle saying—and that I *allegedly* grew pot for her biological father.

"I honestly think Nicole's a bit unhinged," Claire continues, shaking her head slightly. "Or maybe what happened to Dick messed with her head." She pauses, watching me. "She told me you were the person who found him?"

The memory digs in its claws. Hearing Rocket barking. Letting myself in with my key. Feeling the echoing of emptiness of something wrong and then finding him sprawled at the bottom of those steps, still warm but gone.

"Yeah," I say, my voice ragged.

She presses her palm to my upper arm, wrapping it around in a squeeze. "I'm sorry, Declan. I shouldn't have asked about it. That must've been so awful. I can't even imagine..."

I pull onto Main Street and park in front of the flower shop. "You know where you're supposed to go?"

"Nicole told me to find her," she says, her gaze on the road. "It can't be too hard. There are only, like, five businesses here, and she has neon hair."

Still, I can practically hear my mother telling me it's never too late to do the right thing. It'll take me half a minute to get the plant starters where they need to go, and after that I don't have anything going on today other than grabbing a beer with Rex later.

"I'll take you around," I say.

She stares at me again, her hand still wrapped around my arm, sending heat pulsing through me. Maybe I'm not the only one who feels it, because she glances at her hand on my arm and releases it self-consciously.

"Why?" she asks. "You just said you don't want people talking about you."

"My mother wouldn't have liked it if I'd left you to fend for yourself. You've never been here before."

"It's about two blocks long, from what I can tell. I've walked across Central Park in the dark. I'll be fine."

"If you have no survival instincts, I have even more of an obligation to save you from yourself," I insist.

"You really want to stroll down Main Street with me?"

I want to if it means I get to be around her a bit longer. But I don't want to admit that, either to myself or her, so I shrug. "People who hang out at the bluegrass bar in the middle of the day buy a lot of pot."

Her eyes widen, and I see the moment when she realizes I'm fucking with her. She shoves my arm, but her eyes are laughing, and I feel a warm glow inside.

"You are such an asshole."

"I told you your father would be right to worry."

Her eyes are sparkling, and I feel an urge to kiss her right here on Main Street, in front of anyone who's close enough to see through my windows, and that urge is unsettling enough that I close down again.

"Let's go," I say gruffly, and she salutes me before getting out of the truck.

CHAPTER THIRTEEN

CLAIRE

Declan's such a strange mixture of things. He can be funny and kind of brash; quiet, for sure; but there's always this banked intensity in him...a fire that's ready to burn, for good or for evil.

But he couldn't possibly have hurt Dick Ricci. I'm sure of it. And I'm *mostly sure* that I don't just feel that way because I have never, ever been this desperate for a man. Still, I have to admit that he was right, yesterday. It would be disastrously stupid for me to get mixed up with him when he lives next door to me for who knows how long—a month, at least, if I decide I need the money and the half-a-house badly enough to fulfill the terms of the will.

If that's even what the will stipulates. Declan was right—I'd be a fool to take Nicole's word for it. She's manipulative and unpredictable, a loose cannon of a person.

Still...I can't deny I'm a little excited about going to talk to Mrs. Rosings with her. Maybe it's my desire to see Mrs. Rosings, who is also a bit of an oddity. Maybe it's just the thrill of doing something that feels so completely different from what I've been doing for the last seven years. It's like I was a Barbie in a hermetically sealed box, and someone is finally playing with me.

Actually, that sounds a bit dirty.

I glance at Declan, walking beside me—all of the humor washed from his face and his stoic, stony expression back in full force.

I don't know why he decided to walk with me. I'm pretty sure he doesn't know why he did it either, other than what he said about his mother.

"What's your favorite place in Marshall?" I ask. "And don't say the bluegrass bar."

He gives me a half smile before looking away. His dark hair's a little long on top, and it nearly dips into his eyes. It's unspeakably sexy. "Wasn't going to. My favorite place is out at my property. I could never get sick of the view."

"That's a little dismissive of Marshall and its two blocks of fun."

He smiles, looking down, then says, "Spoken like a true New Yorker."

"Are you one too?"

"Nah," he says, but he doesn't offer up more information. Of course he doesn't. This man treats information like it's currency, and he'll go broke if he gives too much away. He glances up and then nods at a coffee shop. "Look in the window, see if you spot her."

"Are we taking turns playing Peeping Tom? Because I'd prefer not to look like a weirdo alone."

"You want me to play Peeping Tom with you?" he asks, his tone wry, but there's a glimmer in his eyes. A remembrance of how things were yesterday.

"You seemed to like it well enough yesterday."

He shakes his head, his mouth turning up at the corners. "Look through the window, Claire."

I'm smiling as I do. No Nicole, although one of the elderly guests has bright pink hair.

"On to the next place," he says.

"It's your turn to look like a weirdo," I insist.

He doesn't comment, just leads the way down the sidewalk to

what looks like is either a coffee shop or a gas station, there's no telling. "Most of the seating's around back," he tells me.

I tap my bare wrist and raise my eyebrows. "Well, what are you waiting for?"

He shakes his head again, but I can see the humor on his face as he rounds the building to check. It's like something has lifted inside of him, and I'd like to think I provided some of the scaffolding.

We check another few places, talking easily in between, before Declan pulls out his phone, swears, and glances at me.

"You've got to make your delivery," I comment.

"Yeah. Why don't you come with me, and we'll track them down afterward?"

"Man, you really don't have much faith in the mean streets of Marshall," I say. I'm pleased, even though I know this can lead nowhere good. Hell, if he found out Nicole thinks he's a potential murderer, he'd brick himself off so thoroughly, he'd probably never speak to anyone again.

Which is precisely why I shouldn't be wandering around with him, looking for her. She doesn't strike me as someone who takes care in what she says to other people. I wouldn't put it past her to accuse him of murder to his face in one breath and offer him a swig from a flask the next.

Still, I can't seem to say no to him, and not just in the way I struggle to say no to anyone. The problem with Declan is that I don't *want* to say no to him.

He watches me and shifts his weight on his feet. I'm struck again by what a powerful man he is—so much so he crushed the armrest on that plane. If I reminded him of it, he'd probably say something about it being cheap plastic, and he'd be right. But *I* couldn't have crushed it. I probably couldn't have even gotten it to crack if I'd put my whole weight into the effort.

Maybe that should make me worry, given what Nicole said about him, but it doesn't. My gut tells me he's trustworthy—to an extent—and he'd use that strength to protect but never harm me. I want it to be true.

"Maybe I need help carrying the starters," he says, "and this is my way of asking."

Laughter bursts from me. He could probably carry ten of them without breaking a sweat.

"There are kinder ways of saying no," he says flatly, and I find myself touching his arm again, like I can't help it—like his skin is magnetized instead of very warm and hard, the muscles underneath the surface a bit hypnotizing.

He glances at my hand and then brushes his fingers softly against it. I drop the hold. "I'll help you," I say. "I'm terrible at gardening, though, and I wouldn't be surprised if the plants spontaneously die after I pick them up."

"I'll take my chances."

We walk companionably back to the truck, and he responds to my questions about gardening. Neither of us mention pot. Or Richard Ricci. Or Nicole.

When we get to the truck, he lowers the tailgate and hands me an enormous flat rectangular box filled with little plant starters. I'm embarrassed by how much it delights me, looking down at those little green leaves, imagining the plants stretching up and growing fruit or vegetables. I've never had a garden before. There's never been room for one. The closest I've ever come is my dad's little herb garden, stationed by the window that gets the most light in his brownstone.

"What are they?" I ask as he picks up a second box.

"Melon and squash," he says, closing the back of the truck with his foot.

"Who bought them?"

"A restaurant. They like to grow some of their own produce round back, but mostly they like to *look* like they grown their own produce when the guests go back there to sit in the garden. They can point to the melons and tell themselves that's what they got in their dessert, but it's really just for show. Still, the pay's decent. Not very hard to get a melon to sprout."

"Huh," I say, thinking this over, "that's brilliant. Still. It *is* better to cook with fresh ingredients when you can."

This gets me a sidelong look as he leads the way down the sidewalk. "You like to cook too?"

"Sometimes, but I'm more of a baker. Is there a bakery here in town?"

"One just closed down last week," he says as he passes a couple of the businesses we've already peeked into. "It was only open a couple of months. A lot of people drive the fifteen minutes to Asheville if they want something special."

My first thought is that this is bad news for someone with a mind to open a bakery—clearly the people of Marshall don't know how to appreciate the glory of a perfectly baked Cronut or Bronut, as it were—but then my mind turns the seemingly plain piece of paper over and finds a golden ticket. There'll be room for a new bakery, and maybe the old building is up for rental. If it was already a bakery once, then it's still set up to be one. The kitchen would be established, which would lower the cost of renovations, and...

And I'm being ridiculous, but I still hear myself saying, "Can you show me the storefront?" There's a little flutter of excitement in my belly even though I'm still pretty sure that I won't be staying here. I just like to dream. To think about what could be if I were more daring or adventurous or *different*.

Declan pauses in his walking, studying me like I'm someone interesting. A gorgeous red-headed woman walks past us and waves to him, but his eyes are on me and he doesn't seem to notice. I feel myself blushing. It feels good to be the one he notices, probably too good.

"Sure. We can go there next," he says. "But I'm guessing you don't just have a thing for empty buildings with crap all over the floor."

"I hope you don't mean that literally," I tell him, adjusting my hold on the box.

"You're not just someone who enjoys baking. That was you downplaying it. It's what you want to do for a job."

"When you put it that way, it sounds like a pipe dream. Embarrassing." I sigh and nod toward the sidewalk, but he doesn't take the hint. "That's why I worked for Agnes so long. She has this reputation of helping her assistants launch their own businesses. But it never happened for me."

He gives me a sidelong look. "I think you're reading the situation wrong. Sounds to me like she valued you too much to let you go."

"That's an optimistic way of looking at it," I say with a sigh. "I think she only kept me there for so long because she knew she could boss me around."

He seeks out my gaze, and when I give it to him, he says, "She took advantage of your assumption that she'd uphold her end of the bargain because you were upholding yours. But you shouldn't feel sorry for being a good person, and it sure as hell doesn't make you any less capable. If you want to do it, I expect you will." Then he grins at me, his eyes lighting up. "Still, I'm glad you got her drunk on public television."

I smile at him, warmed by the assurance even if I'm not convinced I believe him. At the same time, I'm conscious of having said too much. He knows so much more about me than I do him.

"Yeah, guess so. Shall we?"

We start walking companionably, and he must sense my need to talk about anything else, because he shifts the conversation to Marshall. A couple of minutes later, he comes to a stop and nod nods to a storefront next to me. A restaurant—Vincenzo's—with large plate glass windows looking onto Main Street. Currently the red velvet drapes are drawn. "We're here. They're closed, but Mark's expecting the delivery."

He shifts the starters in his arm and knocks on the door—and five seconds later, it's opened from the other side.

But I don't need a photo of Mark to know it's not him standing there. Because it's a woman who's shorter than me but has a *much* more forceful personality. My big sister.

CHAPTER FOURTEEN

"Oh, good, you found us," Nicole says. "Damien said I was taking chances again, but you're smarter than you look."

"*What are you doing here?*" I ask in a seething undertone, not bothering to pretend to be polite.

"Come in," she says. "Chop, chop. Don't let in all that warm air. You'll run up poor Mike's air conditioning bill."

It's no coincidence that she's here, at the exact place Declan was supposed to show up. She expected me to come with him. She's trying to intimidate me, or maybe him. This woman is like a magician, or someone who has read Machiavelli too many times.

I feel Declan shifting on his feet beside me. Is he going to call her out for kidnapping his dog?

But he obviously doesn't want to be drawn into whatever's going on here, because he just asks, "Is Mark here?"

She laughs. "Shit, I've been calling that guy Mike for the past ten minutes. Yeah." She swings a thumb over her shoulder, drawing my attention to the shoulder bag drawn tightly across it. "He's showing Damien his garden in the back. They're talking about dirt. Sometimes Damien really takes things too far."

At least she hasn't accused Declan of murder yet, or admitted she's a private investigator. Because something tells me that Declan might take off if he knew that. There's something he doesn't want people to know, and he wouldn't want to live next door to someone with a proverbial shovel collection.

Declan nods without speaking and then takes the starters from me, easily holding one set in each hand, proving once and for all that he definitely didn't need my help. "Thanks, Claire. Are you okay here?"

With her, he means.

I could tell him no. I *want* to tell him no, but I find myself nodding like one of those desk toys. "Yeah. Sure. Thank you for the help."

He nods once to Nicole. "Nicole."

"What about those stick shift lessons for the Jeep?" I blurt out.

"Stick shift," Nicole repeats, bursting into laughter as if she's a twelve-year-old boy with an addiction to dick jokes.

He nods to me, ignoring her. "We'll talk."

But I'm pretty sure he doesn't mean it. Finding her here set off his internal alarms. He may not know what's going on, but he knows something is, and he doesn't like it.

I watch him go, feeling regret and something almost like panic. It's stupid, since he's barely told me anything about himself, but I feel like he's the only person I trust here, in this unfamiliar place, and he's walking away from me. Leaving me with *her*. I'll need to be careful with him. The last thing I want to do is start relying on someone who's so hot and cold, someone who has secrets so big most of his life seems to revolve around hiding them.

"What are you doing?" I hiss to Nicole.

"What am *I* doing?" she says, waggling her eyebrows. "You've been here less than twenty-four hours, and you're already trying to lock that player down. I admire your hustle."

I glance at the back of the restaurant, trying to make sure no one can hear me, then whisper, "You're the one who keeps pushing us together. You kidnapped his dog this morning."

She laughs. "Hardly. The mutt showed up at our back door, and I let him in, as any concerned citizen would. It's not my fault your boyfriend's never heard of a leash. Besides, we need to talk to him. He's a person of interest—"

"The dog?" I ask in disbelief.

She rolls her eyes. "Declan, and you're the obvious person to befriend him. It was a well-thought-out maneuver."

"Well, he's not going to talk to me now," I say. "He thinks you're up to something."

"Correction," she says, lifting a finger. "He *knows* I'm up to something. But rattling him was only part of the reason I came here."

I glance around at the fancy dining area, taking in the square tables with the fancy chairs and dishware set out, ready for diners who won't show up for another several hours. "You wanted some lunch?"

"Very funny," she says with a sharp-edged smile. "No. We ate some of your crack muffins before we left. Damien and I had a few questions for Mark. But I did know Declan was supposed to make a delivery, and I wanted to catch him off-guard. Did you see the look on his face?" She angles her head, studying me. "That fine man is hiding something, and it's not just his stick shift. I *love* it when people try to hide things from me."

I shrug, my pulse racing for reasons I couldn't name. I know she's right, but I guess I'm hoping his secret is something mild—like he's on the run from hundreds of dollars of parking tickets or selling contraband honey. But in the back of my mind, I know it must be something bigger. "That doesn't mean he did anything bad. You hide a lot of things. No one in town seems to know you're a private investigator...or that you're Dick's daughter."

"How much did you tell your boyfriend?" Nicole asks with a hard look.

"Only the second part."

"Good. Keep it that way. I like to keep my own dirt packed down neat. But that doesn't mean I don't want to dig up everyone else's. We're all hypocrites, Claire. Don't let anyone convince you otherwise. You ready to visit the old lady?"

I glance at the back, frowning, but the door steadfastly stays closed. "Aren't we going to wait for Damien?"

I want to wait for *Declan*, actually. But if I say so, she'll make another smart-ass remark, and I'm suddenly exhausted—as if she has a special way of siphoning my energy.

"Damien's a big boy." Her smile grows wider. "A *very* big boy. And he's going to see if he can catch ride with your boyfriend. Get him talking. Speaking of Declan...I think it would be better if we let him sweat it out a little. You know, let him wonder if it's just a coincidence that we showed up here to talk to Mike, or if we're keeping tabs on him for some reason. A little paranoia is good for the soul."

"You're not normal," I mutter under my breath.

She laughs again, sounding genuinely amused. "Why the fuck would anyone want to be normal?"

"*I* want to be normal."

"Then you're lucky you have me around to make sure you never get what you want."

I want to tell her to fuck off. Maybe I could set off on my own to look for the lawyer's office or that storefront Declan mentioned. But I don't, of course. I hate myself for it, but I follow her out to her car like I'm a little duckling who imprinted on an asshole.

She whistles a tune as she drives, not bothering to make conversation, so I'm the one who has to ask, "What are we going to say to Mrs. Rosings?"

"I'm gonna leave that to you," she says carelessly, her gaze trained out the windshield.

"Excuse me?" I say, alarmed. "You're the private investigator. I'm just—"

"An out-of-work personal assistant. So I'll bet you're really good at bullshitting people and getting them to do what you want."

I'm taken aback for a second, because I'm the person who always goes along with things. I'm the *agreeable* one. I'm nice, aren't I? But she's right. I've had to be commanding for Agnes—to get her the unreasonable things she wants—and I never struggled to make demands on her behalf. Why am I so more willing to take a stand for other people?

Nicole pulls up beside a stone wall with a gate, behind which a mansion looms. There's street parking in this part of town, or at least she decides there is—because she parks the car at the curb.

"This is where she lives?" I ask, impressed.

Way to go, Mrs. Rosings.

"Yeah," she says, studying it. "Ugly, isn't it?"

It is, kind of. But ugly in the way that only a really expensive house can be—the grandeur giving it an air that goes beyond ugly. It has wood siding with piping, as if it's an oversized cake, and an asymmetrical window that provides a view of a spiral staircase.

"Well, let's do this," she says, removing a sheaf of papers and a small box from her cross-shoulder bag before reaching for her door handle.

"What's that?" I ask.

"A bequest from Dick. I hope to Christ it's a golden mold of his dick. Damien wouldn't let me open the box."

"Is that the will?"

"Yeah." She gives it a shake. "Want to see it?"

She says it so easily that I immediately distrust the offer. "Did you...do something to it?"

Surprised laughter gusts from her, as if she's delighted by my accusation. "Like what? Are you worried I used it as a Kleenex, or are you asking if I doctored it and printed it out at Staples?"

"The second."

"I didn't do anything to it. Swear on our father's grave. But if you don't believe me, and I wouldn't if I were you, then you can pay a visit to his lawyer. Very sweaty guy in Asheville. I'll give you the address and you can go tomorrow."

I think of the Jeep. I think of Declan offering to give me driving lessons. I say, "Can I borrow your car?"

"I gave you the Jeep."

"You know I can't drive stick. Hell, you probably knew before you ever met me. It's like giving a person who's allergic to peanuts a snack pack from Planters."

She laughs. "Hardly. It's giving my sister an excuse to get lessons from Hot Stuff."

"I don't think he's going to follow through," I say, trying not to sound too sad about it. "He offered before he knew you were stalking him."

"Oh, he'll follow through. But sure. You can borrow the car, or Damien will bring you if you're worried about driving on the highway."

I am, but I don't want to tell her that. "Where will you be?"

"I've got plans. I'm going away for a few days. Damien'll be around if you need anything."

Rather than ask follow-up questions she almost certainly won't answer, I take the will from her and start paging through it.

"There's a lot of legal mumbo-jumbo," she says. "Page seven is where it gets good."

I flip ahead and find the page of bequests. Sure enough, it's written there in ink. His house, car, and insurance policy, divided between his biological daughters. His dog, to Declan. This random box, to Dahlia Rosings.

"Flip the page," she says.

I do, and find confirmation that a DNA test verified that I'm his biological daughter.

I look up at Nicole, and find her watching me with eyes like mine. It sends a shiver through me. "He didn't leave a note for me or anything, did he?"

"If he did, I haven't found one," she says, giving me a smile that would look sympathetic on anyone else. "It's like I said, he didn't know he was going to kick it. I think he was just paranoid. Guilty conscience and all that."

"You said he worked in construction. Why would he be paranoid?"

"Maybe he built a lot of shit houses and worried a beam would hit him, or a pissed off homeowner."

But from the way she says it, I know there's more to it.

"Was he in some kind of trouble?"

She snorts. "What trouble wasn't he in? I told you, a lot of people thought he was a dick. He liked to gamble, plus he screwed up a bunch of building jobs. Messed around with a lot of women, including married ones. We might be looking into this for months."

The thought is oppressive. What am I going to do if I'm stuck in Marshall for months? I think again of that empty storefront, but without any money to rent it out, it's as inaccessible to me as an open storefront on Fifth Avenue in Manhattan.

Still. If I *do* stay, I'll have to get some sort of job. I've never had this much free time loom before me *ever*. While my mother was a free spirit, she left most of my parenting to my father, who believed idleness was a gateway drug to harder stuff. So I worked hard in school, and out. Running bake sales and fundraisers and cookie exchanges. And then I started working for Agnes, and my entire life was devoted to making hers easier. When I think about it, my whole life has been a long stream of working, of building things for other people. It's terrifying to consider all that free time, waiting to swallow me.

Maybe Lainey will come. I don't want her to get fired—that's a toxic wish—but I *do* want her here. I want to feel less alone. My mind flashes to Declan—to the way he smiled at me earlier after he tried my muffin. But my mind is stupid. Declan's told me ten different ways that he doesn't want to get mixed up with me, and I should be smart enough to listen.

"Well, let's do this thing," Nicole says, climbing out of the car and leaving me with the will. I tuck it under my arm and get out too, just as she's pressing the buzzer at the gate.

"Hello?" asks a familiar voice.

"Hey," Nicole says. "We're Dick Ricci's daughters. We're here with a bequest from his will."

The gate buzzes without her saying anything else, not that I'm surprised. Mrs. Rosings is a woman who clearly doesn't think much of social niceties. Maybe she believes she's above them. I also get the sense that she's bored, same as I've been, and eager for something to happen.

"Why do you think she has such an extensive security system here in Marshall?" I ask Nicole as we walk toward the house. "Doesn't seem that dangerous."

"She's rich. Rich people always think someone's going to nab their shit." She shrugs. "And you know what, a lot of the time they're right."

The front door opens as we reach it, and Mrs. Rosings peers out at us with a shrewd expression. She's in another of those rich people caftans, only this one is a deep emerald green. Nicole led the way to the door, and she's a person who has much more natural command than I do, so it doesn't surprise me that Mrs. Rosings notices her first.

"Well, let's have it," she says, holding out her hand.

Nicole gives the box to her. Then she steps on my foot—a little too hard—and I clear my throat. "Hi, Mrs. Rosings."

The older woman's gaze shifts to me, and the only sign that she recognizes me, and cares that she does, is a slight widening of her eyes. She laughs, then shakes her head. "When you're as old as I am, life loses the ability to surprise you. You've managed what I'd thought impossible. You're Dick's daughter, too?"

"So I'm told."

"Well, come in. Both of you." Her eyes twinkle. "Might be that I have a glass of gin for you. I know how you like to drink in the middle of the day."

Nicole grins at me. "Look at you, getting a reputation as a lush."

I could say no. I could object that I'm not a day drinker, but instead I find myself saying, "That sounds like just the thing. Thank you, Mrs. Rosings." And no shit, ten minutes later, we're drinking gin fizzes in a fancy drawing room—a drawing room!—that would put Agnes Lewis to shame, from the crystal chandelier to the fireplace that obviously hasn't hosted a fire in at least two decades, because no soot would dare leave a mark. I'd already surmised that Mrs. Rosings is rich—but this goes beyond rich into the territory of filthy rich.

Above the never-used fireplace are two framed photos—one of a woman with black hair and big green eyes, the other of a handsome man with a strong jaw and brown eyes. Her kids?

"So, have you discovered that the boy you were publicly fornicating with lives in town?" Mrs. Rosings asks me, mischief in her eyes.

Fantastic. Nicole turns toward me with a grin. "I *knew* it."

"Let's not exaggerate," I say. "Declan kissed me. Once. We thought the plane might be going down." No need to tell them about the other times he kissed me, or the way I can still feel his hard body pressed against me.

Mrs. Rosings makes a sound of disagreement and sips her gin fizz. I have to admit, she can make the hell out of a drink.

"Speaking of fornicating," Nicole says, and if I had any energy left to stop her, I'd really try. "I've heard you and our father were doing the dirty deed before he died."

Mrs. Rosings purses her lips. "What a woman does in the sanctity of her own home is her own business." She glances at me. "What she does in an airplane, next to other people, is *everyone's* business."

"Of course," I demur. "We're just trying to piece together what happened to him at the end."

She plays with the rim of her drink, peering off into the distance. "It's natural to want to make sense of something senseless, but sometimes the story is as simple as it seems. Dick liked to drink and take pills that weren't prescribed to him, and he wasn't half as good at home improvements as he believed himself to be. The stairs in that house are uneven, and he tripped."

"Were those pills prescribed to *you*?" Nicole asks pointedly.

Well, shit. I half expect Mrs. Rosings to kick us out, but she actually laughs. "Yes, in fact. The authorities told me so. I have arthritis. It wouldn't have been the first time he'd stolen my pain medication."

"But you kept going back for more?" I mutter. I can relate to that more than I'd like after seven years of Agnes yelling in my face and telling me to stay late, again. Of her asking me to do menial tasks for her just so she could watch me squirm.

Mrs. Rosings smiles again, her lips barely tipping upward. "There was something about him. A certain charm. It was intoxicating."

Nicole gives me a knowing look that I'd rather not interpret.

There's a buzzing sound, and Mrs. Rosings pulls a phone out of the pocket of her kaftan and frowns at it. Shaking her head, she stuffs it back in. "My personal assistant quit, and it's impossible to plan a wedding on one's own. It's almost enough to drive a woman to drink."

There's something ironic about that, given that she's sipping down gin at lunchtime, but it would take a stronger woman than me to point it out. Besides, something else has captured my attention.

"You're getting married?" I ask. Does her fiancé know about Dick?

"No need to sound so aghast," Mrs. Rosings comments with polite amusement. "Although I'd certainly be within my rights if I wanted to get married again, I never will. Why clip your own wings? It's my son who's had the fool idea to get married, and he and his fiancée need all the help they can get."

An idea sparkles in my mind, and before it has a chance to crystallize, I blurt, "I have to be in town for a month. I can work for you temporarily. My father's an event planner, and I've helped him out for years."

Or at least my resume says so. But I've also helped Agnes Lewis plan dozens of high-profile events. This can work. I can make some money while staying at the cabin and fulfilling my end of the will. I won't have to face that void of free time.

"Your father was Dick Ricci," Mrs. Rosings says flatly, "and although he was not a man without talents, I wouldn't have trusted him to plan a child's birthday party."

"I won't argue with that," Nicole mutters—and I wonder, again, what it was like growing up with him, for as long as she did grow up with him.

"Not *that* father," I say. "The man who raised me. And I worked for Agnes Lewis in New York City. Directly. I was her assistant for years."

This captures Mrs. Rosings's attention. "And you could secure the proper references, I suppose?"

I consider this for a moment. I won't be getting any recommendation from Agnes or Doug, that's for damn sure, but I have a couple of friends at the office, and they've been texting me real-time updates about the morning show incident. "Yes, of course."

She gives a doubtful shrug. "Sure. You can start on Monday." She points a rigid finger at me. "But no drinking on the job."

"Even if you offer?" I ask, lifting my glass as if to cheers her.

"I won't. So you might as well enjoy that."

I provide Mrs. Rosings with the direct contact information for my friends at Agnes Lewis, and Nicole and I leave soon afterward.

Back in the car, my half-sister gives me a shrewd look. "Nicely played."

"I figured I could use something to keep me busy while I'm here."

She flinches and then whistles through her teeth. "You actually *want* to help some spoiled rich kid plan his wedding? And here I thought you'd found an in with Mrs. Rosings so you could find out what's in the golden cock box."

I shrug. "She didn't kill him. You heard what she said. She'd have no reason to kill him. Besides, if the cops already talked to her about the medication, then they must have considered the possibility and thrown it out."

She waves a finger at me. "You're too trusting. The rich rarely get held accountable for doing fucked-up shit, and this lady is clearly loaded."

I don't know what kind of life she's led, other than that Dick was her deadbeat father, but she's hard and flinty. Would I have been like that if I'd known him? Would we have been different if we'd grown up spending time together?

I clear my throat, trying to focus, and ask, "So you're going away tonight?"

"For a few days. Like I said, Damien will take you to see the lawyer. You can pull some intel on Mrs. Rosings, and when I get back, we'll be golden."

"Have you gone through Dick's stuff yet?" I ask haltingly.

"We'll do it when I get back," she says. "I saved all the fun stuff so we could do it together."

I'm terrified to find out what she means.

CHAPTER FIFTEEN

DECLAN

Text conversation with Rosie, Declan's burner phone

> I miss you.
>
> I know Seamus made it sound like we're doing great, and it's OK, but we should all be together.
>
> It's messed up that we're not together. Seeing you just made me realize how much we're missing out on. Shay too, even if he's too much of a dumbass to say it.

> It's still not safe..

> It's been over two years. No one's looking for us. I doubt anyone was ever looking for us. You're just punishing yourself, but you've got to stop.

I set the phone down on my kitchen table, then tap it with my index finger. I'm not so sure she's right. I've *felt* like people are looking for me lately, their phantom stares beating into me.

But maybe that's just my awareness of Claire, right next door. So fucking close.

I've seen her a few times over the past several days—once, out on the back deck of Dick's place, staring up at the stars over the mountains, the gold of her hair backlit from a soft glow within the house. I meant to look away, but I stood riveted to my window like a damn stalker pervert—a Peeping Tom—soaking in the sight of her. Because I have a soul-deep craving for good things, and there's no question she qualifies.

Another time, she left some letters on my porch, which I guess must have been mis-delivered to her house—a first since the postman has memorized everyone's addresses.

I've seen Damien run her to town several times over the last five days, and each time I feel the burn of guilt, because I promised to teach her to drive the damn Jeep, and it was a promise I had no business making.

Nicole hasn't been around, which doesn't ease my mind, because there's something off about her. I'm convinced her presence in Vincenzo's the other day, right before I was due to show up, wasn't a coincidence. I asked Mark what they'd talked about, and all he'd say was that it concerned "business." Mark is a bookie on the sly, taking bets on everything from major sports to how long it'll take the town to remove the Christmas wreaths in January, but paranoia suggests Nicole's been asking around about *me*. Trying to figure out my deal. Maybe because of this matchmaking fixation Claire thinks she has.

I can't have anyone wondering too hard about who I am or why I'm here. So Claire is ten times more untouchable than when she was just my tempting neighbor.

Still. I want to know how she's been getting on. And I want to figure out a way to give her those driving lessons so I can sit in the car next to her, her warm, sweet presence beside me. Yes, I'm truly fucked, just like I told Rocket the other day, because that need is getting stronger than my aversion to being noticed.

When I first came here, I figured I deserved to be alone—that part of my punishment would be to live out the rest of my life secluded from Rosie and Seamus and everyone who mattered, living in this small, Podunk town where no one gives a shit about me. But wants have a way of asserting themselves—and it turns out that even someone who'd rather keep to himself most of the time still has a need for other people. It started with my next door neighbor insisting on being my friend, but it didn't end with him.

My Declan James phone buzzes, probably with the request for some rare, niche plant that a rich person can neglect until it withers, and I sigh before picking it up. Then I jolt a little when I see the message is from an unknown number.

> Hey, man. This is Damien. I got your number from Nicole. I'm tied up in a meeting in Asheville, and I got a sinking suspicion I left the oven on this morning. Can you go check it out if you're home? There's a key in the fake rock by the front porch. I'll owe you one.

I frown at the phone as if it just gave me the finger. Then I type out a response.

> Can't Claire do it?

If it makes me sound like a prick, so be it. I want confirmation that she's not over there if I'm going over.

The three dots of death appear, followed by his answer.

> I can't get ahold of her.

The hairs on the back of my neck prickle. She doesn't have a car she can use, so unless she went for a hike—which doesn't seem like her thing—where the fuck is she?

I could ask Damien follow-up questions, but Dick's cabin is literally next door, and I don't have anywhere to be for a couple of hours. So I text back,

I'll check.

Then I give Rocket a rub and head for the door, still feeling that prickle on the back my neck, kind of like what happens to Rocket's back on the rare occasions we encounter another dog on one of our walks. I have a powerful need to know what Claire's doing, to reassure myself that she's not in any kind of danger.

I head to the house next door and retrieve the key from the fake rock, giving my head a rueful shake, because it's obvious as hell it's plastic and Mother Nature had nothing to do with it. The protective part of me doesn't much like the setup—because if you felt like breaking into a secluded house in the middle of nowhere, you'd know exactly how to get in. Of course, it's not very likely that a person who'd want to profit from a break-in would choose Dick's place as their target, especially with my better-maintained house next door, but you never know—desperate people do desperate things.

I unlock the door, and a puff of sugared, heated air hits me in the face, so maybe Damien was right to worry about the oven.

"Claire?" I call. No one answers, but I hear a soft padding sound in the kitchen.

Maybe she's here, and she couldn't hear me because she's listening to music.

Maybe I'm intruding.

I should turn and leave, but I told Damien I'd check the oven... and I also want to have eyes on her so I can make sure she's okay.

I step inside, feeling a burst of *familiar* as I take in the crappy wooden wainscoting, the musty smell, and the curling edges of the carpet in the front room. Most of that familiarity is good—slugging down coffee or whiskey with Dick and shooting the shit, throwing balls for Rocket and laughing when they got caught under the sofa— but my head wants to summon a fucked-up image of what I saw on my last visit. I bury it six feet down beneath dirt, because I don't want to remember. It stays buried because I'm good at shoving things down. Still, I avoid looking at the bottom of the steps.

I head toward the kitchen, walking slowly, just in case the person in there is actually an intruder. Not very likely, since typically a thief's first impulse wouldn't be to stick around and bake an *I'm sorry* batch of cookies. But when I reach the threshold, the only thing I see from the opening is Claire's softly swaying ass as she turns on the tap. The sink is full of dirty dishes.

I stand stock still, riveted, watching her ass as if it's a pendulum about to slice me open. Listening to the soft murmuring she's doing under her breath to whatever song is spouting in her ears. There's no reserve in her right now, no self-consciousness. This is Claire in her element.

It's wrong to stand here, to soak her in when she doesn't even realize I'm here, so I shake off the haze and step forward. "*Claire.*"

Her hand scrabbles for something in the sink, settling on a rubber spatula. She hurls it at my head as she whips around, the projectile coming toward me so fast I don't have time to duck. It doesn't hit hard, but it leaves sweet-smelling batter smeared across my face before it falls to the linoleum floor.

"Holy shit," she says, her hand lifting to her mouth. "I'm so sorry." As if realizing she's speaking loudly, nearly shouting, she flinches and removes her earbuds, setting them down on the counter.

I lick the corner of my mouth. "Vanilla. Nice. Thanks for the taste."

She grabs a dishtowel from the counter, her eyes rounding, and steps into my space. Her hand lifts to my face, and she starts wiping away the batter. When she reaches my lips, she looks up, her eyes meeting mine, then holds my gaze as she slowly wipes the rest of my face, her soft touch radiating through me.

"I'm sorry," she repeats, and even though I know better, I reach for her hand, holding it to my cheek for a moment before squeezing and releasing it. She drops the towel but doesn't step back, and neither do I.

"You already said that. But I'm the one who let myself into your house and startled you. It serves me right that you beat me with your spatula. I'm lucky you weren't using a rolling pin."

She's standing close enough that I imagine I can feel her breath across my skin, warm and sweet, like whatever's baking in the oven. "What are you doing here? I'm pretty sure I locked the door. I always lock the door. New York reflexes."

"There's a key in the very fake-looking rock outside. Damien asked me to stop by. He thought he might have left on the oven."

She frowns. "The only thing either of them have prepared in here is a Pop-Tart. And Nicole burned it."

I shift on my feet, suddenly feeling like a tool. *Of course* she was here. I'd known that the second I smelled the sweet scent wafting from the kitchen. The only reason I'd still came in was because I'd wanted to lay eyes on her. The rest had been a lie I'd told myself. The business of why Damien had wanted me to stop by in the first place was something I could think about later, although maybe Claire has a point about their weird match-making game. I wouldn't mind that much, under other circum-stances.

"I don't know," I say, "but I figured I'd do the neighborly thing and check." I scratch my head. "He said you weren't answering your phone."

She purses her lips. "I was in the zone. I never check my phone when I'm in the zone. It drives my dad crazy."

It's probably time for me to leave. I've broken into her house, interrupted her baking. But I find myself saying, "Do you make a habit of beating him with spatulas too?"

"I have, before," she says with a little smile. "I'm jumpy."

There's a dusting of flour on her cheekbone, and without letting myself think too hard about it, I lift my fingers and wipe it off.

Her lips part, and she must really want to make me suffer, because she licks them.

"Normally I'd be at work right now," she says in a rush, "but Mrs. Rosings is getting a chemical peel. Well, she didn't *say* it's a chemical peel, but she told me she was going to the dermatologist and would be 'a little under the weather,' and I can read between the lines. Besides, no one has skin like that when they're seventy unless they pay for it."

"What?" I ask, dumbstruck by everything she just said. The last I'd seen of Mrs. Rosings was the white of her hair as she walked away from us without a backward glance. I'd figured it was the last I'd ever see of her.

"A chemical peel. You know, they burn off the top layer of skin." Her lips lift again. "Actually, I don't really know what they do, but Agnes used to get them all the time."

"It was the part about Mrs. Rosings that threw me...and you working for her."

"Oh, I didn't tell you," she says, stepping forward and capturing my arm in her hand. Heat razes through me. "Mrs. Rosings lives in Marshall. She's organizing her son's wedding, for some reason, and I'm helping her." Her mouth scrunches to the side. "Sort of. She has very decided opinions about what she wants, and I have to be honest, most of them are bad."

"How did this happen?"

"I guess she and Dick were...*involved*. She was named in his will, so Nicole and I went over to deliver her bequest." She frowns. "How come you didn't recognize her? You said he used to bring women over to your deck."

I snort. "Does Mrs. Rosings strike you as the kind of woman who'd be impressed by my mountain view? She wasn't one of them. Your father wasn't what you'd call a one-woman man."

"Like you."

I'm not sure whether I'm imagining it, but I hear a hint of accusation in her voice. I stoop to grab the rubber spatula and return it to the sink. "Different. I don't make a habit of pretending to be something I'm not."

Or can't be. But it comes down to the same thing. It also means I shouldn't be here, talking to the very woman I've vowed to stay away from. It means that I shouldn't be happy that she'll be sticking around—that I'll see her, or at least glimpses of her, every day. But there's no denying the warmth the thought puts in my gut. Or the feeling of possibility it creates. "You'll be here awhile, then."

She puts a hand on her hip, drawing my gaze there. "Don't sound so disappointed."

"I'm not. Just making an observation."

She watches me for a second, her golden gaze shaking something loose inside of me, then says, "Dick put it in his will that Nicole and I have to stay at the house for a month before we can inherit it."

My first thought was, of course he did. Dick liked playing any kind of game. He was Mark's best customer, always betting on one thing or another, and he could get other people in on the action by the sheer force of his enthusiasm. He's the one who came up with the Christmas wreaths bet. Almost the whole town took part in that one, and I'm convinced it's what pressured the mayor into ponying up the money to pay Rex, the go-to guy for odd jobs, to take them down.

Dick had given him plenty of crap for it, on account of he'd done it the day before Dick and a few other guys had predicted. Of course, that was probably more the mayor's doing—a not-so-subtle fuck you—but Dick had never expected anything of the people who were "in charge of shit." He'd thought little guys should stick together.

I'd never partaken in any of Mark's gambles, because I'd seen firsthand what gambling could do to people, and to their loved ones long after they died.

But Dick had lived to play the odds. If there wasn't a chance to win—or lose—he wasn't interested. The only thing he liked better was cheating the system so it slanted in his favor.

Could be he'd figured his daughters were the same way. Or maybe he considered it his last chance to sucker other people into playing a game with him. Either way, it means I get at least three more weeks of Claire.

"He liked having his way," I say, clearing my throat. Feeling a pulse of emotion. Of missing the old bastard, partly. Of relief, that she'll be around for a good long while. Of worry, because I'm not supposed to care, but I do.

"Don't most men? I'll bet *you* like having your way."

She doesn't say it seductively, but that's the way the words hit anyway, standing there in this sweet-smelling kitchen with a woman who's half sunshine. "I do," I admit, my voice gruff. Nodding to the oven, I ask, "What are you baking?"

Her eyes widen, and she darts for the baking mitt sitting out on the counter. "Shit!"

Reading the room, I open the oven door for her, letting out a puff of sweet-smelling steam, and she darts her gloved hand inside to retrieve the tray of shell-shaped cookies. Madeleines.

They smell delicious, but she's already shaking her head as she sets them on the counter and I shut the oven door. She takes off the glove and gently presses one of them.

"They're overcooked," she says, sounding crestfallen, and she's so fucking cute, I can't help but laugh. She throws her mitt at me, still warm from the oven. "You should never laugh at someone who's just ruined a whole tray of madeleines. It would be like if a whole spread of starters died."

"I've killed plenty of plants in my day," I say, smiling at her. "When I was seven, I fed my favorite potted plant a cup of coffee."

"You didn't!"

"I did. I'd overhead my father saying coffee grounds were good for plants, so I figured if the grounds were good, a whole cup would be even better. And I added creamer because my mother said coffee was no good without it."

"I'll bet you were adorable," she says with a smile. "You probably got away with murder."

My smile slips, but I nod to the pan. "You're making madeleines. You bring that with you? There's no way Dick had a specialty pan for them."

She laughs. "No, Mrs. Rosings had two of them. She gave it to me after telling me a long story about her cousin Jennifer."

"The one with herpes?"

Her laughter is delighted this time. "Yes, but this time she had scabies."

"Poor Jennifer." I nod to the pan. "Have you made them before?"

"They're my white whale." She tucks some hair behind her ear. "You know, from *Moby Dick*."

I smile at her. "I read the CliffsNotes, same as everyone else in high school. Well, maybe not you. You don't strike me as a Cliffs-Notes kind of girl."

"Not normally. But there are only so many synonyms for water one person can take." She prods the same madeleine as before and sighs. "I can never get the texture right."

"Can I try one?"

"If you want to torture yourself by eating a subpar madeleine," she says, but she seems pleased that I asked.

It's still hot, but it slides right out of the tray, and I feel the weight of her gaze as I bite into it. I'm probably burning my mouth, but it's worth it. I can't think of a single thing wrong with it. Then again, I'm in the burned Pop-Tarts camp of baking. I'm also getting the sense that Claire's a perfectionist.

"It's perfect," I say, partly because I want to see how she'll react. "I'll happily accept your reject leftovers."

"Oh, they're definitely not perfect," she says. "The crumb feels wrong."

My mouth hikes up. "I might know someone who'll let you in on her super-secret madeleine recipe."

She tilts her head. "Oh?"

"We'll see what she can do for us," I say, then pull out my burner phone, which I always carry with me *just in case*, and type off a text to Rosie.

When I glance up, I'm surprised to see Claire frowning. "What's wrong?"

"Nothing," she says, but her tone is tense, and I get the sense it's not about the cookies.

My phone buzzes a few times, rapid fire, with Rosie's response.

> Why? Are you baking something to impress a woman?
>
> You never bake and you NEVER try to impress women.
>
> Here it is. I look forward to getting an update later.

So that's one of us looking forward to that.

"Got it," I say, showing the screen to her. "She won some kind of prize for them, but it was in middle school, so don't get too excited."

"Rosie," she says slowly, reading the screen, and I kick myself mentally for being a fool again. "Is she one of your...*friends*?"

For a second, I'm undecided. I shouldn't share Rosie's name, but at the same time, what harm will it do? Rosie herself always says I'm too careful, too closed off. That the life I've been living is no kind of life. Besides, I could dismiss the hint of jealousy in Claire's voice with a few words, and I want to. Even though we haven't made any promises to each other, I don't want her to think I'd casually text another woman, an ex-*something*, with her around. So I say, "She's my little sister. The one who likes to bake and has an Agnes Lewis obsession." I eye the counter. Claire's got all the ingredients still laid out, but it's not a mess, the way it is when Rosie gets it into her head to make something. "Do you have any ingredients left?"

"Yeah..." she says, her eyes questioning.

"So why don't we give it a try?"

"You want to make madeleines with me? Don't you have somewhere to be?"

"Here. I promised Damien I'd check on the oven, and I wouldn't be doing my neighborly duty if I left you here with it on."

"You really want to make madeleines with me?"

Fucking her would be dumb, but this is stupider.

She's already started to mean something to me, and if I spend more time with her, she'll become more important. I can already feel my life stretching to make space for her. My gaze searching her out every time I get back to my house, or someone leaves hers. And the messed-up part is that right now, at least, I don't care.

Maybe Shay and Rosie are right, and I've been taking too hard of a line. Maybe no one cares about us and no one's looking. Maybe...

"You're seriously going to make madeleines with me in the middle of the day?" She's grinning, her whole face lighting up with it.

"Unless there's a plant emergency."

"Does that happen?" she asks.

"What do you think?"

She shakes her head slightly as she reaches for an apron on the hook by the back door—something she must have bought or brought with her, because Dick sure as hell never wore an apron.

"I think you'd better put this on."

I glance down at the front and snort at the slogan *Eat it or Starve*.

Actually, maybe it did belong to Dick.

CHAPTER SIXTEEN

CLAIRE

This is by far the most exciting thing that's happened to me since Nicole left. I went to the lawyer's office with Damien on Monday morning and learned that Nicole had been honest about the terms of the will, including the necessity of staying in the house for a month in order to inherit it. If we fail to comply, it will be donated to The Treasure Club, although we'll be allowed to keep all of his other belongings.

I googled The Treasure Club. It's a strip club run out of Asheville, which basically tells me everything I need to know about Dick Ricci. What a strip club would do with a shitty cabin in the woods, I honestly don't want to know.

I spent the other half of Monday polishing Mrs. Rosings's silverware. I'd thought she was fucking with me when she asked me to do it, but then she busted out the microfiber cloth, making it clear that even though she might very well be fucking with me, she still expected the work to be done. We've also done some prep for the wedding over the last few days, which felt strange since I have yet to meet or speak to either member of the happy couple.

"Are you sure they want us to do this?" I'd asked before our second trip to the flower shop on Main Street.

She gave me a cold, dead-eyed stare and said, "What they want is immaterial," so at least I'm not marrying her son, I guess.

Another plus: the internet was installed the other day, so I can now use my laptop in addition to squinting at my phone and trying to expand the text until it's readable—something I've had to do since there's still no sign of my suitcase. It's a situation that's been giving me a fair amount of anxiety, and the half a dozen phone calls I've made to the airline have done nothing to help the situation or abate the anxiety. I've had to continue borrowing clothes from Nicole's stash and supplementing it with a few things I bought on Main Street.

I've talked to Lainey multiple times and even consented to another Tarot drawing over FaceTime. I got the DEATH card again, which wasn't reassuring. She didn't get fired from her job, so I didn't push her about coming to Marshall, even though I really, really want to.

I've talked to my dad, to whom I've continued to sugar-coat this whole fucked up situation, telling him about the pretty sunrises and mountain views with one hundred percent less possible murder.

And I've glimpsed Declan in passing—storing up those little moments like I'm a squirrel with puffed-up cheeks.

Basically, time has passed, but nothing interesting has happened. It's like I'm back in my little cubicle outside Agnes Lewis's office. Passing time. Watching life go by. Existing. Only I find it much harder to tolerate it than I used to.

But now...

I've never baked with a man before. Honestly, I've avoided it in the past because I had a couple of ex-boyfriends who liked to watch me bake. I hated the feeling of being observed, which made me self-conscious of something that's usually natural to me. I burned cookies. I sunk souffles. I baked atrocities no one in their right mind would want to eat. And then there was the boyfriend who'd begged me to bake naked, as if there's anything sexy about getting flour and eggshells stuck all over your body...

But I want to bake with Declan—to share this thing I love with him. Watching him measure out ingredients with precision is making me gooey inside, like a perfectly baked cookie. Maybe I have a baking kink I never knew about.

While we prepare the recipe and then wash the dishes, Declan tells me more about his landscaping business. He also talks about his sister, but it's as if he's trying to hold the truth away from me and little pieces are falling off despite his best efforts. Rosie likes baking, yes. She learned from their dad. He ran a small construction company, but he loved watching baking shows, even though people gave him shit for it. She works at a bakery, but it's only one of her millions of interests.

I reciprocate by telling him about my dad and Lainey. About my Bronuts. About Mom and the Tribe of Light.

"So do they believe the world's about to end?" Declan asks, his gaze on the microwave timer. Four minutes left until the moment of truth. We're sitting at the kitchen table now, companionably, as if we've known each other for years. Except my body is achingly aware of every little thing he does—of the fine details of him. The way his hair hangs over his eyebrows a bit when he dips his head at a certain angle, or how his eyes aren't just brown but a little green.

"Of course," I say. "When it happens, they're going to ascend to the Great Beyond in a rainbow—seven of them for each of the colors. My mom's a purple. The rest of us are fucked, I regret to tell you."

He snorts, then shakes his head. "Sorry. You know, I get why people are drawn to cults. It's a messed-up world. There are so many things out there that can make a person sad and angry. Bitter. And none of us know if there's any point to any of it, or if we're just ants, trying to make it to the top of the hill. It feels like a kinder interpretation—that we matter, that we have purpose, that something good is going to come of all of it."

"If you're a member of the Tribe of Light," I say, raising my eyebrows. "Not so kind to the billions of people who aren't. Honestly, I don't know why you'd want to spend eternity stuck with a handful of the same people anyway. Don't you think you'd end up hating all of them?"

"I don't know," he says with a slight smile. "I wouldn't mind spending eternity with you if you keep making perfect madeleines and rejecting them for other people to eat."

"Don't you think every madeleine would be perfect in the Great Beyond?" I ask, getting up and putting on the oven mitt as the timer starts counting down the final seconds.

Declan turns in his seat to continue watching me. I can feel his gaze everywhere—every pore, every imperfection—but when he's looking at me like that, I don't feel imperfect, like a madeleine that hasn't achieved peak texture. I feel delicious. "A person can always find imperfections if they don't stop looking for them. I'd prefer to have imperfect madeleines here than to wait for a place that probably doesn't even exist."

I breathe in the hot, sugared air as I open the oven. They smell right. Then I carefully take out the pan, my eyes seeking out the right color. They *look* right. "So you think I'm a perfectionist?" I comment as I set the pan down on the stovetop.

"Yes."

I smile at his directness. "I guess. But I have to be. Do you know how many people want to open bakeries in New York? It's insane. I'd be better off trying to open one here." I poke a madeleine, burning the tip of my finger, and glance over at him, my eyes wide.

"What's the crumb feel like?" he asks, one corner of his mouth lifting. He's teasing me, but I don't care.

"Perfect," I say, feeling excitement bubbling up. "Your sister is a genius."

"They could taste like sawdust." His eyes are shining, and he looks so handsome, so gleeful and sinful, that I feel myself taking a step toward him before I remember he's off-limits. He's made himself that way.

"They won't," I comment. "They smell like the Great Beyond."

"I don't know," he says, his mouth twitching. "If the ascension happens in a rainbow of light, I'm guessing the Great Beyond probably smells like Skittles." He pauses, studying me. "You said you'd be better off opening a bakery here than in New York. Would you really stay here if you found a place?"

"You'd prefer it if I left," I say, sounding a little sulky to my own ears, like a teenager who hasn't gotten her way. I kind of dislike myself for it. But maybe it's only natural to experience some arrested development when you get plunked into the house of a father you didn't know existed.

"Never," he says, and seems to mean it. He gets to his feet and steps toward me. My breath quickens as he gets closer, because I don't know what he means to do, but I know what I'd like him to do. But he removes a hot madeleine from its mold and breaks it in half, making my breath come out in an aggrieved huff.

"Did I ruin everything?" he asks, mischief in his eyes.

"Yes."

"Let's try it at the same time. Open your mouth, Claire."

I could tell him he's being bossy. Aggravating. But suddenly my whole body is an aching, pounding awareness. Without thinking, I do as he's ordered.

His eyes take me in as he places part of the madeleine on my tongue, his callused finger brushing my lips, and it feels like an unholy sacrament. I almost whimper when he pulls his finger away and places the rest of the madeleine in his mouth. Then we both chew at the same time.

It doesn't taste like sawdust, but the balance isn't quite right.

There's too much vanilla and not enough salt. But I can work with it.

"Yours tasted better," he says.

I don't mean to, but I grab a handful of his apron and pull him closer, the way I've been wanting to for the past hour or so. I look up at him, so much closer suddenly, and say, "You know exactly what to say to a girl, but then I guess you get lots of practice."

His eyes darken, and he leans down to me, his hair brushing my forehead, his lips so close they make me ache. "Maybe I'm naturally charming."

"I'll bet."

His hand drifts up to the small of my back. "And I'll bet you taste like your madeleines, Claire. Like vanilla and cream."

Then the door creaks open at the front of the house, and Damien calls out, "Claire?"

The magic leaks out of the moment, leaving behind several madeleines I don't want to eat. I can see sense restoring itself to Declan. Something like panic fills his eyes. We're not supposed to be doing this; we're still neighbors. He glances up at the kitchen clock and mutters under his breath as Damien steps into the kitchen.

"Ah," Damien says with a smile as Declan clicks off the oven. "I can see you have everything under control." His eyes alight on the madeleines, and his grin stretches wider. "Mind if I try one?"

"They're like the three bears' madeleines," I say. "The first batch doesn't have the right texture, and the second doesn't have the right flavor, but if Declan's sister and I baked some together, they'd be just right."

I can tell it was the wrong thing to say, because Declan immediately takes a step toward the door.

"Thanks for checking the oven, man," Damien says, his eyes sparkling, and it hits me that Nicole's not the only one who's in on the joke. He did this on purpose. Part of me is grateful, and the rest of me is livid, because no good can come of throwing me at a man who's made it very clear he doesn't want to date me. A man who has some secret buried in his past that's bad enough that he feels compelled to keep it there.

"Anytime," Declan mutters, then nods to me.

"The car," I blurt. "You said you'd help me with the Jeep."

His jaw flexes, but he nods. "I'll come by to talk to you about it. Look, I'm sorry to duck out like this, but I have to put in some bushes in Asheville."

I seriously hope that's not a euphemism for visiting one of his friends with benefits. Then again, I don't have any right to tell him not to. The line he established between us may have blurred to the point of disappearing today, but he just took a metaphorical Sharpie out of his pocket and re-traced it.

I watch, crestfallen, as he leaves.

Damien pops one of the perfect texture madeleines into his mouth, following it up with one from the first batch.

"You did that on purpose," I comment, once the front door has been closed. "Because Nicole wants me to be like Mata Hari."

He shrugs. "I like keeping my wife happy. But she's right more often than she's wrong. You two like each other. Before you showed up, that guy only said a couple of words in front of us."

That gooey cookie feeling takes over in my gut. "Really?"

His mouth twitches up. "He sure wasn't offering to stick around and make cookies."

I shift on my feet. "Well, it doesn't matter. He's not interested in a relationship...or anything."

He shrugs as if he couldn't care less one way or another. "Not the vibe I got."

"What vibe did you get?" I ask.

His grin expands, taking over his face. "That man is one forced meeting away from cracking."

I shake my head, feeling such a strange combination of

emotions. Hopeful. Annoyed. Pissed off. Excited to see what happens next. Because I'm still on this roller coaster ride of *things are happening again.*

"I barely know anything about him. He has secrets."

Damien's expression is incredulous. "Don't we all?"

"*I* don't," I say with a sigh, taking some Tupperware containers out from the bottom cabinets for storing the madeleines. I don't want to eat them, but maybe Damien will. Or Mrs. Rosings.

Or Declan, a voice in my head whispers.

"I don't have any secrets," I reiterate.

"That so?" Damien asks, his eyebrows still hiked up. "I have this theory that everyone has at least one."

I set the Tupperware on the counter and consider his words. I'm about to double down again, to insist my life is an open book, start to finish, and the only secrets I have are my hatred of my dad's bran muffins and the fact that I never liked Lainey's former fiancé. But my mind hits a snag.

A late night in Agnes's office...

She'd gotten drunk at a happy hour and then holed up in her office for two hours while I wrote an editorial for her. She'd left to get dinner and insisted that I stay. I can't even remember what I was supposed to be doing other than that it was menial and unimportant, a power play. But she'd left a leatherbound journal out on her desk...

"Well, maybe one," I admit softly, my gaze distant. I can still feel the pages beneath my fingers as I flipped through it and realized what I was holding. The book was full of dirt on other lifestyle gurus and celebrity chefs. A couple of news anchors. An actor. I didn't know where she'd gotten it all from, or even if it was true, but I'd photocopied every last page, my heart racing, every ambient sound in the empty office making me flinch. Even though I knew Agnes didn't care enough about me to create a test so elaborate, it had felt like one.

The next morning, the book was gone. I didn't say anything to her, and she didn't say anything to me, and that was that...other than the photocopies in my possession.

Damien nods to the small table in the kitchen, and I find myself sitting down again. "You want to get it off your chest?" he asks.

I'm about to tell him no, to say it's none of his damn business, and if everyone else gets to keep secrets, then so do I. But I realize it's been bothering me, that book. It's been scratching at the back-side of my brain. Because I haven't told a single soul. Those photo-copies are part of why I'm so anxious about my lost bag, sitting somewhere in Charlotte, because they're tucked inside of it. I'd put them in there hoping that I might get the balls to use them.

That I might...get even, I guess.

I worshipped at the altar of Agnes Lewis for years, and she treated me like I was nothing. No, worse than nothing. Like I was dust on her shelf. Dog shit on her shoe. A dent in her car.

There's a part of me that wants to show her there's more to me, and a part of me that still questions whether there is in fact more to me.

"Yeah, maybe," I tell him softly.

And the story comes spilling out. He's a good listener, nodding in the right places.

"It doesn't matter, anyway," I say at last. "They're gone. I'm never going to get the bag back. I've called, like, a dozen times at this point, and they always say the same thing. Call back in another day. Bags turn up all the time. They're never bringing it here."

He hums under his breath. "Maybe not, but that doesn't mean it doesn't matter. You go around lighting fires, you're going to get burned someday. Agnes will get hers."

"I don't know about that," I say bitterly. "Seems to me there are plenty of people who get away with murder."

He watches me for a second before kicking back in his chair. "You're not wrong, but unless someone's a real psychopath, something like that sticks with them. It leaves a mark. You can get away with a crime, but it's not the same as being truly free of it."

"Speaking of psychopaths, where's Nicole? She's been gone for most of the week. I thought she was only leaving for a couple of days."

His flat look tells me he didn't appreciate the turn of phrase. "She'll be back," he says with certainty.

"You don't think she abandoned us?"

"She's not the abandoning type."

"Where do you two live, anyway?" I ask, realizing I don't even know that. I've been so overwhelmed with change that it hadn't occurred to me to ask.

He smiles again. "Asheville."

"You live less than twenty minutes away?" I ask in disbelief. "Why do you even need this house?"

"We don't," he tells me. "Don't particularly need the money either. *You* do."

Oh. *Oh.*

"You don't have to do all of this for me," I blurt, even though I sort of need them to. It's the people pleaser in me who's talking, the woman who's been primed to give but never receive. "You must have your business to take care of, and—"

"We're still taking care of it," he says. "Nicole's on a job we booked a while back, but she's also tracking down some leads related to Dick. He had a lot of female friends around the area."

"She said you were talking to someone about the stairs," I say.

"Sure. They're not up to code, surprise, surprise." Damien continues. "But the cops don't care. They say Dick might have messed with them himself. It's impossible to prove otherwise, although I'm inclined to believe he wasn't the kind of man who cared about routine maintenance." He nods to a piece of the wood siding, detached from the wall with an old, rusted nail protruding from it. "But Nicole's chasing down some leads, and you're working at the Rosings woman's house. We're doing our due diligence."

"We're not going to get the insurance money, are we?" I ask, feeling like a bit of an asshole for caring, but he's right. They might not need it, but I do.

He shrugs. "Maybe. Maybe not. If we don't, there's still the house."

I eye the piece of crappy siding, barely attached to the wall. "I have a feeling it won't get top dollar."

He snorts. "You'd be surprised. You got a postage stamp of property around here, you can sell it for something."

It occurs to me that I haven't even bothered to check what real estate goes for around here, which is a mark of how distracted I've been. "That's good, I guess." I pause, my mind whirling, then ask, "How did you and Nicole meet?"

This is a point Lainey and I have been debating in our phone calls. Was it at some private investigator's conference? Online? At a bar? Nothing seems wild enough to fit them.

He gives me a lazy grin. "She was following a guy I'd been paid to tail."

"Really? That's pretty romantic."

He laughs, his eyes glimmering. "That's one way to put it."

I'm about to ask follow-up questions, possibly several, but my phone buzzes with a text from Mrs. Rosings.

I glance at it and find a request for half a dozen random things I'll need a car to retrieve. Well, well, I guess she's feeling better.

Sighing, I ask Damien for a ride.

CHAPTER SEVENTEEN

DECLAN

I'm a dick.

It's Sunday afternoon, and I still haven't gone around to check on Claire or talk to her about the Jeep. I know I should tell her I can't help and steer her toward someone who can—toward Rex, probably—but I keep putting it off.

Because I want to be the man who steps up for her. I want to feed her cookies, teach her to drive stick shift, and tell her that she looks like she's made from gold, with her golden eyes and blonde hair—and the invasiveness of those thoughts is no less than stunning.

Truthfully, I haven't thought about a damn thing other than Claire Rainey. It doesn't help that my sister keeps calling and texting, asking for updates that don't exist. I've only seen glimpses of her over the past few days—walking to and from the car with Damien, her hair a blur of gold.

I went out for a beer with Rex last night to get my mind off Claire, but I guess the town's bored of gossiping only about the people we've all known for years, so the three hot topics of discussion at the bar were Claire, Nicole, and Damien. By now, everyone knows they're expected to stay at the house for a month in order to inherit it. The Marshall gossip collective is also aware that Claire got fired from her job as Agnes Lewis's assistant because of the throwing-up-on-national-TV incident. No one knows what Nicole and Damien do, other than that they don't seem to mind racking up charges on their platinum credit cards.

Within five minutes, it became extremely fucking clear to me that the only reason Rex had asked me for a drink was to pump me for information I didn't really have and had no inclination to give him. Judging by the glances the people around us kept casting in our direction, half the bar was in on it. But he'd accepted my one-syllable answers with something like grace, and we'd slid into a conversation about sports, which I felt pretty lukewarm about given that the only teams I care about are from a state I can't publicly acknowledge I'm from.

When I got home from the bar, I eyed the house next door for a few minutes. I could see a flash of gold through the window, and I knew all I had to do to see her was grow a pair and go up and knock. But I didn't. Because if she knew everything about me, she'd run—or maybe ask Damien for a ride to the police station so she could turn me in.

I've spent most of the day trying to find projects to do around the house, falling short with everything I try, even though they're simple tasks. I can't concentrate enough to nail in a loose floorboard, let alone do anything more complicated, but I still decide the grout in the bathroom needs to be replaced. It's simple, tedious, and time-consuming, so it should be perfect. My mind keeps wandering, though, and I'm getting nowhere.

Rocket's been following me around like he feels lost too, so after wasting the better part of an hour, I decide to give up and look down at him. "You need to go out, buddy?"

His tail wags like it wants to come clear off his body, and he scurries out of the bathroom and heads to the front door to retrieve my shoes—a trick Dick spent weeks teaching him, because that's the kind of guy he was—too lazy to get his own shoes, but not to tackle the much harder task of teaching a dog to get them for him.

I feel a pulse of grief, but I breathe through it as I slip on the shoes and find Rocket's leash. Snap it on. It's a pain in the ass to put it on every time we leave the house, especially since he used to freely roam back when Dick was alive, but I've made sure to put it on every time we leave the house after his "dognapping" last weekend. I still don't know what Nicole and Damien are up to—with my unsteady income and lack of a social life, I'm hardly a gold-star candidate for Claire—but it's a constant discomfort, knowing they're there, next door. Knowing she is.

I go to open the door, and the person standing directly outside it, fist raised as if to knock, shrieks—prompting me to yell in surprise and Rocket to start barking.

Then my brain catches up and finds the visitor to be Claire. *Claire*, as if my thoughts drew her to me. She's wearing a black sleeveless dress, probably another lender from Nicole, with a short-sleeved cardigan over it. She's taller than her sister, though, and the dress shows off her long legs.

"I'm so sorry," she blurts. "I didn't mean to scare you."

"I wasn't scared," I say automatically, even though I just made a sound that contradicts that statement. It hits me that this woman has only known me a little over a week and has seen me act like a coward twice already—a pathetic record. One that makes me think again of my uncle. *Soft, like your mother. You'll never amount to anything.*

She gives me an *if you say so* look I've gotten countless times from my sister, and I shift on my feet. "There's nothing wrong with being scared," she says. "It doesn't make you less of a man."

"Being scared of something that should scare you, sure. Being scared of you? That *does* make me less of a man. So I couldn't possibly admit to it."

"Your secret's safe with me," she says with the slightest of smiles.

I watch, chest constricting, as she leans down to pet Rocket. Her dress gapes at the front, giving me a glimpse of heaven, and then she catches me looking, her eyes dilating, her mouth forming a perfect oh of surprise.

I clear my throat. "You're here about the Jeep. I've been meaning to come talk to you about that."

"No, I'm not, actually. I..." She pauses, laughs. "You were about to go for a walk with your dog." She blushes, the pink flush on her cheeks making her eyes sparkle in the low lighting of the porch. "It's just...I...kind of got locked out of the house, and I was wondering if you had a spare key."

I squint at her. "What happened to the fake rock?"

Her lips twitch with humor. "It's not there anymore. Damien got rid of it after you told him it was a security hazard."

"Isn't he home?" It's a stupid thing to say, because clearly he mustn't be if she's over here, asking for my help. But my brain's struggling to work properly.

"No," she says. "I think he left to pick Nicole up from the airport. I went out to take a walk, and when I came back, the door was locked. I must have used the doorknob lock without realizing. You know...New York reflexes."

I pause, working through this. No, I do not have a key. Yes, I can get past it easily if it's a doorknob lock.

"I don't have a key, but I can get you in."

Her eyes widen. "Oh, I don't want to break anything."

"Won't need to break it. You got a couple of hair pins?"

Her upper teeth capture her lip. "No, not on me."

Rocket paws at my pant leg. I hand his leash over to Claire, who takes it readily enough. "Wait down here. I'll be right back."

As I run upstairs it hits me that I should have invited her in. It would have been the gentlemanly thing to do, but I don't really want her in my space, among my things. It'll be harder to banish the memory of her if she's actually been inside, if her scent is attached to my walls, my space. I grab a couple of hairpins from my bug-out bag and jog back downstairs. When I get there, I see Claire bowed down over Rocket, her hand cupped around his soft little face, and warmth unfurls in my gut. Shit. Shit. *Shit.*

"Let's go," I say, my voice harsher than intended.

She gets up and looks at me, eyebrows lifting when she notices the bobby pins in my hand. "You have women's hairpins in your bedroom?"

I snort, because I can tell she thinks I have a closet full of discarded women's things up there, hairpins and sweaters and panties. "No one but me has ever been here before."

Her eyes widen. "Really? Why not?"

Because if you want to keep to yourself, it's best to do so thoroughly. This is a place where I let myself keep out traces of Rosie and Seamus and the life that was before—and even if they're only things I'll understand the meaning of, I still don't want to share them with strangers. I'm too greedy for them.

But I settle for saying, "For the reasons I've told you. The hairpins are part of my bug-out bag."

From the look on her face, she neither has a bug-out bag nor is aware of their existence, so I say, "It's something you prepare in case of emergencies. You know...if you have to leave at a moment's notice."

Her eyes widen. Maybe she wants to ask which emergency would require women's hairpins, or she would if she weren't in the middle of one.

"Well, let's go."

Rocket whimpers when I try to put him back in the house. "Oh, we should bring him," Claire says, her fingers brushing against mine, sending a sensation through me like an electric jolt that pulls memories from my brain. Claire's golden eyes, her lips soft against mine, her hand weaving into my hair to pull me closer...

Her mouth, open to receive that madeleine, and the way she pulled me to her by the front of my apron.

Fuck. I keep thinking of what I wanted to do. Of what I would have done if Damien hadn't picked that exact minute to walk through the door.

"I don't want to ruin his walk," she insists, pulling me out of my head. "I can hold his leash while you're working."

"You think he'll get a kick out of watching me break into your house?" I ask, letting the knuckles of the hand holding the leash brush against her hand.

"Well, he was my bio-dad's dog. From every account, it seems like the kind of thing Dick would have enjoyed."

Indeed.

I nod. "Far be it from me to rob him of simple pleasures."

We walk over to the other house companionably, neither of us feeling the need to talk. My hand brushes against her arm accidentally, and it feels good, so I do it on purpose the next time. When we crest the porch, I hand over Rocket's leash, and she takes it with such solemnity I almost laugh.

I bend over the knob. It's dark, so fucking dark, and I'm going to need my flashlight to see what I'm doing. I grab my phone from my pocket and switch the light on, then hand it to Claire so she can shine it on the knob.

It takes half a second to turn the lock.

When I look back at Claire, on the other end of that flashlight beam, she looks stricken. Maybe I should have made it last longer. She's afraid now, maybe of me, maybe of the thought that she's been living out there, in the woods, with a lock it takes half a second to break. I try not to be sorry for the former; I'm grateful for the latter —she *should* be careful. I'm home a lot, but I'm not always home.

"Use the deadbolt," I say as the door creaks open, pocketing the pins and reclaiming my phone from her. "It would have taken longer for me to break in if you had."

"But you still could have done it."

No point in lying. "Probably."

"Why?"

There's no need to answer her honestly other than I want to. I take a second to ask myself why, and I acknowledge that it's because I want her to know me. I've been giving her the little pieces I can dispense with without telling her the thing that sent me here. Clearing my throat, I say, "My uncle taught me. He was another man your father wouldn't have approved of."

"Would you like to come in for a minute?"

Yes.

"No, I'd better take Rocket around." Rocket licks my leg at the sound of his name and proceeds to plant his butt down like he's in no hurry and would happily sit here all night on this porch that used to be his. It hits me that it has to be strange for him—living next door to his old home, not knowing what happened or why, only that it did.

"Okay." Claire bites her lip again, and my dick gives a faint twitch. "But there's something else I wanted to ask you."

I'm curious, and also wary, because whatever it is, I want to give it to her—even if I should say no. "What is it?"

"Do you know much about flowers? I feel like the local shop is giving me the runaround. I mean...sure...the flowers I'm looking for are rare, because they smell really bad, and no one in their right mind would grow them, but the heart wants what it wants."

I pause, considering. "Why are you getting flowers? Did you and Nicole decide to do something for Dick? Because if so, I don't think you need to worry about floral arrangements. He didn't like flowers. Said the only use for them was to get a women to... Never mind."

She sighs, visibly deflating. "Dick really was a dick, wasn't he?"

I shift on my feet, wanting to put an arm around her or lead her inside and pour her a drink. But it's not my right to do those things, and if I do them anyway, it'll be hard to know when to stop—what line I can't cross before it becomes too late, and all I see is her.

"No, Claire," I say gruffly. "He wasn't just bad. Most people aren't just anything. He was funny, and he could be generous. Caring. But it was always on his own terms." As I say the words, I feel them in my gut. Not just about Dick, but about my uncle. A worse man than her biological father, to be certain, and yet, there were moments when I'd felt close to him. When I'd believed he truly cared about me. I think about the good times every now and then to balance the bad.

The people we lose never really leave us. They haunt us whether they intend to or not, and my uncle haunts me in particular. When I walked into this house a few weeks ago and found Dick sprawled at the bottom of the steps, I nearly had a heart attack, because for a second it was my uncle's face I saw on his body. My uncle, dead a second time.

But Dick's accident was an accident, and the universe doesn't care enough about me to haunt me specifically. I'm just unlucky, I guess.

"I'm sorry," she says, touching my arm, and it feels wrong—her apologizing for my loss when he was her father. She smiles. "You know, get rid of the generous and caring part, and he sounds like Nicole."

"At least you're willing to admit I'm funny," a voice interjects from inside the house, making both of us flinch for the second time tonight. Even Rocket flinches, then cowers against my leg as Nicole steps out of the back hallway in a robe, a towel wrapped around her hair.

"I thought Damien left to pick you up," Claire asks, still gaping at her.

"If he did, he's going to be sorely disappointed. I took an Uber.

Damien probably had a job in Asheville. We haven't all lucked into indentured servant jobs with rich old people."

"Wait..." Claire glances outside and then back at the door. "Did you purposefully lock me out?"

"Did you purposefully leave the door open?" Nicole asks. "I had to take a shower. I didn't want some pervy neighbor sneaking in."

I clear my throat. "As your only neighbor, I can assure you that you had nothing to worry about."

"Here I am, in my robe," she says, giving him a pointed look. "And here you are at the door."

I shake my head, torn between beating a retreat and laughing, because fuck...is she ever Dick's kid. I don't see it as much with Claire, but there are glimmers here and there. Her sense of humor. Her vibrancy. The way she wants to grab life by the balls but hasn't let herself try yet.

Nicole waves a hand in dismissal. "Oh, we all know you'd only try to peek at Claire in the shower."

"On that note," I say, nodding to Claire. "I'm going to go walk Rocket. But if you want to take a drive in the Jeep on Wednesday, I'm free from noon onward."

"Yes," she says, her eyes widening. "That would be great. I'll take the afternoon off. And about the flowers..."

"I'll text you."

"You don't have my number."

"It's okay," Nicole says, "*we* have his number."

I gave it to her, when she first came by with Rocket, so I shouldn't feel uneasy. But I do. There's something uncanny about this woman. She knows too much and is too damn curious. This is twice now that she's gone out of her way to guarantee that Claire and I run into each other—because I'm guessing it was no accident that she locked the front door. Maybe three times, if you count the oven incident with Damien.

Nicole's unpredictable. Dangerous. But I'm truly fucked in the head because what I don't like is that I'm leaving her alone with Claire.

"You okay?" I ask her.

"Are you worried a woman in a bathrobe is going to kill her?" Nicole asks with a snort. "If you're worried about anyone, it should be the person who was almost left naked and helpless in the bathroom, the door open for anyone to come in. Really, Claire. You need to pay more attention to your surroundings."

"I don't think you're ever helpless," Claire replies. Turning her attention to me, she insists, "I'm okay." She drops her hand from my arm. "Goodnight, Declan. I'll see you on Wednesday."

Well, shit. That gives me three days to learn how to drive stick shift.

Then again, I brought down my uncle, a drug kingpin in Western Pennsylvania. I've done harder things.

CHAPTER EIGHTEEN

CLAIRE

"You did that on purpose," I say to Nicole a few seconds after the door closes behind Declan.

"Did what?" she asks with a snort.

"You weren't really in the shower."

She waggles her brows. "You want to take off my robe and check?"

"No. You're the type of person who'd lean into a ruse. I'll bet you really did take a shower."

She grins before whipping off the robe, revealing an acid yellow tank top and cut-off jeans. For someone who's supposedly a private investigator, she sure doesn't seem to mind attracting attention. "But thank you for the props. I normally would have gone for the full effect, but I was working with a small window of time."

I shake my head. "You're truly demented. Why do you care so much about throwing me at Declan? I told you. There's no way he hurt Dick. He *liked* Dick."

"I hope he doesn't like dick. That would really get in the way of my plan to get you laid."

Sighing, I say, "I guess I walked into that one. But, seriously, why do you want me to sleep with him if you think he's a potential murderer?"

"It's like I said. I think you'd have fun with the whole Mata Hari thing," she says, her eyes sparkling. "It would do a lot for your personality."

When I glower at her, she lifts both hands, palms facing out. "Okay, okay. I'm pretty sure he didn't kill our father. And I want to help because I'm a good wing woman." She shrugs, tugging off the towel around her dry hair. "Besides, I can tell you like him. You've got this whole moony thing going on whenever he's around, and it's obvious to me you need help...both of you, actually. Damien told me about the whole cookie thing—what a missed opportunity. I asked him to lock you out of the house that night so you and the hot neighbor could finish what you'd started, but he has principles sometimes."

"How inconvenient of him," I say, rolling my eyes.

"It just means I think more of your coping abilities than he does. But he did steal some of hot guy's mail so you'd have to deliver it."

"You guys are unhinged."

She shrugs. "Let's go get drunk. It's been a long few days."

"Are you going to tell me what you were doing while you were gone?"

She lifts her eyebrows. "What do you think?"

I sigh and toe off my shoes. I suddenly need that drink—maybe two of them—but that's the effect of being around my half-sister for more than two minutes. The last several days have been comparatively peaceful.

Boring, a voice in my head whispers.

I follow her into Dick's kitchen and sit at the table, watching as she pours each of us some of the bourbon I threw at her last weekend.

"You missed me, didn't you?" she asks as she sits down across from me, shoving one of the drinks in my direction. When I don't answer, she clinks the glasses together. I hold back a smile, because I might not want to admit it, but I kind of did miss her.

"Are we going to start going through Dick's stuff?" I ask.

She nods, then throws back the contents of her glass, and I remember again that this is different for her. Dick wasn't just a mysterious figure with a house full of weird stuff; he was her father. "What was he like when you were a kid?" I ask before I can stop myself.

"A shit," she says, banging the glass back down on the table. "There was nothing he liked more than fucking people over...and fucking people who weren't my mother." A side of her mouth lifts. "But, sure, he could be funny sometimes. I'm not convinced that makes up for giving me a lifetime's worth of trust issues."

"You have trust issues?" I ask, surprised. She comes off as invincible. Fearless. As a person who'd be a terrible boss rather than work for one. I'd love to have even a sliver of that boss bitch energy—that willful insistence on being herself—but it appears to have skipped my side of the bloodline. Or maybe it came from her mother.

She snorts. "Why do you think I wanted to become a private investigator? I always have a copy of Damien's phone."

"Seriously?" I ask, cocking my head. "He's so devoted to you."

"He is. Tell that to my issues, though. Damien gets it. It's become a kind of game with us. He tries to lead me down rabbit holes, and I do the same with him. It's foreplay."

"You guys are...."

"Not normal, you've said. Neither are you, you know. The way you volunteered to be that Rosings woman's bitch..." She grins and shakes her head. "It was like you were going for the last slice of cake at a birthday party."

I shrug and take sip of the drink. "I like to keep busy, and I'm used to worse."

She raps a palm against the table. "Well, that's a ringing endorsement. She's used to worse, ladies and gentlemen. Isn't there anything you'd like to do? Any dreams you have? Or do you pin all of your hopes on other people?"

I think of the bakery that lives only in my head—the red-and-white-striped awning, the built-in shelves, the glass bake case filled with my as-yet-to-be-renamed Bronuts. "No dreams," I say thickly. Because I'm not going to hand-deliver my dreams to her as if she won't crush them.

"You're lying," she says. "But that's okay. I would have lied too." She's still watching me, though, her gaze hawk-like. "What happened with Agnes Lewis?"

"You know everything," I say, suddenly tired. *Desperately* tired. "Surely you already know."

"I want to hear it from you."

I don't know what possesses me, but I find myself telling her about Doug's grudge. The fizzy drinks. And Agnes word-vomiting and then vomit-vomiting.

"And you're the one who got blamed?" she asks, her tone harsh.

"I was *always* the one who got blamed," I say, surprised by the bitterness in my voice. A the time, I'd told myself it was okay—that it was part of paying my dues and *everyone* paid their dues. Even Agnes had paid her dues, back in the day. Or so the story went. Her father was a famous film director, so when you got right down to it, she was a nepo baby.

"People only walk all over you if you pretend you're a carpet," she says, lifting her eyebrows. "If Dick Ricci taught me anything, it's that people take advantage of people pleasers like my mother."

I rub my chest. It occurs to me that I should have learned that lesson from my own parents—from watching my mother cheat on and use my father, again and again. He still loves her. If she called him tomorrow to say that she realized the Tribe of Light was a racket, he'd probably buy her a plane ticket and pick her up from the airport. I love him, and he's strong in his own way, but I don't want to be like that.

I find myself thinking about the burn book. About the photo-copy tucked into the suitcase that will probably never be found. That's the one thing I didn't tell Nicole about, although for all I know she and Damien are the type of couple who tell each other everything.

Nicole's still looking at me, waiting for some kind of response, so I say, "You're not wrong. My parents had that kind of dynamic too, but the opposite."

"So why don't you grow a pair?" Nicole asks. "You can."

"My high school anatomy teacher disagrees with you."

She shakes her head, smiling ruefully, like she can't even with me. "Let's get started. But I'd suggest you drink more of that first. Mom tells me that Dick used to have a truly extensive porn collection."

"WHY ARE THERE DVDS?" I say with a groan. "Why couldn't he keep everything on his hard drive like a normal pervert?"

"He didn't have the internet, and knowing him, he didn't trust digital files," Nicole says, snickering at the title of the DVD—*Little Titty Women, Big Time.* "At least he had diverse taste." She points to another DVD case—*DD Titties.*

"Where's the trash bag?"

She shakes her head. "Nope. They're hilarious, and we're keeping them. You get half of them."

"I hereby bequeath my half to you."

"But you already gave me all of the weed shit. I mean, I under-stand that you can get more from your boyfriend, but I feel you're being overly generous."

I throw a copy of *Tony's Titty Club* at her, thankful that she had black latex gloves. Also wondering why she had a big box of black latex gloves.

We've gone through half of the contents of Dick's closet now. There's weed paraphernalia but no weed, about thirty losing scratch-offs he kept for unspecified reasons, a Sam's Club treasure trove of condoms, and a lot of old clothes. One of the T-shirts—*This is How Eye Roll*—made Nicole's face pucker up for half a second before she shoved it into the donate pile—ten times larger than the keep pile—with a wry comment. I made a mental note to myself to put it aside later. Because something tells me she bought it for him and he kept it. She might not want it now, but it obviously means something to her.

She starts taking more DVDs out of the box—most of them porn, along with *Free Willy* and a box set of *Leave it to Beaver*.

"I get it," Nicole comments after I express my confusion about his organizational system. "They're porn DVDs and DVDs that sound like porn."

She finds a tiny key at the bottom of the box and glances at me with shining eyes. "The motherload."

"You think it's important?" I ask, unimpressed. "It could go to anything."

"He hid it in his porn and movies that sound like porn box. It's important, although we'll have to go around fitting it into locks, like we're a porn version of Cinderella."

Sighing, I add the keep pile to a half empty box containing other "keep" items. Even though I didn't know this man had existed until he no longer existed, it's emotionally draining to go through his things. I'm reminded again of all the things that have outlasted him —ridiculous porn DVDs and the condom wrapper that fell out of one of his pairs of pants.

I pull another box over and open it, gasping at the sight of the framed photo on top. Dick Ricci with a woman who resembles Nicole and a small child. He doesn't *look* like a cheating asshole. Then again, my mother doesn't at first glance look like an occultist.

"You have blond hair," I say.

"Bite your tongue." She grab the photo from me and sets it face down on the floor. "It was only blond for a few years before it turned pink."

"Mhm," I say.

"With a short stop at brown."

I remove a photo album next, and Nicole opens it with a huff before setting aside and grabbing the one beneath it. I'm prepared for her to set that one aside too, but after opening it, she shoves it toward me. "This one's yours.

"Mine?" I ask, my heart beating faster.

"You've got this people pleaser expression that really hasn't changed with age," she says with a half-smile. "I would have recognized you anywhere."

That and she's probably seen childhood photos of me in the deep dive she inevitably did after learning about me.

Heart thumping, I open the album. It's full of photos of me at different ages. A newborn. First time walking. First food. First day of school...

I stop turning the pages and look up at her. "It doesn't mean anything," I say, closing the book. "It's just...my mother must have sent them to him, but it doesn't mean he cared. Anyone can keep photos. Hell. I still have a frame with the photo of the model inside. It doesn't mean I care about him."

"Fuck Richard Ricci," Nicole agrees, lifting an imaginary drink to me. She glances at her empty hand. "And fuck this. I'm getting the bourbon."

She gets up, pausing to touch my shoulder for a second before she leaves the room, and for a second, I'm glad for it.

I don't want to care.

I don't want to think about him, thinking about me. Or to wonder if he's ever regretted his decision to leave Nicole's life and to not be in my life at all. I don't want to think about him at all, other than to be annoyed that his last gesture was to give us a homework assignment—and to die in a manner that's open for interpretation, and inviting of mistrust.

I definitely don't want to feel heat behind my eyes as I open the album again and turn the pages. As I see my life through someone else's eyes.

It seems so small...

By the time Nicole comes back with the bourbon, the tears are falling silently down my cheeks.

"No," she snaps, grabbing the album from me and slamming it shut. "Not happening." She stacks my album on top of hers. "We're burning them."

"What?" I ask, caught off-guard.

"You heard me, don't play dumb. We're going to burn them, and it's going to feel therapeutic and shit. You need to remember he's not your father, Claire, and I didn't have a father. I had a kickass mother, and she was more than enough."

"I didn't," I say with a half-hearted smile. "But I'm guessing you know all about that."

"Who knows, maybe that wrinkled little man really *is* the reincarnation of god," she says, her lips twitching. "But if so, she should have black-bagged you and brought you to California. I'd kidnap you if I found the key to salvation. No way would I leave my only sister behind to burn."

"Thanks, I think." I feel something dangerous—a softening toward my sister. A *warmth*. She shoves the bottle of bourbon at me, and I glance at it, thinking about my father's aversion to germs. Then again, I risked drinking from Mrs. Rosings's flask when I thought the end was upon me, and it feels like a different kind of end is upon me now. I take a swig and hand it back. "Are we really going to burn them? Don't you think we might want them at some point? Like that T-shirt you put in the discard pile?"

She snorts. "Why the fuck would I want that? I used my allowance to buy it for him for Father's Day, and he left me and my mom five days later. Fuck that shit. I'm glad he kept it, but only because I hope he sadly wept into it. But no, Claire, I don't need to feel bad about him or the shit he left behind for us to clean up, and neither do you. If we owe him anything, it's to figure out what happened to him so we can collect that damn money, and his ephemeral spirit can fade away happy, knowing he did exactly one thing for his children."

I look at her in amazement. And I acknowledge, for the first time, that my sister, for all her flaws, is a badass. "Okay," I say slowly, getting to my feet. "Let's do it."

CHAPTER NINETEEN

CLAIRE

Victory flashes in Nicole's eyes, and to my shock, she hugs me, the bottle of bourbon trapped between us. "I knew you had it in you."

"I didn't," I say quietly, but now that the idea's been planted, it sprouts. "But you're right. We don't owe him grief. We don't owe him *anything*."

"That's the spirit," she says, nudging my arm. Then she lifts the arm with the bourbon. "Out to the fire pit!"

I head outside with her, assuming she knows her fire-starting shit, and promptly trip over a gaping hole in the ground—small but deep.

I go down hard, and Nicole tuts her tongue. "Defeated by a land beaver. That's got to be a new low."

"What the hell is a land beaver?" I ask, groaning as I pick myself up. A quick glance over the dusky ground shows there are another couple of holes within view.

"A cool term for a very uncool animal."

"Not making it any clearer," I say following her toward the fire pit, picking my way carefully now.

"Gophers."

I've heard of them but never seen one in nature. The extent of the wildlife we see in New York are pigeons, rats, mice, and squirrels, so the thought of a gopher infestation is pretty exotic.

"I'd like to see one," I say, getting a snort.

When we reach the fire pit, it turns out Nicole only has a Bic lighter in her pocket, plus the brush around the fire pit, which is damp from an earlier rain.

"This is harder than it looks," she says with a sigh. "I hate it when something is anticlimactic."

Then she looks up, her gaze drilling into the dark night, lit only by our house, the house next door, and thousands of stars. She points a finger at something behind me. "Him."

I turn and see Declan, out walking Rocket again. The dog has on a reflective vest, so clearly Declan cares more for his safety than he does for his own.

"You!" Nicole calls, louder. "Hot stuff."

Declan veers toward us, his gaze catching mine. I can barely see it, but I can *feel* it—it's a brighter burn than the bourbon.

"How afraid should I be?" he says as he gets closer.

"Do you know how to start a fire?" Nicole asks.

"Depends on what you want to burn," he replies. "I'm partial to my house." His gaze settles on me again. "And your sister."

I swallow. "As it happens, I'd prefer not to be burned too." I gesture to the box we brought outside, only then realizing that he might take offense to what we're doing. Dick was his friend. But I don't want to lie to him, and if he's going to start the fire for us, it seems only right that he should know what's going in it. "We're going to burn up some photo albums we found in Dick's things."

"Are you sure?" he asks, his eyes on mine. There's no judgment in gaze, and I'm more grateful for that than I probably should be.

I pause to consider, but it's a less complicated decision for me than it is for Nicole. All I'm doing is destroying photos of myself—of a life that Richard Ricci chose to watch from the sidelines, never involving himself in even the smallest of ways. I hate him a little for that. Or maybe I hate him a lot for it. And despite what I said to Nicole, despite the fact that I have an amazing father and didn't need another, I'm still sad. But all of me, even the sad part, wants to see those photos burn. It's not just because of him, but because of what I've come to realize—I've let so much of life pass me by, and it's time to stop.

"Yes, you?" I ask, shifting my gaze to Nicole.

She laughs. "I'll take any excuse to start a fire."

It's a glib response, but when I look into her eyes, so like mine, I see an expression in them I've seen often enough in the mirror. She's not feeling glib. She needs this. She wants to burn away the part of her that wanted his approval. She wants to turn it to ash and blow the ash into the ether, sending a smoke signal to her father's soul. *I don't need you. I never did.*

Declan nods solemnly, then hands me Rocket's leash, the brush of his fingers against mine awakening my nerve endings. "Hold him for me? He likes fires and has the survival instincts of a male praying mantis."

"I'll protect him from himself."

"You're good at that," he says. Then he shocks me by reaching up and tucking my hair behind my ear. "You smell like bourbon again."

"You're just jealous," Nicole says. Grabbing the half-empty bottle from the box, she holds it out to him, "Want some?"

He shrugs and then takes it from her, knocking back a swig, and I must be truly gone for him, because I feel jealous of the bottle.

How's Declan going to start the fire? My mouth gets dry as I think about the muscles in his shoulders working, his chest getting sweaty from the effort. I remember watching some eighties movie where a guy turns a stick around in circles and magically causes a blaze, but if it were that easy, wouldn't more people die in fires? Then there's the rock-to-rock method, another mainstay in movies...

I watch, riveted, as he gathers dry brush and sticks from areas he seems to magically detect and arranges them in some kind of prede-termined order in the fire pit. There's something sexy about the capable, easy way he does it—like he starts fires every day and thinks nothing of it. Something tells me he didn't learn how in the Boy Scouts. Maybe his uncle taught him—the same one he's so certain my father would have disapproved of.

"How are you going to get it going?" I say, unable to contain myself anymore. "Are you going to use the rock method or the stick method?"

I feel his smile everywhere, as if it had reached out and stroked me. "I have a special trick."

"If you whip out your dick, I'm going to laugh before I hit you," Nicole says.

But Declan doesn't give her the reaction she probably wants. He's still looking at me as he pulls a lighter out of his pocket.

"Ah, I'm an idiot," I say.

"At least we didn't have to say it," Nicole interjects. "But I have a lighter too. It got me nowhere."

"You didn't really try," I comment, my gaze on Declan.

"I could definitely have pulled off the rock method, though," he says, his eyes sparkling in the dusky near dark. "I just want to save you ladies time."

The brush takes, the fire whooshes into being, and Nicole roars into the night. And I must be a little drunk because I roar with her.

"Are you going to dance around the fire too?" Declan asks with a grin, and he looks even better by the light of the fire he made with his hands. A little wicked. *Very* capable. The longer hair in front is dancing in the breeze, like even the wind wants a piece of him.

"Look at you with the good ideas," Nicole crows, and she really does start dancing. I might not have joined her if I were sober, but the bourbon's kicked in hard. I glance at Declan and find that he was already watching me. There's a glimmer in his eyes, an appreci-ation, and suddenly I don't want to just dance around the fire because it's fun—I want to do it because I know that he's here watching me.

"Let me take Rocket," he says, his voice husky. "I don't want him getting any bright ideas."

Our hands brush again as I hand the leash over, and this time he surprises me by squeezing my hand before releasing it. My heart beats faster. Has he changed his mind?

Have I changed mine?

It would still be messy as hell to get mixed up with someone who lives next door, not to mention he's made it perfectly clear he's not a one-woman man. For all I know, he was with one of his friends-with-benefits earlier tonight, a thought that makes me want to grit my teeth or maybe have a full-on, feet-kicking tantrum.

"Dance for me, Claire," he says in an undertone that makes me achy with wanting. But my whole life I've done things for other people. I want him to watch me; I want him to want me. I desperately want him to touch me, but I also want to dance for myself.

So I do. Nicole and I dance around the fire like witches, like heathens, like people who don't give a shit about what they might look like, and the whole time I feel Declan's gaze beating into me. Undressing me.

I have never, not once in twenty-eight years, felt so alive. And when we stop, breathless and laughing, Nicole nods to me. There's something serious in her face, almost somber. Intention flashes in her eyes. "It's time."

I pick up the box of photo albums, intending to dump the whole things into the flames and be done with it, but Declan grabs my hand, smoothing his thumb over the back of it. "Not the plastic. There would be fumes."

"So we have to take the photos out to burn them?" I ask.

I'd hoped never to have to look at them again, but Nicole nods resolutely. "Good. It'll be a more personal fuck you this way."

She starts with her book, peeling the photos out and feeding them to the hungry flames. Declan's thumb makes another pass over my hand, probably intending to comfort but revving me up instead. Then he steps back, giving me space to feed the flames.

So I start to do it too. In goes the photo of me in my pull-ups. Me frowning over spinach for the first time. Me eating my first cupcake, years before my real father would teach me to bake them. *Me, me, me*, my face curling and blackening and bubbling. And it feels like another awakening, like a new beginning. Like witchcraft, out here with the mountains in the background, the soft glow of our houses behind us.

"It feels surprisingly good to burn things," I say, glancing behind me, my hair whipping in the summer breeze.

"Don't make a habit of it," Declan says with a smile. I wonder, again, if he's sad about what we're doing. But he still doesn't seem judgmental. He's an observer. A witness.

I throw in a photo of my middle school graduation. Senior skip day. Senior prom, which Lainey and I went to without dates because we were just that cool—and no one asked us. High school graduation. The first three-tier cake I sold to a private client. My first day at Agnes Lewis. There are only a half a dozen photos after that, and it doesn't take a genius to figure out why. My mother had eventually stopped sending them. Maybe she'd already heard about the Tribe of Light, or maybe another obsession had overtaken the inconsistent interest she'd taken in being my mother. But at the back, behind the last photo, of me smiling fakely at the camera next to Agnes, who'd just threatened me with physical harm for bringing her the exact coffee she'd asked me to order, I find something unexpected—a folded piece of paper with my name on it. My heart quickens, and without looking at either Declan or Nicole, I tuck it into the pocket of my cardigan.

That done, I glance at Nicole, wondering if she found one too. Wondering what the fuck it means and whether I even want it to mean anything. Maybe it would have been better if both albums had gone directly into the flames. If Richard Ricci hadn't been allowed this last chance to say something to me. Because words can be more harmful than silence.

But before I have a chance to ask her anything, a familiar car pulls up to the house and parks. Damien emerges from it, and Nicole squeals and runs to him, meeting him partway to the bonfire.

He wraps his arms around her and buries his face in her neck. "You've only been home for a few hours and you're already starting fires?"

She glances up at him. "Would you expect anything less?"

"Never. I'll get the marshmallows."

I feel rather than see Declan step closer to me, the front of his shirt brushing my back. His hand skates down my arm, the calluses sending hot shivers through me as I remember what they felt like tracing the line of my torso—as I imagine what they'd feel like touching all of me. Then he gently removes the empty album from my grip. It's only then that I realize I had it in a death grip. Its cover is plastic, and Declan tucks it back into the box without comment. Then he returns, standing close enough that his heat is radiating toward me, or maybe that's entirely in my imagination since I'm standing next to a literal fire. His little dog is sitting by his side, such a tiny fuzzy thing next to this mountain of a man, and it's such an appealing picture that I wish I had my phone to capture it. I wish it were something I could keep forever.

"Do you feel better?" he asks, his words full of concern, as though my answer is important to him.

"I do," I admit, but there's that note, burning a hole in my pocket.

"Good." He glances at Nicole, now making out with Damien, and grabs up the bottle of bourbon, pouring the equivalent of a shot into the dirt next to the fire pit. "Slainte, you old bastard."

The little dog wags his tail and starts lapping at the dirt, surprising laughter out of me despite my throat, which suddenly feels like it has a tennis ball lodged in it.

Declan turns to me. "He has a taste for the good stuff. Dick's doing, I guess."

"Why not pour it into the fire?" I ask.

"I figured you like having eyebrows."

"You're a smart man."

"Doesn't feel like it right now," he says, giving me a sidelong smile that makes my heart beat faster.

"Agnes always said a person doesn't need to be both smart and pretty, but she's a terrible person, so who knows."

His mouth lifts. "You think I'm pretty?"

"You *know* you're pretty. Everyone thinks so."

"I only care that you think so," he says, then takes a swig from the bourbon bottle before setting it down.

There's a warm feeling inside of me, as if I'd downed that bourbon, but I don't have time to sink into it, or to do any of the things I want to do to Declan, because Nicole and Damien come back to the fire. She's riding on his back, and he's got a bag of marshmallows in one hand. "Looks like I've been missing some party," he says with a grin.

"Who says it's over?"

It takes me a second to realize I was the one who said the words.

CHAPTER TWENTY

DECLAN

Conversation with Seamus, Declan's burner phone

I'm worried about Rosie.

She hasn't gone to work in a few days, so I swung by the bakery. They said she quit.

Fuck. Why? I thought she liked this one.

Damned if I know, but she's been off since you were here. She said you seemed depressed, not yourself.

I told her you were always a miserable bastard.

But she says you shouldn't be alone.

You can tell her I identify as a miserable bastard.

You know why we can't be in the same place.

Do I? Or is this another case of big-brother-knows-best? Because, if so, I can give you a documented list of twenty times you've been a dumbass.

Nah. I'm selling myself short. Fifty.

I was worried about you too, for the record.

I slip my phone back into my pocket after reading Shay's last message and checking my alarm. It's set for six-thirty on Monday morning, and I've got a job in Asheville at seven-thirty. If I had any respect for my future self, I wouldn't still be out here at one in the morning, drinking bourbon and beer and eating marshmallows with Claire, Nicole, and Damien, gathered in lawn chairs around that bonfire of memories as the photos within it crumble to dust.

But I'm too busy living to think about what trouble might be lurking tomorrow. Worry about Rosie is dancing at the edges of that feeling, but it's so nice to finally feel that way, in the moment and enjoying it, that I can't stand for it to end just yet. Even if my own memories keep dancing into view in those flames.

One of those memories is of sitting at this same fire pit with Dick, drinking beers and talking, Dick wearing one of his Hawaiian shirts. He'd had dozens of them—ridiculous since we were about as far as a person could get from Hawaii while still remaining in the same country. He'd always said he'd get there someday, although to my knowledge he never had.

"Do you regret whatever brought you here, Dec?" he'd asked that night, leaning back in his chair and smoking a joint.

At that point, that had been the closest he'd come to flat-out asking me about the trouble that had driven me to Marshall. To living near a city but not in one, hidden away in the woods, alone.

I'd thought about it a moment before saying, *"Yes and no."*

My non-answer had made him laugh, and I figured he was going to give me some shit about it, but instead he said, *"I understand that, bud. Sometimes the right answer for you has to be the wrong one for someone else."*

Had he been talking about leaving Nicole and Claire? Had he

had a reason for abandoning them, beyond knowing he didn't have it in him to be a parent? I can't respect him for that. Then again, I'd never thought he was a good man—just a man I'd liked, despite myself.

I'm not a good man either, although if I said that to my sister, she'd probably punch my arm and tell me I'm an idiot. That I definitely know is true. I'm an idiot for being out here right now. For picking the lock earlier. For setting this fire. And I am most definitely an idiot for offering to teach Claire to drive stick shift when I don't know how to do it myself.

Seamus would have a fucking field day with that one, not that I ever intend to tell him. He's a car nut, so he'd take it personally if he knew—and tell me I'm pussy whipped, of course.

Nicole sighs and says, "I think we need some of those weird cookies Claire made. Declan, did you know my sister is a baking goddess?"

"I may have noticed that," I say, captivated by the way Claire's blushing. Her eyes are bright in the firelight, her hair rustling in the wind. She looked like a fucking goddess earlier, dancing around the fire—a goddess who went and got herself stuck in Marshall. Next to me. I feel myself leaning in closer, like I can't help myself, like I'm a wolf circling a lure even though I know it's laced with poison.

Then again, what man could resist her?

"Let's not exaggerate," Claire mutters. "It's just a hobby."

Nicole skewers a finger at her. "Never undermine your accomplishments. Let someone else try to do that for you—and then kick them in the balls. Because, let's be honest, it's probably going to be a man who does it."

"I take offense," Damien says lazily.

I clink beer bottles with him across the fire. We switched to beer from booze about an hour ago. "Amen, brother. My sister's friends were vicious to each other in high school."

It's only after I say it that I remember I'm not supposed to talk about Rosie, or myself, or my life before. But it's hard to remember why that's so important right now, sitting out here with them. Having fun in the first time since...well, since I baked with Claire the other day.

Nicole huffs. "And why do you think that is? Because women are pitted against each other by men, which is so fucking stupid. There's space for all of us." She trains a look at Claire. "Even twenty-eight-year-olds who wear boring clothing and smell like senior citizens."

"Are you talking about me?" Claire asks, her brow wrinkled.

"If the smell fits..." Probably in response to Claire's confused expression, she adds, "You always smell like Chanel No. 5. I've never met a woman under fifty who regularly wears that shit."

Claire lifts a hand to her collarbone, the fingers spread out, and I want to layer my hand over it. I want to tip her head up and kiss her and suck down her scent—not the Chanel No. 5, but the scent of apples and rosemary that underlies it, probably from her shampoo. "Agnes gave me a bottle for Christmas. Every Christmas, actually. I have seven of them. Last year, she must have been pissed at me, because it was just a travel bottle. That's the one I have with me."

"You like it so much you brought a travel bottle with you?" Nicole asks, gaping at her. "You know, she probably gave it to you because she wanted you to smell bad."

"Shit," Claire says, her eyes widening. "You might have a point. Why do I still wear it? She expected me to, every day. If I didn't wear it, she'd make a passive-aggressive comment... I got used to it."

"Go get it," Nicole says with shining eyes. "We'll add it to our death fire. That woman doesn't hold any power over you anymore either. This is the fire of absolution!"

Claire gets up and actually takes a step toward the house, which is when I realize they're both loaded. I'm drunk, but not *that* drunk.

"Let's not throw flammable liquid in the fire," I say, getting up and taking her hand. To my surprise, she weaves her fingers through mine. Awareness floods the place where our skin is touching—little zips of sensation spooling and unspooling. "Come on back to your chair. I don't think that would end well for any of us."

She watches me, her pink lips parting, and I wonder if she feels the same combustibility between us. There's this feeling that something is drawing us together—and the world will fucking blow up if we let it happen, and will blow up anyway if we don't. "Oh, you're probably right," she says softly, a hint of huskiness in her voice, and lowers back into her chair. I sit back down beside her, feeling the ghost of her hand in mine.

"Besides, if we do, this whole damn place will smell like Chanel No. 5 for months," Damien adds. "Nobody wants that. I don't like the stuff either. No offense, Claire."

"Seriously, none taken," she says, lifting a hand. "*I* don't like it. But I wore it every day for seven years. For *her*. And, you know, I don't think she even said thank you to me. Once."

"For the Chanel No. 5?" I ask, riveted without quite knowing why. Maybe because it's hard to imagine Claire in that other life. Bound to an office chair. She seems so vibrant—as if the land and sky met to make her—and every office I've ever been to is the very opposite. A box, with pet people inside.

"For anything," she says. "I've done thousands of things for her —*millions*—and not a single thank you."

"Has Mrs. Rosings ever said thank you?" Nicole asks with a giggle.

"Have you?" Damien retorts.

"The thank you is immer— immma—." Claire frowns and then snaps her fingers. "Immaterial. It's immaterial. It's her complete inability to care about other people that makes her terrible. I'm going to write a comment on her Facebook page," she adds, fumbling into her pocket for her phone.

"I'll be taking that," I say, reaching in, trying not to feel the swell of her hips, or the intimacy of reaching inside something so close to other places I'd like to explore. She's drunk, and I may not be a good man, but I'm a better man than to take advantage of a drunk woman.

I tuck the phone into my own pocket.

"You're bossy too," Claire says with a pouty look. "People are always telling me what to do. I'm tired of it."

"Hallelujah, sister," Nicole crows, lifting a bottle that has to be empty at this point.

"But *you're* probably the bossiest person I've ever met," Claire adds. "Even more so than Agnes."

Nicole shrugs, making no argument. "I use my powers for good. When I like people."

Claire nods. "Yes, I think that's actually true. Agnes doesn't like anyone except for herself. And maybe Doug." She scowls. "I *hate* Doug."

"So why'd you fuck him?" Nicole asks, making me bristle. I have no right, and I know it, but I don't like thinking about other men touching Claire, earning those breathy little sounds of pleasure.

"I don't know," Claire says airily, waving a hand. She misjudges the size of the gesture and strikes the side of my shoulder. She absentmindedly rubs where her fingers struck, and I restrain the urge to hold her hand in place. "You know, he thought the female orgasm was a myth."

Nicole laughs. "Because he's never given one to anyone. I'd feel sorry for him if he weren't such a dipshit."

Anger forms a fist in my gut—that fucker didn't deserve to touch Claire or even fantasize about touching her.

Claire continues, oblivious, "I think I was just bored. I kept waiting for something to happen. Waiting, waiting, waiting." Something inside of me comes to attention—like a dog perking its head at the sound of "treat." Isn't that what I've done too? Isn't that who I've been? I've waited for someone to find me, for someone to make me pay, and that's all I've done. Claire sighs. "It went on for years. But nothing did happen. So sometimes I made things happen. Like with Doug. Or when I convinced Agnes that pigtails were coming back into style for grown women. Otherwise, it was the same old shit, day after day, year after year, until two months ago."

"What happened two months ago?" I ask as she continues to absentmindedly rub my arm. I don't ask for any information about Doug, because I have a feeling knowing more about him won't make me feel any less inclined to drive all the way to New York so I can crush his legs. Jealousy isn't a usual emotion for me, and I decide I don't care for it at all.

"Lainey and Todd broke off their engagement because he's a cheating *douchebag*, and I got fired, and Nicole called me, and then I met *you*. And now everything is weird and interesting. It's like..." But she trails off, staring at the fire, maybe taking in the curled coal at the bottom of it—what used to be photos.

"Damn straight it's interesting," Nicole says, lifting that empty bottle again. "And this roller coaster just left the station."

I catch another smirk from Damien, and I smile back. "I think it's time to tuck it in," I say.

"Is that a penis analogy?" Nicole asks with another wave of the bottle.

"No," I say immediately, then amend it to, "I don't think so," because I don't actually know where the saying came from. "But it *is* time for us to get some sleep."

"No way," Nicole says. "Didn't you just hear me? The roller coaster just left the station. We can't push it back. Gravity would be against us."

"Why are you so hung up on roller coasters?" Claire asks with another frown. "You're right, though. This is a big moment. I'm seeing everything so clearly now. It's like when you take your glasses off, and you can see."

"Aren't glasses supposed to help you see?" Nicole asks. She's put the bottle down and is waving a stick at the fire. The end catches flame, and she holds it, watching as the fire travels upward before dropping it into the flames.

"You're right. And I had some reading glasses!" Claire says. "They were only like one-point-five, but they helped me on the computer. Agnes said they made me look like a bug, though, and wouldn't let me wear them at the office. Like, what the fuck? But, you know, my dad actually calls me Bug as a pet name. So maybe she had a point."

"Probably," Nicole says thoughtfully. "We'll get you some new glasses that make you look like a badass."

"There are glasses that make people look badass?"

"If there aren't, we'll make them. Maybe we should start a new company. A badass glasses company." She frowns. "On second thought, no, that sounds boring as fuck. But maybe we can find other people we can pawn the idea off on."

Damien and I exchange another half smile over the fire—the look of two men whose women are wasted, a thought that gives me immediate pause, because Claire's not mine. She's my neighbor. My desire. Maybe even my friend.

But she's not mine. When I did what I did, I gave up my right to other people. Or at least that's what I've been telling myself so long I don't know how not to believe it.

"What other symbolic things can we do with the perfume?" Nicole asks. "Why don't we bury it?"

"Veto," Damien says, leaning back in his chair. "Right now, you'd be lucky to get it half a foot under, then I'd accidentally step on it someday and get flooded with Chanel No. 5."

Nicole starts laughing hysterically, rocking back and forth on her chair. "Let's donate it to a nursing home," she says through laughter.

"Hey, that's actually a good idea," Claire says. "They might like it."

"Or you could give it to your new overbearing boss."

"No, I'd rather give it to the nursing home. Besides, Mrs. Rosings isn't much older than my real dad, and she scares me. I don't want to inadvertently piss her off."

I laugh. "Yeah, she scares me too."

"Really?" she asks, turning toward me in her chair—the motion so sudden it almost topples over.

"Really."

She smiles slowly. "Add that to the list of mysteries of Declan..." Her eyes widen. "I don't even know your last name."

"I don't know *your* last name."

"Rainey."

I put out a hand, and she takes it, her grip sending another jolt of need through me. "Claire Rainey, I feel privileged to meet you. I'm Declan James."

I hear a snort from the other side of the fire. "No, you're not."

"Yeah," Claire says with a grin. "You're messing with me, aren't you? That sounds like a cowboy movie name."

But ice is running down my spine, because the way Nicole said it...it sounded as if she knew...

You're being paranoid, a voice in my head insists.

Still. The spell is broken.

"Time to..." I stop myself from saying "tuck it in." "Time to get some rest. I've got to get up early."

"You and me both, my man," Damien says with a groan, getting up from his chair.

"You got any sand for the fire?" I ask.

He nods. "Dick kept some in the shed."

I knew that already, but it seemed impolite not to ask, like I'd be saying I know this place better than they do, and even if it's true, it's theirs now. They have the power to tell me to fuck off and stay away, and even though that seemed like the wise course of action before last weekend, now I wouldn't like it.

"I'll get it," I offer.

When I get back with the sand, they're both gone, leaving only Claire behind. Well, shit.

CHAPTER TWENTY-ONE

DECLAN

Claire tries to stand from her chair but wobbles. "I'll help you."

"That's okay," I say with a smile. "I'd rather play it safe and keep the drunk girl away from the fire."

"I'm twenty-eight," she says belligerently. "I'm a *woman.*"

"My mistake. Keep the drunk woman away from the fire."

"How old are you?"

"Thirty-one."

She sighs and glances at the house. "I'm sorry they went inside. That's really rude. I told them it was rude. But Nicole pretended she was feeling nauseous."

I cock my head. "You sure she was pretending? She slugged back most of that bourbon herself."

"I could tell," she insists, then adds, "She's always trying to get us alone together."

I don't dispute it. It's clearly true, although I still don't fully understand why her sister would go to so much effort to lockdown a deadbeat gardener for her. "I don't understand why she'd do that, but I don't mind being alone with you."

They're small words, because truthfully there's little I want more than I want to be alone with her—and at the moment, I want it more than I fear it.

"Really?" she asks brightly.

"Really. Now let me put this fire out, and then I'll see you back to your house."

"Are you going to pick the lock again?" she asks.

"I will if I need to." I glance back at her, taking in the sight of her by the softer glow of the fire. A little drunk, a lot tired, and so damn beautiful it would make an angel weep and a devil burn.

"It made me so wet, watching you do that," she says conspiratorially.

I nearly fumble the bag of sand. "Jesus, Claire. You're not making this easy."

I'm tipsy enough that I don't really know what I mean by that. She's not making it easy to stay away from her, I guess.

"Good," she says, pursing her lips.

My cock mostly hard and my heart throbbing, I finish dousing the fire, making sure there's not a spark of it left to cause destruction we don't want. I feel a slight pang of regret when I see the crumbled ash at the bottom of the pit—all that's left of a hundred photos of Claire. But I saw them go into the fire, like watching her life go by on fast forward. Claire as a cute-as-hell baby, a toddler, a little girl, a preteen, a goody two-shoes teenager, and Claire as the assistant to Agnes Lewis.

I don't hit women—wouldn't, no matter what—but I'd destroy Agnes in other ways if I could. Anyone who'd look at Claire and want to crush her is a monster.

Claire must see me looking, because she tries to get to her feet again, manages it this time, and touches my elbow. "You know everything about me now, but I still don't know anything about you."

"I *don't* know everything about you," I say, slipping an arm around her waist and telling myself I'm doing it because she needs support. "I don't know what your favorite color is."

She snort-laughs, leaning into me in a way that makes my heart swell as I start walking her back toward the house, lights still glowing inside. It's nearly pitch black, but the stars are twinkling overhead and the moon's glow is buttery soft against her skin. The breeze carries the scent of our campfire, flavored with wildflowers. It feels like the witching hour, a time of night where anything can happen.

"There's all this pressure on everyone to have a favorite color. I feel like people only choose one because they're cornered into it. I mean, come on, aren't I allowed to like more than one color?" She scrunches her face. "I guess that's probably how you feel about your friends with benefits."

"No," I say, my hand moving over her lower back, trying to memorize the feeling of it beneath my fingertips. "And I told you. I haven't been seeing anyone."

She halts her steps before we round the side of the cabin. "But you could be seeing me if you wanted to. You could see *all* of me."

Fucking A. She's going to kill me. I thought my death would come at someone else's hand, but I was wrong. I'm going to die here and now, incinerated by Claire Rainey. I make my hand fall from around her back, because I can't touch her right now.

Clearing my throat, I say, "You're drunk, Claire. This isn't a good time for us to discuss this."

"In vino veritas," she says in a dramatic voice, lifting her arm and holding it out horizontally like she's an actor taking a bow.

"So you were sneaking wine, too, huh?" I joke. "Should've known. I mean it, though, I can't—"

"Does that mean you *can* when we're sober?" she asks, eyes twinkling.

"We're neighbors." I take a small step closer without meaning too, eliminating more of the short distance between us.

"I've decided I don't care."

"That's good of you," I say, my heart thumping. It's one of those moments when the air seems drunk on possibility. I'd thought I was past the point of possibilities, so I can't seem to find it in me to shut this one down. I want her, and I want her bad.

"Not tonight," I repeat.

"What if I can do a field sobriety test?" she asks, laughing as she tries to walk in a straight line, arms out, and fails miserably.

"Now it's a hell no," I say, smiling at her. Because she's cute as hell, and being around her is addictive. I'd defy anyone to be in a bad mood when they're around her. Except for this Agnes Lewis woman.

She takes another step, and I capture her hand and draw her in close. A gasp escapes her, and she peers into my eyes. "You know, I do have a favorite color—it's green, the color of the moss in the winter and of those little flecks in your eyes. You have beautiful eyes. When I thought they were the last thing I was ever going to see, I was at peace with it. I want you, Claire. I haven't...I haven't let myself want anyone in a long time."

"Declan," she says, gripping my arms. "You need to kiss me, now."

"There's a lot you don't know about me," I say, groaning, feeling torn in two by all the things going on inside of me. Wanting her, needing to protect her by staying away, and needing to keep punishing myself, the way I think I deserve. I'm not sure which will win out, but right now they all seem likely to destroy me.

"So...start talking." She gives my arms a squeeze.

"You'd look at me differently if you knew everything." I know I should stop. I can't tell her. I can't tell *anyone*. The more people who know, the more likely it is that someone will come for me—and everyone around me, including Claire, could suffer for it. I look down, feeling my hair tumbling against my brow. "It would be unfair of me to get involved with you, knowing that."

"And I suppose you won't tell me."

"I can't. But I wasn't exaggerating. Your father would fucking hate me if he knew about my background."

"Can't you tell me some stuff?" she asks. "Other than your favorite color?"

"You know I have a sister," I say haltingly. My mind supplies: *a sister who just quit her fifth job in two years, and she really seemed to like this one.* The worry rears up again, but I swallow it. "And that my parents are dead. I have a younger brother too. Seamus. He's less than a year younger than me." I regret the words after they come out, because I've put myself in a position where I can't see that line in the sand again. I want to tell her things, to let her in. I want to know her, and for her to know me.

"You're the oldest," she comments.

"How'd you know?" I ask, brushing a lock of hair behind her ear.

"You have this air of *I know best.*" She pauses, her expression contemplative. "Like my sister. You know, she's definitely crazy, but I'm starting to like her."

"I like both of them," I say, which isn't to say I trust them. Something about Nicole and Damien sets me on edge. There's this look they keep giving each other, like they know more than everyone else and it amuses them. "I'm the oldest," I confirm. "It's on me to look out for Rosie and Shay."

"They're both adults, I'm guessing?" she says, a slight smile playing on her lips.

"More or less."

"And did you always do landscaping?"

"Is this a job interview?"

"It's some kind of an interview," she says, her lips tipping up at the corners, "but I hope you don't expect to get paid for sex. I've only been here for a week, and Mrs. Rosings hasn't given me a paycheck yet."

Despite myself, I'm smiling again. "No, I haven't always done landscaping. I used to work in construction, but I've always liked plants. My mom and I took care of a greenhouse together when I was a kid. It was my favorite place in the world."

She lifts a hand to my face, guiding it down my cheek, and ends with her thumb on my bottom lip. My dick is as hard as a fucking rock, but what's more distressing is the feeling in my chest—soft like the bottom of one of those upside-down cakes Rosie likes to bake. Soft like a guy who keeps a greenhouse with his mother and doesn't like hurting people for the sake of it. Claire does that to me. She's done that to me from that first day, when I thought I was toast. She made me feel, for a second, anyway, like maybe it wasn't so bad to be toast. "See, that wasn't so hard."

"It is hard," I say without thinking. "*Very.*"

I mean it two ways, and she doesn't miss either meaning, her gaze traveling downward in a slow but sure way that spreads fire through my body.

She glances back up, licking her lips, her hand still on my face. "You're going to take me driving on Wednesday? Maybe we can go out to dinner too."

"I can't do that, Claire," I say, swallowing. Because what I say next might be the end of this, whatever this is, and I don't want it to be. "We can't see each other out in the open. I can't have people talking about me, speculating. If we do this...it would be as friends with benefits, basically. Exclusive. We'd spend time together here, at our houses. That's all I can offer."

It's more than I should offer.

She lowers her hand, and my heart is thumping so fast, I'm surprised we can't both see it rising and falling from my chest in a cartoon pantomime. She's going to say no. I don't want her to say no. I'm not sure I can handle the disappointment if she does.

She studies me for a moment, then says, "It's because of that thing you can't tell me—the thing you're afraid would put me off."

"I *know* it would, because you're a good person, and you need to know that I'm not. I meant what I said the other day, Claire. I'm a bad man who's done bad things."

"I disagree," she blurts. "You care about your brother and sister, and you obviously cared about your parents."

"Everyone likes someone," I say gruffly, making myself take a small step back.

"Only someone who values life would choose to make a living growing plants," she argues, and although she doesn't know it, that one stings.

"When someone tells you they're not to be trusted, you should believe them," I say gruffly. "I'll bet your father told you that."

"He did," she says with a slight nod. "But I've followed his advice for most of my life, and where did it get me?"

"It got you here, I guess." Although a few seconds ago I'd meant to end this conversation and walk her the rest of the way to the house, I *am* a bad man—a man who's no good at denying himself. I pull her to me and rest my chin on top of her head, holding her to my chest. "I'm glad you're here."

"You're confusing."

"I know," I say softly. "I'm sorry."

She pauses, then says, "You said we'd have to keep it quiet, but Nicole and Damien would obviously know. And my friend Lainey. I tell her everything."

"You'd agree to that?" I ask, pulling away enough that I can look down at her. Then I shake my head. "Don't answer me now. I want you to think about it. We'll talk when I see you on Wednesday."

"Okay," she says silently. A second later, she grabs my shirt, catching me by surprise. "But you're going to kiss me right now, Declan. I need to make an educated decision."

"You're—"

"Too drunk for you to fuck, yes. But not too drunk for you to kiss. I want you to. I've wanted you to all week."

A groan escapes me, and I'm not about to tell her no. I've wanted to kiss her all week too. To pull her to me and forget everything, the way I did for a few seconds on that plane, when all that existed was Claire and me. Our connection started in that moment, when we thought we were breathing our last breaths and found a reason to enjoy them. But I would have still liked her, wanted her, no matter where we met. It would be impossible not to feel those things for Claire, but if we'd met in a different way, maybe they would have been more controllable.

When she tugs me down to her, my shirt still balled in her fist, I let my hand cup the back of her head so I can draw her closer. The second our lips brush, wild need takes ahold of me. It just feels so good, so *right*. I suck in her bottom lip and run my tongue over it, and the hand that's not holding the silky mass of hair runs down her back to the swell of her ass, learning her shape. Touching her in the places I've admired.

A sounds escapes her, and she releases my shirt and surprises me by slipping a hand beneath the hem and branding her palm against the bare flesh of my chest—her touch arcing electricity straight down to my dick, which has claimed all of the blood in my body and most of the functioning of my brain. Her palm roams around, learning me the way I'm learning her, while she makes those little sounds of pleasure that funnel directly into my mouth, and it's driving me mad. *She* is driving me mad.

She lifts onto her toes to get better leverage, her kiss becoming more forceful, her lips hot and sweet and soft against mine, although there's nothing soft about the pressure she's applying. Her tongue is weaving with mine in a dance that's familiar but not, because it's different with her. All of this is different, *better*.

Because you care about her, you dummy, I can hear Rosie say.

I want to back her into the side of the house and push her bra down so I can capture her nipple in my mouth again. I want to lift that dress up so I can bury my head between her legs, and my dick very much wants to sink into her sweet heat until both of us get a release—but she's drunk, and even though our houses are secluded and no one's likely to see us messing around outside, her sister and brother-in-law are in Dick's house. In fact, if Nicole's as interested in what's going on between us as Claire thinks, I wouldn't be surprised if she's watching us put on a show.

That thought's almost enough to deflate my dick. Almost. But then Claire's searching hand tracks lower as our mouths keep fighting to find the perfect angle. Her warm fingers slip under the waistband of my shorts and brush over my dick, captured in my boxer-briefs, and that sensation—her hand on me, even if it's just a whisper through the thin fabric, is too much. It feels so good it almost hurts.

I pull back, panting, and tug her hand away from my dick. "Not now."

"Wednesday," she says with a smile. "I need to give you something to look forward to." Then she hiccups. I laugh, my blood hot and heart racing, and then for no fucking reason at all, since she's perfectly capable of walking, just not in a straight line, I sweep her up into my arms.

She looks at me with startled eyes. "Well, hello."

"If you've forgotten that we've spent the last few hours together, I feel like a real asshole for kissing you."

"Not for letting me touch your dick?" she asks as I stride toward the front of the house.

"You took that liberty all on your own."

"I can still feel you," she says, snuggling closer, and I grit my teeth together and deliver her to her door.

It's not locked, possibly because we found each other just fine without any intervention.

"Bring me upstairs," she says.

I'm about to tell her it's not a good idea, but I see a glimmer of fear in her eyes, and I remember. Dick tripped down those stairs drunk, and even though I doubt she'd fall, she's thinking about it. Now, I am too, and nothing will do but for me to carry her up and see her safely to bed. So I do, and after I set her down on the mattress, I find myself drawing up the blankets so they cover her.

"You tucked me in," she says, sounding delighted by it.

"I guess I did. I think I'm going to get you a glass of water too."

"Are you going to sternly tell me to drink it?"

The way she says it, coy, makes my cock stir, and I nearly groan. "Yes, Claire."

"Good," she says with a soft smile, and I get her a glass of water and an Advil from the kitchen downstairs. It's still strange to be in here, now that it's theirs and not Dick's. It feels like the soul of the house has changed. Maybe that's because of the bonfire we had tonight. Something has been exorcised from this place—or maybe from Dick's guilty conscience. Because they may not have seen that he was troubled, but I did. He'd made bad choices, and he'd felt the weight of them. It was something we'd had in common.

He would have understood what they did tonight, and he wouldn't have held it against them.

Would he hold it against you if you fuck his daughter?

Shaking off the thought, because the answer is so obviously yes, I take out her phone and set it on the counter. She's probably too drunk to cyber-harass her ex-boss tonight, but it'd be better not to take the chance. If she wants to get revenge, I'll help her, but planning vengeance is best done sober.

When I get upstairs, Claire is asleep, and she looks so beautiful, her head cradled on her pillow, her eyelashes resting on her cheek, that my chest feels soft again. No doubt about it, she's making me soft. I'm not sure I can afford it—and I'm not sure I can stay away.

I set the water down on the table beside her bed. But if I don't get her to drink it, she's going to have one hell of a hangover tomorrow, so I kiss her forehead, then touch her cheek, wanting to rouse her without scaring her.

When her eyes open and she sees me, a smile lifts her lips. "Is it Wednesday already?"

I laugh. "No, unfortunately. I brought you some water and an Advil. This is me being stern. I'm not leaving until you drink it all."

"I thought you wanted me to listen."

I hold back another laugh. "And when I say I'm not leaving, I'm going to stay here and tickle your feet until you do. That won't be pleasant for either of us."

"What's wrong with my feet?"

"Nothing, but feet don't do it for me."

She surveys me for a moment as if judging whether I'm serious. I must be tipsier than I realized, because I am.

I mime going for her foot, and she scrunches it up and pulls it away. I wrap a hand around it, and she arches it in my grip in a way that makes me wonder if I am in fact a foot guy—or maybe just a foot guy for her—and then I start tickling the sole.

Screeching with laughter, she says, "Stop, stop. I'll do it."

Releasing her foot, I give her the glass of water and the pill. She glances up at me over the rim of the glass. "I'm going to have to pee if I drink it all."

"That's between you and your bladder."

She looks at me through my eyelashes, watching as she takes the pill and downs the water.

"Thank you for taking care of me," she says. "A bad man wouldn't bother. A bad man would have taken what I've been offering."

Fuck me.

Is there anything more alluring than a beautiful woman telling you exactly what you want to hear?

"Don't saint me just yet," I say, then kiss her on the lips once more—a soft brush, because I don't trust myself to stop if I allow myself to have more—and I leave.

It's not until I'm home that I realize I left the wrong phone. But when I go back, it's not on the kitchen counter. I start to panic when I spot it on the round kitchen table. My heart slows back to a nearly normal pace as I make the switch.

Close call.

CHAPTER TWENTY-TWO

CLAIRE

I wake up on Monday morning to the bleeping of my alarm clock with a hangover and a dry mouth that tastes like rotten marshmallows.

Crap.

The last thing I remember was trying to seduce Declan—possibly multiple times—despite being so drunk I couldn't walk straight.

"Smooth move, Claire," I mutter. He hadn't seemed too put off, but then again, it's hard to judge other people's perceptions when your own are impaired. My mind travels further backward, and I remember what he said, or most of it. I think he told me he wants to be my fuck buddy, exclusively, which is mostly good news.

Only "mostly," because I can already tell I'm going to be stupid over him. He's funny and complicated and interesting, and easily the most attractive man who's ever wanted to kiss me. I like him. I *really* like him. And I'm desperate to know whatever it is he thinks he needs to hide from me. Especially if he's got some kind of secret family, like in one of those books Lainey always tries to push on me.

My second alarm goes off, reminding me that I have to get to Mrs. Rosings to help her with yet another thankless task connected to the wedding of a couple I've never met. A second gush of memories from last night hits me.

Agnes.

Chanel No. 5.

That bitch. I get up, groaning from the ache in my head, and march to my dresser. I pick up the bottle and throw it at the trashcan, only remembering when the bottle is airborne that we'd decided to gift all of the perfume, presuming I get the rest back at some point, to a nursing home. And also that I'm shitty at throwing things, another genetic gift I must have gotten from Richard Ricci, since my mother was the pitcher for her high school intramural softball team.

The glass bottle hits the floor with a tell-tale crack that makes my eyes fly open wide, especially when the stench hits me. Shit. *Shit.*

I fight a wave of nausea as I grab a couple of towels from the closet and mop it up, then carry them to the bathroom to wash them in the washer-dryer combo set up in there.

Sighing, I get ready for the day, and then plod downstairs toward the alluring scent of coffee. Damien's sitting at the kitchen table drinking coffee, and there's a plate of buttered toast in the middle.

"It's for all of us," he says, grinning at me. Probably because I look and smell like a senior citizen.

"Bless you."

His nose twitches, but he doesn't say anything about how generously I've shared my perfume.

"Your phone was on the table when I came down," he said, nodding to it. "I'm guessing Declan left it there so you wouldn't resort to any late-night texting." His eyes are dancing, and he doesn't look hungover at all, the jerk.

"She would have deserved it."

"No doubt."

I grab some coffee and toast and sit down, and we carry on with our breakfasts in blissful silence for a few minutes until there's a racket in the other room, and then Nicole emerges with a suitcase.

"Did you bathe in that stuff just to fuck with me, Claire?" she asks, laughing. She doesn't look hungover, but at least she has the decency to look tired. "Thank God I'm leaving again, because I think I'd burn the whole house down just to get rid of the smell."

"The bottle bro—" I start, then catch myself. "What? You're going somewhere?"

"I'll be back in a couple of days," she says.

"You just got back yesterday," I say, dropping the toast before I can get in a third bite.

"Hence why I'm leaving 'again.'"

My mouth gapes open for a second, and then I find plenty of words. "I thought we were both supposed to live in this house for a month to get the inheritance. You've barely been around since I got here."

"I'm the executor of the estate," she says with a laugh. "I'm the one who gets to decide whether the terms have been fulfilled."

"That's bullshit!"

"Besides, Damien's going to stay here to keep an eye on you. Legally speaking, he's my other half."

"Guilty as charged," Damien says, his eyes warm as he watches her. He's always looking at her like that—like the world revolves around Nicole instead of the sun. I wonder if he knows she's crazy and just doesn't care. I remember not caring either, last night. Now, in the light of day, befriending my sister seems like less of a good idea.

"But I thought we were supposed to be looking into what happened to Dick, and so far we've done nothing."

"Untrue," she says, lifting a finger. "What do you think I've been doing all week? I had some other stuff to take care of, sure, but I was also tracking down a couple of leads. Besides, I think we've agreed it probably wasn't Declan—although you should plan on *very* thoroughly investigating him." She winks theatrically. "Speaking of...is he upstairs? I know he brought you in last night."

"No!" I protest. "I was drunk, and he has this thing about being a gentleman." Then I blush, because I said too much, and in front of Damien.

Damien sets down his coffee cup, his gaze on my sister. "And if he *were* upstairs, I'd have to rough him up for taking advantage of your sister."

Nicole preens, and I remember what she said about their interesting form of foreplay. "Declan's a big guy," she says, "but so are you. I'll bet you *could* take him. Who would you put your money on, Claire? Your man or mine?"

"No one's punching anyone," I say, annoyed. "And you don't have to defend my virtue, Damien. I'm not some Victorian virgin."

Nicole breathes out a laugh. "You might as well be, if you've only boned men like Doug."

"There've been plenty of other—" I glance at Damien.

"Don't cut yourself off on my account," he says with an amused grin.

"I'm not having this conversation with either of you right now," I say, turning back to Nicole. "Where are you going anyway?"

"I *will* tell you. But only when I get back. This is a secret mission. If I told you what I was doing, the whole thing would be compromised."

"I think you just get off on seeming mysterious."

"Absolutely. Speaking of... You have an assignment while I'm gone. You need to get into Mrs. Rosings's box." Her nose wrinkles again, and she laughs. "That sounded dirtier than I intended it to. I love it when that happens."

Damien finishes his coffee and gets to his feet, grabbing Nicole's bag. "Let's go. The Chanel's going to do me in."

"Amen," Nicole says, lifting onto her toes to kiss him.

"Bye, Claire," Damien says with a wave.

"But—" I manage, but they're already out the door.

Alone, sandblasted by Nicole's sudden departure, I check out my phone as I finish the toast. My pulse accelerates when I see I have three missed calls from Lainey.

I immediately drop the toast and call her back, and she answers on the second ring. "Are you okay?" I ask. "Did someone die? Is my dad—"

"He's okay," she says in a rush. "Sorry, I wasn't thinking. I just... I..." I hear a sob on the other end of the line. "That fucker's engaged again. *Already*."

"What?" I ask, shocked. Because she has to be talking about Todd, and their engagement only ended two months ago.

"It's the woman he was fucking around with. They grew up together. Summered in the Hamptons," she adds with a huff. "I think he sees her as his equal, and I was always this...mistake. A blip in his life. He thought I was pretty and fun, and before he realized I was a loser, we were engaged. That's what his mother thought."

"No, she didn't think that, Lainey. She just has one of those faces that always looks constipated. She's probably had a lot of work—"

"She told me that herself after she had two glasses of sherry. I didn't tell you because...I was embarrassed. But they're right. I *am* a loser. I'm barely hanging on to a job I hate, and I don't make nearly enough money to afford to stay in New York without a rich boyfriend. I'm almost thirty, and I have nothing to show for it. I'm a poser, just like my parents."

"What about the Tarot idea?"

"I keep getting the Death card. I'm starting to think it's magnetized. Either that, or I have shitty luck, and it's bleeding into everything."

"Or maybe you keep getting it because you're supposed to come down here too. I've been trying really hard not to be needy and beg you to come, but I really, really want you here. Please don't tell me no. There's plenty of room at the house, so your rent would be free, and you could get a job somewhere while you figure out what comes next. We can do it together. And if the money comes through, we'll have enough funds to actually do something. *Please*, for the love of God, say yes."

She laughs through her tears, and I can see her in my sad little apartment, surrounded by those boxes that aren't good for a person's soul to see every day. "Lainey, I think this is supposed to happen. It's going to be so good for both of us, I promise."

"Yes," she says loudly. "Fuck. *Yes*. I'm coming to Marshall, North Carolina." She sighs, then says, "I'm going to take care of clearing out your apartment, though. So it'll be a week or two."

Excitement floods me, drowning out the hangover for at least half a second. "I can't even tell you how happy I am right now." I glance at the clock above the stove. "But I'm going to be late if I don't leave soon, and Mrs. Rosings will make five passive-aggressive 'back in my day' remarks, and I'm much too hungover right now to handle it."

"Hungover?" she asks with renewed interest. "Were you drinking with Declan?"

Memory wraps around me, warm and cocooning. Declan, telling me I'm beautiful. Declan, kissing me. Declan, carrying me into the house...

I clear my throat. "Yes, but don't get too excited. Nothing really happened."

Other than me wrapping my hand around his *very hard* cock, no in-flight magazine getting in the way this time. But I don't have five minutes to tell her about it, or even two, and it feels a little...private.

It's an unexpected thought, because usually I tell Lainey everything. I even told her about the time Doug and I had sex on the copier machine, and it made a photocopy of my ass.

"I'll call you later. Screw Todd. He's boring, and he likes boring things. You couldn't be boring if you tried."

"*I did*," she said with a sound that's half laugh, half sob. "I went to the opera. I bought three collared shirts. Four, but I returned one of them because it made me look like my mother. I listened to people talk about their investments. I don't think my mother's ever going to forgive me. Me marrying Todd was, like, her social-climbing dream."

"Nothing good can come from trying to please someone who doesn't want to be pleased. I wore Chanel No. 5 for seven and a half years because Agnes told me to, and apparently it's an old lady's perfume. Did you know that?"

There's a pause over the line, and then she says, "Yes, but it doesn't smell *bad*."

"A ringing endorsement. Okay, I love you. This is going to be great. Don't freak out."

"I'm not freaking out," she says. "But do you think I should get a dumpster and just throw all of my boxes away so I can start fresh?"

"No way. We can sell the expensive shit Todd bought you on eBay if the insurance policy doesn't come through."

"You're right," she says with a sigh. "I hate it that you're right."

"I'll hire people to pack up the rest of my stuff," I say. "You don't have to do that."

I don't have the money to make that offer, but I *am* working for a very rich person who will be paying me in another week, so I can figure out a way to make it happen.

"I'll do it," she insists. "I need to keep busy. It'll help me feel useful."

We've hung up with each other before I realize that I have a problem: Damien just left to bring Nicole to the airport, or wherever, and I still don't have a car I'm able to use.

"Shit, shit," I say to myself. Then I glance out the window hopefully, checking out Declan's driveway. *Gone.* He'd mentioned having to leave for an early job, so it's not a surprise, just a disappointment—even though it's probably for the best that I don't bathe him in Chanel No. 5.

I quickly log on to Uber. There's only one vehicle available in Marshall right now, so I select it, down the rest of my coffee, and go outside to wait.

A red truck pulls up, and to my surprise I know the person behind the wheel. "You do Uber, too?" I ask as I open the passenger door and climb in.

Rex grins at me, his nose wrinkling only slightly from the Chanel as I shut the door behind me and buckle up. I'll take that as a win. "I'm all about getting people where they need to go. You're going to Smith House, so I guess you've met our resident black widow?"

"What?" I ask, confused. "You're talking about Mrs. Rosings?"

He whistles and then clucks his tongue as he pulls out onto the road. "No one's told you yet? She's been married three times, and each of her husbands died within a few years of the wedding."

"And the people in town blame her for that?" I ask, lifting a hand to my throat. I'm half intrigued, half offended for her. Mrs. Rosings can be a bit of a pill—honestly, she seems to enjoy being that way—but there's something I like about her. She has an iron spine, and she has no compunction whatsoever about potentially pissing people off. I'd like to siphon a little of that quality for myself, although only a little.

"When you put it that way," Rex says with a self-effacing grin, "it makes us sound terrible. It's just that they all had weird accidents, and she's never been very friendly, so when she inherited the Smith House estate, people were salty about it."

"Weird how?" I ask, my pulse picking up. Would Nicole know about this? It's the kind of thing she would know, but it's strange she never mentioned it...

Then again, Nicole doesn't exactly have a personality that

invites other people to idle chatter. Maybe no one ever told her because it's mostly unfounded gossip. Except, if I've learned anything from working in an office for seven years, it's that sometimes seemingly unfounded gossip has a kernel of truth at the core of it. Maybe Mrs. Rosings was behind Dick's death after all.

"Well, one of them died from food poisoning, and her third husband died in a plane crash."

"I don't see how that could possibly be her fault."

"True. But the second one, the father of her kids, died in an accident at Smith House. He was the heir, you know. Adrien Smith. He fell while he was picking apples from a tree in the yard. It made people suspicious, how that went down. Everyone in town loved him."

"Okay," I say. "I can see how all of this would lead to gossip, but don't you think it's a little unfair to blame a woman for being a three-times-over widow?"

Rex grins at me again. "You have a knack for putting a man in his place."

Do I?

I rewind our conversation. It hits me that I've been bolder here, in Marshall. Partly because, in the beginning, anyway, it felt like it didn't matter. I wasn't going to stay, so what did it matter if Declan thought I was too forward or Nicole or the other people I met thought I was disagreeable?

But now I'm staying. Can I still be Bold Claire?

"Sorry," I mutter, then retract it. "Actually, I still think it's bullshit, but I'm sorry if I made you feel bad. I doubt you're the person who started the rumors."

"I'll accept that," Rex said with a quick glance at me. "How've you been getting along with Nicole and Damien? I heard some talk in town that Nicole's your sister."

"More gossip." I shrug. "But this time they're right."

What if they're right about Mrs. Rosings? a voice in my head insists. Because if she knocked off a couple of husbands, it wouldn't have been that hard to get rid of a drunken ne'er-do-well.

He shakes his head and whistles under his breath. "Your father got around, didn't he? Well. Can't say my mother was any different. I don't get why people take the trouble to get married if they're just going to step out with someone else."

"I agree with you there," I say.

"Did you find Dick by doing one of those DNA tests? That's how I found my real dad."

"No, it was written into his will."

He snorts. "Mine wasn't any too pleased to find out about me, and the man who raised me washed his hands of me as soon as he found out I wasn't his."

"Sorry, that's horrible," I say with a grimace, thinking of my own father—the most mild man in existence, and he'd transformed into a warrior the second I'd suggested that I didn't need to be his problem because he wasn't biologically my father. I was glad to be his problem.

Rex shrugs as if he couldn't give a shit, or maybe stopped giving a shit years ago. "He was kind of an asshole, anyway," and for some godforsaken reason I start laughing.

He looks surprised for a second, but then surprised laughter trips out of him too. "You know, you're the only person who's ever laughed when I've told them that," he says, and I wipe at the corners of my eyes.

"I'm so sorry," I say through gusts of laughter. "It was the delivery...it was just..."

"No, I'm glad," he says as he passes a car. "It's better to laugh about it."

"That's the spirit," I say with a small smile. I shift, and that's when I feel it, in my cardigan pocket—the slip of paper I pulled out of the back of that photo album last night. I'd forgotten all about it.

I reach down to touch it and feel the crackle of paper inside, which makes anticipation tingle down my spine. But I don't want to open it in front of Rex. Based on what little I know of him, it's possible everyone in town would know what it says by lunchtime.

Rex and I talk about other, lighter things for the next few minutes that bring us to Smith House. I tip him, I wave to him, and then he's gone, and I'm five minutes late, and *I need to open the letter.* Glancing at the gate, I step to one side of it and then tug the note from my pocket.

I open it.

> Claire-
>
> If you're seeing this, I'm probably dead. Oh well. I never took great care of myself, and my body is feeling old and tired these days.
>
> Finding out about me probably wasn't the greatest surprise, but I hope having half the house and half the insurance money will help. Your mother has kept me updated on your health and well-being all these years, and since she told me you have a good father, I decided to do the responsible thing and stay away. Trust me, Claire, it WAS the responsible thing. By now you know Nicole, and you've heard how poorly I did the dad thing. I'm going to be frank with you and admit I wasn't too great at life in general, but I DID have fun. I hope you do too.
>
> Maybe you're wondering about the one-month stipulation in the will since you have a job in New York. Sorry about that, but it's my humble opinion that you can do better than being some woman's servant. You might decide to stick it out with her and say fuck it to the house and the money, and that's your choice. We all have a choice, and it's been my habit to make the bad one. The thing is: I

never knew my brother, and I wanted you and your sister to know each other. I'm forcing that chance upon you, kid, like I wish my own deadbeat dad had done for me.

I'm sorry for being myself, but I could hardly help it. If you need help with anything connected to the house or property, ask Declan. He's a friend and a mostly good guy, which is all any of us can hope for if we're being honest.

I wish I'd known you, kid, but that's a selfish wish, and I've done enough selfish things to last anyone two lifetimes.

Love,
Dick

He's a mostly good guy...

The gate swings open, nearly hitting me in the face.

"You're late," Mrs. Rosings says blandly. "What are you reading? A love note from that gardener?"

I wish. Emotion is pricking behind my eyes, and even though I'd promised Nicole I'd never give Dick any of my tears, I'm very close to breaking that promise. This note makes him more real—a person rather than a concept. A curiosity that will never be satisfied.

I wish I'd known you too, you jerk. I wish I'd seen the side of you that Declan saw.

"It's from Dick," I admit.

She flinches. "He left a note?"

I lift my hands in a staving-off gesture. "Not *that* kind of a note. It's one of those *if you get this, I'm probably dead* notes."

Although now that I think about it, it's a little coincidental that he'd write me a note like that before dying an untimely death.

"Well, I suppose he had to be right about something eventually," Mrs. Rosings says, prompting me to gasp. I think again of Mr. Smith in the apple orchard. Of her first husband and the mysterious case of food poisoning. Could she really have had something to do with it?

"Were you surprised when you heard he was dead?" I ask slowly.

She sniffs. "No. He was self-destructive. Brash. But I'd hoped to be wrong. Now, get into the car. Don't dally. We're going to look at a venue on the other side of Asheville."

I can't help but frown. "Don't you think that's something Anthony and Nina should be here for?"

She lifts her chin and looks down at me, despite being at least four inches shorter. "No."

Can't argue with that. I drive her car—a sleek sedan—marveling again at how quick and abrupt the change is from sleepy small town to medium-sized city. Neither of us speak much. I'm wrapped up in my thoughts and hangover, and she's not the kind of person who's inclined to fill awkward silences. If anything, she likes extending them to make people uncomfortable.

I follow her directions to a goat farm with an events center attached.

When we arrive, I give her a sidelong look. Is it considered in vogue to get married at strange places so you can then tell people you got married in a strange place? Sure. It makes for good social media. But this doesn't feel like something Mrs. Rosings would go for at all. "Are we in the right place?"

She makes a sound perilously close to a snort. "You would have heard from me by now if we weren't."

We get out of the car, and an elderly blonde woman with a purple cane emerges from the house. She sees us and grins. "Welcome, welcome to paradise."

Fuck. I haven't had enough coffee for this.

We spend the next two hours touring the goat farm and exploring the event space, which—no joke—has an indoor pen for the goats and a stained glass window of a goat eating hay. The smell in the event venue almost makes me lose my toast.

"And if you *do* get flowers, I'm afraid they'll have to be arranged very high. The goats like to munch on them," the woman, Stella, says. "Now...I'm an artist, and I would be more than happy to paint a portrait of the happy couple after the ceremony. They'd have to stand still for about half an hour, but it would make for a very happy memory. *Very* happy. And my husband is connected with a local brewery, so we could get you competitive pricing."

As if Mrs. Rosings would offer only beer at her son's wedding. But to my shock, she says, "I'm interested. I'll let you know within a few days."

"Splendid," Stella says, beaming. "*Splendid.* You know, I don't offer this to everyone, but if you'll send me a photo of the delightful young people, I can Photoshop them into the venue with some of the goats, give them a real feel for what the ceremony will look like."

Mrs. Rosings's eyes shine with mirth. "Yes, that would be most acceptable. Thank you."

I'm barely able to keep my feet as we head back to the car and get in.

Don't say anything, Claire. None of your business, Claire.

And I wouldn't have commented on the situation if it had been Agnes. Or if the last week of my life hadn't happened. But it only takes five minutes for me to shoot a look at her and say, "Mrs. Rosings, do you want this wedding to be awful?"

She tips back her head and laughs, immediately pressing a hand to her mouth as if she's done something unspeakable. "It took you long enough to ask. I was starting to think you might be a real dullard."

"*Why* do you want the wedding to be awful?"

"You don't have children yet," she says. "When you do, you'll understand."

"So you hate your son's fiancée?"

"She's an uppity, irksome being, to be sure," she says. "But she's not the problem. *He* is the problem. Imagine, engaging yourself to a woman who refuses to show your mother any common courtesy. A woman who expects your mother to pay for the entire wedding *and* plan it."

"Did you offer to do those things, Mrs. Rosings?" I ask with suspicion.

"To teach my boy a lesson? I'd do worse. I'd do anything to save that boy from himself."

"You know," I say. "This whole thing could really backfire on you. What if his fiancée loves goats and smelly flowers?"

"*No one*, however distasteful, wants a goat eating the backside of their dress."

"What's your end game?" I ask. "Do you want to break them up? Or are you hoping she'll suddenly take an interest in the proceedings if you do a bad job?"

She sighs, suddenly sounding weary. "When you get to be my age, sometimes you just cast the die for the interest of seeing where they lie." It's so similar to a thought I've had about Nicole, and her seemingly inexplicable actions, that I find myself smiling.

"But if I had it my way, he wouldn't marry her," she continues. "She's subtle enough, but you don't get to be my age without learning to read people. She's only interested in him because she wants Smith House and the Smith fortune, and if he were thinking with his brain rather than what he's got between his legs, he'd have realized it by now. But truthfully I'd prefer for my children not to get married at all. Marriage is a mistake. A trap. And he's walking right in because a pretty young twit is holding the right lure."

"That's an interesting sentiment for someone who's been married three times," I say before I can think better of it.

I feel her watching me as I merge onto the highway. "So you've heard the whispers around town," she says with a soft, throaty laugh. "People do love to talk."

"I think they're ridiculous. Only a woman would get blamed for having bad luck." I think but don't add, *But if you poisoned my bio-dad and gave him a push, blink twice.*

"Only a *successful* woman. They can't stand that their precious Smith House is in the hands of a woman who didn't grow up there. But Adrien Smith wasn't the god among men they think he was."

Shit, there's a sheen of dislike in her eyes. Hatred. But if the police don't exactly give a shit about my biological father's death, something tells me they gave many shits about Adrien Smith. So they would have done more than their due diligence in investigating his death.

"Why were you seeing my father, Mrs. Rosings? Dick Ricci, I mean. I...did you know he was involved with other women?"

"You think I wanted more of him than what I got?" she asks with a snort.

I think of her lovely home. Her put-together life. Her beautiful things. "No. I suppose not."

I feel her glancing at me. "When you get to be as old as I am—"

"I will," I say shortly. "Either that or I'll die. I'd prefer to live."

"Well said," she tells me, sniffing in approval. Or at least I'd like to think it's approval. "I've spent most of my life being serious. Doing what's expected or prudent, and when you see the end approaching, you question all the decisions you've made for other people. I got involved with Dick for no greater reason than because I felt like it. Because life is too short to avoid the things that will give you pleasure. But I was perfectly content for him to live his life and for me to live mine. I will never, ever again sign over my power to another person."

I think about Declan's offer, and about the way he makes me feel alive and so full of wanting I might burst from it.

I don't think I can be as glib as Mrs. Rosings, or that I'll be able to keep him at arm's length, but it doesn't matter. I already know what I've decided.

"What was in the box, Mrs. Rosings?" I ask softly.

"That's between me and the dead," she says.

And I nod, because she's right. Even though I do have every intention of breaching her privacy when the opportunity presents itself. Because I need to know it wasn't her—I need that knowledge for myself as much as anything.

"You know," Mrs. Rosings says contemplatively. "Your perfume smells lovely."

CHAPTER TWENTY-THREE

CLAIRE

"It's stalling again," I say, glancing over at Declan in fright. "What do I do?"

He swears under his breath, something that's happened at least half a dozen times since we started our driving lesson. It's pretty obvious he regrets offering to do this for me, and possibly even meeting me. At this point, I'm starting to take it personally.

I didn't *ask* him to teach me to drive the Jeep. He offered. It's not my fault that I'm not an expert at it after two hours. The only thing I've instantly been good at is baking, and I'm pretty sure that's not going to help me out of this current five-alarm-fire mess.

Truthfully, Declan seemed to bring his bad mood in with him when he showed up at the house earlier. And, sure, maybe it didn't help that Damien was waiting in the living room with me like an overprotective father and cracked jokes about knowing where to bury bodies—at least I hope they were jokes—but, honestly...

I'd been looking forward to seeing him, barely sleeping, and now it feels like he'd rather be anywhere else, and...

And I'm still stalled in front of a green light in the four block radius that passes for downtown Marshall. A woman who pulled up behind me in an enormous Buick honks her horn five times, then rolls past in the left lane. She looks like she's at least eighty and is still wearing curlers in her hair. She flashes me her middle finger as she passes. I'm usually the kind of person to take elder abuse rather than dish it out, but I'm upset enough to reciprocate and wave my index finger around like it's a flag.

"I thought people in small towns were supposed to be friendly," I say, trying not to hyperventilate. There aren't any cars behind the Buick, not yet, but it's only a matter of time. Soon there will be a pileup of them behind me, and I'll probably end up in the Marshall newspaper.

"Common misunderstanding," Declan says, but he looks stressed out too. His temples are shiny from sweat, and his hair is a delicious mess that I'd appreciate more if he weren't acting like a dick. That's another problem: it turns out the air conditioner doesn't work in this beast anymore, and it's a hot day, enough so that I suddenly have more sympathy for the unbaked cupcakes I slip into the oven. "They're shittier to each other, but there's a real community feeling about it."

I try the gas pedal. Nothing happens. Unease slides down my spine. I can feel people watching us from the sidewalks. Oh God, they'll probably have a nickname for me by tomorrow, and I'll only find out because Rex will tell me.

Declan swears again. Then, in a softer voice, he says, "Don't get anxious. You're doing just fine."

"I know I'm not," I say, my voice edged with panic. "If I were doing fine, the car would be moving. What am I doing wrong?"

He layers his hand over mine on the stick shift, and even though my whole body is tense and terrified, I feel his touch pass through me like a wave, turning me liquid for half a second before I remember that we're in the middle of the road, and we're stuck, and—

"We'll get through this together," he says, running his fingers across my hand as he tries to guide me through shifting the gear. "Now..."

I try, but by now my whole body is stiff and awkward with panic, and the awareness of the people watching us is overwhelming. "Oh, this is bad. This is really bad."

"Get out and circle around," he says. "I'm gonna slide in behind the wheel."

"What?" I squawk. Does this mean he thinks I'm incapable of learning? Am I doomed to own this Jeep but never be able to drive it?

"Claire," he says in a low rumble. "Please."

Since we're still stuck in the middle of a road, at a light that has turned red again, I comply.

"Having some car trouble?" asks an older man standing on the road watching us as if we're his favorite episode of the Andy Griffith show. He's wearing a newsboy cap and smoking an honest-to-God pipe even though it has to be five thousand degrees outside. "That thing's a beast. I always told Dick he'd stop up traffic with it. You must be—"

Someone honks their horn behind us, and I realize I'm standing in the middle of the road like a deer caught in the headlights listening to this man try to make casual conversation with me. Coming alive, I wave a hand at him and run around to the passenger seat. "Yep, I'm Dick's biological daughter, Claire," I call out. "Lovely to meet you. Enjoy the smoke."

Declan doesn't look at me until he's got the car moving again. Then he gives me a glance, the corner of his mouth twitching up the slightest bit. "Making friends?"

"Yeah," I say, leaving it at that, because I've decided I'm pissed. The more I think about it, actually, the more pissed I am. Everything he offers on his terms, his way. How is that fair or just? If we weren't in the middle of the road, in a hugely stressful situation, I'd give him the what-for. I'm sick of taking what I'm offered and being told to ask for no more. Besides, he's the one who offered to take me driving. Why should I have to apologize for that?

Declan drives another couple of blocks, then pulls over. "What?" I say, my voice hostile. "Are you going to tell me I'm doing a bad job? Because I realized that when I stalled in the middle of the road."

His eyebrows wing up and he pings his fingers against the wheel. I can see the anxiety playing on his features, the unease. I hate that we're back to this, that the easy playfulness of the other night is gone. It makes me feel so damn tired.

"No," he says, his voice halting. "The other day...you wanted to see the storefront for the old bakery." He nods to a red-and-white-striped awning a couple of cars down, and a gasp escapes me.

Declan smiles for what's maybe the first time today. "Looks like the kind of place that would serve some kick-ass madeleines, don't you think?"

I smile at him, feeling a surge of at least partial forgiveness. It's not his fault he's a shitty driving instructor. After all, it's not like he's a professional. If I were trying to teach a nearly thirty-year-old woman to drive and she kept stalling in the middle of the street, I'd probably be sweating too.

"Let's get out and take a look," he says.

So we do, Declan putting a hand around my back as we make our approach, and even though my back has to feel swampy with sweat, he doesn't pull away. I decide that I don't want him to.

The windows are papered over, so I can't see inside, but there's a little box nailed to the door of the former bakery filled with brochures with the information for the realtor. I don't have the money to rent or buy this place, obviously, unless the insurance payout goes through—or Nicole agrees to sell the house and the sale goes through in record time.

But I've always found excuses not to go after the things I want. So I march up, grab one of the brochures, and stick it in my purse.

I feel Declan come up behind me. He murmurs into my ear, "When you're excited about something, you—"

But I don't get a chance to hear his insight, because someone grunts and says, "Dec."

I turn back to see a man with buzzed blond hair and a pair of rimless glasses that probably would have passed Nicole's coolness test. He's maybe thirty or forty, but it's impossible to tell because there's something ageless about him. Although he's not tall, he had broad shoulders and looks like he spends a lot of time at the gym.

"Mark," Declan says, so at least they've established that they know each other's names. Then it clicks: Mark is the man who owns the restaurant Declan brought plant starters to a week and a half ago.

"I saw your friend take one of the flyers," he says, nodding to me with the interested look of someone who's used to knowing everything but doesn't know me. He knows who I am, though, I'm guessing. Probably everyone in town does. "Place went off the market a few days ago."

All of the sunken bakes I've ever made seem to have returned to exact their revenge on my gut. Of course it already got snapped up. The location's perfect, and it even has that adorable awning.

"Oh," I say softly. It's not even a word, really, but it's all I've got right now.

Declan swears under his breath, then nods in my direction. "This is Claire. Claire, this is Mark."

After we exchange nods, Mark says, "Nicole's your sister?"

"That is my misfortune, yes," I say, even though I'm not altogether sure I mean it anymore.

He nods again. "Your sister asks an awful lot of questions. I'm sorry about your father. Dick was a good guy."

He looks like he means it. Then again, some people are excellent liars.

I nod, very much wanting this interaction to end so I can pout, and he takes the hint and delivers a third nod before moving on. He looks back once, though, maybe because he's curious about why Declan and I are here together, checking out someone else's shop.

My heart breaks a little, knowing this place will never be mine. It wasn't going to be mine anyway, but the possibility had been there. I'd been able to see it in my head.

"I'm sorry," Declan says, taking my hand, and the shock of his touch courses through me. There's an entreaty in his gaze. "Last time, it took them a year to fill it, so I thought..."

"It's okay," I say brightly. "It's probably too small, anyway. I'd obviously have a full house around the clock, and you don't want people to be packed in together like sardines."

"Course not." He runs his thumb over my wrist. "What you should really be looking at is a baking warehouse. You could be making shitty, mass-produced snack cakes."

"The dream."

But my voice hitches as I say it.

Something passes over Declan's face, and he leads me back over to the Jeep, which I've decided I loathe. I feel something crack inside of me when he doesn't even suggest that I slide behind the wheel.

It's irrational, since he just implied that I could open a successful bakery on my own, but my first thought is—*he doesn't believe in me*. There's a stoic, resigned look on his face that seems to validate it.

We hit a red light at the end of the downtown area, and this time Declan's the one who stalls. I watch as a bead of sweat travels down his forehead, and even though we're stuck in the middle of the road again, and the car is hot, and both of us are obviously in bad moods, part of me wants to lick it. Is it gross to want to lick someone's sweat?

It is, I decide, and it's given me a different reason to be mad at

Declan, because he drives me the kind of crazy where I actually want to lick sweat.

"Is the car the problem?" I ask. "Maybe the car's the problem."

"The car's *not* the problem," he snaps back, messing with the stick shift and the pedals. That third pedal is what makes this so tricky, I decide. Too much going on. There's a reason I've never been interested in having a threesome.

"So *I'm* the problem?"

He doesn't respond, just keeps fiddling, and we start moving again. I feel anger building inside of me again, like a bread dough rising—although each silent minute is like an hour, expanding the lump of dough by two, three. I'd like to let him have it, I decide, although I'm not going to do it while we're driving the potential death trap car.

Neither of says anything else until we reach the driveway leading to Dick's house. Damien's car is gone, so Declan pulls into the premium spot, closest to the house.

Then he breathes out a sigh, taps the wheel as if deciding something, and unbuckles his belt before turning to me in his seat. "There's something I've got to tell you."

He looks bothered by it, maybe even tormented. It unfairly makes him hotter, which makes me madder.

This is it, I think as I unfasten my belt. He's going to tell me that he's decided it was a terrible idea to kiss me. He'll tell me that we shouldn't do this, and we *can't*. Logically, I know it's probably for the best if I don't start a no-strings arrangement with a man who lives next door to me, but I feel a crushing sense of disappointment. It's ridiculous to feel this awful about the end of something that never actually got off the ground, but I do. Worse than I have about any of my real breakups.

And all that awfulness only makes me madder, at Declan and also on myself, because I knew better, and I went and pinned my hopes on him all the same.

"I had no business offering to teach you how to drive," he starts, passing a hand back through that dark, black-as-pitch hair. It tumbles back down so quickly he shouldn't have bothered.

Here it comes...

I try to brace myself, but my heart is beating fast. So fast I'm surprised it's not filling the car with its percussive beat.

"I had no business doing it because when I offered I didn't know how to drive stick shift."

My mouth drops open.

"I figured it would be easier to learn," he continues, acting tormented, "but Rex has spent the past two afternoons trying to teach me. I'm not a natural, not even close, so it's fucked up of me to try to tell you what to do when I barely know how myself. I just..." He taps the wheel again. "I wanted to help you, and I made the offer before thinking it through. I didn't want to let you down. But I did, obviously, and it was irresponsible as hell. I'm so damn mad at myself."

"Why didn't you let Rex teach me directly?" I ask. "He probably wouldn't have minded." I'm still struggling to process this information. A second ago, I thought Declan was trying to push me away again. I was ready to rage at him and then go inside and rage-eat a whole pint of ice cream. But it turns out he's been spending his free time trying to learn something so he could have the dubious pleasure of teaching me. It's...

No one's ever done something like that for me before. *Ever.* Doug wouldn't even make me a photocopy of his notes from a meeting I'd missed. And this man, who is so much more than him, learned how to drive stick shift for me.

Declan's jaw works, then he says, "Because *I* wanted to be the one who helped you. I didn't want to let some other guy get to do it. I know how stupid that—"

I grab the front of his shirt and pull him to me. That's all it takes, a tug—and his lips are on mine again. *Where they belong.*

They're soft but demanding, and the brush of his short beard against my face sends sensation rushing across my skin. It's such a relief, such an immediate pleasure, that a pleased sound escapes me. He must like that, because he leans in closer, his hand burying into my hair, tugging on the nerve endings in a way that makes me gasp again. He swallows the sounds, his mouth still on me, *always* on me, and my hand scrabbles under his shirt, needing to touch his flesh again. His chest is as hard and hot as I remember, a little sweaty, and I want all of it. All of *him*. I'm keyed up, blood boiling, and it's a little like that moment in that plane...adrenaline is pounding through me, wanting a release, making me want him more.

He lifts his mouth from mine, finally, but only so he can kiss my neck. It must be sweaty, but I can't find it in myself to be self-conscious, I'm too full of need to think about anything but getting Declan all over me. Inside of me. His mouth travels down to the crux of my collar bone, and he buries his face into the top of my shirt, like he can't be bothered to even pull away for the half a second it would take him to push it down.

I don't think I've ever been with a man who's so desperate for me he can't help himself, and it feels like my whole body is an ember of burning need. His hand travels up my thigh, up my skirt, and dear God, I'm going to explode if he touches me there...

His fingers feather across the top of my panties, and that slight contact makes me quake.

"Declan," I breathe against his hair. "I can't believe you did that for me."

"It would have been more impressive if I'd been any good at it," he says with a soft smile, his fingers brushing over me again, making me squirm.

"I guess I'm easily impressed. I need you. *Now*."

His answer is to pull away slightly, leaving my shirt pressed down from the pressure of his head against it.

"I need *you*."

"Thank God."

A smile lifts his lips slightly, a wicked smile, a *warm* smile, and then he kisses me again, soft and then hard, claiming my lips, and his hand stays under my skirt, stroking me through the fabric—and I know he has to feel how wet I am. How eager.

I half expect myself to be embarrassed by it, but again, I'm not. For the first time in my life, I'm not self-conscious about wanting something dirty.

He pulls back, which I don't like, then says something I do. Breathing as hard as I am, his dark hair dipping over his forehead, his eyes burning for me, he says, "Come with me."

Right now, I'd follow him off a cliff.

I press another kiss to his lips, then another, because it's a freedom I don't take for granted. I can kiss my hot neighbor now. I can kiss him, and no one but the two of us and the birds will ever know. "Okay."

He's out of the Jeep so quickly I almost get whiplash, and he comes around and opens my door, helping me down.

"Are we going inside?" I ask, my pulse quickening. I've thought about bringing him upstairs to my room. About stripping him down in my sad bedroom so I can have a positive memory attached to the space in addition to broken perfume bottles, lost suitcases, and the ghost of the deadbeat father I'll never meet.

"Yes," he says taking my hand. He weaves his fingers through mine, and the feeling of his calluses—put there by hard, sweaty work—makes me melt. He starts walking away from the car in long, capable strides, and I go with him. He doesn't lead me toward either of the houses, though, but down his side of the hill.

I give him a sidelong glance, and he explains, "There's something I'd like to show you."

"Is it your dick?" I say, sort of joking. Mostly not.

"You want to see my dick?" he asks, giving me a look that burns me to a crisp.

"*Yes.*"

He shakes his head slightly, the longer pieces of his hair resettling with the movement. Hopefully that's just surprise and not a no. I don't think I could handle a no. "Fuck me."

"I'm trying to. I've *been* trying to."

He stops and licks his lips, and I remember that armrest again, how he cracked it like it was an egg. Maybe I'm being naïve with him, and with Mrs. Rosings—trusting that they are what they seem to be even though there's evidence they both have secrets. But Damien was right. We all have secrets—each and every one of us—and I don't have it in me to be afraid of him. I want him to handle me, and handle me well. I want to give myself the kind of experience that won't fade into a disappointing memory halfway through.

"I've been thinking about you nonstop," he says, his gaze pulsing into me. "Ever since we got off that plane."

I lift onto my toes to kiss him again. He puts his big, strong hands around my waist and lifts me. And I squeal and wrap my legs around his waist, feeling his hand curl around my ass to support me.

He starts moving like that, as if I weigh nothing, and starts climbing down the hill. I kiss his chin and then the side of his face. I kiss just below his ear, and his hand moves over my ass. I am more anticipation than person, my whole body throbbing with need. My body wants him, and wants him *badly*. But it's not just my body. I've collected little bits of him over the past couple of weeks, like a crow searching for shiny objects and using them to tell a story full of missing pieces.

He keeps moving, humming slightly in his throat as I kiss his face, his beard, his lips.

"We're here," he says, setting me down, and to my surprise, my legs actually carry me instead of turning instantly to gelatin. In front of us is a little glass-encased greenhouse at the bottom of the hill—partially hidden from above by the trees in between our location and the houses. The door is metal, made to look like vines crowding together.

"I didn't even know this was down here," I say with a gasp.

"I don't advertise it," he says, giving me a significant look.

My eyes widen. "Because this is where you grow all the weed."

"Among other things," he confirms.

Alarm threatens to fizzle my high. "You grow other drugs?"

He shakes his head. "Drugs aren't the only plants worth growing, Claire."

Eyes dancing, he opens the door and stands back to let me enter. I step inside and gasp. Because I asked about flowers, and here are some next-level flowers. Orchids, arcing up in fat purple and yellow bunches. A pot of pink begonias with yellow centers like eyes. And dozens and dozens of dahlias.

"Declan..." I pause, turning to face him as he steps in behind me and closes the door. "This is amazing. You grew all of this yourself?"

"Yes. No offense, but I'm not going to sacrifice them for some rich guy's wedding. They were my mother's favorites."

"This place is partly for *them*," I say, understanding clicking into place. "For your family."

He shrugs. "Some of the stuff in here is. It's my way of missing people, I guess. You can mostly grow the same plants here as in Pennsylvania. Weather's different, but not much."

Emotion swells my throat.

He can't tell me much about his past, for whatever reason, but this is his way of sharing himself. Of giving me as much as he can of the person he left behind when he came here.

And, shit, I can feel myself tipping into something that's going to be more dangerous to me than Doug or any of the dumbasses who came before him ever could be.

CHAPTER TWENTY-FOUR

DECLAN

What am I doing?

Sitting next to Claire in the Jeep earlier, stopped in the middle of the damn road, I felt the full extent of my stupidity. Who the fuck offers to teach someone a skill they don't possess themselves?

A pussy-whipped idiot, I can hear Seamus saying, shaking his head in a better-you-than-me way.

It's not like me to get tied up in knots over a woman—you could say I've made an art of avoiding it. But here I am, in the thick of it, and I brought her down *here*.

Other than a few things spaced out around my house, this is the only truly personal place I've allowed myself. The only spot where I can be who I am—Declan O'Malley, not Declan James. And I wanted to take her here. To fuck her down here, sure, but also to show her this place that's mine. To prove to her, and maybe to myself, that I may be a man who breaks things, but I can build them too.

As we walk inside, I can't stop casting glances at her, trying to see this place through her eyes. Her eyes don't hide the way she's feeling ever—in the Jeep, I felt her rage toward me, and it fed my own, directed at myself. And now...I see the understanding sparking in their golden depths. She knows this place is important to me; she understands why. And it's that ability in her to understand what's unsaid that makes her so special. It makes me want to disassemble all of the walls I've built to keep Declan O'Malley from view. That still scares me—it shakes me to my core—but it also fills me with wonder. With warmth. With *need*.

I lead her over to the hip height table on the far side of the greenhouse, where there's a big tub of rosemary. "You know, it took me a second to understand what Nicole and Damien were talking about the other day with the Chanel No. 5."

"Oh, please let's never talk about that again. I broke the travel bottle in my bedroom, and it's haunting me. It'll never go away."

I take her hand again and run it gently over the plant. "But this is what you smell like to me. Rosemary and apples. It reminds me of the house where we grew up. We had big rosemary bushes on either side of the door."

She beams up at me, bathing me in her light, and I'm struck again by how generous she is in sharing it. I pluck a piece of the rosemary off the plant and step into her space, lifting it to her lips. She opens them for me, soft and pink and so fucking delicious, and I feed her the piece of rosemary. My dick is so hard it hurts. The sight of Claire in this space is intoxicating. Exhilarating.

I lower my head and kiss her, and she tastes of rosemary. I need her in this place—I need her *now*. It feels like I've been waiting for years instead of only a couple of weeks.

I guide her down to sit on the table next to the pot of rosemary. Her knees splay open naturally, as if she knows what I need and has a mind to give it to me. Good. I get down on my knees beside the table and she gasps as I tug down her panties from beneath her skirt. It's hot as hell to see her like this, completely dressed other than her panties.

I should say something, but she gave me the green light, and right now all I can think about is burying my face in her and then burying my dick in her. It's been all I can think about for days.

Maybe I can finally exorcise her from my mind—or at least recapture a few of my brain cells so I can function again.

I spread her thighs wide and pull her to me, breathing in the scent of rosemary and flowers and Claire. Just Claire. I'm in trouble, and I know it, and I don't give a flying fuck, because I'm kissing her soft thighs. She's so wet for me. Wet because she's been fantasizing about fucking me, and that's the greatest gift I don't deserve. I'm selfish, because I'm going to take it anyway. And, if I'm very lucky, take it again and again. As much as I can have of her, for as long as I can have her. Because she won't stay. She may not see it right now—that Agnes bitch may have blinded her—but she's the kind of woman who's going places. I'm guessing that's why she never got the promotion she wanted, never got a boost. Because you don't terrorize people into wearing your favorite perfume every day if you're not secretly afraid of them. If you don't worry that if you fail to keep them in line, you'll walk into the office one day, and they'll be sitting in your chair.

She's going to have her dream job, dream life—and if there's one thing I know about myself, it's that I'm going nowhere at all. After what I took, I'm lucky to be alive, so the small existence I've carved out will have to be enough.

Right now, parked between Claire Rainey's thighs, it feels like enough. Because this is a big moment, the kind that will leave a mark on me—a *scar*, because even though she's going to move on, I'll still going be thinking about her. About her laugh, and her smile, and her smell, and the soft skin of her thighs as I kiss my way up to the place I've dreamed of tasting.

I have it bad, but I'll worry about that later, when I don't have my mouth on her. Her hand weaves in my hair as I make my way to her center, and a sigh escapes me as I tug her closer to me by the thighs. I suck and lick and savor her. And she still seems to taste like rosemary. Her hand flexes in my hair as I show her the attention she deserves, and she says, "Oh my God, Declan. You don't need to—"

I pull her closer by the thighs, burying my face where it wants to be, because she has to understand I want this as much as she does —and also that I don't intend to be one more lazy asshole who's going to let her down or pretend the female orgasm is a myth.

Her hand fists in my hair until it hurts, and one of her shoes falls off. I slip the other off as I stroke her with my tongue and then gently run my teeth over her clit. She rocks toward me, nearly falling off the table, but I hold her steady—almost shaking with the need for her to come around my tongue. I need to feel the change and know I was the one who brought it about. To know that I can do this one thing right. I need to see the look on her face when she tumbles over the edge, and I need to kiss it. To capture it so it can become part of me.

"Declan, I'm going to—"

She bucks against the table, and the rosemary pot crashes to the ground, breaking, and the scent of rosemary is everywhere—and she *is* coming, I can feel it. I feel her body moving with it, clenching around my tongue. I pull her even closer, until she's nearly sitting on my face, burying myself in her taste, in her scent, in her pretty pink center.

She's making a sound I want to bottle, and her hand is still tugging on my hair. Finally her body relaxes, and I pull back so I can see her face, so I can kiss her and let her know how fucking good she tastes.

She's looking at me with wonder in her eyes. "That was...I didn't know it could be like that."

"It's always going to be like that."

The words fall from me, because I want them to be true. I want her to be mine, and I want to keep her. Even if I know that I shouldn't let a woman like her, a bright, sparkling light, hitch her star to a man who has to hide in the shadows.

The expression on her face slips into worry much quicker than I'd like as she eyes the broken pot on the floor, the dirt. "I ruined your plant."

I run my fingers over the bottom of her tank top, then pull it off in one quick gesture, revealing the blue lace of her bra, blue like the Carolina sky. It's pretty, but not as pretty as what's beneath it, so I take that off too, my mouth dry again, my dick a constant ache.

"Fuck the plant," I say, kissing my way across her chest, pausing to suck in one perfect nipple and run my tongue over it. "Rosemary grows like a weed."

"So my hair smells like weeds?" she asks, her voice breathy.

I glance up as I release her nipple. "I happen to like weeds."

Her hand reaches out and grabs the bottom of my shirt, the way she did it earlier, as if she always wants to have her hands on my chest. "And I'd like it if I weren't the only one half naked."

"Do what you'd like with me," I say in a challenge. Because I need her to undress me, to touch me. To want me.

Her eyes light up, and she leans back slowly. Then she tugs my shirt off, getting it caught around my neck for a second, making us both laugh. Once it's off, she runs her palms over my chest, her touch seeming to shoot straight down to my cock but also sink in deep. Because it means something.

Then she steps off the table and reaches down to unbutton my jeans. Then she unzips them. And everything inside of me is attuned to her as she lowers them down with a whisper of fabric. She pushes down my boxer briefs next, and I toe off my shoes so I can step out of the clothes. She's in nothing but her skirt, a little slip of a thing, and I'm completely naked. So fucking ready for her. Needy and hard and lost.

"You're beautiful," she says softly, wrapping a hand around my dick.

I'd laugh if, again, she didn't currently have her hand around my dick. "*I'm* beautiful?" I ask, stepping forward, crowding her. "You're so fucking beautiful to me, it's hard to believe you exist. Maybe the last couple of weeks only happened in my head, and we're still on that plane."

Her lips part, her hand comes around my waist, settling on top of my ass, my hard dick caught between us. She may not even be conscious she's doing it, but her hand starts moving on my back, rising and falling, her touch radiating through me. "And I have a hard time believing you like me that much."

"Then I'll have to keep showing you," I say, although I feel an instant dislike toward all the people who've pulled her down.

I pull down her skirt and fist her hair, rosemary-scented sunshine, kissing her hard as I back her toward the glass wall. Her lips part for me, and they press back in a bid for more. A flowering vine waves through the air next to us as we reach the glass. She breaks the kiss and angles her head back to look at me. "You brought me here as a way of showing me, didn't you?" she says, her head tipped up to me. "This is your palace."

"And in this one place I am king," I say with a self-deprecating smile. The truth is, I could have been a different kind of king if I'd had a mind to. One with power. But instead I ran.

"Then fuck me where you're king," she says, and I'm so turned on I'm surprised my heart doesn't stop hammering in my chest. I turn back toward the heap of our clothes and claim a condom from my pants pocket. I roll it on, watching her, standing there against the wall of my greenhouse, in the middle of the plants that saved me.

I step toward her, drawn in. Not fully in control of myself.

She meets me halfway, and I pick her up again, needing the feel of her against me to remind me that we're both real.

I kiss her, and kiss her, and I pick her up and carry her back to that table. "Thank you for giving us space," I say with a smile that's probably as feral as my voice sounds. I lower her back down to the table, smiling at the sight of her spread out before me, her long blonde hair tumbling off the side of the table, her rose-tipped tits bared, the vee between her legs ending in short trimmed blonde curls. The table's just big enough for most of her body, her legs spread off to either side. I step in between them, looking down at her. Taking her in. She's beautiful, more beautiful than every flower in this greenhouse, or the view from my deck.

"I'm thoughtful like that," she says, the last word coming out with an "*oh*," as I reach down and rub her still-sensitive clit with my palm. Her hand reaches for my dick again, and she runs her hand over it.

"I'm going to need that back," I say, capturing her hand and pinning it next her head. From the look in her eyes, she likes that.

"I hope that means you're going to give me what I want," she says.

I run my hand over my length, line myself up. Find myself looking into her eyes as I sink into her, a couple of inches at a time. Wanting to let her adjust. Wanting it to last. Wanting to fuck her hard, without restraint, but holding back.

I feel her clenching around me already, her body pulsing. "*Declan*," she says. "*Declan*."

And for a minute, as I lower down to kiss her, my cock captured in her slick heat, I feel like a fucking king. I release her arm and stand back up, wrapping her thighs around my waist, tugging them for leverage as I pull out and thrust in again. It feels so good I'm having trouble pacing myself, already feeling the tingling sensation low in my back that my need for her is going to send me over the edge sooner than I'd like. Then again, almost anything would be sooner than I'd like, because I can't think of anywhere I'd rather be than here, inside of her. I bring one hand to her clit, needing her to come with me if I'm going to be pushed over the edge. I have to give her enough to make an impression.

"Oh my *God*," she says, reaching for me, and I pull her up so she's sitting and I'm standing, her legs still wrapped around my waist as she rocks against my cock—and I lower my head to nuzzle her tits, because I haven't given them enough attention, and they deserve it. They deserve a damn parade held in their honor. And then I kiss her again—a deep, searching kiss, like I might find the meaning of life inside of her mouth, and fuck, maybe I will. Because I feel closer to it than ever before. I feel meaning hovering around me and her, whereas before there was just being.

Leave it to me to become poetic over a woman after all these years of dicking around and avoiding anything that might matter.

"I'm going to come again," she whispers in my ear, as if it's a secret.

"Good," I say. "Because I'm not going to last much longer."

I give her another thrust, my hand working her in time with my dick, and I feel her fall her apart around me, and this time I get to watch all of it—her eyes wide, as if I've surprised her pleasantly, her pink lips parted, and her hair a beautiful mess.

I feel like one lucky bastard.

One lucky bastard who just opened a door he should have kept padlocked.

And the way she clenches around me and throws her head back, as if the pleasure coursing through her is too powerful for her to hold it up straight, is what throws me over the edge. I pump inside of her one more time, and I'm gone. I lower my head to her neck, breathing her in, and then she's kissing my hair. "So much for the myth of the female orgasm," she says.

And I do something I'm not sure I've ever done seconds after coming—I laugh with her.

CHAPTER TWENTY-FIVE

DECLAN

"You're sure you want to do this?" I ask Claire as I slide into the passenger seat of the Jeep after loading up the back.

It's Friday afternoon, and I need to install a couple of burning bushes at a business in Asheville. Claire got off work early, so she offered to come help. I didn't say no because I can't seem to get enough of her. I want all my days saturated with Claire, to help make up for the blank, long days I've spent without her—*and all the days you'll be without her in the future,* an unhelpful voice whispers in my head.

We decided to take the Jeep, which we practiced driving yesterday afternoon. Both of us have gotten the hang of it, but I want to make sure she's totally comfortable with it before she brings it out alone. Granted, there's dick-all I can do from the passenger seat, as we've both seen, but it makes me feel better to be there—to have eyes on her. To be able to talk her through any tough spots, something I'm better at now that I'm not gripped with the guilt of having agreed to teach her something I suck at.

"Yes," she says resolutely as she pulls out of the driveway without hesitating or stalling. Pride fills my chest. "I have to admit I'm not used to playing in the dirt, though. My dad's a bit of a clean freak, and we didn't exactly have a garden. The only plants we had were the windowsill kind."

I layer my hand over her thigh, and she glances at me, her eyes sparkling. "We both make things," I say. "When you mix things in your kitchen and put them in the oven, or fry them, you're creating something out of smaller parts. You're making them into something bigger, better, than they could have been on their own. It feels like that when I plant things too, like I'm bringing possibilities to life. I want to share that with you."

She shakes her head, giving me a sidelong glance that blazes through, her eyes big and gold and warm for me. "You always say you don't have a way with words, yet you keep proving yourself wrong. Thank you, Declan. I'm glad you're sharing this with me."

So am I. But even though I've been happy for the last couple of days—happier than I can ever remember being—I feel on edge. Part of it is because I'm worried about Rosie. I spoke with her last night, and she acted like quitting the job was no big deal—she doesn't like to be tied down, never has—but I sense a greater discontent behind it. She's up to something, and I don't know what, and I'm too far away to do anything about it. But that's not the only reason I feel like I'm walking the razor-side of a knife. It can't go on like this. I can't keep letting Claire in without *actually* letting her in. But it's impossible to tell her everything, isn't it?

Still. I feel the pulse of wanting to. Of wanting to lay myself bare before her and let her decide whether to stab me or expiate me.

I breathe in a jagged breath, taking in her rosemary scent, and let it out, calmer already. I feel Claire watching me as she pulls onto the highway to Asheville. "You know, I've barely spent any time in Asheville," she says, "other than going to that lawyer's office and a couple of stores. Do you like going there?"

"Sometimes. But I like Marshall better. It's...it fills me with calm, being out here with nature. Having the mountains in my backyard."

She smiles at me, because she knows that already—she probably knew it within hours of meeting me. "That's because it's where you belong. Sometimes we're not born where we belong, and we have to find it."

I turn a little in my seat, needing to see more of her, my hand still on her leg, soaking in her warmth. "And how about you, Claire? Have you found it?"

I want her to say she has—that she's found it here in the mountains, with me, and maybe even with Nicole. But I'm also scared of that possibility. I'm scared of showing her all the stains on my soul.

"I think I'm in the process of finding it," she says, smiling at me, her expression filling me with hope edged with worry. "Maybe that process will be complete when I fall in a bucket of dirt."

"Things always seem clearer to me when I have my hands in dirt," I say with a grin, letting my fingers slide over her thigh. Wanting to cling to the levity to keep from falling over the edge. Wanting to hold on to her for as long as I can.

We talk easily for the rest of the drive, and when we get into the city, I direct Claire to the spa that's the site for the installation. She parks in the lot of the small building with the sign shaped like a lotus flower. The bushes I've brought will go to either side of the door.

After we speak with the business owner, an older woman with a soft demeanor, we get to work, unloading the shovels and fertilizer, followed by the bushes, their roots still wrapped in moist burlap.

"Aren't they a little plain?" Claire asks me in an undertone, like she's worried the woman might hear us through the brick or glass and get insulted. Or possibly that some of her clients will—the spa is still open for business, giving people manicures and pedicures, and whatever the hell else they do.

She's right. The bushes are green and full, but not particularly decorative. But they're much more than they seem.

I take her hand and run it over the profusion of green leaves. "I wouldn't call them plain," I tell her, leaning into her ear, "they're lush and green, and you already know how I feel about green things, but in a few months the leaves will change. The trees will be a sea of orange and yellow and green and red, and these bushes will reveal their secret. They're called burning bushes, because in the fall, they'll look like they're on fire. They'll turn scarlet, and every last leaf will look like a budding flower."

She glances up at me, her lips parting prettily. "That's beautiful."

My lips tip upward for half a second. "You're like that, you know. I feel like you've been changing color before my eyes, becoming more yourself. It's beautiful to watch."

She lifts up on her toes and kisses me, softly and sweetly, and I feel the warmth of it swallow me up. Putting an arm around her waist, I say, "Now, Claire Rainey, it's time to put you to work."

It's sweaty, dirty work, and by the time we're done, I can tell Claire's tired. But we did it right, and the bushes look upright and healthy, like they'll take to their new home just fine.

"You were right," she says, grinning at me. "They're not plain. They add something that was needed here. Something that was missing."

Life, brimming to either side of the door, making the place inviting. Spas are supposed to be relaxing, or so Rosie tells me—she'd know, since she's worked at one—and we've made this one more so.

I can tell Claire understands the feelings coursing through me —the sense of worth this gives me. Bringing life to the world. Making it more beautiful. And I take off my gloves and pull her close.

"I'm so dirty and sweaty," she says, laughing.

"So am I," I say into her hair. "Let's go home, and I'll draw you a bath and make you dinner." Because I want to take care of her. I might not be any good in the kitchen, but I need to show her how much I appreciate everything she's been doing for me. I need to let her know how I'm feeling without telling her the things I dread sharing.

She glances up at me in surprise. "You want to take me to your house?"

"The hard thing will be getting me to let you leave," I say with a smile, halfway meaning it.

"That means something to you."

"*You* mean something to me." And then I kiss her again, letting her know how true it is. How she's cut to the core of me. How badly I want to keep her.

CHAPTER TWENTY-SIX

CLAIRE

"I feel like I'm a teenager about to get caught by a security guard for smoking on school grounds," I say contemplatively, leaning into Declan's chest. I might be addicted to his chest—it's so hard yet warm, so *capable*. I'd destroy all of his shirts if I could get away with it. He's in nothing but grey sweatpants right now, and I feel like I should write a letter to the female equivalent of *Penthouse*.

Four and a half days have passed since the greenhouse. At the time, that was easily the hottest experience of my life, but he's already co-opted the top five, then the top fifteen. We've driven the Jeep together. Planted bushes together. Made dinner and baked madeleines that would make an American weep and a French person shrug. Snuggled our way through stupid movies, talked until midnight. He even brought me on a hike with Rocket yesterday, on which I very notably did not kill myself.

He's let me into his house—his sanctuary, where he's invited no one else. I haven't spent the night there yet, but I've seen the photos of his brother and sister he has on display, laughing together. Of the greenhouse he had with his mother. And he hasn't tried to hide them or tuck them away. He's told me about them.

The one thing he hasn't told me is his secret, the one that's required all these smoke screens, but I haven't pushed because I know that it's already required so much trust on his part to give me what he has. To show me this side of him. Maybe, with more time, he'll finally be comfortable showing me the rest.

I hope so, because I have to admit that I'm falling for him. Falling *hard* and fast and deep for this beautiful, complicated man who both speaks in poetry and can be delightfully dirty.

It doesn't hurt that we've had lots and lots of sex.

I've become positively bohemian, because while he's rocking the only sweatpants look, I don't have on underwear or a bra on under my dress. In the past, I might have been scandalized by myself, but it feels right—it feels *incredible.*

We're out on his deck now, the one my biological father used to sneak women out to. Both of us are reclined in a single lounge chair, my back to Declan's front—a perfect position for me to feel that he's half hard.

I have to admit, Dick knew the right way to seduce a woman. It's a beautiful view, not interrupted by ugly, half-dead trees with gnarled trunks the way ours is.

"You were the good girl in school, weren't you?" Declan asks with amusement. "I'll bet you arranged all of the bake sales."

"I did," I admit. "And you were the bad boy, corrupting all the good girls behind the bleachers."

"Maybe, but I never wanted to corrupt anyone. I always thought it was bullshit in *Grease* when Sandy gave herself a makeover. She was fucking perfect the way she was. But if you want to smoke a joint, we smoke a joint. I'm not about to tell you what to do."

He hands me the joint we're smoking, and I take it, choking a little when I inhale. The joint was my idea. Because I *was* a good girl in school. And out of it. And every day of my life until I got fired for something that wasn't my fault. And being a good girl, a girl who listened and said sorry for things I didn't do ...it never really did all that much for me.

Truthfully, the blunt's not doing much for me either. Or at least I don't feel like it is. I'm already riding the high of Declan. I've been riding it for days now, and it seems to just keep getting better.

He rubs my back, then takes the blunt, stubbing it out in an ashtray. "You know, I got something for you."

My eyes widen in disbelief. "You did?"

"It's not a big deal."

"Let me be the judge of that," I say, glancing over my shoulder at him.

He smirks at me. "You'll have to get up if you want me to get it."

"But I think I'd like to lay against your naked torso for the next month or two." *Maybe forever.* Sighing dramatically, I get up and watch him disappear into the house, his sweatpants riding low.

I melt back into the chair, my mind a pleasant fuzz, and he's back a couple of minutes later, holding something behind his back. He looks a little embarrassed, the way he does when he's alarmed by something and doesn't think he should be. Or when he does something sweet but doesn't want to be thanked for it.

Too bad.

"You're being ve-*ry* mysterious."

He smiles and hands me a small, hard case, longer than it is wide. I glance up at him in surprise, then snap it open and find a pair of reading glasses with tortoise-shell frames and a sticker saying they have a strength of plus one-point-five.

I gasp, then take them out. "You've given me the gift of sight!"

Actually, they're not going to help me much now—it's reading things close to my face that's the problem, but I can't think of the last time a man did something like this for me.

Because a man has *never* done something like this for me.

"Wait a second," I say, lifting a finger. "How'd you know my prescription?"

"You told us the other day when you were drunk," he said, his mouth an amused line.

"Oh. I kind of remember that."

He reaches out his hand for them, and I hand them over. Then he gently slides them onto my face, his fingers sending cascades of pleasure through me as they carefully brush my hair behind my ears.

"Do I look like a bug?"

"Not even a little." He sits back down and pats his lap. "Come here."

He doesn't need to tell me twice. I straddle his lap and am instantly distracted by his perfect tattooed chest, bracketed by two muscular arms. "God, you're pretty."

He laughs and shakes his head. "I think we know how pot affects you now. I don't dislike it."

"No," I say, giving his arm a shove and then keeping my hand wrapped around it. "It doesn't affect me at all."

"Of course not. Are you going to wear glasses when you have your bakery?"

"Let's be honest," I say, feeling deflated. "I'm probably never going to have one."

He angles his head, studying me, *seeing* more than I intended to show him. He has a habit of doing that, but it's balanced by the vulnerability he's shown me. "You're not just saying that because the place on Main Street was already rented, are you?"

"I know you have a different interpretation of things, but Agnes didn't believe I could pull it off," I say. "She'd be in a position to know, wouldn't she?" I instantly feel like a bit of a baby, talking about my old boss as if she's an adult and I'm a child. As if she can still tell me what to do. But there's no denying that part of me still feels that way. She's *the* Agnes Lewis, and I'm no one. A woman who won't even wear the reading glasses she needs unless she gets permission from her boss.

"Nope. I'm sticking to my interpretation. She didn't want to let you go. I don't know her, obviously, but she doesn't strike me as someone who likes being outshined."

I gape at him. "You think *I* could outshine Agnes Lewis? You're definitely high."

He gives a wry shake of his head. "Nah. Doesn't affect me like that. And I *know* you could. You don't see it, but everyone else does. There's something about you that draws people in. You even thawed Mrs. Rosings."

"I forgot to tell you what I found out about Mrs. Rosings the other day," I say, still holding his arm like it's a stress toy. Truthfully, for me, it is. "Do you know what they call her in town?"

"Nah, I don't pay attention to that stuff. Never have."

I tell him about her three husbands and the black widow claim, and he rolls his eyes when I say it was Rex who told me.

"Rex is a good guy, but he gossips like a twelve-year-old girl half the time."

"I think I should object to that, on behalf of twelve-year-old girls."

He lifts his eyebrows. "I have a little sister. You can't hide the truth from me. I know all about what Tracy said about Rob at the home game."

I snort. "Must have made an impression."

"Things that are repeated a thousand times typically do." He wraps a lock of my hair around his finger, and I feel the tingle at my scalp, and a warm, syrupy feeling inside of me, like I was transformed into a tall stack of pancakes.

I think of his sister. I've seen him shoot off several texts to her over the last few days, and I know he talked to her the other night. "You miss your brother and sister."

"Yeah." He runs a hand back through his hair. "Not just that, though. I miss being a part of something bigger."

I angle my head, studying him. "You could always join the Tribe of Light."

"No thanks." He puts his hands around my hips, and I barely stop myself from dry-humping him like a teenager. I'm infatuated with him, completely and utterly. "I'd rather stay here with you."

I lean in to kiss him, only realizing I still have the glasses on as I get close. I move to take them off, but he captures my hand. "I like them."

So I kiss him harder, the bridge of the glasses bumping against him. When I pull back, he says, "You know, I'm still not giving Mrs. Rosings my plants, but I've been thinking about it, and I can probably help you source flowers for the wedding. I've got a friend who has a pretty extensive greenhouse, and he owes me a favor."

"Do you have plant connections across the state?" I ask with a snort. "Like an organized crime ring for plants?"

Something passes over his face, but then he runs a hand over my hair, his fingers ghosting over my scalp. He keeps touching my hair and playing with it. Once upon a time, I used to hate having my hair touched. I'd worried it would make me look mussed or less put together, but when he does it, it feels like there's a hotline from my scalp to the vee between my legs. When he does it, I want to look mussed, used. *His.*

"Something like that," he murmurs.

"The thing is, she admitted the other day that she doesn't even want this wedding to happen. Like, she offered to help her son and his fiancée just so she can sabotage it." I frown. "Now that I think about it, it's kind of offensive that she hired me to help her. Anyway, unless they're really ugly or smelly flowers, like the ones she had me looking for, I'm guessing she's not interested."

"So what you need is a *shitty* flower hookup," he says with amusement. "I might be able to help you there too. Although one person's shitty flower is another person's dream, so she'll want to be careful. My sister loves lavender, and I think it smells like soap."

"Don't be unfair to lavender," I say. "It's the soap that's co-opted its smell, not the other way around." Because I can't help myself, I ask, "What's your sister like?"

I brace myself for him to shut down and turn away. To say I should go home.

He tucks my hair behind my ear and runs his thumb across my bottom lip. "Besides her perfect-texture, subpar-taste madeleines? She's funny. Smart. Not afraid of anything. You'd like each other. You could have boring hour-long conversations about pastries."

He watches me for a moment, his eyes warm, his hand finding my knee, and I think he's going to say something profound. Then he says, "Sun's going down."

"Really?" I ask in disbelief. We've been talking and fooling around all day, pausing only to make sandwiches in his kitchen and feed Rocket. It passed in a blink. This weekend has passed in a panting, life-changing blink.

"Come with me," he says.

"I'm sitting on you. You can't go anywhere unless I let you."

He smiles and slides a hand under my ass, standing and bringing me with him. "You were saying?"

"I'm not complaining."

He carries me to the edge of the deck before setting me down, and I gasp at the sight of the layered colors forming on the horizon, over the mountains. I'd been so focused on him that I'd barely noticed. I glance over my shoulder, feeling a glow inside that matches what's happening in the sky. This is another moment of doing instead of just existing. I feel so exquisitely alive. "It's beautiful, Declan."

"Turn around and hold on to the railing."

His voice is husky and full of promise, and I'm instantly wet as I turn to face the mountains and grip the rail. I feel his hand on my thigh, flipping up my skirt. I feel his breath at my neck as he leans in to kiss me, his teeth nipping me like I'm delicious.

"You're spoiling me, you know," I say, my pulse picking up as his hand finds my slickness. "No one's ever acted like I'm irresistible."

"I'm glad you've only come across stupid men before. But appreciating you isn't the same as spoiling you," he says against my neck, his lips pausing to kiss me again, his dick hard against my back. "You'll know when I'm spoiling you."

I'd thought it was impossible, but I get a little wetter, my whole body arcing back toward him.

"We can't do this out here, can we?" I ask. "What if someone—" I'm cut off by a guttural sound that escapes me as his fingers find a spot that make my joints feel liquid.

"Hang on to the railing. And we can do whatever we'd like. Even if Damien comes back, he won't be able to see us from the front of the house."

He could if he decides to go out on the deck, but I'm not about to say that, because I desperately, desperately don't want him to stop. I hear him pulling something out of his pocket, then there's a rustle. I want it to mean that he's pulled out a condom, but I don't look back, because there's something exciting about not knowing for sure. About not knowing when it's going to happen. He reaches under my shirt and cups my breast, his fingers finding the nipple as he continues to kiss my neck, his other hand finding its way under my skirt again.

I hold on to the railing for dear life, because I feel myself falling. "Lean forward and look at the sky, Claire," he breathes into my ear. "Watch the sun set over the mountains while I fuck you."

So I lean forward and push my butt out, my hands wrapped around the wood. My breath stutters in my chest as he withdraws his fingers—his clever, clever fingers—and then he lines himself up, his warm heat surrounding me. There's so much filthy promise hanging in the air like honey. Then he slowly eases in, stretching me deliciously.

He swears under his breath, then kisses my neck again as he starts moving inside of me. "You're such a *good girl*, Claire. So wet for me."

I think he's halfway teasing me with the good girl comment, and if anyone else had said it, I might have left. But I've never been so needy in my life, arching back to take him deeper, even as I keep my hands on the railing.

He has one callused hand palming my hip, using it as leverage for fucking me, and the other roams over my body, slipping under my clothes to do dirty, delightful things to me, while I hold on for dear life. He kisses my neck, my hair, my cheek, but when I look back at him, desperate for his mouth on mine, he smiles and shakes his head slightly. "I don't want you to miss the sunset. Face forward."

And for some reason that makes me even crazier. I've never been this wild, this undone. I already feel the first quakes of an orgasm pulling at me. *"Declan,"* I say, desperate, although I don't even know for what, because I'm pretty sure I've forgotten every word I've ever learned. *"Declan."*

And he layers one of his hands on top of mine, the other finding my abdomen, as he thrusts in one final time, breathing hard in my ear, and that's all it takes for both of us. I know because my knees melt, and I'm only kept upright by the pressure of his hands on me. He leans into my neck again, his forehead sweaty, and kisses me. Then he's pulling out, which I'd like to object to, but before I can say anything, he turns me around and kisses me hard, his hand finding my hair again. And it hits me that right at this moment, for the first time in my life, I feel precious to a man. It's probably the power of the orgasm that does it, but the thought puts tears in my eyes.

He kisses me once more, softly, then pulls back slightly, his eyes widening when he notices. "Are you okay?"

"Yes, yes," I say, feeling stupid, and wipe at my face. "That was just really, really good."

"So good it made you cry?" he asks, lifting one eyebrow.

"Yes, actually. Don't brag to your friends. I'm told Rex gossips like a teenage girl."

"I would *never*," he says, his tone so adamant I know it's true. Not that I would have believed otherwise. He's a man who knows how to keep his own counsel—and how to keep quiet to protect the people he cares about. For now, anyway, I'd like to think I'm one of them.

I'd like to be one of them forever.

I lift my hand to his jaw and trace it. "I know."

"I need to go take care of the condom," he says. "I'll be right back."

So he could tell I needed a minute without making me ask for it. I watch his back as he goes, noticing the bunching and flexing of the muscles, and I feel the crush of misgiving. In the beginning, I was determined to be cautious with him, but that's gone by the wayside. I like him too much. If he pushes me away now, there's no way it'll be a clean break. As long as I live here, I'll have to see him. Walking his dog. Heading down the hill to the greenhouse. Maybe bringing women home. What'll *that* feel like?

The dull ache in my chest, like someone's been hacking at it with a butter knife, suggests it won't be good.

My phone rings from the small table beside the chair. It's next to the ashtray with the joint, and I get another burst of *what the fuck am I doing?* It's not like me, to let myself have the things I want without first worrying what they might cost.

I pick up the phone and see Lainey's name, then immediately answer. For all I know, she's drunk and on the verge of sending Todd a text that will embarrass her for the next five years. Best friend duties *demand* that I answer, regardless of what's going on with me.

"Hello," I say, my voice a croak.

"Claire," she says in a burst, "have you seen the news? I couldn't believe it. Agnes's burn book got released to the public, and Doug got fired."

CHAPTER TWENTY-SEVEN

CLAIRE

"What?" I ask, lowering down into the chair, shock washing through me. "Start from the beginning."

"You didn't know?" she says, sounding pleased as hell that she gets to be the one to fill me in on the hot gossip.

"I don't know anything, I've been—" *fucking Declan for the past few days,* "—busy." I've told her about the developments with Declan, but she probably doesn't realize just how immersed in him I've been.

Declan returns from inside. When he sees that I'm on the phone, he kisses my forehead and walks back into the house, giving me privacy.

"What happened?" I hiss.

"Well, I don't know everything, but apparently the burn book went live this morning. Of course, Agnes put out a statement saying it was a hoax, but then a bunch of people saw Doug being marched out of the building with a box of his things. Everyone's saying it's real, and he got fired for sucking at his job. It's *all over* the internet."

"What the actual hell?" I ask in disbelief.

I think again about that leather journal, sitting out on Agnes's desk.

About the photocopies tucked into my suitcase.

And I wish that I'd had the balls to do it myself.

Who did?

I can't believe it was actually Doug, even though I suspect he would have had access to it. Why rock the boat? He was Agnes's human pet—the one person who ever got praised by her in meetings. The mascot of Agnes Lewis. He'd have to be *insane* to leak that book.

Insane...

I hear a crunching sound, and when I glance around the side of the house, I see a car pulling into the driveway. It's nearly dark now, but there's enough light left for me to see the two people sitting in the front seat. There's a flash of pink.

I know someone who's bold and more than a little crazy...

I know someone who might hold a grudge against Agnes and Doug, on my behalf.

Could my sister have done this?

My heart starts beating faster; my pulse elevates. I grab my underwear from the side table and tug them on. Then I start trying to put on my bra one-handed and nearly fall.

"Lainey, I have a lot of stuff I need to tell you—a lot—but right now I need to go."

"What?" she practically shrieks. "Wait until you hear what Agnes said about Martha Stewart. And I saw a photo of Doug looking sad! I'm going to text it to you. Maybe we can blow it up and put it on your wall."

"Gross. I don't want a photo of him on my wall."

"What about the bathroom? Ew. No. As I'm saying that, I realize it's gross."

I hold back an almost hysterical laugh. "Look, I'll call you back as soon as I can. I just...everything's all right, but I need to go."

"Okay, you're being extremely mysterious," she says slowly, giving me the chance to fill her in. But I can't. Not until I talk to

Nicole. So I let the silence linger until she sighs and says, "I also need to tell you about quitting. Call me soon."

"I will."

My phone buzzes a second later with an image of Doug holding a cardboard box that's so full it looks on the verge of collapsing. His face is almost comically sad, his mouth drawn down like a caricature. I don't have it in me to feel bad for him. Or Agnes. She used me. She took advantage of my willingness to please and my foolish dream.

I finish putting on my bra, slip on my shoes, and then pause at the back door. Do I knock? It feels weirdly formal considering what Declan just did to me out here, but I don't want to barge into his space without him. I know he values his privacy. I glance inside, but there's no sign of him.

There's a murmuring sound of muted conversation, though, so I enter through the sliding glass door. It opens into a little dining area, attached to the living room and kitchen through open doorways that are too small for me to see more than a rectangle of each space. Rocket pads over to me from the entrance to the kitchen, wagging his tail, so I stoop to pet his head.

"What happened?" Declan says in an undertone. There's a pause, then, "Fuck. *Fuck.*"

I take a step toward the front door, feeling awkward suddenly. Did he forget I was out there? Should I leave from the back?

But Rocket whimpers and pads at my leg, and I hear Declan say, "I've gotta go. I'll call you back."

He steps out of the living room, his whole body humming with agitation. It hits me that he's been relaxed all weekend, his guard down. But it's back full force, and because of that, so is mine—as if we were in a bubble and it just burst.

"I'm sorry, Claire. I've got to leave town for a couple of days."

"A plant emergency?" I ask, giving him an out, even though we both know it must be a personal matter, related to that part of his life that's cast in perma-shadow. The part that I'm not allowed to know about. There's a tugging feeling in my chest—a want that hasn't been filled. We've danced around his past for weeks, small bits of information leaking through but nothing major. This, I sense, is major.

"Yeah," he says wrapping a big hand around my waist. "An oak caught Dutch elm disease."

"Silly oak. Didn't it realize it was the wrong species?"

"Trees aren't known for their intelligence," he jokes. Neither of us are smiling. He pulls me to him, close enough that I can feel his heart beating fast. "This last week has been...well, you'd give Sandra Dee a run for her money. You're fucking perfect."

"I'm not perfect," I say, feeling my cheeks burn. "No one's perfect."

"That's not how I meant it," he says, his tone intent. "I told you I'm not good with words. What I meant is that you're perfect the way you are. There's nothing about you that should be changed." His lips twitch. "No leather jacket. No final makeover montage. I like you exactly the way you are, Claire Rainey."

My mouth drops open to object. "But I'm too agreeable. I go along with everything."

"I've seen no evidence of that," he says with a partial smile. And I realize he's right—I've never really been like that, with him. Maybe because right after I met him, I saw the vulnerability he usually keeps so close to his chest. We saw each other on that plane, everything else stripped away.

I let a hand lift to his beard, to the angles of his face. "I'll bet you say that to all your friends with benefits."

He scratches his head, looking conflicted, then says, "That's not how I see you. But I can't—"

"You still think you shouldn't get close to anyone, and you won't tell me why," I say sadly, my voice thick.

He swallows. "I want to, but I can't yet. Not until I talk to my brother and sister. It doesn't only concern me."

I'd gathered as much from what little he's said. And while I want to push him, I don't. His secret is big, or at least he thinks it is, and we've only known each other for a couple of weeks, even though it feels much longer. So it makes sense that he's not ready to tell me everything. I have to admit I'm not ready to show all of my cards either. Because if he finds out Nicole and Damien are private investigators, he'll worry that Nicole will take a back-hoe to all of his secrets. Frankly, it might be a legitimate concern, especially if she just went rogue and took care of Agnes and Doug on my behalf.

If he knew about them, he'd push me away. Maybe he'd even blow town altogether, a thought that chokes me. I've seen his paradise down the hill and the joy he takes in his work, and I hate the thought of him being torn away from the existence he's carved out for himself because of me, my illegitimate father, and my sister.

Still, there's something I do need to tell him.

"Agnes," I say, slightly breathless. "She's finished." I explain what happened with the burn book and Doug, plus my suspicion that my sister was behind it, and he does me the courtesy of not acting impatient, even though he's obviously worried about whatever he was told on that phone call.

"They deserved it," he says, unwavering. He tucks hair behind my ear, then kisses just beneath the lobe. "They deserve worse, honestly. But why do you think Nicole did it?"

He doesn't really get it...

He hasn't been left notes adhered to tables with knives, or experienced the subversion of Nicole. Or at least he doesn't *know* that he has.

"She's been away from the house all week, and she knew about the burn book," I settle for saying. "She'd give Machiavelli a run for his money. I really think it was her."

He considers this for a moment and then nods. "I like her more if it was. You deserve to have someone to stand up for you, to stand by your side. I wish I'd been the one to do it."

It goes without saying that he thinks he can't be that person for me, but I'm glad he at least wants to be. That's something, right?

I lift up on my toes and kiss him, and he kisses me back hard, his hand wrapping into my hair as if it can't help itself, and I get the sense that he wants to recapture what we lost.

"I've got to go," he says when he pulls away. "But it shouldn't be for more than a couple of days."

Worry wraps around me in an uncomfortable squeeze. What if he doesn't come back? But he's in a hurry, obviously, and so am I, so I kiss him one more time and then hustle out of the door, Rocket giving me a parting lick on my heel.

My head feels buzzy and weird, because of Declan, and Agnes, and maybe a little bit because of the pot. But I go over to Dick's house and stride inside with purpose pounding through me. I *will* find out what Nicole did. I *will* find out why.

I hear noise in the kitchen, and when I walk in, Damien and Nicole are sitting at the table having a drink. Nicole seems relieved to see me. "Oh good, you're okay. The glasses are certainly something...and you look like you've been getting some very *thorough* stick shift lessons this weekend."

I lift my fingers to my hair self-consciously, then feel pissed at myself for giving in to the impulse.

Damien rises and kisses the top of Nicole's head. "I'm going to leave so you two can have a private discussion."

He goes, taking his drink with him, and winks at me on his way out. Both of them are in high spirits. But is it because they've been reunited after a few days apart or because they toppled a lifestyle goddess?

I sink into the chair Damien just left, and Nicole pours me some bourbon. I ignore it, my gaze on her.

"Were you in New York City?"

Her smile widens, showing teeth, like she's a vampire. "*Ding, ding, ding.*"

"Damien told you about the burn book. You brought down Agnes, and you made it look like Doug's fault. Why?"

She looks a little puzzled by the question, and for a moment I think I got it wrong. For a moment, I'm...disappointed. I'm surprised by the realization that I want it to have been her—and it takes me a beat for another thought to follow in the wake of that one. I want it to be her, because if it *was* her, she did it for me. If it *was* her, then I played a hand in the downfall of the woman who made my life hell for years—and the man who mistreated me.

"That's a stupid question," she says finally. "So I'm going to give you a stupid answer. Will you believe me if I say I did it because of the Chanel No. 5?"

"Maybe," I say, my pulse picking up again. Because this sounds an awful lot like a confession.

She gives her head a small shake, smiling slightly, her hair giving her the look of an impish fairy. "It's simple, Claire, and it's for the best if you understand. You're my sister. If someone fucks with you, they fuck with me. And *no one* fucks with me. After our talk the other night, I knew Agnes and Doug were owed a lesson, and there's nothing I enjoy more than playing teacher."

It hits me like the Jeep I can finally drive that two people have made massive gestures for me this week—Declan, learning how to drive stick shift for me, and Nicole, taking down my ex-boss. It's hard to wrap my head around it, even though my life and my very personality have been shaped by a much larger act of kindness—by my father's decision to raise a baby who wasn't his. I struggle to believe I deserve it, but I know Nicole's not a person who'd take kindly to that kind of protestation.

"I can't believe you did that for me," I say instead. "I'm...I'm speechless."

"You're talking an awful lot for someone who's speechless."

"I'm metaphorically speechless," I say, grabbing the glass of bourbon and taking a long, calming sip. "I...I saw the photo of Doug walking off with a box of his stuff."

Her teeth gleam like an apex predator's. "I know, I'd like to blow it up and hang it on the wall."

I laugh. "That's exactly what Lainey said, but I'd prefer not to have to look at him every day. How'd you do it?"

Her approving look suggests this is a question she was waiting for me to ask. "The photocopies in your suitcase helped."

My mouth puckers. "You have my suitcase?" Without it, I have a grand total of four outfits I've been rotating, some Nicole's, some purchased from a very cheap secondhand store downtown. "How long have you had it?"

"Oh, don't get your titties in a twist," she says, as if it's no big deal to steal someone's baggage and go through it. "You might have made a few phone calls, but at the end of the day, you were content to let it stay lost forever. I'm never content to let anything go. So I drove up to Charlotte after taking care of some other business last week, and I made enough of a stink that someone listened. Lo and behold, they found your bag, same as they would have done if you'd been more of a squeaky wheel, and they gave it to me."

"Why would they give it to you?" I ask, feeling my cheeks heat, my ire rise. I don't know who I'm more pissed at—her, the TSA, or myself.

"Because I had the claim tag, obviously. You really need to keep better track of your things. I was going to give it to you as a surprise the night we had the bonfire, but we got distracted, and then Damien told me about the burn book, and it gave me an idea. I like to follow through on my ideas before anyone can talk me out of them."

"It's fucked up that you went through my things," I say.

"Probably," she admits, watching me, "but I find it interesting that you object to that, and not to me messing with Doug and Agnes."

"I'd like to have my bag back."

"It's already in your room."

"So I guess you released the pages to the press. But why would that require you to fly to New York?"

She clucks her tongue. "They would never have dared to press publish if I'd been that direct. I broke into your old office and sent a scan of the pages from Doug's computer. In case that wasn't enough to truly fuck him and Agnes over, I found the original book and had it couriered to the offices of Gabber Media. Traceable to him, of course. Do you think he cried?" She asks it conversationally, as if we're discussing the weather.

Gabber Media is infamous for their takedowns of poorly behaving public figures, so she definitely did her research.

"You could have gotten caught," I say, impressed and a little horrified. "Arrested."

"Oh, Claire," she says, her tone almost pitying. "If you're so scared of everything, you're never really going to live. You'll spend the rest of your life as an indentured servant to someone who's braver than you."

I have that stabbed-by-a-butter-knife feeling again. Except maybe I've been the one doing the stabbing all along. I take off the glasses and rub my eyes. "I don't know whether to thank you or tell you to go fuck yourself."

She laughs. "I get that a lot." She plays with her glass of bourbon, watching me, then says. "I've got something else to tell you. I'm not sure how you're going to take it, since things have obviously progressed with our neighbor." She lifts a shoulder. "Sorry about that. I shouldn't have encouraged you, but I only found out some of this shit today. It seemed like it would be better to discuss it in person."

I lift my fingers self-consciously to my hair again, feeling the mess of it. "What are you talking about?" But a part of me already knows. She poked into Declan's business, as surely as she's always poking into mine—and she found something.

"Well, his name isn't Declan James, big surprise. I'd already figured that part out. But he left his burner phone over here last weekend, and I duplicated it. It was a bitch to figure out the password, but I broke through eventually. Found out some interesting information about our buddy."

My heart feels like it's stalled in my chest. "You're certainly good at invading people's privacy."

"His real name is Declan O'Malley, and his uncle died about two years ago. Get this, Claire..." She taps the table. "Rory O'Malley took a header down a flight of stairs."

A chill runs down my back. "You're not saying..."

She waves a hand. "I'm not saying anything other than that it's a *mighty* coincidence, don't you think? And get this...Declan and his brother and sister moved away after their uncle died. All of them. And after they moved, they vanished." She kisses her fingers and then spreads them, lifting them into the air.

I think about everything Declan's said to me.

That he's hiding and can't get close to anyone.

That I'll judge him if I find out what he's done.

That he's bad and has done bad things.

I take a big slug of the bourbon.

"I haven't even gotten to the good part," she says, her eyes shining.

"There's a good part?" I mumble.

"The uncle was this big kingpin. Organized crime. Drugs. I mean, fuck, it fits, right? We already know Declan's been growing weed in his greenhouse. So what about this for a theory—our dad finds out that Declan offed his uncle and confronts him, so Declan says, hey, what worked for one guy will work for another and, kaput. Dick goes for a spin down the stairs."

"I don't believe he'd do something like that," I say, mostly certain of it. Because it doesn't fit the man I've come to know. Because despite what he's said to me, more than once, I see goodness in him. Still, my mouth's dry; my stomach's a drum.

"You never know what someone's capable of," Nicole says, punctuating the statement with a poke to the air. "But I can't make sense of why he'd stick around after offing Dick. Sure, everyone thinks it's an accident or suicide, but why take the risk? And don't even get me started on how messed up it would be for him to fuck around with you if he killed your father. So what I'm saying is that he's either innocent, or he's a real psychopath. Either way, you should probably stay away from him until we're sure. I would have told Damien not to let you spend time with him today, but I didn't realize you were planning to. And I didn't think it would be a good idea for me to go over there and extract you."

I take another slug of the bourbon, but it doesn't give me the usual wash of heat. I feel like I'm made of ice and wood. Fuck. Fuck. *Fuck*. I don't want any of this to be true, but Declan's made no secret of the fact that he's running from something, and he flinched from talk about organized crime earlier today...

In my head, I can hear him telling me that he's the kind of man my father has always warned me away from. He's right. My father was worried about me dating my high school boyfriend because he had a job at the bowling alley. Apparently, bowling alleys are dens of iniquity in my dad's imagination, so I can only imagine what he'd think about all of this...

"Nicole," I say, my voice choked. "I...I don't want it to be him. I really, *really* like him."

I'm falling in love with him.

I expect her to make some careless quip about my shitty taste in men, but instead she fills my glass to the brim. "I like him too," she says. "I thought he would be good for you. I still do...if he's not a murderer. But remember that we don't know shit yet. He's back on the suspect list, but he's not the only suspect."

"Should I talk to him? Should I ask—"

She's already shaking her head. "What's he going to do if you ask about his uncle and he *did* knock Dick down the stairs to keep him quiet? He'd run. Or if he's really a psycho, he'd send you down the steps too. No. Avoid him. Tell him you're busy with family shit, and you'll have the peace of mind of knowing it's mostly true. In the meantime, maybe I'll dig up enough to clear his name. Speaking of suspects, fill me in on Mrs. Rosings. Did you get into the old lady's box?"

"No," I say with a sigh, debating whether to tell her that Declan's going to be out of town for a couple of days. I decide not to. If I tell her, she'll want to dig into that, too, and it was obvious he wanted privacy. She might do it anyway, once she notices his car is missing, but I'm not going to offer up the information. Instead, I tell her about Mrs. Rosings and the black widow stuff.

"Oh, shit," she says, sounding delighted. "I knew I liked her. She has this certain *je ne sais* fuck about her."

"Do you listen to half the things you say?"

"I don't make a habit of it, no. Well, obviously you need to check out her house and get more info. That's your assignment for the rest of this week."

"And you'll be looking into Declan?" I ask softly, feeling like a traitor for saying it, even though everything she's said about him makes sense. Even though a reasonable woman would doubt him, and herself. But I'm still reeling, and I know how much he'd hate for someone to go digging into his metaphorical backyard...

But is it because he knows they'd find a body there?

"I will be," she says, lifting her glass.

I try to lift mine and splash my hand.

"You and your murderous boyfriend really have a thing for wasting my bourbon."

"I kind of hate you right now."

"Drink up, you'll feel better."

So I drink it down. But I don't feel any better. My mind is full of worries now, spinning around each other and forming new worries.

"Who else are you looking into?" I say after a moment. "Who else did Dick piss off?"

She kicks back in her chair, leaning it on the two back legs. "I've talked to a couple of contractors he flaked on. Two women he was seeing at the same time. Another woman whose husband left her because she had an affair with Dick. But honestly, I'm guessing it's impossible for us to find everyone he ever pissed off." She angles her head and lifts her glass. "I might have resented the salty bastard, but he did know how to have a good time."

"Yeah, no kidding," I mumble.

These past two weeks, *I've* been having a good time. Like maybe that part of my bio father rubbed off on me just by being here in this place. But I don't know what I'm going to do if it turns out...

He didn't do it. He wouldn't have.

Nicole would probably tell me I'm being naïve, a Pollyanna, but I refuse to believe Declan had anything to do with Dick's death. His uncle, though...

Maybe he did have something to do with *that*.

I try to shake off the thought and focus on my conversation with Nicole, but I feel Declan's hands ghosting over me, his whisper in my ear.

"What about the Treasure Club people?" I ask. "Do you think they could have done it to try to get the house?"

She laughs with feeling. "You think a bunch of strippers banded together, force-fed him drugs, and tripped him down the steps? You know, I'll bet that's how the bastard would have liked to go out."

"Probably," I agree, because it fits the Dick I've gotten to know. It's a strange thought, but in some ways I *have* gotten to know him.

"But I don't think so. No one's given us a hard time about being here or tried to get us to leave. I don't think they're after our shitty house. If someone did this, I'm guessing it was personal...or because Dick knew something he shouldn't."

"If?"

She shrugs. "There's still the chance it was an accident."

"I hope it was an accident," I say with feeling.

She shrugs again.

"Seriously? You want it to have been murder?"

"No," she says, laughing. "Dick might not have been much of a father, or a person, but he didn't deserve to be murdered. But if it was an accident, we'll have a harder time proving he wasn't responsible for his own death."

"Oh." I trace a finger around the rim of my glass. "Damien mentioned that the two of you don't really need the house...or the money."

"No," she agrees. "His grandmother died a few years back and left us a lot of money. But I want it for you. I'm going to give you my half of the house."

Here she is again, acting like I matter. A few weeks ago, she didn't know I existed, and I didn't know she existed. Dick might not have done much for us, but he did bring us together. It makes me think of that note...

"Thank you," I say, meaning it. "*Thank you.*"

"Don't get all mushy on me." But she's smiling a little.

"Nicole, did Dick write a note to you? He wrote one to me."

She studies me for a second. "Where'd you find yours?"

It's not an answer, but I hear an answer buried within it. "In the back of that photo album."

"Oh shit," she says, straightening out her chair. "He really should have been more careful with his things. What'd it say?"

"I'll show you mine if you show me yours."

She shakes her head. "Not yet."

"It wasn't..."

"No, it wasn't a suicide note."

I'm disappointed that she won't let me see it, but I don't press her. "Okay. Can I...can I see your house sometime?"

"Why?" she asks, her expression amused. "This place not doing it for you?"

"No. I...I think I'd like to get to know you a little more."

She winks at me, her expression pleased. "I knew I'd grow on you."

CHAPTER TWENTY-EIGHT

CLAIRE

Text conversation with Dad

Bug, you didn't answer my call. Everything okay?

Did you see what happened to Agnes? She shouldn't have forgotten the Golden Rule.

Maybe it's small of me, but I sent her Congratulations! balloons.

God, I really love you.

Text conversation with Declan

This is going to take longer than I'd hoped.

I can't stop thinking about you, Claire.

Same.

Let's make some more madeleines this weekend. We can make a picnic for our next hike.

Doesn't sound very bad boy of you.

I told you I had a thing for Sandra Dee.

I wasn't lying to Declan—I *can't* stop thinking about him. He doesn't need to know that some of my thoughts have blood spatter on them now.

After what Nicole told me, my mind keeps spinning hundreds of what-ifs, each worse than the last. I know she's been looking into him, trying to figure out if he's a…

Well, a *murderer*.

I call Lainey on Monday night to give her an update. Part of me wants to hold back the worst of it—to avoid giving her a bad impression of Declan—but she has a right to know everything if she's going to be moving into this fucked-up situation. So I let it all spill out, and it's a relief to tell her. To share this bizarro version of my life with someone who's known me since I was a toddler.

"Holy shit," she says at the end. "Your life is like a Lifetime movie. We should write a screenplay about it and sell it."

"Let's not make that our career plan just yet," I tell her. "But it's starting to look like I'm not going to get the insurance money. We'll still have the house."

"I have an idea for a business that won't have any start-up costs at all," she says, practically buzzing with enthusiasm. "I've circled back on the Love Erasers idea."

"You don't think it's too soon after Todd?" I ask, because I do. Lainey's told herself she's over the whole thing, but I know she's not. She's barely scratched the surface.

"No. It would be therapeutic. And there are other services we can offer. Like…what if someone wants to get even with a shitty ex? We can help them!"

"So instead of paying for therapy, you want to take your repressed rage out on other people's exes?"

"Exactly!"

"We'll figure it out once you're here," I say, which feels kinder than saying no. I have enough of my own shit to deal with without getting weighed down by strangers' baggage. I'd prefer to start some kind of catering business on the off-chance that we can get Dick's kitchen certified without spending thousands upon thousands of dollars.

There's a pause over the line, then she says, "Are you okay, Claire?"

And, just like that, I feel like crying. "No, not really," I say through a tight throat. "What if I'm falling in love with a murderer?"

"You wouldn't be the only one," she says. "I watched this documentary on—"

"Not helping."

"I know," she says. "I'm sorry. But I doubt Declan killed Dick. It sounds like they were friends. I mean sure, most people are killed by someone they know, but my guess is that he didn't do it. You have a good people sense."

"Are you sure about that? I worked for Agnes for seven years, and I willingly had sex with Doug."

"Yes, but I don't think you were under the delusion either of them were good people."

"And I stuck with Agnes for years and Doug for months. What does that say about me?" I ask, feeling a pulse of panic in my chest.

"That you want to be wrong about people. That's a good thing. It means you care about people and want to give them a chance."

"And in both of those cases it fucked me over."

"But you gave Nicole a chance, and she pulled off a pretty badass move. You gave me a chance, and I'm a great best friend."

I still feel unsettled by the time we hang up, but at least she tells me she's coming this weekend, with an ETA of Sunday afternoon.

Less than a week, and Lainey will be here.

Less than a week, and I'll officially be making Marshall my home for who-knows-how-long.

What'll life look like in a week?

He didn't do it, I tell myself. *He didn't kill anyone. The worst he's ever done is grow pot, and that's barely a crime anymore.*

And, like the ostrich I am, I pretend to believe it.

His car is gone all day Monday. All day Tuesday, too.

He texts but doesn't call.

I worry.

I pine for him.

I fear for my sanity.

ON WEDNESDAY MORNING, Mrs. Rosings has me fold her collection of linen napkins into perfect triangles while she tells me stories about people I don't know. We're sitting at a table in the drawing room. It's unclear to me how we're supposed to successfully transport the folded napkins wherever they need to go, or why she needs them, since I don't get the impression she holds a lot of dinner parties. This isn't the first time it's occurred to me that she doesn't need a full-time assistant, for the wedding or otherwise. She's either lonely, or she feels bad for me because I'm poor. No, from what I know about her, I'm guessing it's actually option C, and she's lonely *and* bored. The busy work is fine by me, though. It's about all I'm capable of at the moment.

Someone buzzes at the front gate, prompting me to flinch, and she lifts her eyebrows and says, "Are you going to answer that?"

"Am I? I doubt they're here to see me."

"In my day..."

"Yeah, yeah," I say, and this is one of the rare occasions that she smiles when I interrupt her.

I answer the buzzer, and an unfriendly male voice says, "Who are you?"

"I'm Mrs. Rosings's assistant, Claire."

The man makes a rude noise. "So she suckered someone else into working for her?"

I glance at Mrs. Rosings with interest, because I still haven't learned what happened with my predecessor.

Sighing, she waves a hand regally. "Let him in."

"Come in, sir," I say, which prompts a swear under his breath. "We're in the drawing room."

"Who is he?" I ask, turning to look at her.

She seems excited, as if something interesting is finally happening, and she doesn't quite know what to do with herself.

"My boy," she says, glancing at the door to the dining room. "Anthony."

I perk up, too, mostly because I've been very curious about this missing-in-action son and his hated bride-to-be.

"Were you expecting him?"

She lifts her eyebrows again, appearing very pleased with herself. "Yes, I felt sure I'd finally warrant a visit."

Moments later, I hear the front door open, so presumably Anthony has a key, and then he stomps into the room moments later. I recognize him from the photo hanging above the fireplace in the drawing room, only he's had a business man glow-up in the years since it was taken. He's wearing horn-rimmed glasses and a casual suit, if a suit could be said to be casual. His hard jaw is shaved to precision, and if not for his eyes—large, brown, and long-lashed—he'd look too severe. He's holding a sheet of paper that he proceeds to shake in the air.

It take me half a moment to process what I'm looking at—it's a mock-up photo of the goat farm we visited the other day, with two figures with the faces of Anthony and his as-yet-nameless bride badly Photoshopped onto them.

"You went to see this place without Nina and me?" he says to his mother, barely giving me a glance. He's not shouting, but he's not *not*-shouting. "You gave them a *deposit*?"

"A lovely surprise, don't you think?" she asks, her eyes bright with glee. If he figured a visit would get her to behave, he clearly can't read a room. This is what she wanted.

"When you told Nina you wanted to help with the wedding, she thought you were being nice, Mom. She was excited. She told you she wanted to have it here at Smith House, and you smiled and nodded." He shook his head, swallowing. "But you were up to your usual shit. Unbelievable."

She feigns a look of innocence that slides into an expression that's almost earnest. "I thought you would enjoy it, Anthony. It's the kind of thing that would have made you laugh, back in the day. Your sister was in hysterics when I sent the photo to her."

He shakes his head, his jaw tightening. "Unbelievable," he repeats with venom.

"Yes, you already said that. Now, there *is* a catering package, but I'm afraid that they only offer roasted goat for the main course. I know Nina's diet is restrictive."

"We're obviously not getting married there." He glances around, his accusatory gaze falling on me for a second before returning to her. "Did your asshole boyfriend put you up to this?"

"Honestly," Mrs. Rosings says, crossing her legs. "I'm seventy years old, Anthony, don't you think it's a little gauche to call someone my boyfriend?"

"You didn't answer my question."

She sighs. "Richard wasn't my boyfriend, my dear, just a friend, and he's *dead.*"

My mouth falls open, because for some reason I'd failed to connect the dots. This guy knew my biological father. He *disapproved* of him. Maybe Dick was even the reason for the obvious friction between Mrs. Rosings and her son.

Anthony flinches. For half a second, I think he's going to stay something really crappy like "Good," but he swallows, looks down at the polished floorboards, and says, "I'm sorry, Mom. I didn't know."

She sniffs. "Maybe you would if you'd answer any of my calls."

"I've been—"

"Busy. Yes. So have I." Something like victory flashes in her eyes. "I have a feeling I'll continue to be very busy, unless there's someone around to help me make decisions. I may have been married three times, dear, but so much has changed... If I made an error in judgment about the venue, I'm sorry. We can fix it. Together."

He glances at me and then the folded tower of napkins. "It looks like you have help."

"Hi," I say brightly, holding out a hand. "I'm Claire, the asshole's daughter."

He flinches as if I'd slapped him. "Sorry. I've been unspeakably rude. I'm Anthony."

"That's okay," I say, "the common consensus is that you were right about my father."

His phone beeps, and he draws it out, muttering something under his breath when he sees the screen. "I have to go," he tells his mother.

"Yes, of course."

"Mom, you need to stop this. I'm marrying Nina, and you'll have to get used to the idea."

"You think I went to the goat farm for my health?" she asks, tipping her head. "Why, my cousin Jennifer caught West Nile Virus at a goat farm."

I'm beginning to think Jennifer is either very unlucky or very made up.

Sighing, he shakes his head and nods. "Nice to meet you, Claire. Good luck. You're going to need it." Then, to his mother, "We'll talk."

He leaves the room, and when the front door closes behind him, Mrs. Rosings nods once, still seated at the table. "That went well."

"Did it?" I ask in disbelief.

"He's flustered," she says, sticking her bottom lip out slightly. "I'm getting through to him."

"How do you figure?"

Her lips tip upward. "Nina saw the photo, and you can be assured she wasn't the slightest bit amused. It's given him doubt. Only a dullard wouldn't be amused by such a thing, and my boy is no dullard."

"I don't know, Mrs. Rosings," I say. "He didn't seem very amused either."

"Oh, he was. He has an *excellent* sense of humor. Eventually he'll realize he doesn't want to spend the rest of his life with someone divested of one."

"He knew Dick?" I ask, still caught on that detail.

"Yes," she says, taking one of the perfectly triangle napkins and fussing with the seams. Apparently, she agrees with me that something perfect could always be more perfect. "I met Dick because he was working on one of Anthony's properties."

I swallow, trying to process that. Anthony and Dick, working together. That has to mean something, doesn't it? But Anthony seemed genuinely surprised to hear Dick was dead...

Of course, people can pretend to be surprised...and it's strange that he hasn't been in touch with his mother if his bride-to-be has her heart set on getting married at Smith House. It's almost like he's been keeping his distance on purpose. Because of guilt?

"What kind of property?" I ask through my dry mouth.

She waves a hand. "Oh, it was a mess. Anthony blamed Dick, and I'll be honest with you, he was right. Dick cut corners. He didn't build the staircase to code, and it destroyed the budget."

My pulse is racing, my mouth dry.

Mrs. Rosings sighs, not seeming to notice my discomfort. "I'm afraid my boy will never forgive me for what I did."

"For what?" I ask. "My bio-dad? The goats?"

"Oh, this goes far beyond the goats," she says mysteriously.

"Was your previous suggestion a horse farm?"

She smiles, shaking her head, and glances above the fireplace at those framed photos. A young Anthony and his sister, equally shrouded in mystery, although I have confirmation that she, at least, finds terrible Photoshop as funny as the rest of humanity. "I'm going to take a nice long soak. You can leave after you finish with the napkins."

I hold back from giving her a salute, barely.

When she closes the door behind her, I take out my phone to text Nicole an update, but it occurs to me that this is my chance to look in the box we delivered to her.

I know where it's being kept—I saw Mrs. Rosings place it above the fireplace, next to three small urns that presumably contain some of the ashes of each of the husbands she's lost. It feels appropriate, if macabre.

Heart pounding, I set down the last napkin and make my way to the fireplace. Feeling like a thief—a very bad one—I quickly take down the box and crack the lid open.

CHAPTER TWENTY-NINE

CLAIRE

"No fucking way," Nicole says, rocking back in her chair with a grin on her face. It's after eight, and she just got home from who-knows-where. We're sitting in the kitchen and having a check-in session and a beer. "No way," she repeats, slapping the table again.

I pull out my cell phone and draw up the photo. She takes a look at it and then slaps the table a third time, palm down.

Grinning, she says, "This is proof that dreams really do come true."

Then she bellows Damien's name, making it sound like an emergency. He races into the room, nearly skidding on the linoleum, his worried expression easing when he sees us sitting at the table.

"Damien, take a look at this, will you?" she asks.

I hold up my phone obligingly, and he whistles. "That looks a lot like a golden dick."

"Right?"

"Is it your father's golden dick?"

"Yes," she says. "You know, at times like this, I almost like the guy. This is...well, *golden*, for lack of a better word. If you're on death's doorstep, you know exactly what to get me before you go."

He ruffles her short hair. "Don't give up hope for your birthday, Nicole. I'd hate for you to have to wait until I'm dead to get something you'd truly enjoy." He glances between the two of us, then says, "I'm going to make a phone call. I'll see you all later."

I watch Nicole as he leaves the room. "How'd you know?" I ask. "There's no way that was just a lucky guess."

She shrugs. "He used to tease my mom about it. Say he was going to get her his dick cast in gold for Christmas or her birthday or whatever. It was an ongoing thing, but I never thought the old bastard would actually go through with it. I'm guessing it's not really gold, but he must have really liked Mrs. Rosings after all. I really wish I'd put in a bet with Mark."

"The guy who owns Vincenzo's?"

"Otherwise known as the local bookie."

My eyes widen. "No way. Do you think he could have—"

"Had a problem with Dick?" she asks, rocking. "It did occur to me, abso-fucking-lutely. Can you imagine how many bets Dick must have put in? He probably got plenty of things right—and if there's one thing a bookie doesn't enjoy, it's losing money. But we already went to talk to him, as you know, and he has an alibi. Plus, a few people around town have told me they were friends. I guess Dick's the one who encouraged him to take the odds on a bunch of random shit, not just sports games or whatever, and it's made him a lot of money. So he's probably not our guy." She shrugs. "One weird thing...he mentioned Dick won a lot of money over the years." She sweeps the ramshackle room with her eyes, lingering on all the signs of disrepair.

"Doesn't seem like it went very far," I comment. Then I remember something Rex told me weeks ago. "Rex said Dick was kind of a prepper. Or that he would have been if he could be bothered to put in the work."

Nicole snorts.

"What if he didn't, you know, believe in banks."

She lets the chair slam down. "Do you think he buried treasure in the back yard? It would be just like him to do that and not leave a map."

"Wouldn't a hidden stash of money be another reason for someone to try to kill him?"

She nods, and then something flashes in her eyes. "You tripped over that hole the other day, and there were more. What if they weren't from land beavers, but the person who made them dug them so we'd assume that? What if they've been roaming around at night, looking for his stash?"

Well, shit. The thought of someone roaming around back there with ill intent sends a shiver through me. We're miles away from the small downtown area, miles away from anything.

"What do we do? Go out there with a back hoe?" I ask, my ignorance about all things related to construction showing. But my worry is twined with a surge of adrenaline that feels a little like excitement.

"Or pay attention to anyone else who goes out there with a shovel," she says pointedly. "I'll get Damien to install cameras." She allows for a dramatic pause before pointing out, "Declan would have access."

Disappointment digs into me. She's right that he'd have access, but I know—or at least I want to believe—that he wouldn't tear up the land he loves. Especially not for that reason. "He doesn't seem to care about money."

"Oh, my sweet, sweet sister. *Everyone* cares about money. Especially the people who don't have a lot."

I don't really agree with her. If Declan cared about money, he'd sell the pot, not give it to people. Of course, he may have been lying to me about that, and if I say anything to her, I'm pretty sure the word naïve will be thrown around. Perhaps not without reason.

"What about Mrs. Rosings's son? I mean, she claims he has a

sense of humor, and Dick messed up the staircase. Maybe he saw it as poetic justice to arrange an accident on the stairs for him?"

"You're vicious," she says with a grin.

"I didn't say *I* saw it as poetic justice."

She inclines her head, acceding the point. "It's definitely worth exploring. I'll look into their connection."

I want to ask questions about Declan; I also very much *don't* want to ask about Declan. His car was in the driveway when I got back from Mrs. Rosings's house, so I knew he's back home. He hasn't texted me, though, and things feel too unsettled for me to drop by unannounced.

From the way Nicole's watching me, she knows who and what I'm thinking about. But she's even more stubborn than I am. So I just sit there, and she just sits there, and finally she says, "I don't have anything new on your boyfriend, but he was definitely running a growhouse for his uncle. I suspect he was also running money for him through the family construction business."

"Okay," I say slowly, struggling to take that in. Declan, funneling money from organized crime. Growing weed, potentially for a lot of people.

He said he didn't sell it, but it occurs to me now that he said he didn't sell it *here*.

What else did he grow for his uncle?

What's the line I'm unwilling to cross? Declan joked about making a bad impression on my father, but in all seriousness, what would my dad, my *real* dad, think of him?

He'd tell me to run.

He'd stay up all night worrying.

He'd have a heart attack, and it would be all my fault.

But it's impossible to divorce my logical brain from the way Declan makes me feel—alive and happy and *valued*...

Like I'm enough, just by being me.

I want him to be enough, just as he is, too.

I want to help him with his greenhouse and walk Rocket with him and pretend I enjoy hiking.

I want to bake together and have adventures.

I run the pads of my fingers over my collarbone, feeling panic brewing inside of me, fizzing and bubbling and toxic. I'm in over my head. I'm in over my head, and I feel like I'm drowning...

"I see the look on your face," Nicole says, scrunching her mouth to one side, "but it might not be as bad as you're thinking. It's possible the guy who took over for the uncle is the one who popped him off, and Declan and his brother and sister ran because they didn't want to become collateral damage."

"I'll bet that's what happened," I say, but the words have the mouthfeel of a disappointing cake. Dry. Dusty. *Wrong*.

If that's what happened, he probably wouldn't be carrying around a guilty conscience. Yes, growing drugs is illegal, but he obviously doesn't mind too much if he is willing to do it here. Equally, funneling dirty money is wrong, but the way he's been acting...

It goes deeper than that.

I feel something inside me unspool as I make a decision. I'm not going to sit around catastrophizing. I'm not going to be the Claire who parked herself in an office chair for years, dreaming about a future she was doing nothing to achieve and smelling like a perfume she didn't like.

I'm going to find out exactly what's going on so I can properly freak out about it.

Which means I need to talk to Declan. I need to talk to him *now*.

"I'm going to take a walk," I say, my voice faint, more echo than person. But the words are defined and unshakeable.

"Wear the reflective vest I got you," she says. "I hung it on one of the hooks by the front door."

I look at her in surprise. "Why'd you do that? To make me look stupid or keep me safe?"

"Both," she says with a wink. Then, in a softer voice, she says, "If it goes badly, tell him that I know all about his history, and if he hurts you, I will *ruin* him. I know where his brother and sister are hiding, and I'll ruin both of them too. All that will be left of them is a whole bunch or ruin. It'll make what happened to Agnes and Doug look sweet and gentle."

I raise my eyebrows, my heart beating fast in my chest. "You know where I'm going, and you're not going to try to stop me?"

"I've always believed in solving my own problems. I'm not going to get in your way if you're stepping up to confront yours." She shrugs. "And I wouldn't have stayed away from Damien if I were in your shoes. You know...when we first got together, there were plenty of barriers against us too."

"Like what?" I ask.

"He's from this incredibly wealthy family—"

"Not making me feel better."

She grins. "But they're dicks. They hate me, obviously. They'd probably have me popped off if we weren't so much better at cloak and dagger shit than they are. And then there was his ex-girlfriend... she pretended they were sleeping together behind my back."

"What'd you do?" I ask, because she obviously did *something*. She's not the kind of person who'd take that kind of thing and carry it around for years. She's a woman of action, the way I want to be. The way I hope I'm becoming.

"I punched her in the face."

"Good to know," I say. "I'll keep that one in my back pocket." It takes me a second to realize I'm borrowing Declan's father's phrase. It clutches at my heart with wispy hands.

"Don't do anything I would do," she says, her expression shifting to just sideways of serious. "This is the kind of situation where being careful is probably a good thing. For you, anyway.

Obviously we won't turn him in if you like him. You can tell him that too."

I doubt he'll take it as gospel. But I nod and get up from the table, then stoop and take a swig of my beer. Glancing at my sister, I say, "He may not even be home. He's been off dealing with something."

She has the grace not to suggest that whatever he's been dealing with might be criminal in nature, but fuck, it really might be.

"If he's not, you'll try again later."

I nod, something caught in my throat. "I will."

"You're going to be okay," Nicole says as she runs a hand through her hair. Half of it sticks straight up, but it has the nerve to look good. "If he turns out to be a bad guy, I'll find you someone else."

I laugh, nearly snorting beer. "Do you moonlight as a matchmaker?"

"Sort of," she says. "I've decided I consider myself more of a love fixer."

"Like fixing broken hearts?" I ask, rubbing the sore area in my chest.

"No, more like in the organized crime way. Like, you've got a problem? I'll fix that shit right up for you. That's me. And Damien, because he doesn't have a choice."

"I heard that," Damien says from the kitchen doorway. But there's a fond smile on his face as he enters the room and heads to the refrigerator, grabbing a beer from the door. Turning to us, he leans back against it, looking like he belongs in an advertisement for expensive jeans, and adds, "But it's true. She has me wrapped around her finger. Guess what she made me name our P.I. Agency?"

"I couldn't begin to speculate."

"The Fairy Godmother Agency." He crooks two fingers to make quotation marks. "'Because we make wishes come true.'"

"You must really love her."

"You have no idea."

She grins at him, and he snaps his teeth at her, the click audible from across the room.

"You two are disgusting," I say, from the depths of the gooey, broken feeling in my chest. In my mind, I see Declan, baking with me. Getting those glasses for me. Trying to learn how to drive stick shift for me...

I've known him for less than three weeks, but it's been a transformative time in my life. An awakening. And there's no denying that I have stronger feelings for him than I've had for any of the men who've flitted through my life, or even the ones who've planted their feet in and stayed awhile. That has to mean something, doesn't it? That kind of connection isn't easy to find, so it shouldn't be easily let go of either.

I don't want to lose him.

"You'll be disgusting too, once we finish fixing your love life," Nicole says.

"Have we figured out whether we've been trying to set her up with a murderer?" Damien asks, quirking his brow.

"Working on it," Nicole says, pausing for a swig of her beer. "She's going over there to talk to him."

His expression turns big-brother serious. "If he tries anything..."

"I know, I know," I say with a sigh. "You're both very frightening, and I'll make sure he knows it." I sigh again and speak my fears out loud. "Even if he had nothing to do with Dick's death, he's not going to stay. Not when he finds out what we know. He came here to hide. No offense, but no one wants to hide next to a couple of private investigators with no respect for personal boundaries."

"Maybe. Maybe not. I guess we'll see what he's made of," Damien says firmly, and Nicole hums her approval and gets up, going to him. He wraps his arm around her, pulling her in.

I steel my spine. "I guess we will."

I guess I'll see what I'm made of too...

I turn to go, pausing in the entryway to agonize over the reflective vest. But I decide that I'd like to keep some of my dignity intact.

No reflective vest.

When I step outside, it's spitting rain. The drops are small, but they seem pissed off. I pause, wondering if I should wait until later, but then I realize I'm being Old Claire again—the Claire who'd photocopied the pages of Agnes's burn book but hadn't done anything with them, who'd broken up with Doug but hadn't had the balls to stand up to him. I don't want to be that woman anymore. I'd prefer to be the version of myself I've been becoming—the woman who speaks her mind.

So I step into the rain and eye the house next door.

Declan's car is still in the driveway...

I approach the house through the pissed-off rain and the wind that whips my skirt around my legs. Then I get close enough to see them on the screened-in front porch, sitting side by side on the swing—a beautiful blond woman with a purple streak in her hair, her side pressed against Declan, her head cradled against his shoulder in a way that suggests she's not there to install high-speed internet.

My chest caves inward like a chocolate souffle that hasn't been given enough love. I'm guessing she didn't come here to talk politics or try to convert him to the Tribe of Light. The way they're leaning into each other suggests they're *quite* familiar with each other. Is this one of the women on his list? A girlfriend he decided he didn't need to mention to me?

A wife?

I'm an idiot.

Declan's eyes catch mine, widening, and he pulls away from his friend, his mouth opening to say something. Brave Claire goes into hibernation, probably to never return. I turn and run.

The logical thing to do would be to run toward the house, but I don't. I race down the hill, the ground turning to mud under my feet, rain splashing my hair and my face and my everything as I dodge trees.

CHAPTER THIRTY

DECLAN

"Fuck. *Fuck*," I say, feeling the urge to splinter wood with my fist. I know from experience it wouldn't make me feel better for more than a second, but that second, oh.

"Was that *Claire*?" Rosie asks. She seems delighted by the possibility, as if Claire didn't take one look at us and run off into the night.

My sister has personally taken an axe to what passes for my life. The call I'd gotten on Sunday night was from Seamus, who'd gotten in touch to let me know Rosie had disappeared. I'd driven to fucking New York, and Shay and I had spent all day Monday trying to track her down. Then she finally responded to the hundreds of texts and messages we'd sent, saying, *Isn't it in bad form not to greet your guest?*

Turns out she'd arrived in Marshall on Monday morning and let herself into my house—my uncle had taught me the lockpicking trick, and I'd taught my sister and brother. Let no one say my sister doesn't do whatever-the-fuck she wants—including shutting off her phone because she didn't care to explain herself to two men who "always tell her what to do." As if she weren't as stubborn and mulish as the two of us combined.

So I went home, pissed off and seeing red. And, sure enough, there she fucking was this morning, waiting for me in my own house like she was queen of it.

She apologized for making Shay and me worry but insisted that if she'd given either of us any warning, we'd have done something to sabotage her. Sabotage, like we were rival spies. She has it in her head that she's going to *save* me, like I'm some shivering puppy stuck in the rain, not a thirty-one-year-old man capable of making his own bad decisions. But that's Rosie for you. I've told her I'm taking her home tomorrow, but she pointed out that she's a grown woman, and even if I kidnap her back to New York, she'll take the next flight out, and we'll have to do this dance again.

She came here because she heard something in my voice when I spoke about Claire, and she was convinced that if she didn't intervene, I was going to fuck up the only thing that has made me happy in years. She insists that I need to tell Claire the truth—everything—because it's the only way I'll be able to really be with her.

Shay, who's been more or less unhappy with me for years, surprised the fuck out of me by agreeing.

I'm less certain. I've only told one person since I left New York, and now he's in the unfortunate position of being dead. He's not dead because I told him, but even so, it's an unpleasant record.

Honestly, I haven't figured out what to do about Rosie yet. I can't keep her hidden in the house for however long she chooses to grace me with her presence, but I also can't start introducing her around town.

And now...

I saw the look on Claire's face. She thinks I stalled on seeing her because I'd arranged to bang another woman. Panic pounds through my veins. I can't let her think she doesn't matter to me. Because she does. A lot. The last few weeks have felt different than the sludge of time before them. Something inside of me broke when I found Dick dead at the bottom of those stairs, but Claire has pieced it together and pulled out parts of me that were buried for years. With her, I don't feel like I have to constantly be on my guard. I can be myself without worrying where Declan James ends and Declan O'Malley begins—because the truth is they're both me.

I get to my feet, my heart pounding. "I've got to go after her. She thinks we're..." I toggle a hand between us, and Rosie scrunches her nose.

"Gross."

"Thanks a lot," I say, taking the two steps to the cabinet on the porch and rustling through it.

"What the fuck are you still doing in here?" Rosie asks. "Your awesome, madeleine-making girlfriend is down there. You shouldn't be looking for rain boots or whatever. *Go.* And remember what we talked about."

"It's for *her*," I growl, finding the umbrella and grabbing it. I'm in too much of a rush to use it, so I tuck it under my arm and blast out of the house, my head whipping around to look for her. I see flash of white down the hill, visible through the grabbing tree branches, and I'm about to run down after her when I notice Nicole standing on the porch of Dick's house, Damien behind her. She points to her eyes, then me. I don't know how the fuck to respond, so I reciprocate the gesture and then race down the hill, nearly wiping out from the mud slipping beneath the heels of my shoes.

A few minutes later, I can see her at the bottom of the hill, near the greenhouse. She's stopped running and is standing there in the driving rain, staring up at me like she finally sees me for the fucking waste of life I am. She looks upset, but I can't tell if she's crying, because the rain is coming down hard now.

I head toward her through the mud, taking out the umbrella and popping it up, and it's just as insufficient as the pink plastic one was the day we met.

"*Claire.*"

"I'm not getting under that umbrella with you," she says, her bottom lip pushed out. I hold it out for her to take, but her hand doesn't budge. Fuck it. I drop it, because I'm not going to stand around half-heartedly dry while she gets soaked.

"Let's talk in the greenhouse," I say.

"No, I'm not going into your *growhouse*."

There's something about the way she says it...

I angle a look at her, and she crosses her arms over her chest, her wet shirt stretching across her tits in a way that might have been distracting if she weren't looking at me like I were whatever's currently on the bottom of my shoes. Part of me is glad she's finally seeing me that way, that she's no longer looking at me like I'm the man who makes flowers bloom. I've given her so little to hang onto, so few assurances and guarantees.

It's no wonder she doesn't trust me—she shouldn't. She deserves more—she deserves everything—and I want to be the man who gives it to her, even though I know my own flaws and imperfections. My absolute inadequacy. I want to keep what we've been building and let it grow. It may be impossible, but I want to give it a chance. The hope that's been trying to seed in my heart demands it.

"I know what you're thinking," I say, speaking loudly because the rain is driving down, making water stream down my face in wet rivulets from my hair. "But she's my sister. Shay, he's my brother, he called me the other night and said Rosie had left home, and I drove to New York to help him search for her. When I got home, she was waiting for me. She was...I guess she was worried about me. I told you. There's no list. There are no other women. There haven't been. There won't be."

Her mouth parts, and she glances up the hill. I don't, because I don't want to take my eyes off her. She looks like a vision, her wet clothes only reminding me of that day, of the way she rocked against me next to the van with the busted tire. Also, if I look up there, the only thing I'm liable to see is Nicole and Damien with a couple of shotguns standing on the edge looking down—or maybe the two of them doing shots with Rosie. Either way, I'd rather not.

"I'm sorry," Claire says in a small voice. "I feel foolish."

I span the distance between us and wrap her up in my arms, surprised by the instant serotonin hit when she's pressed against me. I hold her because, right now, I can. But I've made a decision, or I'm halfway toward making one, and it's the kind of thing a man can't walk back from. Once she knows everything, there's a good chance she'll be running away from me because she understands rather than because she doesn't. But it's time to take a risk.

"Why wouldn't you make assumptions?" I say into her wet hair, gripping her tighter and reveling in the way her arms have wrapped around me, fisting my wet shirt. "I've given you no reason not to." I pull back enough that I can look at her. "But I need to talk to you, Claire. If we're going to keep seeing each other, you deserve to know who I am. All of it. Then you can decide."

She stiffens in my arms. "You'd really tell me?"

"Yes," I say, the word like dust in my mouth. "*Yes*."

"I have something to tell you too," she says in a rush. "Something I should have said a while ago."

That's unexpected but not unwelcome. If there are skeletons in her closet too, maybe they can dance with mine. But there's no way her secret is equally heavy—not with a soul like hers, bright and blinding and smelling of madeleines.

I hear Shay in my head again, *pussy-whipped*, only this time maybe he'd say it with half a grin. Earlier, Rosie thrust her phone at my face and insisted I talk to him so he could speak sense to me since I wasn't listening quickly enough or well enough for her.

"There's a chance she'll turn me in," I'd told him, and he'd grunted in agreement.

"Sure. But I agree with Rosie, man. You haven't been living your life. What's the difference between what you've been doing and a prison?"

There *is* a difference, of course. I have my greenhouse, full of life that I've helped create. I have my dog. I have the view of the sun going down over the mountains, and the pleasure of stepping onto the deck with a cup of coffee in the morning and soaking in the sounds of peace. Those things aren't nothing, but they're not living either. Not fully. I've been in stasis for the past two years. Not imprisoned but not free. Not engaging in anything except for when Dick conned me into being his friend...or on the rare occasions Rex backs me into getting a drink. Taking numbers only from women who were interested in sex, no conversation necessary.

Maybe it's foolish, telling Claire what happened. Ripping my chest open and letting her see the wounds I've hidden inside. But she's made me want more than just okay.

Her hand travels up to my jaw, and when I look into her eyes, I feel like I'm on that plane again, sitting between two possible futures. Life and death. Redemption and total destruction. And what do you know?

I'm compelled to do the same thing I did then. I lower my head and kiss her like both of our lives might depend upon it. Her hand finds my hair and grips it tightly as she kisses me back the same way, the rain falling down on us as if it's a blessing or a curse, or maybe both. Rain helps things grow. It washes away the ash left behind by destruction. And yet, rain itself can be destruction. Right now, though, with Claire in my arms, kissing me like she doesn't want to let me go, it feels like absolution.

Even if there's a very good chance she won't absolve me of shit. But I still want her to be my confessor.

She makes a noise in her throat, and I pull her closer, needing her sounds, her lips, her taste. Needing it to wash away everything that came before and everything I worried would come afterward. She nuzzles closer, our teeth clashing as the angle changes.

"Fuck, I missed you," I admit. It's only been a couple of days, but they've been tense days—the kind that make a man want to grind his teeth to dust—and I've longed for her. For the way all the colors look brighter when she's with me.

She pulls away slightly, panting. "Let's go to the greenhouse."

"My growhouse, you mean?" I ask, lifting my eyebrows.

She bites the lip I just sucked. "Like I said. There's something I have to tell you too."

Nerves prickle across my skin. She knows something, but what? And from whom?

Maybe I'm being a dumbass, but I swing her up into my arms. Because it might be the last chance I get to pretend that she's mine.

I didn't intend to fall for her.

But I'm not too oblivious to notice when I'm hurtling down a cliff.

She makes a sound of surprise but then wraps her wet arm around my wetter head, holding me close like she feels it too—the pulse of what might be goodbye. When we get to the door, I swing it open and then set her down inside.

"There's a chair in here," I start, but she shakes her head, water drops flicking from her hair. I feel them coursing down the collar of my shirt, my neck. My fucking underwear are wet. I'd suggest changing before we have our talk, but the only thing I have in here is a gardening smock.

Would I like to see her wearing that, and nothing else?

I'm only human, but it wouldn't be conducive to the conversation we're about to have.

"I'd rather stand."

I nod, because I'd rather stand too. It's better to take bad news standing, because it forces you to be strong enough to keep your feet.

"Declan," she says, biting her bottom lip. "I think I'd better start. Damien and Nicole...they're private investigators. The insurance company won't pay up because they claim Dick's death could have been suicide, so Nicole's been trying to prove it was an accident, or that he was...you know...that he might have been murdered. She's been looking into the possibility."

My spine has turned to ice, but I don't move. Don't talk.

If Claire felt like a fool earlier, I feel like the first sentient life-form, gifted with only a brain cell or two. The signs were there all along. The way Nicole and Damien showed up at Vincenzo's to talk to Mark on his day off, when he's only open to receive bets... Nicole's possible revenge on Agnes Lewis and Doug...and then there's the way Nicole and Damien have kept throwing me toward Claire. Did they do it hoping information would shake loose?

Did Claire know that's what they were up to?

A feeling of betrayal scrapes at my throat.

"That's not good," I say woodenly. "You know..."

"That you've been hiding something big, yes. I'm sorry. I was worried you'd run from your life here. From me. I didn't want you to have to lose everything again..." She sighs. "That makes me sound too selfless. I didn't want you to go." She swallows and then says the thing I've lived in fear of for two years. "They know who you are, Declan. Nicole found out on her last trip to New York. When she heard about your uncle, she was worried..."

"She thinks I killed Dick," I say, swearing, then run a hand through my drenched hair. I pace a few steps before I can look at her again, shaking my head. "*You* think I might have killed him."

But she's shaking her head, her eyes troubled. "No, you liked him. Besides, I know you too well to think you'd do something like that. You're not a murderer."

Hot emotion floods me, nearly making me stagger. Because I want to agree with her. I really do. But I say, "That's where you're wrong, Claire. I am."

CHAPTER THIRTY-ONE

DECLAN

Her eyes widen, and I expect her to run again, the way she did earlier. Because everyone knows being a murderer is worse than being your garden-variety player or asshole. But she stands her ground, staring up at me. "You're talking about your uncle."

At least she doesn't believe I killed her father and kept it from her. At least she doesn't think that of me.

"I am," I repeat, feeling a burning inside of me, like everything is in danger of being flash-fried. I glance down, water dripping off my hair.

"You had a reason," she says, a statement more than a question.

A bitter laugh escapes me, but I'm laughing at myself, not her. "Everyone has a reason for the shit they do. That doesn't make it okay. He's dead because of me. End of story."

Finally, I look up at her, because I need to prove to myself that the light has gone out of her eyes when she looks at me. But her eyes have the same buttery, golden gleam. She looks alarmed, naturally, but she doesn't flinch from my gaze.

"Claire..."

"That may be the end of the story, Declan, but I'd like to hear the beginning. You want someone to judge you, but I refuse to do it without knowing everything."

"I don't want you to be good to me right now," I say, feeling like something inside of me is broken, stabbing holes into my gut from the inside.

"I can tell, but I'm not being good or bad to you," she says matter-of-factly, then sits on the floor, cross-legged. My heart clenches at the sight of her making herself smaller, more vulnerable, after I just told her I'm a fucking murderer. I don't deserve her trust —I deserve it less now than I did five minutes ago, and yet she keeps presenting it to me on a platter. It makes me want to be burned in fire and reborn. "I'm just listening. We owe each other that much at least, don't you think?"

"You should run," I tell her, my voice ragged.

"I'd rather not get wet," she says, punctuating it by lifting up the bottom of her shirt and squeezing a small cascade of water onto the ground. Her gaze meets mine again. "Besides, I'm not in any danger, am I? Nicole and Damien made me promise to warn you that they'd get stabby if you hurt me, but I don't think I need to. I think you'd protect me from harm, just like they would."

Of course I fucking would. But I don't say so. I try to swallow back the feelings inside of me, same as always, but they don't go down easy.

"Dick knew about this, didn't he? You said he helped you with some things. I'm guessing those things were hiding under the radar."

"He didn't know at first," I say, wiping my mouth. Then, because I don't want to tower over her, especially not after throwing around words like "murderer," I sit on the ground across from her, my knees bent, my arms balancing over them and my head bowed because I can't look at her right now with the shame thick in my mouth, my soul. "And not everything. But I didn't kill him, Claire. I know what it must look like... When I found him like that, at the bottom of the steps..." Suddenly it all rushes through me, and my eyes feel hot, but I'm not going to cry, sitting here with my confessor angel. I refuse. "It was like I was back there again," I say, swallowing. "I didn't do it, but part of me wondered if it was my fault anyway. If I was cursed, and I'd given my curse to him. I don't think anyone did it to him, though, Claire. It's like I told the police. No one was there, and there weren't any signs anyone had been. He'd always drunk a lot. Taken pills. He carried a lot with him."

"So do you," she comments, watching me. "Carry a lot, I mean."

I nod once, feeling more water drip from my hair.

"Okay. I'd like to know everything," she says softly, watching me. "If you're ready to tell me."

"I was going to tell you anyway. Tonight," I say. "It...it feels important for you to know that."

She nods, and I can see in her eyes that she's not only saying she believes me, she does.

I swallow. "Our parents died when I was twenty-one. Shay was twenty. Rosie was just eighteen. Shay and I were both in the family construction business, but my dad did the finances, so I didn't know what he'd been up to until he died. We were running at a deficit, and instead of giving up, he'd started borrowing money from his brother." I breath out a sigh. "Then he borrowed more money so he could try gambling his way out of the mess, and everyone knows how well those stories turn out..."

"And your uncle was involved in...organized crime."

I nod, my jaw tight. "My mother didn't like him, so we barely knew him. But after my parents died, he showed up and told me it didn't matter that I was family—he couldn't be seen giving anyone breaks. There was proof of what he said...my father had signed an agreement. So my little brother and I could either give up our kneecaps, the family business, and the house, or I could do him a few favors when he needed them." I look away, wipe more water off my forehead. "I didn't feel like I had a choice. I had to protect Shay and Rosie, and I didn't have any skills other than building and growing things. Shay and I hadn't gone to school. Rosie was in college, and I had to help her with tuition on top of everything else. So I told him yes, but I said I wasn't going to hurt anyone for him. Ever. He told me that he didn't rule his house with violence, only intimidation when it was necessary, and I decided to believe him. But there was always one more favor. Usually it was hiding money for him, but when he found out I'd gotten my mom's green thumb, he recruited me to grow for him, which I guess you already knew." I glance off, feeling shame heat my neck. "I didn't say no. The money was good, and the business needed help. We'd been broke, worse than broke, and it seemed like a chance to build something. I opened an off-shore account for my savings so he couldn't touch them."

She nods mutely, taking it all in. My confessor. I always figured I'd end up telling this story to someone in a police uniform. How lucky am I to get her instead?

"Then he asked me to do something I wasn't willing to do…" I pause, taking in a deep breath, because it fucking hurts. Even now, my feelings toward my uncle are complicated. I hated him. Wanted to ruin him. But part of me loved him all the same. "He wanted me to move harder drugs through the growhouse. But he told me I couldn't keep pretending to keep my hands clean. It was time to grow up. Be a man. That's when it really hit me, how deep I'd let myself get. Rosie had been out of college for years, and I had the business out of the red. Partly with dirty money, but I'd learned how to run a business by then. So I told him I was done. I'd paid my debt, and more, and I wanted out." I run a hand back through my sopping hair. "And the next thing I know, he's telling Seamus he wants to help him open an auto body shop. But I knew what he was really after. He wanted to move more money through Shay. Maybe stolen cars. He was tying us to him so tightly we could never leave. So I decided I had to talk to him. To appeal to him as my uncle.

"I didn't set up a meeting because I didn't want him to be

prepared for me. I went over to his house. Broke in through the back door, the way he'd shown me, and found him upstairs. He came out of his study to greet me just as I came up the stairs. He wasn't surprised to see me. He'd known I'd come looking for him after what he told Seamus.

"He said it had taken me too long to grow a pair, and maybe he'd be better off working with my brother. He was needling me. Trying to get a reaction." Shame licks at me again, sickening. "And I was worried he was right. Seamus has always been a hothead. Then my uncle told me I was too much like my parents—soft like my mother and complacent like my father, content with a smaller piece of the pie. We were pussies, both of us, in a cage full of lions. He'd been the only thing keeping us afloat, but I'd disappointed him again and again. Maybe Shay would be less of an embarrassment. Or Rosie."

I swallow, feeling myself there again, feeling the flecks of spit as he yelled in my face and the twisting sensation in my gut that I'd fucked everything up, maybe for the last time, because he was never going to let us go. By then I'd realized he never let anyone go—if someone tried to leave him, they paid and kept on paying. Sometimes with their lives. He'd said he didn't exercise violence, but there'd been signs. At first, I'd been oblivious, trusting. But I'd learned never to take anyone at their word.

"I told him he needed to stay away from my brother and sister, and he said the only way he would was if I stepped up and did what needed to be done. If I entered his business fully."

"You told him no," she says softly, her eyes intent on me.

"I said I'd have to think about it, and he told me not to think too hard, because otherwise I might have an accident. People who were ungrateful often did." I swallow. "From the way he said it, I understood that my parents' accident wasn't an accident."

Her eyes widen.

"It happened in a split second. We'd been pacing around the top of the stairs while we talked. I shoved him, and he fell." My voice quavers on the last word, and I press my palm into the ground, needing to feel something solid against it.

"It was an accident," Claire says, her gaze intent.

I shake my head. "I wouldn't call it that. I saw the stairs behind him... In the back of my mind, I think I knew. Part of me wanted it to happen." I pause. "And I should have called the police. An ambulance. Someone. But I didn't. He was..." I take a deep breath. "He was dead. I checked. But maybe they could have...I don't know. I changed the security footage so it wouldn't show me breaking in. If someone had seen that..."

"They would have assumed you'd gone over there to hurt him."

I nod, feeling miserable. "Maybe I did. Maybe a part of me knew what would happen—that only one of us could survive, and I chose myself. The police declared it an accident, and if anyone believed otherwise, I didn't stick around long enough to hear it. I knew whoever stepped in to take over would be cleaning up. Getting rid of anyone considered loyal to my uncle. We probably would have been on that list. Either that, or they'd have tried to get us under their thumb, same as we'd been under his. I was done."

I don't mention the other part...that *I* could have taken over. That Seamus had wanted the both of us to do it together. *We don't have to do it like him,* he'd said. *We can make it our own.*

But I'd never wanted that kind of power. I'd only ever wanted quiet things. Simple things. The pleasure of watching something grow, of making a beautiful woman moan. Of building something.

"Why didn't you hide with your brother and sister?" she asks. "Why send them to New York and send yourself here?"

I give her a half smile. "I told them it was safer for us to split up, because I was the one they'd look for if anyone came looking. But that's not the only reason. I killed him, Claire. My own uncle. I deserved some punishment, didn't I? That's not the kind of thing you should be able to walk away from."

CHAPTER THIRTY-TWO

CLAIRE

"Declan."

This is both so much worse and so much better than I'd feared. I get up and take a tentative step toward him, and when he doesn't move away, I span the remaining distance. I rethink hugging him, because I'm still soaking wet—and then rethink it again, because so is he. He also needs it—I can see that in the lines of his body, in the way he won't look at me.

A surprised sound escapes him when I get down and wrap my arms around him, but he doesn't shrug me off. Thank God. He doesn't reciprocate either.

"You're not a monster," I say, because I could see in his eyes that he thinks of himself that way. He doesn't believe he's deserving of love or a life, because he took one.

Maybe I'm being naïve to trust a man who just admitted he knowingly worked in organized crime for several years. But I've gotten to know Declan. It's obvious he'd do anything for his brother and sister. For me. And I've seen how much he loved his parents, even though his father fucked him over. How much he cared about Dick, even though Dick was, by most accounts, well named. And I've seen the love and care he puts into nourishing his plants. It wouldn't be fair to define him by the worst things he done.

Besides, a part of me understands how it must have gone down. Didn't I spend years under the thumb of a more overbearing personality? I know what it's like to bend to the will of someone powerful, someone who can make you feel like a god in one breath and a crushed ant the next. I *know*. There's a thrill to living your life like that, teetering between salvation and annihilation—just a breath or a whisper away from either.

There were moments with Agnes when I could see my dream— the awning, the sign, the line out the door. She'd even talk it over with me like it was a done deal before reaching into my head and snatching the vision away the next time her latte wasn't a perfect 155 degrees.

I can see Declan is disgusted with himself for having allowed his uncle so much power over him and his siblings, but here's the thing—when you get yourself into a situation like that, under someone's thrall, it happens so slowly you don't register what's going on. In the beginning, Agnes wasn't sending me to airports to pick up her coat from lost in found, or to ten different stores to find her favorite discontinued brand of lip gloss. She'd tested me, one disagreeable task at a time, until she knew I'd do anything. And that's what Declan's uncle was doing, escalating so slowly that Declan didn't realize it until it was too late. Until they stood at the top of that staircase...

Maybe I'm a bad person, but I don't regret that his uncle's dead. He wouldn't have stopped. People like him never do. Not unless someone takes a stand and stops them. And I don't even think Declan intentionally did that—it's more like karma reached out and decided to plant his uncle in that exact spot when he said those exact words.

Would my real father want me to be with such a complicated man?

Absolutely not. But he operated by the "what she doesn't know won't hurt her" rule for twenty-eight years. Maybe it's my turn to play that card.

"You're not a monster," I repeat, lifting his hand and kissing the back of his knuckles and then the palm. A tortured sound escapes him, and I dip my head and kiss his neck—his Adam's apple, his bearded chin. His nose. He watches me with an expression of disbelief, almost of wonder as I say, "No one is just one thing. We're all a mixture of good and bad. I've seen the man you are, and you are not a monster." I press a hand to his chest, feel his rapidly beating heart, and lift my lips to his brow to kiss him there too. His eyes have an entreaty in him, like he wants to believe me but can't bring himself to, so I repeat it again. "You are *not* a monster."

A gasp escapes me as Declan finally wraps his arms around me, pulling me onto his lap. And I lean up and kiss him. I tell him again, this time without saying anything, that I see him and like what I see. He makes a brutal sound and sinks his hand into my hair, pulling me closer, kissing me like it is, again, his last act. His lips and teeth and tongue all seem bent on consuming me. I know with sudden certainty: no one else will ever kiss me like this, treat me like I'm irreplaceable. And I kiss back him the same way, showing him how much I want to keep him, how little I want to return to my life before. The Claire before. This person I'm becoming is the one I want to be, and he's been part of teasing her out.

As he sucks in my lower lip, I reach for the soaked hem of his shirt and shove it up, and he pulls it off with a fluid movement, revealing the crow on his sculpted chest, and in seconds he has my shirt off, too, then my bra. I crowd into his warmth, wanting to soak it up, to bottle it up but never to sell it. Because I'm going to keep everything to do with him in a locked cabinet in my soul and save it only for myself. His hand flexes in my hair, and he pulls back slightly. "I need you. Fuck, I need you so bad."

"Then take what you need," I say, using the words he said to me a week ago in this same place. I rock against him, feeling how much he wants me. And knowing, again, it's never been like this with anyone else. It will never be like this with anyone else. Feeling a desperate need to make him stay.

He swears, his hands lowering to my hips as I move against him. "I don't have a condom."

"I'm on the pill. Are you—"

"I've always used protection. Are you sure?"

I rock against him again. "Oh, I'm sure."

He shoves my shorts and underwear down, his hands trembling slightly, and I get up so he can finish undressing too, our clothes forming wet heaps on the ground of the greenhouse. A chill tries to work through me, but it doesn't get very far because he pulls me to him, his heat soaking into me and making me warm from the inside out.

"The things I want to do to you..."

"Thousands of pages couldn't cover all the things I want to do to *you*."

He spears a hand into my hair and holds on, the nerve endings lighting up. "I want you to straddle me, like you did that first day."

"You mean when I dry-humped you by the side of the road?" I ask, almost needing to squirm against the tide of need that sentence pulls from me.

"Yes," he hisses, hiking my thigh up around his waist. His hand finds me where I'm wet and desperate for him, and I make a sound that's frankly embarrassing. But from the way his cock pulses against me, he likes it. "I've been thinking of it ever since."

So had I. Then again, my imagination has been very free with Declan. He's unleashed a side of me that's been slumbering my whole life, waiting for someone to kiss it awake.

He's still playing with me as he leans in and kisses my neck, just beneath the ear, and then trails kisses down to my breasts. Groaning, he takes my nipple into his mouth and sucks, and what his hand

and his mouth are doing make my knees threaten to buckle. He must sense it because he sits and guides me down to him.

"Declan," I breathe against his lips, his cock captured beneath me. I rock against it, the pressure hitting perfectly right, and I feel like I did that day on the side of the road—lost to him. Lost to sense, reason, and logic. My fingers trace the crow on his chest, and I send up a wish for him—that he can let go. That he can be free. That he can be mine. Feeling feverish, I rock harder, bursts of pleasure lighting up my body each time I do. I grab the back of his hair, and I kiss him.

"That's it, baby," he says, pulling away slightly, his eyes finding mine. "You take what you want."

What I want is him, so I lift up, adjust him and then slowly lower down, taking him in deep, watching his eyes as they flutter with pleasure. "I want you," I say. "I want *you*."

"Then I'm luckier than I deserve," he says, his voice strained, and he thrusts into me as I press down. He's in so deep, so deliciously deep. He kisses me, his lips and tongue claiming me as his cock does—the same way I'm claiming *him* each time I press against him, asking for and getting more. Kissing his lips and his neck and his bearded chin. I want *everything*. I want time to go slower, to give me more of this, to let this moment stretch out forever—to take over everything that will come afterward and all the uncertainty and anxiety that came before. I want him, and I want him here, and I want him always.

I don't know where that thought comes from, but I don't have time to explore it, because I feel it coming. I feel a bigger release than I've ever had edging up on me as he kisses me and thrusts inside, all the while looking at me like I'm someone he adores. And then he captures my back with his hand and rocks forward, pushing me to the ground—a cold contrast to the hot, muscular man on top of me—and guides my legs around his hips as he strokes in deeper, hitting me at exactly the right angle to make me lose my mind.

"That's it," he whispers into my ear, chasing the words with a kiss. A stroke of his cock. Taking my hands and pinning them above my head, which instantly makes me even more feral as the waves of pleasure ripple through me, filling each limb, each cell of my body. "That's my girl."

I squeeze around him, I feel his breath come in faster pants, and then he's burrowing his head into my neck, his cock swelling inside of me, and his body shudders and then settles into mine. And he's mine, in that moment he's really mine. He kisses my neck and then turns us onto our sides, his cock still buried inside of me.

"I can't get enough of you," he whispers to my mouth.

"Good."

I feel his smile as much as see it. "I'm fucked up."

"I think I am too," I say. "So it's not really the turn-off you might think it is."

His hand soothes up and down my back and then he pulls out. "I'll be right back."

I sit up, watching, because I can't bear to let him out of my sight right now. But he retrieves a towel from a cabinet at the side of the greenhouse, runs it under the tap, then comes back. He strokes it between my legs, making the sensitive skin light up again, asking for more, please.

He sets it aside, then gathers me in his arms again, with me facing him. My heart is swollen and large, and I feel it in my throat as I say, "I don't want you to push me away. And I really, really don't want you to leave."

"Your sister and her husband know everything," he says into my hair, his hands flexing on my back.

"Yes," I say, "but she's known for half a week, and she hasn't done anything about it. I don't think she's the type of person who feels obliged to...well, anything, to be honest."

He pulls back to look at me, and I can tell from the set of his jaw that he doesn't particularly trust Nicole to do the right thing—or the wrong thing, depending on a person's perspective.

I trace the tattoo on his chest. It's beautifully rendered, the ink whirling over his pec. "What's this from?"

His mouth twitches and he captures my hand against his hot flesh. "It's the sign for my uncle's organization. I wanted to remove it, to get laser treatments or burn it off if I had to, but I felt like I deserved to be marked."

I purse my lips. "You know, crows are seen as a positive sign. They stand for transformation and change." I pause, considering if I should share what I have to say, then decide screw it and do: "They can also symbolize someone trying to send a message from the other side. A good message."

There's a benefit to having a best friend who occasionally dips into crystals, the Tarot, and symbology when she's feeling maladjusted.

His smile spreads. "Look at you finding the sunshine lining."

"Oh no," I say, flexing my hand against his chest—I'll never get tired of touching it. "Don't you call me a sunshine girl. I can be downright dour if I don't have my caffeine."

"I don't think you're an anything girl. You're a woman who can't help but find the good in other people. Mrs. Rosings has been giving you the runaround, but you're still helping her, and it's not because you need the money. Or because you're looking for an Agnes replacement. You saw the same thing in her that you did in me."

He's looking at me like he couldn't possibly look away, and I feel an answering glow inside. "What's that?" I ask.

"That we were both lonely as fuck."

My heart quails and aches and grows.

I kiss Declan's jaw, his lips. I let myself push the wet hair off his forehead. "I'm not going to let you be lonely ever again. You're going to get so sick of me."

His smile is sad, and worry pounds a steady beat in my chest.

He's going to leave me. He's going to take that bug-out bag and bury himself away somewhere no one can find him, not even Nicole and Damien.

I weave my hands into his hair, as if I can force him to stay by sheer force of will. "I can understand why you don't want to trust a person who's so obviously a loose cannon, but I've realized something about Nicole. She wants to be there for me. She wouldn't do anything to hurt you, because she wouldn't do anything to hurt *me*."

"So I guess I'd better not piss you off," he says with a half-smile that doesn't meet his eyes.

"I would never let her hurt you, even if you *did* piss me off," I say intently, because he needs to know that I'm not going to throw a hissy fit if he blows me off to go plant a tree or whatever.

He dips his head to kiss my neck. "I believe you." From the look in his eyes, he does, but he still doesn't trust Nicole. I don't really blame him, because there's no denying she does whatever she wants.

I pull back and cup his jaw. "Don't leave without saying anything to me. Don't do that."

He's already shaking his head. "I wouldn't."

He doesn't object that he might decide he needs to go, but I decide I'll have to settle for the assurance he's offering. At least for now.

"Do you really think Dick was murdered?" he asks. He's intentionally changing the subject, but I don't have it in myself to shift it back to one I'd rather avoid anyway.

So I tell him about the bequests, all of them written as if Dick knew the end was staring him in the face. And I tell him about Anthony Smith. Mark. Mrs. Rosings. And all of the other women Dick might have screwed over or pissed off.

As I talk, I think of Dick, giving Declan that dog in his will. He must have done it because he knew how much Declan would miss him—how much he needed at least one other person to know him. It hits me that everything in Dick's will was geared toward him dying sooner rather than later. Was he just paranoid, the way Nicole thinks, or had he known it was going to happen? And if he'd known, was it because he'd planned it or because he sensed it was coming?

Declan runs a hand over my wet hair. "Claire...there was no one in the house. No sign anyone else had been there. No car. Nothing."

"Yeah, but if you went over to kill someone and wanted it to look like an accident, would you park in their driveway?"

He inclines his head, then says, "You don't want to think he did it to himself."

He's right, of course. I feel like I've gotten to know Dick, in a way, and I don't want to believe he killed himself. "Do you?"

His throat works. "No. He had his demons, but I don't think he... I still think it was an accident."

I nod slowly, not truly believing it, not sure he even believes it. "Maybe."

He leans in and kisses my neck. "But I'll help you look into it. Whatever you need."

"You will?" I ask in disbelief.

He gives his head a small shake. "I must be a real shithead if you're this surprised."

"No, it's just... I know you've avoided getting involved in the town."

"Maybe it's past time for me to stop avoiding things."

My heart swells, because it's almost as if he's promising he's not leaving, or at least not leaving yet.

His mouth tics up in one corner. "You look like someone just gave you a recipe for the perfect madeleines."

"I feel like it."

He takes my hand, weaving his fingers through mine. "Do you want to come meet my sister?"

"As much as I hate to say it, I think you should probably put on a shirt first."

CHAPTER THIRTY-THREE

DECLAN

They're not safe around you. You should go.

It's a voice I've heard before. It won't shut the fuck up, to be perfectly honest.

It felt like an unburdening, telling Claire the truth—it felt like I was taking some of the weight off the scales damning my soul. I'm honored by the way she's withheld judgement and accepted me. Knowing her as I've come to, I didn't expect anything less, but I still don't feel I deserve it. If I were a stronger man, I would have stayed away.

So I'm glad Claire knows everything now, but it makes me feel like insects are crawling over my skin, because Nicole and Damien are next door—they're next door, and they know too.

Claire texted them before coming into my house, and it felt like she was telling her attack dogs to Stay.

The second we got inside, Rosie shot me a withering look, like I'd peed on the carpet, and whisked Claire off for some dry clothes. I'd gone upstairs to change out of my wet stuff, too, and Rocket had padded up there with me, wagging his tail as if to tell me that I'd done a good job, finally, by bringing people over.

Now, we're all sitting in the living room with hot toddies Rosie made—Claire on the couch with me while Rosie sits in an armchair across from us. They're talking about baking, and Rocket's curled up at our feet with a buffalo horn, and it's such a normal scene— such a *comfortable* scene—that there's an ache in my chest. Because I never thought I'd have anything like this again—Rosie and Claire, in my space. Because I still don't think I deserve it. Because that voice in my head makes me abso-fucking-lutely certain I'm going to lose it.

Claire squeezes my hand and gives me a sidelong look. She seems worried, and I wish I could tell her not to be.

"Sorry, did I miss something?" I ask.

"Oh, he's off in his own world," Rosie says dismissively, waving a hand. "He likes to live there."

Claire smiles for a second, but a serious look slips back in. "And what's happening in your world?"

It's been a hellscape, full of brimstone and fire and ash, but a few weeks ago, something changed. The sky opened up, and it rained...and suddenly plants are sprouting up out of the cracks of ruin.

I smile. "Just listening to you two. I'm used to the house being empty. It's nice to have guests."

Her hand flexes around mine again. "I seem to recall you saying that you don't want to learn how to be pleasant because then people would talk to you."

Rosie snorts. "Wow. He's a real charmer. No wonder you fell for him."

I'd throw a pillow at her if one were within reach.

"It doesn't hurt that he's incredibly hot," Claire says, her eyes twinkling.

Rosie mimes covering her ears, but she looks pleased. I can see it now—how worried she was for me, how much better she feels now that she's here. And it hits me that I was wrong to stay away from her and Shay. I thought I was only punishing myself, but I was hurting them too, Rosie especially.

"Did he really have a greenhouse with your mom when you were kids?" Claire asks.

"Oh, yes," Rosie says, her smile more indulgent. "They could grow anything. They grew a tomato that was as big as a melon. People down the street came by to look at it for a week, and then Shay cut it up for a salad without a second thought. Our mom was so pissed she didn't talk to him for a day."

They talk for a while longer, Rosie sharing more stories about the time before. It feels good to talk about my parents, and it hurts because it's part of another life.

Rosie suggests we order pizza, and is appropriately horrified to discover that there's not a single delivery place that will bring one to us.

"Let's make some!" Claire suggests. Her excitement is adorable, and it makes me feel like an ass for not having had the foresight to buy yeast even though I've never made a loaf of bread or a home-made pizza in my life.

We make pasta and heat sauce instead, and when we sit down to eat, I feel it again—the pleasure and pain of being a part of something larger. Of having a family again. Of knowing it can be taken from me.

Still, there's an uncomfortable tugging inside of me—*you should go. They'll be safer if you do. She might not think you're a monster now, but she'll find out.*

"I'll clean up the dishes," I say after dinner, because I like that Rosie and Claire are getting along so well. Because I want them to talk—and also because I need a minute alone to process everything. But I'm still finishing up when Claire steps into the kitchen.

He hair is dry now but messy. She'll probably fuss over it if she finds a mirror, but I like it this way. It's like it's been blown dry by the wind.

I reach for her without meaning to, my hand still wet with sudsy water. She doesn't hesitate to take it, and that ache inside me turns warm. "Stay with me tonight."

Her lips part in surprise, and I realize it's a stupid request—she's soaking wet and would probably prefer to go home to shower. Maybe she also needs time to herself to process everything. To consider what I've told her.

Maybe, I realize, I should have asked her before. We spent most of the last week together, but I've never had the joy of having her sleep in my arms. I was holding back, keeping a slender space between us, because I was convinced she'd reject me once she knew everything—and in the back of my mind, I knew it would break me.

She spans the few steps between us and wraps her arms around my neck, her fingers playing with my hair. "Yes. But I need to go back and get a few things."

"You won't need any clothes."

Her eyes are bright as she studies me. "No?"

"You can wear one of my T-shirts if you get cold. You seem to like them."

"You haven't asked for yours back."

"And I won't. I like thinking about you wearing it, lying in your bed. Touching yourself while you think about me."

"Do you have a camera in my bedroom?" she teases, her hand still playing with my hair, sending zips of sensation across my scalp.

Fuck, that means she's done it.

My cock takes an interest in that piece of information, but truthfully I'm not just hoping she hangs around so we can have some fun. I want her in my bed. I need her there. I want to wrap myself around her so nothing else can touch her, hurt her.

She lifts onto her toes and kisses me, and I feel desperate in a way it takes me a moment to understand.

I don't want to lose her, this.

I don't want to seam the sky shut and lock myself back up into that hellscape divested of color.

"I still need my toothbrush," she says.

"I have a new one in the closet," I say, not sure why I'm pushing back on this. Of course she can go next door to pick up a few things...

"You really don't want me to go over there," she comments, watching me. "Why?"

It's only then it clicks.

"I'm worried you won't come back," I admit, my voice hitching, because I can't help but feel like less of a man again. Right from the beginning, I've cracked myself open for her, letting her see my fears, my strangled hopes. My softness. "I'm worried they'll convince you not to come back."

She brings her hand around to cup my cheek. "I used to be the kind of woman who could be talked around and told what to do. But I'm not anymore. No one could convince me not to come back. Not even Nicole."

She sounds almost angry about it.

"I know," I say. "It's another irrational fear, Claire. Like with airplanes. Or you, with roller coasters."

Except it doesn't seem so irrational to me. The irrational thing would be for her to return.

"I'm going to go," she says to me, her hand still on my cheek. "But only to prove to you that I'll come back."

I put a hand on her waist. Squeeze lightly, to assure myself she's here. "Okay."

And then I kiss her again because I want to—because if the opportunity to kiss her arises, I'm not going to waste it. Not anymore.

I go to the front door with her and watch her leave, her figure climbing up the steps to Dick's house and opening the door, where she's greeted by a woman with pink hair. Rosie comes up behind me and pats me on the shoulder.

"I overheard everything you said in the kitchen."

A sigh escapes me.

"Don't worry, I have really good earplugs. Top notch." Then she turns me around to look at her. She's fussing with the purple streak in her hair, as if she's not *quite* sure how it got there. When she was a kid, she always used to suck on the ends of her hair. It got so bad at one point that my mom threatened to cut it short. Her hair is a gauge for how she's feeling. How she's feeling right now is apparently anxious.

"Please, *please* don't fuck this up," she says.

I can't help but grin. "From your mouth to God's ears."

It's something our dad used to say, and for a second we just smile at each other. It's like no time has passed at all, until I hear myself murmuring, "I'm sorry, Rosie. I'm sorry I left you. I'm sorry I screwed everything up so badly."

Her expression shifts—sorrow filling her eyes for a moment before her hand tightens around my shoulder. "Now I'm even more desperate for you not to lose her. Because I'm relieved someone's finally gotten through to you. And you need to realize that it would have been worse if you'd listened to Shay."

I nod firmly, even though there was never a chance I would have listened—or allowed him to get sucked further into that life. I would have zip-tied his wrists and dragged him out if I'd needed to.

My sister releases me and nods, then says "I'm going upstairs to call Shay."

I nod, mute. But I don't move. I stand there until I see Claire coming back to me.

I stand there, and something inside of me breaks and is reborn as she walks back up the steps of my porch.

WHEN WE GET UPSTAIRS, I undress Claire slowly, taking off the clothes she changed into at the other house. Making love to her thoroughly, slowly, until she's moaning, her mouth a perfect oh that I capture, sucking down her cries and making her mine.

Afterward, we lay together, talking, and I stay awake long after she falls asleep in my arms. I watch her for a while, soaking in the sight of Claire at peace. Claire, *safe*. Then I head downstairs with a book, Rocket following me.

Something in me already knows that I'll have a visitor. So I'm not surprised when Rocket stiffens at my feet and then races to the door.

I follow him, then look out before opening it to let her in.

"So you're not totally stupid," Nicole says. "You knew I'd come."

"I suspected," I agree. "Would you like a drink?"

She lifts a flask out of her pocket. "I brought my own."

"So you won't mind if I pour one for myself." She gives me a look that my hospitality is time wasting, so I shrug and pour myself some whiskey.

"Do you want to talk on the back deck?" I ask, remembering all the time I spent out there with Dick. Now, those memories are layered with memories of Claire. All of them are good. I've been creating a life here without meaning to, or even noticing. It just happened. Because of them.

"As long as you don't push me off," Nicole says.

"A sentiment I agree with—and return," I reply.

We head out onto the deck and each claim a chair, looking off into the blackness, a few distant stars sparkling overhead with a half moon.

Neither of us says anything for a moment. We just sit there and drink, both of us mired in our thoughts.

Finally, I say, "I'm glad you dealt with Agnes and Doug, but I wish I'd been able to help. I don't like that I didn't have any part in it."

She studies me for a moment before nodding in what looks like approval. "Next time someone fucks with Claire, I'll give you first swing."

We exchange a smile, then Nicole lifts her flask to tap to my glass and we drink together.

"I'm not going to screw you over," she says after another moment. "Not unless you give me a reason to."

"What constitutes a reason?" I ask, leaning back in my chair. "Am I going to get picked up by the cops if I accidentally cut you off in traffic?"

"You treat my sister well, you have nothing to worry about," she says pointedly.

"I know she deserves someone who's—"

A finger jets into the air, interrupting me. "She deserves whatever the fuck she's decided she wants. And if it's you, you should feel lucky, and do whatever you can to deserve it."

"I don't know if it's safe for me to be with her," I grind out. Because for so many years, I've been looking over my shoulder—waiting for someone to come, to make me pay. Because, my uncle's death was, in many ways, a relief. It was freedom. But freedom paid for by blood is never truly free.

"No one's looking for you," she says. "The police think the guy who took over for your uncle did it, if anyone did, and his people could give a shit about you and your siblings. They're happy you're gone. If you were to randomly show up, sure, they might feel motivated to kill you to keep you from taking a piece of their pie, but as long as you stay away, they couldn't care less. You can believe me when I say that, because I'm good at collecting information. I collected *your* information."

"Because you did something with my burner phone."

"You left it out in a kitchen that was half mine. It was practically an invitation."

I shrug, because it was a stupid mistake, and I own it. Besides, her words are a relief. I've wanted to believe it. At certain points I've dared to...

This means Rosie can stay with me. It means Shay could join us...if he wants. It means I don't have to be alone, and I've only been keeping myself that way as a punishment, the way both Claire and Rosie have told me.

Except Nicole knows...

She lifts her eyebrows at me, almost as if she knows what I'm thinking, and maybe she does. Maybe the ability to read me runs through their blood, because Dick could do it too. "You want something on me so if one of us slips we can be assured of mutual destruction?"

I gape at her. "You'd do that?"

She shrugs. "Sure, why not? You'd be a fool to try to ruin me. I'd eviscerate you, and that's nothing on what Damien would do—but if it would make you feel better, I'm not opposed. I've done tons of illegal shit."

I can't help but laugh as I shake my head. "No, I'm good."

"You're just being polite. You're going to hire someone to go through my shit, and I'd honestly rather give you what you need."

She's not wrong.

"I'll send you proof that I staged the whole Agnes thing, how about that? If you turn me in for helping your girlfriend, you'll be a double asshole, so it's only appropriate."

"Okay," I say, pausing. Then, "Thank you."

"Claire says you don't think our old man was murdered."

I shake my head. "No, but I'm not the private investigator."

"You know, I keep going back to Mark."

"He liked Dick," I say, not surprised she'd be suspicious but certain that line of inquiry will get her nowhere. "Besides, Mark was in Charlotte that weekend. Restaurant was closed and every-thing. He had me come in and water the plants."

"I know he has an alibi," she says, "and I've verified it. But it all feels connected to me. The betting. The holes in the yard. Claire and I were wondering if Dick might have buried money back there. Maybe someone lost a big wad to him, and they didn't like it much." She rubs her forehead. "Normally, this shit would all net together in my head, but I can't get it to—"

"You're too involved. It's personal."

Her lips firm into a flat line. "Maybe. But it's not because I care about that asshole. It's because there have been distractions."

"Sure," I say, but here's another thing my dad used to say: don't kid a kidder. An interesting sentiment for someone who got bilked by his own brother, but maybe he knew what to do and just didn't do it. That's something I understand well enough.

"You have a background in organized crime," she says easily, like it's something I talk about at dinner parties. "What do you think about the money theory?"

I nod slowly. "I wouldn't be surprised if he buried a stash. I know a lot of people who have, and Dick didn't trust banks. But it sounds like he left a pretty in-depth will. Why wouldn't he have mentioned something like that?"

She grins, but there's something sad in her eyes. "You don't think the wily old bastard would have wanted to challenge us one last time? He wanted us to stay in his house for a month. I'll bet he was hoping we'd figure it out. Besides, if it's money he won gambling, something told me he didn't pay tax on it. Maybe he didn't want us to have to either."

"What if the instructions were in those photo albums?"

She snorts. "Maybe. He'd figure it would serve us right for not being nostalgic and looking at his shit." Then something sparks in her eyes. "Hey, good idea, Claire's boyfriend."

"Yeah?" I ask, not at all disliking the nickname, even if it means she's forgotten my name. "What's that?"

"I know just where an asshole like my father might have hidden a thing like that."

I don't ask. It's none of my business, really, and if she wanted to tell me, she would. Besides, this peace between us still feels like a new thing, potentially breakable. Which is why what I say next is really fucking stupid...

"You remind me of him, you know. Both of you do, but more you than Claire. He was funny. Loud. Said what he thought when he thought it. Manipulative, too."

She surprises me by tipping her head back and laughing. "Good for Claire. Bad for me, maybe, but my old man did have a passable sense of humor, I'll give him that. And he knew how to make a good puzzle." She rubs her chest, like part of her knows that he did it for her, because he knew who she was. I have to believe he did—he was like that, too lazy to take out the trash, but on the ball enough to research the lives of his daughters. He probably followed every milestone from a distance. It's a lonely thought, a lonely life...

"And he knew what he wasn't," I blurt. "He knew what he couldn't be. I think he cared about both of you as much as he was able to."

"And you?" she asks pointedly. "How much are you able to?"

I look out at the expanse stretched out before us, remembering the first time Dick came out here. Remembering the sight of his body, broken at the bottom of those stairs. Maybe I was on the same track as him—living alone, gearing up to die alone, with only a few people to feel sorry about it. With nothing to do but figure out ways to make my death more dramatic, my legacy something people had to pay attention to, whether they wanted to or not. I don't want that life, or death. The need for something more burns in my chest. "More. I want to be more for her. She's already changed everything for me."

She holds out her hand for a shake. "Then welcome to the family, Declan Whatever-the-fuck-your-last-name-is. I have some work for you to do."

And that's when she tells me what else she's been up to these last few weeks.

CHAPTER THIRTY-FOUR

CLAIRE

It's Friday, and I'm at Smith House, helping Mrs. Rosings pick out ugly favors for her son's wedding. Since the goat lady's wedding venue got nixed, Mrs. Rosings has decided it's a "fair compromise" if she picks soaps from the selection on the woman's website, with names like Grumpy's Garden and Trixie's Trash. Most of them are molded to look like goats' heads. It's a thankless job, and an idea that's sure to get tanked by Anthony or his bride as soon as they find out, but I'm humming as I scroll through the poorly made website.

Nicole and I still don't know what happened to Dick Ricci, and even though Declan insisted that he and Nicole have reached some sort of understanding, and he even gave me his bug-out bag as a promise he won't leave without warning, it's possible he'll still decide he needs to go. But I'm *happy*. For the first time in a long while, I'm not just looking forward to what comes next or wishing away this week in favor of the one after. I'm enjoying myself. Even now, looking through these terribly named soaps, I'm having fun.

Lainey's coming on Sunday, and I've spent the last three nights with Declan. He and Rosie came over for a barbecue last night. Declan and Damien made all the food for dinner, and Rosie and I made the most perfect madeleines to ever bless this earth. Nicole...

drank and instigated a game of Never Have I Ever, which is how I found out more than I ever wanted to know about my half-sister, my brother-in-law, my boyfriend, and my boyfriend's sister. I ended the night nearly sober and impressed. And it was as close to perfect as a night can be.

Nicole and I have agreed that we can start planning Dick's send-off party even though we haven't settled things with the insurance company. Her rationale is that if he was murdered, the killer will probably be at the party, a possibility she sounded excited about but feels like a spider fast-footing across my arm. In the meantime, she's going back to Vincenzo's to talk to Mark this afternoon, while Damien does who knows what, and I promised to try to make an appointment to talk to Anthony. Declan insists he's going with me after he gets finished with his afternoon job, and I haven't fought him on it. I'm not afraid of Anthony, but it's possible he's more dangerous than he appears to be. I'd rather not find out the hard way.

According to Nicole, she also has a surprise for me for when I get off work, and I'm both terrified and intrigued.

"Oh, what's that one?" Mrs. Rosings says, leaning over my shoulder the way she's been doing for the last twenty minutes. She's sitting in a chair next to me, but judging from the amount of times she's leaned over my shoulder, it doesn't give her a good enough of view of her laptop screen. It's ten times nicer than my computer, and used only for tormenting her son, as far as I can tell.

"Wendy's Waste." I give her a sidelong look. "I think it's meant to look like..."

"That's the one," she says with a gleam in her eyes.

"Mrs. Rosings..." I pause. "Isn't it a waste of money to go through with buying two hundred bars of soap, when there's—" How to put this...I can't think of a polite way, so I just go for it. "...no way in hell Nina is going to agree to give them out as party favors."

"She'll do it if I allow them to have the wedding out of this house," she says pointedly. "She'll agree to it, and he'll know, if he has a lick of sense left in him, that she's just using him for the Smith family name and money." Sighing, she sits back in her chair. She's wearing another of her expensive kaftans, but this one has faded colors, like maybe this long, drawn-out, and somewhat one-sided war is wearing her out.

I've learned her mannerisms enough to know she has more to say, probably a lot more, so I shift my chair slightly to face hers. "What if she only agrees to please you because she loves him?" I ask, because it needs to be said.

"Oh, pish," she says dismissively. "I was a gold digger. I know one when I see one."

My eyes widen, because I certainly hadn't expected her to admit that.

"Don't look at me that way. Back in my day, we didn't have as many opportunities as you do. A woman had to take what she could get..."

"Mrs. Rosings, you're not that old," I say. "I'm pretty sure you had the vote back in the 1970s."

Her lips twitch with a repressed smile. "Be that as it may. I did what I did, what everyone in this miserable town thinks I did, and I paid for it. For *years*. But if that girl marries Anthony, he's the only one who'll be paying. I know my son. If he finds out she doesn't love him after the wedding, it'll crush him."

I have about five thousand questions, none of which are appropriate to ask of an employer, even an employer like Mrs. Rosings. So instead I decide to try setting up an appointment with Anthony. Maybe I can pretend it's about the shitty soap.

"Is Anthony coming by anytime soon?" I ask cryptically.

"Probably once he receives the sample wedding favors," she says with a sly grin, but it drops, a shrewd look taking its place. "Why?"

"Oh, no reason. I thought maybe he'd want to talk about Dick."

Her eyebrows rise, and I realize my mistake.

"The person, I mean," I say, my cheeks heating. "My biological father, Dick."

"Why would you want to talk to Anthony about Dick? He hated him."

"I'm trying to form a full picture of who he was as a man," I say, halfway meaning it.

She lifts her eyebrows again, then shrugs. "I have no problem with it. Maybe Nina will assume he's cheating on her."

"Mrs. Rosings," I caution. "Don't try to put me in some kind of compromising situation."

She laughs and sits back, studying me. "I wouldn't dream of it. I've seen you around town with that young man of yours. You *glow*."

That's news to me. I haven't noticed her on the mean streets of Marshall, but then again, I've been so lost in loved-up La La Land, that I probably wouldn't have noticed an oncoming truck before it smashed me in the face. I wonder how Declan will feel about knowing we're the gossip of Marshall.

Then again, he knows this place well enough that he must realize we are—and yet he's still been walking around with his arm around me.

"I'm pretty happy," I admit.

To my surprise, she gives a steadfast nod, as if we've established something between us, then rises from her seat and heads over to the bar. Pours us each something.

"You said you'd never drink with me again," I comment, alarmed by this shift in a character that has always seemed carved from stone.

"I'm glad you've found happiness in love," she says, bringing over the drinks and setting one in front of me. "I never did."

"Not with any of them?" I ask, torn between disbelief and sadness. Imagine having tried three times and failed each.

"No, not with any of them," she says, her voice more than a little sad. "Which is not to say I didn't love any of them. I'm worried Anthony's making the same mistakes."

"Maybe the goat poop soap isn't the best way to express that worry," I say, because I'm done with bottling up my best advice for fear of pissing people off.

She smiles, her eyes glimmering. "No, perhaps not. But it *is* the most enjoyable way."

She's got me there. There's no question she's been having fun, even if behind it I see what Declan did...she's lonely. Which must be why I press her. "You don't think it's...toxic?"

She waves a hand and takes a sip from her drink as if I've driven her to it. "You young people love to throw that word around. My husband Adrien, now *he* was toxic, and this town loved him. He was their promised son."

This doesn't seem like a great reason for pushing her own brand of toxicity, but I can tell I've pushed Mrs. Rosings about as far as she's willing to go today. If I want to get through to her, I'll have to wait.

I take a sip of my drink, and as I do, Mrs. Rosings retrieves a notepad and pen from God knows where and scribbles off a number, handing over the piece of paper. Her penmanship is, of course, impeccable.

"Anthony's number. See if you can subtly let him know he's making a terrible mistake."

"I've never met Nina," I point out. "I have no way of knowing if she's really a gold digger, or you're just one of those mother-in-laws who hates her daughter-in-law on principal."

She gives me a pointed look. "There's nothing preventing both things from being true, although I'd like to think I'd accept a sensible daughter-in-law with open arms." She tilts her head. "*You* wouldn't be entirely objectionable. It's too bad that gardener laid one on you before you could meet Anthony."

I snort-laugh. I can't help it. I feel bad for Mrs. Rosings's future daughter-in-law, whether it's Nina or someone else.

"Put in the order for the Wendy's Waste," she says as if our initial conversation hadn't been interrupted. Her eyes sparkling, she adds, "We'll put them in little satin bags. Expensive. You think she'll realize it's a metaphor?"

"I think even someone who doesn't know what metaphor means would get the message," I say.

Her lips twitch. "Good, because I'm not at all confident she does."

CHAPTER THIRTY-FIVE

CLAIRE

Sitting outside in the Jeep, I grab my phone out of my bag to text Anthony, seeing a message waiting for me from UNKOWN NUMBER, which is how Nicole has programmed her number into my phone, an inside joke between her and herself about how we first met.

> I've learned something interesting. I'm off to talk to Roy. Your surprise is waiting on the kitchen counter. DO NOT DIG WITHOUT ME.

My first thought is who the fuck is Roy? My second is excitement.

Don't dig without me.

Did she find some kind of a map?

We've discussed the possibility that Dick might have buried money in the backyard, but we haven't gotten much further than taking a look at those holes. After a quick glance at them the other day, I had to admit that I know jack-all about holes in the ground and what might have made them, and even though Nicole likes to pretend she knows everything, it was clear she was equally at a loss. So I called Declan, and *he* took a look. He says they're definitely man-made, created by a post hole digger. The pattern seems completely random, so either this person snuck into the yard at night and hoped for the best, or Dick gave them an inaccurate map to mess with them. The only thing we know for sure is that nothing's shown up on the cameras Damien had installed the other day.

I text Nicole

> Don't hold out on me. Did you find a treasure map?

> More information is required.

> New number, who's this?

> Very funny.

> Don't dig without me. If you do, I'll be pissed. People don't like it when I'm pissed.

> Okay, Hulk. Who's Roy?

> You seriously don't remember Roy? He'll be wrecked.

I roll my eyes and open a new message window to text Anthony, tapping the side of my phone as I think about what to say to a man who almost certainly doesn't like me by association. I decide to go for simple:

> Hi Anthony, this is Dick Ricci's daughter. I was wondering if you'd be willing to meet to discuss my father?

There, that's professional. There's an instant three dots, and I straighten up, wondering what he'll say, when his answer pops up on my screen.

No offense, but there isn't much to say. Did my
mother put you up to this?

No.

Thinking fast, I decide to channel Nicole in my next message.

But wouldn't you like to have an insider look at
what she's up to? I'll bet Nina would like to know.

I won't betray Mrs. Rosings, much, since her son has every
appearance of being a tool who completely lacks the sense of humor
she's credited him for...but he doesn't have to know that.

There's a pause, then he writes:

Meet me at the Starbucks in Marshall. At 6:30.

"What if I had plans?" I complain to the empty car. I'm also not
impressed by his selection—there are a few coffee shops in
Marshall, and he picked the only generic one in the bunch. No
question about it, Anthony Smith is a tool.

But is he a murderous tool?

That remains to be seen, but I'm guessing I won't find out at
Starbucks. Honestly, if it's left to me, I probably won't find out at all.

Hopefully Declan's better at interrogating people than I am. I
text him the details for the meeting with Anthony, then leave Smith
House, the gate automatically opening to let me go.

My heartbeat cranks up as I pull into the driveway of the cabin.

Declan's car isn't next door, which I expected—he took Rosie to
help him with a planting job that should keep them busy until just
before our meeting with Anthony.

Don't dig without me.

Is it just me, or does that sound like a challenge?

I head inside the house, dropping my keys on the kitchen

counter, and...I do a double take, because what's waiting there is definitely not what I was expecting.

Little Titty Women, Big Time.

Is Nicole messing with me again? And yet...

I open the box, my tongue captured between my teeth, because who knows what kind of promotional material could be tucked inside, but the box is completely empty other than a folded piece of paper covered in drawings.

My heart starts pounding again. Dick hid this map in here, obviously, and she figured it would be funnier to leave it out for me in the case. She was right, obviously. I unfold it, and press it down on the kitchen counter, ironing out the folds with my thumb. At first I can't make sense of the shapes, but then I turn it one-hundred-and-eighty degrees, and I see a couple of landmarks I recognize. The fire pit. The greenhouse.

The greenhouse.

There's a heart next to it with a red star in the middle—drawn in deep lines that suggest it's important.

I remember again the note my bio-dad left me—*Declan's a good guy, mostly.* He trusted him.

I trust him.

I trust Nicole too, but the shovel leaned up against the counter feels like proof enough that this was a dare—and that she'd be disappointed if I didn't take her up on it.

She's giving this to me, same as if she wrapped it up in pretty paper and tied a bow around it.

Heart pounding, I take the shovel and the porn DVD map and make my way down the hill. On the way, I pass several of the man-made holes pockmarking the land, and it sends a shiver down my spine. Whoever's been doing this has stayed away since the cameras went up, but there's no denying someone was out here looking for something, while we were tucked into our beds, completely unaware. A killer, maybe, in my own backyard.

When I reach the greenhouse, I study the map, and then I see it —a big rock shaped like a heart about ten feet away from the entrance. Well, crap, I should definitely have fit an arm day into my non-existent workout schedule. I take a deep breath, then heave the heart rock with all my might. It budges maybe an inch.

I hear a horn beep up on the road, but my focus is on moving my nemesis rock. I give it another shove. This time it doesn't move at all. If anything, I probably wedged it further into the dirt.

Maybe I *will* be waiting for Nicole.

No, this is more of a Declan task. Nicole may look tough as hell, but her arms are twigs. Declan could probably move it without breaking a sweat.

"Claire Rainey," a familiar voice shouts, and I whirl around, my heart fluttering. Through the brush and trees, I can see a figure standing at the top of the hill. I hurry away from the rock so I can get a better view, stepping around a couple of gnarled trunks, and there she is.

Lainey is standing at the top of the hill in cut-off jean shorts and a checkered shirt, a huge grin on her face. The profound sense of relief I feel—as if a balloon is expanding inside of me—tells me how much I've missed her.

"You said you weren't getting in until Sunday!" I shout as she starts picking her way down. I can already tell she's wearing a pair of shoes that are completely inappropriate for the task.

She grins at me, then makes a face at one of the holes that tried to take her down. A couple of minutes later, she reaches me toward the bottom of the hill. It's wild, having her here. My past, meeting my present. It feels like the space time continuum should explode.

I wrap her up in a hug, pulling her close and burying my head in her neck. She hugs me back hard. "That's for not being around for the Todd bullshit," I say. "I hate that I wasn't. But why are you here early?"

She pulls back. "Your sister surprised you. I figured it would be fun to pull off something like that, too. Why haven't you been answering your phone?"

I wave behind me toward the heart rock, hidden by the trees. "I was in the zone, and I had it on silent. There's this big rock I need to move down there. Remember I told you about the holes in the yard—"

"Yes—" she lifts up one of her wedges, "—one of them tried to end my life."

"Well, Nicole found what looks like a map."

"We're on a treasure hunt?" she asks, her eyes lighting up. "This is the best thing that's ever happened to me."

"Don't get too excited. From what I've learned about Richard Ricci, it could just be the DVD for *Little Titty Women, Big Time.* That's the kind of wild goose chase that would have amused him."

She lets out an amused pfft of air. "After ten hours in the car, listening to the audiobook for *Unfuck Your Life,* that still feels like the best thing that'd ever happen to me. What do we do?"

"We go down there and push."

So that's exactly what we do.

Lainey's not much more physically adept than I am, but she has an edge over me because she's been moving those boxes around like a human game of Tetris. Between the two of us, we get the rock budged out of the way enough that we can start in with the shovel. It's hard, dirty work, and within five minutes, I'm sweating everywhere a body can sweat.

Lainey's taking her turn with the shovel when a thunking sound meets our ears. Her eyes widen, and she shovels more dirt out of the way before I reach down into the pit we've created. There's a metal box inside, locked, and I wiggle it out of the dirt pit.

"Holy shit," Lainey says, crouching down next to me. "We found something."

We did, but it's the work of a second to discover it's locked.

Which is when I remember the key Nicole found a couple of weeks ago.

I tell Lainey about it, and we start up the hill, Lainey pausing halfway up to remove her shoes. We carry the dirty metal lock box inside, setting it on the kitchen counter, so I can run upstairs to get the key.

It fits.

It turns.

Lainey whistles. "That's a lot of money."

More sweat forms on my forehead, in my pits. Because she's right. There's a folded paper note on top of two plastic bags filled with rolls of bills, one hundreds on the outside of each of the rolls. Unless this is an *I got you* situation, where he's wrapped hundreds around ones, or currency-sized pieces of paper, there is, in fact, a lot of money in there. Much more money than I've ever seen in my life.

"Open the note," she urges.

So I do.

> Daughters-
>
> One of the things I enjoyed most about being a father was embarrassing you, Nicole. So I hope you'll allow me this last indulgence. Don't gamble unless you're good at it. I happened to be very good at it. These are my winnings. Spend it well, kids. Have yourselves a party. Maybe you can lift one up for me while you're at it.
>
> Maybe I'm being morose, and I'll decide to dig this up tomorrow, but I feel the end coming soon. When you get older, all the things you've done start clustering around you, threatening to smother you. Maybe I deserve to be smothered by mine.
>
> The bag with the R on it is for Rex. I'll rely on you to

get it to him. You might not believe your old man is capable of regret, but I feel bad about how I won it, and the kid deserves a break.

Yours—

D

My pulse starts pounding harder in my veins.

Rex.

He's been around from the beginning.

He made a comment about the gophers.

He's the one who installed those cameras that have kept our late-night intruder away.

He's the one who seems to know this town up and down, in and out...

And he's also the one, it hits me, whom Nicole calls Roy.

"Oh, this isn't good," I say, dropping the note.

"Seems pretty good to me," Lainey says as she reaches into the lockbox for the bags of money. "I want to count it. I've never had a chance to count this much money, like a fixer in one of those mafia movies."

I grab her wrist, my heart thumping fast. "*Lainey*, I think Nicole's in trouble. We have to get to her. *Now*."

I pull my phone out of my pocket with shaky fingers, see the missed calls from Lainey, and use my fingerprint to unlock it. The first thing I do is shoot off a text to Nicole on the off-chance she's able to answer—

Where are you? I'll come get you.

The next thing I do is call Declan. Maybe my first thought should be to summon the police, but they're the ones who discounted the possibility that Dick's death could be anything but a drunk guy taking a spill down a flight of poorly made steps. Besides, this is a small town, and everyone seems to know Rex—who are they going to believe? A New Yorker who was Dick the dick's daughter, or one of their own?

Declan picks up on the second ring. "Everything okay?"

"No, actually," I say, my voice breathy, and I explain what just happened and my suspicions about Rex.

"I'm on my way," Declan says. "I'll text Damien, too, and you call the police. Stay at the house and lock the door."

"She's *my* sister," I object. "I can't just leave her there without doing anything. If it were me, she'd batter the door down." She'd shown me that. We may not have grown up together, but that didn't matter to Nicole. She'd claimed me, and I wanted to prove that I'd claimed her too, dammit.

"Claire, stay in the house," he says, his tone gruff and desperate. "Damien and I have both dealt with dangerous people before. Let us deal with this. Stay at home. *Please.*"

It's the *please* that does it. The please and the realization that he's right. What would Lainey and I realistically be able to do? I carry around a rape whistle and mace in my purse, and I know Lainey does too, so we'd be able to do *something*, but Rex is taller than us and a man who works with his body. He'd easily be able to overpower both of us, probably even if we attacked him at the same time.

And he also told me he goes deer hunting. That means he almost certainly has a gun somewhere...

More sweat breaks out across my body at that thought, because I don't want Nicole, or Declan, or Damien to be in danger. I couldn't stand it if any of them got hurt.

"Okay," I say flatly. "Okay."

"Promise me, Claire," he says. "I need to hear you promise me."

"I promise. Declan...I'm scared."

He swears under his breath. I hear a sound on the other end of the line, like something being dropped to the ground. I can imagine him throwing his hand trowel. "I want to be with you so badly right now. I hate that I don't have eyes on you. But I swear to God, I won't let anything happen to either of you. I'd die before I let anyone hurt you."

My heart swells. I believe him. If it's in his power, he'll do anything to protect us. *If it's in his power.*

"What about Rosie? You're not going to bring her, are you?"

"No, I'm not bringing her," he says firmly, and I can hear her say something in the background. I'm guessing she's arguing the point, but he'll get his way on this one. He wouldn't let anyone hurt her either. "I'll call you as soon as we have her."

I like the way he says it, like it's going to happen, not just that it might. It's a reassurance he can't give, but I'm still hungry for it. A month ago, I didn't know Nicole was alive. Now, she's entered the small circle of people I'd do anything for, and I can't stand the thought of anything happening to her.

"Goodbye," I say. "Do whatever you need to do to be safe. I mean it. Don't hesitate."

I can feel his smile. "Look at you. Just over three weeks in Marshall, and you're turning into leather jacket Sandra Dee on me."

I feel a pulse of uncertainty. "You don't like leather jacket Sandra Dee."

"Turns out I have a thing for both versions," he says, and my heart feels gooey and large. "Stay safe, Claire."

Then he clicks off, leaving me with my gooey heart and a new worry—that something horrible might happen, and I'll lose both of them. All I'll be left with from this life-transforming month is a house that's more or less falling down and a lockbox of money that my biological father won from gambling on Christmas wreaths and people's lives.

I lower the phone as Lainey watches me. Her feet are filthy

from the trek up the hill, and she just got done with a twelve hour drive with stops, but she looks ready to ride into battle.

"We're not going," I tell her.

I swear to God, she deflates.

"I'm going to call the police, though, and Declan's going over there with Damien."

She nods, twisting her mouth to the side. "They're probably better equipped to deal with this situation. But it would feel kind of anticlimactic to hide in here. Wrong, too."

"I'm going to make that call."

I check my messages first. Nothing from Nicole. Nothing further from Declan. A recipe for gluten-free cupcakes with tofu frosting from my father.

Then I call the local police station. The officer who finally picks up actually laughs when I tell him why I believe Rex might be a danger to Nicole.

"I'd reckon he's the only one who's in danger," he says dismissively. "Rex wouldn't hurt a fly, but your sister, boy..." That's when he makes his big mistake and laughs.

Fury lights in my gut, catching on all the other dismissals I've buried down there over the years. I'm not feeling at all nice when I say, "Listen, *sir*, if you want to keep your job and avoid getting sued, you *will* send a squad car to check on my sister. If I find out you haven't, and something happens to my sister, then guilt isn't the only thing that will plague you. I will do everything in my power to ensure you never work another day in your life."

"As a police officer?"

"As *anything*. Have I made myself clear?"

It's all bluster, obviously, but I learned from the best. How many dressing downs have I gotten from Agnes, in front of half the office. How many have I heard her give to other people?

How many have I written into her speeches?

Enough to give a damn good one, if I do say so myself.

There's a pause, my phone giving a soft buzz that tells me there's an incoming message, then he says, "Yes, ma'am," his voice suddenly all politeness. "I will personally see to it."

"You do that."

When I hang up, Lainey beams at me. "You slayed!"

"A text came in," I say urgently, shifting my phone so I can check the screen.

My heart gives a frantic thump as I check out the notifications on my screen. It's from Nicole.

I click through and frown at the screen.

> Can you wait to come home, actually? I have a
> birthday surprise for you, but I need time to set
> it up.

I glance up at Lainey, horror rippling through me. "This is bad."

"Why?" she asks, peering at the screen. Her brow puckers. "Isn't this good news? I mean, your birthday's not for four and half months, but she's only known you for a few weeks, so—"

I can see it click for her, same as it did for me. Faster for me, because I know Nicole better, and that message is way too nice to have come from her. "Oh, you don't think it's from her."

"No, and I think she told him it was my birthday to send me a message. He's bringing her *here*."

CHAPTER THIRTY-SIX

CLAIRE

"You should leave," I tell Lainey.

She puts her hand on her hip, and before she says a single word, I'm aware she's not going anywhere.

"No," she says flatly. "Now, what are we going to do with the cars?"

Shit, she's right. The second Rex pulls up the road, he's going to know we're here. Her Dodge can be hidden in the garage, but there's no hiding the Jeep. It's a metal beast that will probably outlast the final human on earth.

Then again, Rex might not realize I can drive the Jeep—I've paid him to give me a couple of Uber rides between here and Smith House. He probably heard about what happened last week, when Declan and I kept stalling out on the road and holding up the one lane of traffic.

I tell all of this to Lainey, who nods and fishes her car key out of her pocket. "On it."

I use the interior to access the garage and open it for my friend. The space is full of Dick's crap—a broken bicycle, crates of empty beer bottles he probably always meant to recycle for cash but never got around to doing, and boxes of who-knows-what that Nicole and

I still haven't gone through. Lainey pulls the car in, and it only just fits. Before she leaves the garage, stepping over junk to get out, she grabs her purse and then pauses at her trunk and opens it. After rummaging around for a minute, she pulls out a Yankees baseball bat that definitely isn't hers. My guess is that she stole it from Todd. Not because he plays baseball, but because he's the kind of rich guy who probably has a limited edition bat signed by a bunch of famous athletes.

"Good thinking," I say with a nod. Then, body whizzing with adrenaline, I follow her out of the garage and shut the door behind us.

Only the Jeep is in the driveway. Rex won't know we're home. He'll only assume it's a possibility.

"We're going to put the map back out," I say, my voice shaking. "We'll hide the money, obviously, and we'll lie in wait for him in the greenhouse with our pepper spray. Wait, you have your pepper spray, right?"

She gives me an insulted look.

"Okay, of course you have your pepper spray. I need to text Declan to let him know where we are, and the police...they need to know what's going on too."

"Are you going to call that officer sir again?" she says with a half-smile. But I know bluster when I see it. She's scared now. *I'm* scared. This isn't a situation I've done any preparation for whatso-ever. Lainey's only brush with the law was when she watched that shoplifter walk out with an ugly, expensive shirt without saying something, and then there's me...

A livid boss and a coffee two degrees too cold? Hold my beer. But this?

My only hope is that kicking ass and taking names is somehow built into my DNA, because otherwise we're screwed.

"I will if he needs a polite shutdown," I say. "Nothing works quite like a polite shutdown." I pause, worrying my lip. "You know...

this is all supposition. What if he's innocent, and Nicole really did forget when my birthday is? What if we spray an innocent person in the face with pepper spray?"

"Eh, whatever," she says, heading for the front door. I match her stride for stride. "Remember when we did a skin test with the pepper spray? Milk helped neutralize it."

"So we're going to apologize and splash him with milk?"

She stops me with a hand on my arm. "Claire. If he shows up outside the greenhouse with Nicole, we'll know. But if it'll make you feel better, we'll bring a carton of milk down there with us."

Fuck, she's right. It's only...I don't want her to be right. I *liked* Rex. He's always been nice to me, and I know he's basically Declan's only friend—or was before Nicole, Damien, and I whipped into town. It's chilling to think he's been keeping this from us the entire time we've known him. That he's been sneaking into our yard to try to find Dick's buried winnings while we're all tucked into our beds.

"You're right," I say, taking a deep breath in and out. I lead the way into the house, shutting the door behind us, and hand her the map from my pocket. It's dusted with dirt, so I try to swipe it clean. It's not perfect, but it's as good as I can get. "Can you put this out on the kitchen counter? I need to get my pepper spray."

"Do you want me to put it in the porn case?" she asks.

"No, let's leave it out so Nicole knows we've been down there. Maybe she'll be able to distract him."

She takes it from me, and I grab what I need from my own purse, discarded by the front door, and follow as I take out my phone and plug in a message to Declan and Damien.

> We think he's actually bringing Nicole to Dick's house. Don't worry. We're hiding.

Admittedly, we'll only be hiding so we can jump out and attack Rex, but I don't want to worry Declan. There's a chance they'll get here before we even see Rex—and also that Nicole might overpower him without any help from us.

I'm pulling up the number for the police when I hear the distant rumbling of a car on the road out front. My gaze shoots to Lainey, and she gestures to the refrigerator door.

I shake my head and mouth "fuck the milk." Then I grab the lockbox, and we hurry to the back door in the kitchen, the phone still pressed to my ear. Seconds later, we're picking our way down the hill, Lainey still barefoot and clutching the Yankees bat. My eyes widen as the phone clicks over to voicemail—I hadn't even realized police stations had messaging systems. So I leave a quick message, explaining that Rex is probably on his way to the house, then hang up the phone as we reach the heart-shaped rock.

Lainey takes bags of money and runs them to the greenhouse while I return the lockbox to the hole and start shoveling. I try to time it in my head. If that was his truck, they'll be going into the house now. We have, at most, a minute to pack the dirt and push the rock back into place. She emerges from the greenhouse to help me, and fifty seconds later, we have the rock mostly shoved over the spot where we dug. It looks...

"This looks bad," I hiss. "What are we going to do?"

There's dirt everywhere, like a pint-sized excavator came through, and the rock has clearly been moved.

"This isn't one of Agnes's photoshoots," she says, giving me a push. "We need to get into that greenhouse, now."

She's right. We can't spend twenty minutes out here setting the scene. They'll be down here any minute, presuming we're right about all of this.

We bring the shovel inside and hide behind the wrought iron door. My heart is pounding so hard, I feel like Rex can probably see it from the house. I've never been this worked up, this worried. Everything I've been building here could come tumbling down so quickly...

It could all be over in a matter of seconds.

I realize something in a flash of clarity brought on by adrenaline, the scent of rosemary, and the fear of death—

I'm in love with Declan. It's ridiculously quick, and we have dozens if not hundreds of things to figure out, but it's there, and it's true, and in this moment of potentially facing death—again—I'm not afraid of it. So I pull out my phone and click into our conversation.

> Leave the house, Claire. I'm begging you. Leave
> the house.
>
> I love you.

Lainey, who was shamelessly reading over my shoulder, gives me a wide-eyed *seriously?* look. I nod and tuck the phone away, only then realizing that I must have just scared the shit out of Declan. He probably thinks I sent that because I was about to do something stupid.

Of course, I *did* send that message because I'm about to do something stupid.

There are a couple of open spots in the door's pattern of twisting metal vines, and both Lainey and I press an eye to one. We can see out, but unless he takes a profound interest in the door or approaches the greenhouse directly, he probably won't notice us— and if he does, with any luck it'll give Nicole enough of a distraction to whack him over the head.

Then I see two figures coming into view as they weave between the trees on the hill, one tugging the other by the hands. *Bound* hands. It's them. Nicole's wearing her beanie, but she's far enough away that her features are still crisp, and Rex has the kind of gangly figure that's not easily mistaken for someone else. Worse, it's pretty clear he's either really attached to his cell phone or is holding a gun. I don't have any satisfaction from having been right. I would really, really have preferred to be wrong.

As they get closer, it becomes increasingly obvious that he's not messing around on his phone but is, in fact, holding my sister at gunpoint. Shit. Half an hour ago, this whole situation felt almost fun. At the very least, it was a treasure-map-reading, mystery-solving adventure. But now, it's very real. There's a chance we won't all survive this. There's a chance that I or someone I love will be seriously hurt or even killed.

But I can't back down. I'm not going to. Because not acting would be the most dangerous decision of all.

Lainey squeezes my hand with the hand not currently wrapped around a bat, and I squeeze back, then pull out my pepper spray. Hers is now shoved into the back pocket of her cut-offs.

It's go-time.

Part of me wants to chicken out, to try waiting until a responsible adult arrives. But I am an adult, and right now Lainey and I are the only people who can save Nicole. Because if Rex plans on shooting her, he's not going to wait for help to arrive to do it.

"You already dug it up?" I hear Rex say as they get to the bottom of the hill, his voice different than I remember it. Not jovial at all.

"No, but this is a greenhouse. In greenhouses, people do gardening work. I'm told there's usually dirt involved."

"I've had about enough of your bullshit," he says, waving the gun at her.

"That's too bad, because I was really enjoying this exchange. I thought we were becoming buddies. Stockholm Syndrome for the win."

"You're just like your old man," Rex growls. "Everything's a fucking joke."

"You certainly are."

He shoves her with his free hand, and she staggers back a couple of steps, then glances up the hill and shouts, "Down here!"

I don't think, and I'm guessing Lainey doesn't either, because both of us barrel out of the greenhouse.

CHAPTER THIRTY-SEVEN

DECLAN

Ten minutes earlier

"Go fast, but don't kill us," Damien says, his phone pressed to his cheek. "We won't be any help to them if we're dead."

He's right, which doesn't make me feel any better. We were together when we got the message—Damien, Rosie, and me—working on Nicole's special project.

Rosie wanted to come to Rex's house with us. She wanted to come with us so badly I had to hoist her over my shoulder and carry her back inside the building we were working on, then rush out the door like a kid playing keep-away and lock the accordion scaffolding on it behind me, leaving her beating away at it and shouting obscenities. So there's every chance that'll be the talk of Marshall for half the afternoon.

Only half, because soon they'll find out about Rex.

Rex, who's always talked too damn much, asked too many questions.

Rex, who'd thought it was so funny to take down those Christmas wreaths the night before Dick and a few other people would have won their bet.

Dick must have retaliated. That was his way, to take jokes too far, always. I can get being pissed—I'd been pissed at Dick plenty of times too—but to kill him for it?

It means I never knew Rex. It means I made the same mistakes with him that I made with my uncle, believing he was a decent person, someone with humanity.

My mistake burns, especially because Claire's there in that house with him, probably only feet away from a violent end.

I only got her message after we were halfway to Rex's—

> We think he's actually bringing Nicole to Dick's house. Don't worry. We're hiding.

Then, in response to my message urging her to get the fuck out:

> I love you.

I'd nearly back-ended an old Buick when I saw that. *I love you,* like she was saying goodbye. Like she knew it might be the last thing she wrote. As a gesture, it was like me grabbing on to the last beautiful woman I thought I'd ever see and kissing her.

"Fuck, fuck," I'd shouted, something wild unleashing in me. Because I love her too. Because she *is* good—the kind of person who deserves to be protected and honored. The kind of person who makes the world a better place just by existing. I let myself connect to the world again, and if it's wrenched away from me...

My mind fills with images of Claire.

I can't entertain that possibility, because the thought of anything happening to her makes me want to burn Marshall to the ground, leaving behind nothing but a patch of scorched earth, where not even a cherry tomato can grow.

Damien had pulled the phone from me as I swerved into a gas station to turn around, nearly taking out half the pumps. His jaw flexing, he'd told me, "Go faster," but apparently I'd taken things too fast for him, even.

"Maybe someone will get off their ass and call the cops," I say between my teeth. He's on the phone with the 911 operator, so at least the authorities have been roped in, but it doesn't feel like enough. Nothing feels like enough. Even going this fast, flying up the mountain and taking the curves twenty miles too fast, we're still minutes away. I know better than most that a lot can happen in a few minutes. My parents' car going off the road, my uncle teetering on those steps, Dick taking that fall...

No. Dick, being pushed.

"Thank you," Damien says into the phone. The only sign he's freaking out is the tension he's carrying in his body—every muscle poised as if he's preparing to beat the shit out of someone. He ends the call and pockets my phone. "They're on their way, but we'll get there first. I'm guessing he'll be down by the greenhouse. We've got to assume he has a gun. You got any way of getting us down there without getting shot?"

I don't think Rex will shoot us.

I suspect this has probably gotten bigger than he ever thought it would be, faster than he'd feared it might. Pushing a man and making it look like an accident is easier than murdering several people in broad daylight. Or at least I hope it is. Maybe, for some people, once you cross the line, it becomes easier to cross it again, and again, until there's only a mess of footprints where a line used to be. It wasn't like that for me, but then again, there was no premeditation with what happened with my uncle, no forethought. Just a shove, then lights out.

Damien's still watching me, waiting for an answer.

"A wish and a fucking prayer, my friend," I say. "We can go down on the side opposite my house. Try sneaking up on him from behind the greenhouse."

He nods. "That'll have to do it."

We don't talk for the rest of the drive. We don't talk when we see Rex's fucking truck, parked outside of Dick's house at an angle, the front door still partially open, but I see Damien's jaw flex, and I know I'm not the only one seeing red.

He's down there, with the women we love.

The second I park, we spark into motion—getting out of the car and racing around the side of the house so we can get a look at the lay of the land below. The trees block most of our view, but we can see movement close to where the greenhouse is nestled. A guttural growl escapes Damien as he starts picking his way down the hill, using the brush and trees as cover but moving fast. I'm right there with him. Just before we reach the back of the greenhouse, I hear Nicole shout something. Damien and I exchange a look, and we race toward the front, because fuck subtlety. We need to get to them, and we need to get to them *now*, and nothing on this earth will stop us.

But we're too late.

CHAPTER THIRTY-EIGHT

CLAIRE

Before Rex has a chance to whip back around, Lainey lands him one in the head with the bat. I get him in the face with the pepper spray the instant after his eyes register surprised recognition. He lifts his hands up instantly, dropping the gun, and I kick it, squealing, a primal sound ripping out of me as it skitters away across the ground.

"And we didn't bring you any milk, you asshole," Lainey says, "because you didn't deserve any." She hits him again with the bat while he's wailing and clutching his face, screaming obscenities. He goes down hard, and Nicole, who's freed herself from the knots securing her wrists—which means she probably could have slipped them at any time—jumps onto his back and twists his arms in a way that's probably painful.

That's when Declan and Damien come racing around the side of the greenhouse. Relief radiates through me, because it's over. It's over, and we're all alive, and...

Oh, fuck. I just told Declan I love him.

I distantly register Damien hurrying over to Nicole while Lainey wields the bat, ready to take another crack at Rex if he makes the mistake of trying to get up. He won't. I'm pretty sure he's only half-conscious after that last hit. But my mind is elsewhere, because Declan's sweeping me up off my feet, wrapping his arms around me, both of us sweaty and fearful and so damn relieved.

"You're okay," he says, his voice breaking, his eyes intent on my face. He runs his hands over my cheeks, my arms. "You're okay."

That last time, it sounded like he was assuring himself, and I kiss his nose, his cheek, his lips. "I'm okay."

"I love you too, you insane woman. I've never been so afraid in my life. You do this to me, every time. You're the single most terrifying person I've ever met."

I laugh, riding my adrenaline high for as long as it lasts, and he kisses me hard, squeezing me like he has something to prove to himself—safe, *safe*. I squeeze him back the same way—comforting him and myself. Because he makes me feel alive, and I make him feel at peace, and I want us both to have those things, always.

Then he sets me down, and I almost laugh, because Lainey is snapping a photo of us with her cell phone. Her feet are filthy, and the Yankees bat she used to pummel a man is lying at them, but she still has her cell phone.

"You are *not* putting this on Instagram," I threaten.

"No," she says, "but I figured you'd want some photos to memorialize the occasion."

Honestly, she's right. It's not every day you help apprehend your father's murderer when he comes to dig up buried treasure on the land you've inherited...

It's crazy that this is my life now. All those years of calm, of *waiting*, were building up to one hell of a storm.

"You're Lainey?" Declan asks her, because I've shown him photographs.

"Yes, and you're Declan. Pleased to meet you," she says after pocketing her phone. She holds out a dirty, sweaty hand, but he doesn't hesitate to shake it.

Nicole and Damien are murmuring in low tones, and we turn to join them, Declan holding on to me like he doesn't plan to let go, ever. Fine by me.

Damien has his knee planted none-too-gently into Rex's back—his hands trussed with the same rope he'd used on Nicole—and I can hear the sound of sirens in the distance, suggesting that someone, somewhere, took this seriously.

"There you are, lovebirds," Nicole says, looking pleased with herself.

"Why didn't you free yourself sooner?" I ask, because she obviously could have.

She gives a shrug. "I wanted to see if he'd talk." Damien gives her a knowing look, and she sighs. "And fine, he's taller and stronger than me. I was pretty sure I could take him, but I figured it would be easier if I had backup." Casting a glance at Lainey, she says, "What's with the milk?"

"We'd discussed bringing some down as a pepper spray antidote," I explain, "you know, in case we were wrong. But we concluded that if he came down here with you, he probably didn't deserve it."

Nicole rolls her eyes but grins as she turns back to Lainey. "You've got a good arm. Welcome to the inner circle."

She obviously recognizes her, too, probably because she was all over my Instagram like the sort-of stalker she is. Right now, I can't find it in myself to be mad about it.

Then Nicole surprises me by reaching over and grabbing my hand. Squeezing it. "Thank you, Claire," she says, and I get the feeling she hasn't uttered that phrase more than a dozen times in her whole life.

I nod, slowly, feeling a knot in my throat. It's true that Declan and Damien were seconds away, and they almost certainly would have stopped Rex without anyone else getting hurt. But it's Lainey and I are the ones who did it. We didn't sit back and let someone else take the risks. It feels like I just threw my office chair and set fire to the copier machine. It's magnificent and freeing, and *terrifying*. And I hope I never have to do it again.

"Someone had to show him," I say, swallowing back a lump and leaning into Declan's strong arm wrapped around me. "You fuck with my sister, you fuck with me. And *nobody* fucks with me."

"I've created a monster," Nicole says with something like pride.

SEVERAL HOURS LATER, after we finally leave the police station, we're all sitting around the table in Dick Ricci's kitchen. Declan and me. Lainey. Nicole and Damien. And Rosie, who's still pissed she missed everything because Declan "abandoned" her at his job site. Damien poured bourbon for everyone, and Nicole told us what she'd learned from Rex.

She'd gotten him talking, more or less, and we'd added some pieces to the story over the hours since we were released from the police station.

Turned out he'd taken down those Christmas wreaths the day before Dick and a few other people would have won a lot of money, so Dick had suggested a different bet to the small pool of people who'd lost out—that Rex's dad wasn't his biological father. Half had sided with Rex, half with Dick.

Dick, of course, had been right, and we had the fat wad of cash in the lockbox to prove it.

Who knows what had tipped him off—maybe he was a philanderer who recognized other philanderers. As Nicole pointed out, it would have been perfectly in keeping with his personality if he'd done it simply to be a dick, not knowing whether he was right or wrong.

The end result was that Rex was out the money for the bet, and also out his inheritance, since his wealthy father had cut him off without a cent.

He'd been pissed.

He'd figured that Dick's winnings, at least, were his due.

He claimed Dick's death was an accident, unplanned, and he'd only run from the scene without reporting it because he was spooked.

But Nicole and Damien think the timing—and the amount of drugs in Dick's system, more than what Mrs. Rosings said he usually took—suggest otherwise. He thought he'd put together the perfect murder, one no one would feel called upon to solve, since so few people had liked our biological father.

And we all knew what had happened from there.

Mark and the other high-stakes gamblers had stayed quiet about the feud between Dick and Rex because that had been their deal—none of them talked about their secret bets. But when Nicole had questioned Mark again this afternoon, making it clear that she believed Dick had been murdered over blood money and we might still be in danger, he'd told her about a few of the last bets he'd made. This one was the only one someone might be motivated to kill over, unless someone felt surprisingly strongly about when the daffodils would bloom.

The question we were left with now was how far would he have gone to get that money? Would he have killed Nicole? How about Lainey and me?

He's claiming he had no intention to harm any of us—that he wanted to take his money and run, but there's no way of knowing. He had that gun, after all, and he's proven himself to be someone whose word should be taken with five pounds of salt.

Now, sitting around the table, Declan's big palm on my thigh, steadying me, I feel the full weight of everything that went down this afternoon and over the last month. I feel how much my life has changed—and how much I've gained. I remember, for five seconds, that I was supposed to meet Anthony Smith four hours ago, and he's probably pissed. Something tells me he's not the kind of man who will take "I almost got murdered" as an excuse for not showing.

Oh well.

Nicole smiles at me, then lifts her glass. "Here's to Dick. You were definitely an asshole, but you brought us together, so you weren't an entire waste."

Damien, whose lap she's currently sitting in, hoists his drink up and says, "Here's to Dick. You didn't treat my wife well, so fuck you very much for that, but there's no denying you knew how to make an exit."

It's Lainey's turn, and she lifts her glass. "Here's to Dick, I didn't know you, and your daughter sure didn't know you, but it has to be said you had interesting taste in DVDs."

I snort as Rosie lifts her glass. "Here's to Dick. You meant something to my brother, which means you meant something to me too."

Holding Declan's hand, I lift my glass. "Here's to Dick. You may not have been a good guy, but you were definitely an interesting one." Declan squeezes my hand, his gaze on me, as I swallow the lump in my throat and finish. "I wish you'd given me a chance to know you."

It's Declan's turn, and we all turn toward him, watching him. It's as if we've collectively realized we have one true mourner among us. His eyes are on me as he lifts his glass. "To Dick. I didn't really want a neighbor. I didn't think I wanted anyone, but you proved me wrong. If not for you, I never would have met Claire. I wouldn't have her, and I wouldn't have Rocket, and Rosie wouldn't be sitting here with me. I wouldn't have anything. So thank you, man. Thank you for noticing that I was suffering, and for caring. You might have been a terrible father, and I can't like you for that, but you were a good friend. For a while, you were my only friend. I've missed you, and I will continue to miss you."

There are tears in his eyes, which automatically puts tears in my eyes. Even though we're surrounded by our friends and family, I pull him to me and kiss him.

In that moment, I feel a little love for the father I never knew. While he might not have done anything for me until he died, he gave me the man I love, and my sister, and this house to live in. He gave me the push I needed to do something with my life and the scaffolding to make it possible.

"All right, all right, we get it," Nicole deadpans. "You're in love and shit. It's fucking beautiful. Now, can we drink?"

I pull away, smiling, but Declan tugs me into his lap and kisses the side of my neck.

"Disgusting," Nicole says with a gleam in her eyes, then turns to Rosie. "Aren't you going to heckle them with me?"

"Give me a few weeks. Right now, I'm too happy to see my brother smiling again. I thought he'd forgotten how."

"Well, hallelujah," Nicole says with a grin. Then she theatrically glances downward, "You heard that, you old sinner? Hallelujah, you did something right."

If anyone tried to call her on it, she'd insist there's an onion hidden somewhere in the room, but Nicole's eyes are shining too.

We laugh and we drink. Then Declan and Nicole tell us a few stories about Dick. As moments go, it's beautiful.

We're a little drunk by the time Lainey remembers she hasn't moved any of her stuff inside, and even though the logical thing to do would be to help her with just her suitcase, someone suggests we move everything now, and so we do. She has the smallest bedroom in the house, and the boxes wedged inside fill up the space around the bed.

"You don't want to just throw all this stuff away and start fresh?" Nicole asks.

"I tried to do that," she says, laughing. "Claire wouldn't let me."

"She can sell some of this stuff," I insist. "A lot of these things are expensive gifts from her ex-fiancé. He might be a dick, but he has expensive taste."

"She could just burn them," Nicole says.

"Don't let my wife burn anything," Damien interjects, his eyes dancing as he wraps his arm around her. "She doesn't have a good idea of what constitutes flammable."

I hiccup. "That's true. She tried to burn my Chanel No. 5."

"Hiding it works better," Lainey says, which deserves a shove, so I give her one. I can feel Declan's laughter rumbling against my back.

Rosie, who was looking into one of the boxes with unconcealed curiosity, says, "I've burned things after a breakup before."

"That's what I want to do for a living," Lainey blurts.

"Be a professional pyromaniac?"

"No," she replies, smiling. "I want to help people refresh and move on after a breakup. Everyone says therapy is the way to go, but I just wailed on that guy with my ex-fiancé's prized Yankees bat, and I have to say they're wrong."

Called it.

Nicole snaps her fingers, then points at Lainey. "I think you've got something there, Claire's friend. I'm going to help you with that."

"Here we go," Declan whispers in my ear, and I laugh, feeling fizzy with good will toward everyone.

"I still think it's a bad idea, for the record," I say.

"Yeah," Nicole says dismissively, "but you think everything's a bad idea until someone forces you to see sense."

I could be offended, but she's at least partially right.

Still...

"Maybe we shouldn't make business plans when we're drunk?"

"I come up with my best ideas when tipsy," Nicole says, which seems like an even better reason not to do it. I don't necessarily want Nicole at top form.

"Even so," I say, "I think I'm going to bed."

"I'm staying," Declan says. "I'm not ready to let you out of my sight."

"What about me?" Rosie says, raising her eyebrows.

"There's a perfectly good couch," he tells her with a grin. "I figured we could bring Rocket over too."

"Oh, goody, a sleepover," Nicole says flatly. "Should I get out the face masks?" But she doesn't seem displeased. I think we all feel the urge to burrow in, together.

"I vote for raiding the pantry," Lainey says. "I want some Bronuts, and knowing Claire, there has to be a box of them hidden away somewhere."

I groan, because I'd very much wanted to keep that nickname from Nicole.

"Bronuts?" she asks, sounding delighted. "Tell me more."

Then she throws up a finger as everyone starts filtering out of the room and into the hall. "I need a second with Claire."

Declan gives me a look, and I nod, so he leaves the room with everyone else after giving me a final squeeze. Nicole tugs a folded piece of paper out of her pocket, so apparently she was planning this. My gut tells me what it is.

Her letter from Dick.

"Is it going to make me cry?" I ask with trepidation.

A smile flickers across her face. "I don't fucking know. You seem to cry at the drop of a hat."

I've only cried once in our acquaintance, but I take the paper without commentary. She smiles at me, surprises me by squeezing my hand, then returns to our friends, shouting something, as is her habit.

I unfold the paper, take a deep breath, and read the letter from our father. The last letter I'll probably ever read from him.

Nicole—

If you're reading this, then I'm dead. Fuck, I've always wanted to write that. I don't want to die, but you've got to admit it's a good line. Maybe I died of natural causes—I've never been particularly careful about mixing drugs or going to the doctor, and I've been feeling some chest pain. Or maybe someone finally decided I've pulled enough bullshit and decided to save the rest of the world some trouble by getting rid of me (ha!).

I was a fuckup, wasn't I?

My father was a shitty father, too, and I figured I'd do okay if I could do better than him. But seven years in, I realized I wasn't doing better than him. That I couldn't. Your mother is such a good parent—it always came naturally to her—but it didn't to me. How do you teach good lessons when your natural inclination is to steal the candy instead of buying it, to hit people who deserve it, and to always bite back?

I knew I wasn't any good for your mother, and I realized I wasn't any good for you either. So I figured we'd better cut our losses while you were still young enough to learn some good shit from her. Maybe I was wrong. Probably, I was, and I don't expect you to forgive me. You shouldn't. But I love you the only way I know how. From a distance.

I'm proud of you. I've always been able to find the information I want, so I've followed along. You're pretty good at staying out of the papers, but there are vital records, and I know you're married. I know you have a private investigator's license. That made your old man chuckle. I've always been too curious for my own good, and in that way you're a chip off the old block. Hopefully for you it's only in that way.

The one thing I've regretted is that you and your half-sister never met. (Surprise!) That might sound rich seeing as I've never met her either, but one thing no one ever accused me of is consistency.

I've kept track of Claire, too, and she's a good kid. Smart. Dedicated. But if there's one thing that runs in our blood, Nicky, it's chaos, and something tells me she needs a little push. Someone to challenge her.

That's you, kid. I feel it in my bones.

I know you'll take care of Claire, and I'm hoping she'll take care of you too. That's why I'm being a dick for one last time and asking you both to stay in this house for a month if you want to inherit it.

Spend time together. Do what I couldn't, and be a family. I believe in you, kid. I believe in both of you more than I ever believed in myself. If I did one thing right in this world, it was helping to bring you two into it. I was a shit father, but you're good kids anyway.

Here I am, getting off my soapbox.

Have a party when the month's up, if you would.

Love you,

D

P.S. If I died in embarrassing way, please cover it up.

P.P.S. Be good to Declan, if he still lives next door. He was a friend when I needed one, and this is going to be hard on him.

By the time I finish, there are tears in my eyes. Because, damn him, he was right. Nicole and I did need each other. We *do*. And even though I resent him for keeping us apart for all these years, he finally righted that wrong. I wish it weren't in death. I wish we'd met. But not every wish has a chance to take flight—some we're fated to carry with us, feeling their weight and knowing we'll never have them.

I tuck the letter into my pocket and leave the room, finding Declan standing out in the hall waiting for me. He doesn't speak, he just traces away my tears and then kisses the pathways on my cheeks, which only makes me cry harder.

Because he's a wish I didn't even know I had until it was granted.

"You waited," I say through tears.

"Of course I did." He swallows, tracing the line of my jaw, my neck. "I love you, Claire. Whatever fate put me next to you on that plane—"

I laugh. I can't help it. "It was Nicole. She did it. I don't know how. She put me next to you and Mrs. Rosings because you both knew Dick. She thought you might know something about what happened to him."

"Well, shit," he says, caressing my neck. "Does this mean I have to thank Nicole for something?"

"You're not pissed?" I ask.

He laughs, the corners of his eyes crinkling. "No, Sandra Dee, I'm not pissed. I thought I was going to die, and kissing you was the last thing I wanted to do on this planet. It still is, but now I'm hoping it's at least fifty years off."

"You want to die kissing me?" I ask. The way he's looking at me...the way he's always looked at me fills me up with joy—so much of it I'm sickening to myself. "That's both the sweetest and most morbid thing anyone's ever said to me."

"It's true," he says, his eyes boring into mine, inches away. "But I think we need to put in plenty of practice first."

I inch closer, pushing up on my toes. "Practice makes perfect."

"Spoken like a true Sandra Dee," he says, and then he kisses me like it's the last thing either of us will ever do.

On a Saturday two and a half months after my neighbor died, we're finally holding his celebration of life. This is also a celebration for Claire, although she doesn't know that yet.

"Why won't anyone let me do anything?" Claire complains for the fifth time today. We're in the kitchen, eating a quick brunch before we join Nicole, Damien, Lainey, and everyone else at the venue. Lainey went with them because she's a Claire specialist—the two of them having been friends since they were old enough to walk. So it's the two of us, Rosie, and Claire's father, who flew in last night for the memorial party of the man who cuckolded him. He's a better man than I am; definitely a better man than Dick, a point the deceased wouldn't have argued.

If I owe Dick for introducing me to Claire, in the most round-about way possible, then I owe Chuck that much more for having helped her become the woman I love. So I like him, a lot. Even if part of me thinks he's the kind of nice that's asking to get used up by the world. He's got Claire, though, and me, and now Nicole and Damien. No one's going to mess with him again on our watch.

Chuck wouldn't approve of me if he knew everything. He'd be a fool to. But he doesn't know, and he's the kind of man who doesn't know enough to look for trouble, so even though he'd no doubt prefer to see Claire settle down with a suited banker who lives in the same high rise he does, we get along well enough. He sees in me what I do in him—devotion to his daughter. Truthfully, I don't feel great about lying to him, especially not since I have every intention of marrying his daughter someday, but Claire figures he kept a secret from her for twenty-eight years, so we have at least a couple of decades to keep my past to ourselves before it becomes an issue.

To help even the score, I've let him in on a different secret. Chuck knows where we're going for the memorial party.

Hell, half the town does, but no one's spilled the truth to Claire. Probably because most of them are afraid of Nicole, the rest of me.

Rosie snorts and pushes one of the oatmeal muffins Chuck made last night around on her plate. To refuse such a man would be like kicking a puppy in the face, so we all took one of the dry hockey pucks, which he proudly announced lacked any flour, sugar, or added fat. We're used to Claire's baked goods around here, and Rosie's as a close second—so it's hard to pretend it's edible. Even Chuck has been pushing his muffin half-heartedly around on its plate, eyeing the covered dish of Danishes Claire and Rosie made the other night.

"What was the snort for?" Claire asks as she plays with her cup of coffee.

"Only you would complain about not being able to work," Rosie continues. "We need to get Shay down here so he can talk some sense into you."

"You're referring, of course, to his legendary ability to be so lazy he makes other people lazy," I say, feeling a tightness in my chest at the mention of my brother. He's talked about coming for a visit, and maybe he will, but things still aren't settled between us. I'll always be the guy who screwed up his future by choosing to run rather than dig in my heels and stay. He'd thought he could change the game, make his own rules, but I'd seen enough to know it was the kind of game that ate people up and twisted them. The way it had done to our uncle.

"I am," she says.

"Dad's a party planner," Claire says, gesturing to him. "Why wouldn't you let us help with the planning? And I still don't understand why we couldn't have it here, on your deck. Dick loved it here."

"Which is why we scattered his ashes out back, but we had a different idea for the party," I say. "One he'd like even more." I grin at Claire's father. "Besides, who said your dad didn't help?"

"Dad, you scoundrel!" Claire says, beaming at him. "I used to think you were an open book, but you're the ultimate at keeping secrets from people for their own good."

He beams right back, and I feel satisfaction deep in my gut. The sense of everything being as it should again. Finally. *Finally.* My sister gives me a wistful look, and I know she's missing the way things were. I do too. But I don't miss the man I became, for a while. I don't miss the hollow ache that drove me here to Marshall. I'm ready to leave that part of the past behind, so Claire and I can step into the future.

No one's really eating—we're all waiting, a pattern that Claire and I both have had too much experience with, most of it bad. So I ball up my napkin and throw it at Rosie, who scowls at me, then lean over and kiss Claire on the forehead. "Let's go put you out of your misery, Sandra Dee."

"Oh, thank God," she says, "I was starting to feel—"

"I know," I say, putting an arm around her.

We share a look of perfect understanding, and I feel a little more life sprout in my former hellscape, now populated by rosemary and apples and climbing, flowering vines. We all pet Rocket, tell him he's a good boy, and then board the Jeep. Before we take off, I send off a text to Nicole:

> Bronuts aboard.

When we get downtown, I park on the street, around the corner from our destination.

"You've all been very mysterious," Claire says as I circle around to open her door for her. The Jeep is pretty far off the ground, so I help Chuck down too, earning an incredulous look from Rosie.

My heart starts pounding faster as I lead Claire to the corner we need to round to get there. There's a chance she will think we overstepped. That she won't be totally fucking delighted by our surprise. But I don't truly believe that. We may have overstepped, but she's going to love it, and I'm going to get to see the look on her face. No doubt Lainey will capture it ten different ways on her phone camera.

"Am I being paranoid, or are you all watching me?" Claire asks.

I squeeze her hand, and Rosie answers, "Oh, we're definitely watching you."

I lean in and whisper in Claire's ear. "Just around this corner." She looks up, capturing me with her golden gaze, and I feel a preternatural calm wash over me, chasing the last of my worry away.

"Is this a Nicole surprise?"

"Mostly, but we all helped."

She squeezes my hand, glances back at her father, and then we're around the corner, and the red awning of the bakery comes into view. Turning toward me, she looks into my eyes—and I see the hope in her gaze. It fills my fucking cup. The windows are still papered over, but I bring Claire to a halt and text Nicole again:

> Bronuts landing.

The code wasn't my idea.

Then again, Nicole came up with *this* idea, so I was feeling pretty damn cooperative when she suggested it.

"Declan..." Claire says, her voice a little nervous.

"It's okay, honey. This is good."

And I usher her forward, her father and Rosie giving her sidelong glances. The paper in the window comes down as we get closer, revealing the interior of the bakery—the built-in bookshelves and velvet armchairs, the new bake case I installed. The name, emblazoned in golden cursive, hand drawn by Mrs. Rosings, for the window. Rainy Day Bakery—a name she'd whispered to me one night when she was telling me about her dream.

Although Mrs. Rosings made a fuss about needing to get a new assistant before the wedding, she was happy to contribute to the cause. For all her fussing, she loves Claire, same as we do, and wanted to help.

Rosie is hoping like hell Claire wants her to work in the bakery, but Lainey isn't much for waking up early, so she's offered to fill the gap and help Mrs. Rosings out part time until she can find someone else. Which isn't to say she doesn't have other projects afoot—Nicole's all about her idea to offer services for people fresh off breakups. They've argued about the name, but Claire, the ultimate referee, came up with a solution they both agreed with: The Love Fixers.

Claire turns to look at me, her eyes wide. "It's really mine? But it was rented."

"Yes, by Nicole," I say softly, cupping her face, very aware that her father is next to us, and regretting it at that particular moment.

"But it was rented the week after I arrived."

"She was motivated to keep you around. So was I. As soon as she told me about it, I offered to help."

"And me," Rosie pipes up from beside us.

"Lainey, too," I add. "She helped us decorate it. I installed the equipment and the shelves. We figured we'd have the party here, because it only seemed right. Honoring the old and the new."

This bakery is something else Dick helped build, even though he'll never know it. He would have liked that. Claire showed me both of the letters he wrote, to her and to Nicole, and it brings me comfort to think he does have a legacy.

Although I've never loved construction the way I do growing things, I have plenty of experience. I'd never had as much of a reason to be glad for it as I did in there—building Claire's dream.

"But...but the money from the insurance hasn't come through yet...and..."

"You can work that out with Nicole," I say, "but it's yours."

"It's too much," she says, her jaw working as she looks at the awning, the sign, at our friends waving to us from behind the plate glass window. Her eyes fill with tears. "It's too much."

But I can tell how much she wants it—and how surely she'll do justice to it. I'll be by her side, helping every way I know how—learning to do the things I don't know. Rubbing her back when she needs to get up before dawn to prepare for the day. I've spent the past few weeks researching what it takes to run a bakery, because I want to be ready, and I've prepared some extra starters down in the greenhouse so we can have fresh herbs to use in her baking.

The door to the bakery bursts open, and Nicole and Lainey stick their heads out. Just beyond them, I can see Mrs. Rosings drinking something from a fluted glass. She has the knowing smile of someone who was in on the joke, her preferred place to be.

"Get in here, already," Lainey shouts, "the party's getting started."

Chuck squeezes Claire's shoulder. "I'm very proud of you, bug. You've made a real place for yourself here."

"But I didn't do any of it," she insists. "I don't—"

"Do you think they would have gone to all this effort for someone who doesn't mean anything to them? For someone who isn't worth it?" he asks, turning into a hardass before my eyes. It's obvious he won't let anyone question her worth, including Claire herself, and he automatically rises in my esteem.

"No, I guess not," she says, tears dripping down her cheeks, but I can tell they're happy tears. That this is a sight she never thought she'd see, and she needs an extra moment to let it sink in. "I need—"

"You kids take the time you need," he says. "I'm going to escort Rosie here inside."

"Please do," Rosie says brightly.

"Send Nicole out," Claire says.

I try to follow her dad and Rosie inside, to give her a moment alone with her sister, but she tugs me back. "I want you to stay. This...this feels like one of the most important moments of my life, and I want you here for it."

So I stay.

Nicole emerges from the bakery, grinning like the cat that stole the carton of cream and left the bowl untouched, and Claire wraps both of her arms around her and squeezes.

"I love you. I love you, and I'm so glad you're my sister."

For a second, Nicole looks stunned, like someone just dipped her into a cold pool, and then she pushes away with a grin. "Save that shit for your boyfriend."

"I can't believe you did this for me," Claire says. "How did you even *know* to do it for me? You must have rented this place weeks—"

"Bought." Nicole digs a set of keys out of her pocket. "Bought. It's yours. And if you don't want people to know what your hopes and dreams are, don't post them all over Instagram. "

Claire's eyes get larger as she takes the keys, and fuck, mine probably do too. I didn't know that part. It's obvious she and Damien have money. They drive a Lexus and wear brands favored by my uncle, but this is something else. Marshall's not Asheville, but storefronts don't come cheap.

"But—"

"No buts," Nicole says, giving her a harsh look. "None. But you're officially calling your brownie things Bronuts. They're going on the menu that way, and you're going to advertise them that way, and it's going to be a thing. Plus, you're going to help Lainey and me get the Love Fixers off the ground. That's how you'll thank me."

Claire swallows. "That's hardly equivalent."

"Well, that's the plight of big sisters everywhere, isn't it?" Her grin turns mischievous. "Besides, I've cornered you into staying in this part of the world, which was my intention all along. So you can tell yourself I'm being selfish. You won't be wrong."

Claire shakes her head slightly in disbelief, her mouth curving up. "You're the most generous selfish person in the world."

"Don't go around telling people that," Nicole says with a forced scowl. "You'll ruin my cred. Now, get your ass in there, so we can give Dick the sendoff of a lifetime. I want this party to make Marshall history."

"It won't be hard," I say. "This place isn't known for its ragers."

Nicole puts a finger next to her nose. "It's not known for its ragers *yet*."

Then she turns and swaggers back into the bakery.

Claire turns to me with an adorable lost look, and I lower my head and kiss her. Because she can't look like that without getting kissed—everything inside of me revolts against the thought.

"This is insane," she says in an undertone. "I can't just accept this."

I nod to the keys in her hand. "Possession is nine tenths of the law. Trust me, I'm a former criminal." I wrap a hand around her waist and take a step toward the bakery, bringing her with me. Because I can't let her turn down her dream. Frankly, I won't. "Besides, I think our lives have turned insane. That's not necessarily a bad thing, though. Maybe it's the best thing of all."

With that, we walk into the bakery together, and it feels very much like we're walking into the future. I have to wonder if it's a future Dick saw. I *know* it's one he would have liked.

I sure as hell do.

Next up is Lainey's book, *The Love Bandits*—a madcap enemies-to-lovers, bad boy story involving robbery, mistaken identity, and mild mayhem!

DON'T MISS THE LOVE BANDITS!

I stole his heart...necklace. Now he wants to return the favor.

Lainey

My mother's dream was for me to marry a rich man. So I got engaged to one...and he was a no-good, cheating so-and-so. Now, I'm pursuing *my* dream, running a business helping people who've been through messy breakups.

When a woman comes to me after her ex refuses to hand over her heirloom heart necklace, I know exactly what to do.

I go undercover and cozy up to her ex to steal it back.

Jake is a smooth talker with good game, but so am I. So it doesn't take me long to return the necklace to its rightful owner.

Except it turns out it was never hers...*or* his...

Jake

I know better than to be taken in by a pretty face, but Lainey got me good.

I guess I shouldn't be complaining that her client stole the necklace from me, since I stole it from someone else. But if I don't get it back, I'm toast.

So Lainey agrees to help me. True, her motivations don't match up with mine, but I'm not about to complain. Because suddenly the necklace isn't the only thing I want; I want to make her mine.

Preorder **HERE**

ABOUT THE AUTHOR

ANGELA CASELLA is a romcom fanatic. Writing them, reading them, watching them—she's greedy, and she does it all. In addition to her solo releases, she's lucky enough to collaborate with Denise Grover Swank. They have three complete series and more co-written projects to come.

She lives in Asheville, NC. Her hobbies include herding her daughter toward less dangerous activities, the aforementioned romcom addiction, and dreaming of having someone else clean her house.

Visit her website at www.angelacasella.com or Angela and Denise's shared website at www.arcdgs.com.

Made in United States
Orlando, FL
26 June 2025

62393266R00236